BUILI

UNIVERS

To the coolest cat in town

Thomas Baskerville

The Stirring of Dragons
Universe One

The Stirring of Dragons

Universe One

To those without a universe to explore.
A special thank you to Jamie for his invaluable words of wisdom.

"Even in desperation, love can truly bind one to an inescapable path. Fate cares little for common sense, the universe cares even less for ignorance."

Maximus Baskerville

All the characters in this book are fictional; if they resemble a certain person then I assure you this is a complete coincidence. The names of some characters may resemble names of other people I know; however, that is the only resemblance this book has to the real world. None of the characters are based on my friends or me or represent any opinion I have of a person or subject.

This book is not set in a time or place like ours. A lot of the science and mechanics of the world are also very different from our own but telling you the reason for that will have to wait. After reading all the books in this series, things may still stay unanswered; I would advise that you read things over a few times so that you have fully understood each event before moving on.

CHAPTER 1; INTRODUCTIONS

Tom was a rather thin but talk figure with short brown hair, yellow eyes and normally a crafty but calculated stare that had the means to blank even the loudest of chatterboxes. Tom was a thinker, a tinkerer, the closest thing this world had to any form of scientist.

Cathie on the other hand was well-built and incredibly strong considering her size. Slightly shorter than Tom, yet somehow, she gave off more of a presence than he did. Her long, fiery red hair matched her equally red eyes. Cathie was a fighter, a hunter, a tracker. Skills much more valuable in this world than any Tom possessed.

These two were carefully moving through a thick forest. Despite being the middle of the day, barely any sunlight made it down to their level. The occasional shaft of light broke through here or there, which the two of them expertly avoided at all costs. Despite making good ground, neither one of them had so much as crunched a leaf under their foot, which was impressive considering the number on the forest floor. This skill was the product of nineteen years of surviving in this world, for each of them.

Tom had a bow loaded, but not drawn. The bow was odd in design, as most things were when it came to Tom. Ten arrows were fitted into ten holes in the frame of the bow. The arrows were being held between the frame and five different bow strings all attached to the very same frame.

Cathie on the other hand wielded a large, heavy, two-handed sword. Something Tom could never hope to lift let alone swing. The sword was low in quality and didn't really boast any unique features. The offspring of one of Charlie's rushed jobs, simply so that she had something to swing. She had a bad habit of being a little too rough with her weapons.

There was a snap. The two of them froze.

While Tom did his best to keep as concealed as possible in the ferns of the forest floor, Cathie's senses were working overtime to scan everything around them.

Small tracks, but they weren't fresh. A flutter from above, just a bird. More flutters, more birds. Lots of birds, all taking flight and leaving the general area. Her bare feet eventually noticed the slight vibrations in the ground. Her eyes widened as she realised what had happened. There was no point in being quiet now.

"Beneath!" She yelled at Tom, who acted almost immediately by joining her back-to-back. Both of them had their eyes and ears trained to the ground.

Teeth pierced the ground right underneath them, but they'd been ready for it. Both of them split almost immediately to surround the beast that had emerged from the ground.

They'd done it now. The plan had been to surprise the beast, but it had turned the tables on them. Four legs of pure muscle wrapped in a bone like armour that was thick enough to stop a sword at full swing with nothing but a small scratch. Each leg boasted vicious claws that could dig through the ground as if it were paper. The armour also covered the beasts back and skull.

With small eyes but a mouthful of teeth that simply meant death should you get caught in them, the beast also had a long tail with a mace-like formation on the end made of the same armour that coated most of its body.

A beast well known to the humans of this world. A beast that under these sorts of circumstances, it would be a death sentence to do anything but run and hide. A beast known only as an Earth Dragon.

Unfortunately for these two, they'd come looking for this exact beast. The fight wasn't in their favour. Low visibility out powered and the moment it shrieked, more would be on their way. Luckily for Tom he'd brought something more dangerous with him.

The dragon charged towards Tom with an open jaw ready to snap shut around his entire body. Its head was quickly jerked to the side and thrown against a tree before it could harm him.

Cathie's left hook was nothing to joke about. She'd been smart enough to not use her sword against the thick armoured skull she'd had to aim to save Tom's ass.

Tom circled the dragon while putting some distance between him and it. He didn't do well when things came after him, but that was what she was for.

nerd /o/

The dragon regained its balance and turned to face Cathie. It growled heavily, clearly not too happy about what she'd done. This time it lunged at her with its back legs springing it right off the ground.

It was moving much faster this time, and now it had its full weight behind its attack. Cathie was strong, but she wasn't that strong. This however was exactly what she was waiting for. She'd pissed it off enough to get it to make one big mistake.

She pushed forwards as she drew her sword from her back and sliced at its belly above her. Once she'd got a decent cut, she turned her run into a roll to avoid getting crushed as the dragon landed. She made it in between the back two legs and under the base of the tail, which like the belly lacked the thick armour. One more big slice and the tail came clean off.

Blue, thick blood showered her as the tail landed to her side. Despite this she quickly got to her feet and put as much distance between her and the dragon as possible. Hesitating near a dragon was one of the many ways in this world to guarantee death.

She'd really done it now. A dragon losing a limb to a human was a sign of weakness on the dragon's part to the rest of its kind. If it wanted to return home with any respect now, it would have to do so with at least one of their heads.

The dragon turned with a screech of pain and rage that echoed throughout the surrounding trees. Others would have heard that. It found Cathie as she was running for the trees and began to give chase, but an arrow struck its skull just shy of its eye socket. The arrow merely pinged off, but it got its attention.

The dragon turned to Tom, who was also quite a distance from the dragon. Weaving in and around tree trunks, but not to hide from it. Being a creature that lives underground, the low visibility did little to hinder the dragon from finding him, but this wasn't new to Tom.

Every sound he made gave away his position, any sharp movements would be seen despite the dragons rather poor eyesight. He was making sure to do both to keep its attention on him.

This wasn't the only reason he was bobbing and weaving either. A reason that became crystal clear as the dragon began to form a boulder within its mouth. Once its jaw was at its widest to hold the boulder, it expertly tossed it through the trees and towards Tom.

Tom came to a stop and changed direction just in time to avoid getting crushed by the boulder, which rolled off into a tree, knocking it over.

"Fuck." Tom cursed as he recognised it had hit the tree he'd tied rope to in order to escape into the branches above. There was nothing else for it now. He slung his bow over his shoulder and shoved the arrows in his hand into the black box shaped bag hanging from a strap over his other shoulder.

There was one skill that Tom did possess to aid with his survival, but that was simply because every human was particularly good at this skill. At least, any human still alive that was. The skill was simple and universal but most importantly essential to the survival of a human in this world.

To put it simply, he could run. He could run fast.

The dragon gave chase, knocking over trees with its shoulders and even ramming through a couple with its thick skull.

He continued at full speed until he broke out of the treeline and came up to a small cliff only a few metres high. To most this would look like a complete dead end that Tom was running towards, but that very much wasn't the case.

As Tom approached the cliff, he vanished into thin air. The dragon brought itself to a stop before it risked running straight into the cliff face. For a few vitally quiet minutes the dragon continued to inspect the immediate area.

Human trickery. Humans had an annoying habit of disappearing. Normally they'd do this by going up into the trees and vanishing into the large canopy of leaves, but this human must have used a hidden tunnel in the rock instead.

The dragon bashed its foot on the floor and concentrated on the vibrations for a few seconds. Nothing underground. A trick of the light perhaps?

Eventually, it gave up, and tunnelled away. It had lost them, and now it had to accept its fate.

Tom waited for the vibrations in the ground to completely die down before moving. He'd been stood just the other side of a wooden door.

The door was in the cliff face, although it was rather well hidden. It wasn't even some decent paint job that was responsible either, it was something much more convincing and able to fool even an earth dragon's hearing and smell to hide both the door and the cave beyond it.

"Glad we have you for moments like that." He sighed as he turned to face one of two figures slightly deeper into the cave.

The cave itself was a series of rooms. The main room was communal and acted as a place to cook, eat and generally sit together. Lit up by a few small burning torches hung on the walls, the only exits were the door Tom had just closed to the outside world and a small passageway that led to a series of closed doors deeper into the cave.

One of the figures Tom had turned to face was Cathie, still completely drenched in dragon's blood. The second, was a man of similar height and build to Tom. With longer, brown hair and blue eyes that seemed to angrily stare through Tom instead of simply look at him. This man's name was Patrick. A year younger than the two of them at age eighteen, Patrick gave off a presence which would have anyone guess the opposite.

He slowly walked up to Tom and quickly punched him right in the gut.

"Damn right." He bitterly muttered as Tom threw up a little from the punch as he keeled over. Patrick had more meat on his arms than Tom, not that much more, but enough to make a difference.

"Little much this time, don't you think?" Cathie asked him as she folded her arms at him. Patrick stared at her, equally angry.

"I'd do the same to you if I wasn't guaranteed to get a broken arm out of it." He answered, "At first I thought he was the only crazy one of the group, but perhaps I was wrong."

"It was my idea Patrick." Tom muttered as he finally got to his feet.

"I doubt you took her out there with you against her will." Patrick snapped, still looking at Cathie. Cathie stepped forwards towards Patrick to a distance no one would be comfortable with.

"You have a problem with my decision?" She asked him in a low and borderline threatening tone.

"You know full well I do. So, should you, considering the position your in." Patrick replied, standing his ground despite knowing full well she could easily break every bone in his body. Cathie slowly turned and took a few steps away from him.

"I wasn't in any danger. The two of us made sure of that."

"Bullshit. You two know better than to lead a dragon near home. Something went wrong, but you decided to carry on anyway, didn't you?" Patrick asked the two of them.

"It may have gotten the drop on us, yes." Tom admitted. He could already see the anger in Patrick's face get even more intense.

"Nothing I couldn't handle." Cathie quickly shot at him, "Not as if we were trying to kill it anyway."

"That's a very good point. The hell were you two doing, fucking about with an earth dragon?" Patrick asked the two of them. Tom straightened himself out and reached into his bag. He brought out a glass beaker and walked over to Cathie.

Glass, among other things, was a very rare material to have in this world. Metal alone was hard to shape and forge into swords, but glass required an entire craft that had died out years previously. Not even Tom was skilled enough to make more glass, although he did claim to know how, it just wasn't possible with what they had. Another reason glass was so rare was because it didn't have much of a use other than to look pretty, for most humans anyway. Tom however possessed quite the collection of glassware, something that all of them took rather good care around due to how much time and effort must have gone into crafting such a collection.

Patrick watched as Cathie helped Tom collect a decent amount of dragon's blood from what remained on her leather clothing.

"Need this stuff." Tom answered as he eyed the beaker now half full of the blue, thick liquid.

"Any particular reason you need the blood of one of the most dangerous creatures out there?" Patrick asked him.

"There is a reason. Not a simple form of it though." He responded. There was that look of his, thoughts were going on in that head of his that clearly had no regard for the current subject of discussion. He began to walk over to the passageway. He exited the room and opened the first door to the left. He walked through the door and closed it behind him.

"Arrogant twat." Patrick cursed as he shook his head.

"I assume he's making another one of those mysterious liquids." Cathie thought aloud.

"And you decided to help him?"

"Seemed simple enough. Out of the four of us I was clearly the best choice. Besides, you wouldn't have let me go if you'd known about it."

"That why you decided to head off nice and early? While Charlie and I were doing a fruit gathering?" Patrick questioned her. She didn't answer, but her face pretty much said yes for her in a way that showed she clearly didn't want to admit it.

"Where is Charlie anyway?" She asked, completely changing the subject.

"Good question actually. He should have been back by now. Might have gotten spooked by the dragon you brought to our doorstep."

"Want me to go and look for him?"

"I think you've put yourself in enough danger this morning." Cathie rolled her eyes and quietly scoffed at this, "I'll give him half an hour and then we can both go out and look for him." He suggested.

Cathie rather reluctantly nodded at this.

Just a few seconds later, another man shot through the door and quickly closed it behind him.

"Think I lost them in the forest." He puffed, out of breath and sweating from the full sprint he'd just stopped. Tom and Cathie hadn't even broken a sweat from their escape, so clearly this Charlie had been running for longer.

He carefully opened the door and scanned the immediate area. He nodded, then casually closed the door. Nothing to worry about, he'd lost them.

"More trouble this morning?" Patrick asked him.

"Pack of ice dragons near the lake. Looked like they had slept their last night. Gave me one hell of a fright when I tried to grab a drink." Charlie explained.

Charlie was the same height as Cathie. However, unlike Cathie, Charlie was more about speed than strength. His one-handed sword on his back was a testament to that. He had blond hair of similar length to Tom and brown, nearly orange eyes. Despite his fast and agile fighting styles, Charlie also boasted the title of the strongest man of the group. Although he hadn't yet claimed the strongest human of the group.

"Guess we'll stay clear until they move on. Didn't expect ice dragons this close. The earth dragons are usually very aggressive about their territory."

"Sounds to me like the ice dragons are expanding their territory in this direction." Cathie suggested.

"As if things weren't bad enough." Charlie sighed, "At least we can fight an earth dragon."

"Might need to brush up on your studies Patrick. Remember that earth dragons are the only dragon which don't have wings." She reminded them, "Which means I'm pretty much useless."

"How is everyone with a bow?" Charlie asked them both, "I know that's Tom's thing, but I dread relying on him in your place."

"Can't shoot for shit." Patrick sighed.

"Pretty good shot, but Tom's by far the best." Cathie answered.

"I'm pretty terrible, but some practice will probably fix that. Willing to teach?" Charlie asked as he turned to look at Cathie. He only just noticed that she was completely covered in dragons' blood. He went to open his mouth, but Patrick patted him on the shoulder.

"Tom." Patrick simply answered his question before it left his mouth.

"Of course." Charlie sighed.

"I'm not very good at the whole teaching thing. Ask Tom, he was the one who taught me." Cathie answered as she began to walk towards the front door.

"Where are you off to?" Patrick quickly asked her.

"Stream up the hill. Need to wash this shit off me and my clothes. Won't take long." She answered as she opened the door and walked out. The door swung shut behind her.

Patrick patted a slightly disappointed Charlie on the shoulder.

"Maybe next time mate." He spoke as Charlie let out an equally disappointing sigh to match his posture.

***

Sleep was something Cathie rarely got. She'd spend most nights lying awake in the fur sheets of her bed. Over the many years she'd run out of ways to occupy herself, so she simply let her body rest as it would if she were asleep. Her eyes rarely closed however, and when they did, she shot them back open.

Patrick was always a pain in the ass, but today he'd especially been so. Granted, today she'd been a bit more reckless than usual, but Tom seemed to really need that blood they'd collected.

Tom's mysterious liquids had a rather bad reputation behind them. One let off toxic vapours, one simply exploded, another shone, so brightly they had to bury the damn thing before it drew attention. Yet he continued to mess about with this that or the other.

Clearly, he was trying to make something, but he was also clearly getting it wrong every time. Still, he never answered them when they asked what he was making, or why he was making it. Charlie and Patrick had always pegged the guy as crazy from the start, but Cathie had spent a few years alone with him before they'd met the other two. He'd mix this and that back then as well, and they ended up almost as disastrously, but he'd always seemed determined to finish whatever it was he'd started.

Tom had brought many a perk to their group. Perhaps the main reason Patrick hadn't yet stabbed him in his sleep. Salt from rocks to make food last, doors to protect against the wind, higher quality leather work and basic utensils such as wooden plates and cups, as well as small metal knives. Something of a challenge Tom had issued to Charlie back in the day when they'd first become the group they were now.

Yet these mixtures of doom didn't seem to have any advantage to their way of life. Clearly their intended effect didn't work with all of his previous attempts, but the fact that he was being suspiciously quiet about what he was up to was rather worrying at times.

Tom, like Cathie, wasn't the best around other humans. In fact, other than their own parents, both Tom and Cathie's first human encounters were each other. That being said, she'd never known him to actively try to kill another human. In fact, they'd first met because Tom had saved her from a rather desperate fight for her life, even helped heal her wounds.

Her thoughts were interrupted by the sound of a door quietly opening and shutting. Had she been asleep she wouldn't have heard it, but since she was still very much awake, her ears did their best to listen out for any further sounds.

Footsteps. Towards the front door. She heard it open and shut with equal care to how the first door had been. She quietly got out of bed and quickly dressed herself. She quietly opened her own door and walked out into the passageway.

Tom's door had been left slightly ajar. Her first instinct was to head for Patrick's door, but his rather pissed off face from earlier that day flashed into her mind. She'd gotten Tom into enough trouble already. Instead, she opened Tom's door and inspected the room.

Unlike her own room, which consisted of nothing more than a bed and the occasional sword rack, Tom's room was an intricate mess of objects. The bed against the far wall had a neat pile of clothes on it, something Cathie herself should probably get into the habit of instead of just tossing them onto the floor.

Also, against the back wall and beside the bed was Tom's desk and chair. Upon which lay various sheets of paper with all sorts of notes and drawings. Books lay open and spread about. Glassware also occupied a part of the desk. The very same beaker Tom had put the dragon's blood in now contained a clear liquid that seemed to continue to bubble rather alarmingly. She decided that going near it wasn't a good idea. Beside the beaker was a few other pieces of glassware stained black from whatever liquid had been in them. A wooden bottle with similar stains around the outside was beside that, with the lid firmly on.

The rest of the room was filled with more sheets of paper all over the floor, more books, this time closed, and the odd small contraption that achieved this and that.

She couldn't however locate his bow, which confirmed that he'd not just popped outside to relieve himself. She made a quick stop back at her room to grab one of the many swords. She paused, then grabbed a second just in case. She didn't know what she was getting herself into this time, and Tom seemed to act as a magnet to danger.

***

The cold, harsh forest floor wasn't particularly nice against Cathie's bare feet. Tom had tried many times to create leather shoes for her, but she had a habit of tearing through them after only a few days of use. Besides, she leant to fight barefoot, she was used to it. She'd also had a similar issue with the precisely measured clothes Tom had at first provided her a few days after they'd first met, but after a few attempts he simply opted to make thick leather clothing for her that was too big for her under normal circumstances. It allowed her to freely move despite the protection, something until that point she'd opted not to have, instead using a more vine and leaf approach that barely covered her from chest to knees.

During the summer she'd still wear such a thing, but at this time of year the leaves from the trees were turning brown and falling off. The nights were much colder, and the days began to offer less and less warmth in between the lengthening darkness.

Soon even the leather wouldn't be enough. Soon she'd have to break out her prized collection of wolf furs, but it hadn't gotten that bad just yet.

Cathie had done her best to teach the group how to hide their tracks from other animals. Granted her teaching methods weren't the best, but it was an essential skill that they'd all been very lucky to survive without until that point. However, Cathie also wasn't a fool. Despite Tom's efforts, she found it rather easy to follow the trail he'd left. He'd done enough to stop most from being able to follow, but Cathie never taught them all of her tricks and secrets.

As she reached the edge of the forest her eyes caught a glance of something big and white. She quickly stopped and hid just within the treeline.

Ice dragons. Just beyond the trees the ground gave way to a large lake. Between the lake and Cathie were roughly seven or eight ice dragons.

Very unlike earth dragons, ice dragons were built more or less in the same way a typical dragon was. Four legs that supported an ice cold and pure white body covered in icy scaling. Both wings and a tail designed for flight and a seemingly impenetrable cold aura that surrounded each and every one of them.

They were all drinking from the lake, with their backs turned to her, but an ice dragon made an earth dragon look weak. The flying thing was a massive issue, not to mention the deadly ice breath which could be fired much faster and with a lot more accuracy than the earth dragon's ranged attack.

On the bright side, she was alright at her current position due to them relying more on their eyes than ears. If they didn't see her then they likely wouldn't be aware of her provided she played it smart. She checked the wind, but there wasn't much of a breeze in the first place.

Suddenly every single one of the dragons jerked back from the lake. A few hissed, a few growled. A few began to boom loud dragon tongue. Dragon tongue was a rather complex language that couldn't be replicated by the human throat or properly heard by the human ear.

According to Tom, attempts at communication had been made in the past, but they always ended in blood, without exception, human blood.

She couldn't understand entirely what they were saying, but she could guess the general idea from some past experience of hers. They were confused, alarmed. Something was happening to them, but none of them seemed to know what. Oddly enough they all seemed to turn to one particular dragon.

At first glance that particular dragon didn't seem any different from the rest, but after noting how the other dragons seemed to interact with it, they were very much subordinates talking to their leader.

"The hell is happening to my throat?" One of them suddenly spoke. Cathie made sure her ears heard correctly by running that past second back through her mind.

"Frost, you're speaking in human tongue!" Another dragon exclaimed. The first which had spoken human was the one who appeared to be the leader of this pack.

"So are you." Frost replied. He turned to the rest of the surrounding dragons.

"I can't stop speaking human tongue." One of them announced. What followed was a series of large throats attempting to clear themselves, but there was nothing to clear.

"Honestly I'm surprised you can understand one another." Tom alerted both Cathie and the rest of them to his presence. He'd been hiding on the other side of the lake, within some tall grass that came right up to the water's edge. Now he was standing waist high in it.

"Is this your doing human?" Frost boomed at him. Their eyes all fixed on Tom.

"Glad to know my work wasn't all for nothing." Tom sighed as he shook an empty glass vial in one of his hands. He'd poured some of that bubbling liquid from earlier into the lake.

"A potion maker!" One of the dragons yelled in panic.

"Relax, it won't kill you. Its effects have already come apparent to you." Tom revealed as he folded his arms, "Now we can actually have a chat for once."

"Should I kill him now Frost?" One of the dragons asked as it stepped forwards. Frost however raised a wing to block the dragon's advance.

"Do that, and the second one will gut you before you even make it to the other side." Frost answered. He didn't look in Cathie's direction, but Cathie suddenly had the feeling that he knew she was there. She quietly placed a hand on the handle of the sword sheathed onto her belt. Her second sword lay on her back in waiting, just in case.

"Anticipating an ambush, are we?" Tom asked, "Guess as long as I stay on this side, and you keep to yours, we won't have an issue." He added as he patted the bow on his shoulder for added effect.

"You went to a lot of effort to make yourself heard human." Frost pointed out as he lowered his wing. The other dragons remained on guard, watching their surroundings with sharp eyes.

"I wish to know if it would be possible to negotiate." Tom began. Frost burst out in thunderous laughter for a few seconds before realising that Tom wasn't joking.

"Why would I consider such a thing? Why would you either?"

"Because there aren't that many of us left." Tom answered, "You've no doubt seen what humans can make. Swords and bows. Perhaps we could offer our craftsmanship in return."

"We have no need of your magical tricks." One of the dragons hissed. Frost turned to the specific dragon and gave it a scolding stare before returning his gaze to Tom. He seemed oddly puzzled by what Tom had said, but he was also clearly thinking about something as well.

"Tell me human. It has been many years since the conflict between our two kinds began. Are you aware of why we kill you?" Frost asked Tom.

"I'm afraid not. One of many facts lost a few generations ago." Tom answered. That had in fact been a question that had been asked so many times by the human race in the last few decades that they simply stopped asking, for no answer ever seemed to reveal itself.

"What do you know of the Neutral?" Frost continued to ask. Question after question. Clearly, he wanted to know just how much of the past was in current human knowledge.

"I know not of what you speak." Tom answered.

"Of whom I speak." Frost corrected, "But clearly even that has been lost to time and death." He sighed.

"Sire, you aren't seriously considering…"

"I know little about the knowledge you possess of dragons. You have been most fortunate to address the current king of ice dragons with such a plea." Frost revealed. Tom was very much taken by surprise by this fact. Meanwhile Cathie's grip on her sword tightened, "Yet I cannot speak for all dragon kind."

"I see. So right now, you can only vouch for ice dragons?"

"To stop the other species from killing you, you'll have to have similar talks with their respected leaders, which I'm sure you can imagine being difficult." Tom seemed to take in this new information.

"You wouldn't happen to know how to get to the earth and fire dragons would you?" He asked him.

"You'll have to go much further than that I'm afraid. I take it you probably aren't aware of all the different types of dragon?" Frost asked him.

"There are more?"

"To name a few, the ice dragons are currently allied with both the water dragons and the air dragons." Frost revealed. Two new types of dragon that no human alive today had neither seen nor heard of.

"Clearly we have much more to learn about this world than I thought." Tom muttered to himself.

"Perhaps if your friend would stop hiding in the shadows and join us, I'll happily explain." Frost announced as he finally turned his gaze directly towards Cathie.

Had he known where she'd been the whole time, or had he only just found her exact location. Either way, she found herself oddly recognising the crafty look on Frost's face. He clearly had ideas about the opportunity presented to him.

***

Patrick had dragged Tom into his room and closed the door behind them, but Cathie put her ear to the wooden door just in time to hear what sounded like a painful punch being thrown. She winced, almost feeling Tom's pain for him.

"Really don't appreciate the violence." Tom muttered from what sounded like the ground. She heard him get to his feet only to be slammed once more. This time it sounded more like a knee.

She didn't hear him hit the floor this time however, there was another rather surprising slam from out of the blue. Someone fell back against the door Cathie was leaning on. Luckily it didn't open that way, but that must have been Patrick from the sounds of it.

"Got some fight in you this time." She heard Patrick spit.

"Because this time it's not my fault she was there." Tom answered, "I went alone specifically to avoid this very conversation."

"Clearly you didn't take enough precautions."

"Clearly. It's one thing to get punched for risking her life, I can understand that, but this time its undeserving."

"Fine." Patrick huffed, "I'm sorry."

"Glad you have some reason in there somewhere."

"Now how about we get to the part where you talked to a fucking dragon!" Patrick shouted as Cathie heard another thump.

"Now this was more what I was expecting." Tom winced as he collapsed to the floor once more.

"All these years of being a pain in my ass, risking all of our lives, including the most important life of the group, all to talk to a bloody dragon."

"You wouldn't understand my motives." Tom sighed. Cathie noticed that this time he hadn't even tried to get up again.

"Rather sick of hearing those damn three words."

"What you might understand, is that we now have the opportunity to walk outside that door out there with one less thing to worry about. Now given the situation we're in, I thought it would be a half decent idea to try."

"A bloody dangerous one."

"Hence why I went alone. Figured if it all went wrong, you'd probably not lose any sleep about me not coming back."

"Damn right I wouldn't." There was silence as the two of them seemed to take a break from their argument. She heard Tom slowly get back to his feet until Patrick broke the silence, "You said something about new types of dragons?"

"Ones we haven't heard of before, yeah." There was another pause. Patrick was thinking about something.

"Would be nice to get a look at these different dragons. Possible strengths and weaknesses. Might help avoid some unexpected situations down the line."

"Not a bad idea. You want to use this opportunity to scope them out?"

"Ideally I'd absolutely love whatever dream world you have in that head of yours to become a reality, but even if it doesn't, this works to our advantage provided this ice dragon can guide us to these new dragons."

"Guess we have a fallback plan then." Cathie heard Tom begin to walk towards the door, but she then heard something stop him. A hand pushing against his chest perhaps.

"But if we're doing this, we do it all together. I'm not an idiot, being taken to the leaders of dragon kind will clearly need Cathie with us for protection if shit goes wrong. That means we all go."

"For once we agree on something." Tom muttered. He seemed to be allowed forwards. Cathie stepped back just as the door opened. Tom gave a smile as he noticed her rather poor attempt to pretend that she hadn't been listening in, "Your guardian angel awaits."

"Fuck off!" Patrick shouted from within the room. Tom simply laughed to himself as he walked off, trying his best to walk off the large bruises and slight limp. Cathie slowly stepped into Patrick's room, "Door had a lot more weight to it than I remember."

"You really didn't have to beat the shit out of him."

"Well clearly it's not having the intended effect of getting him to listen to me. But at least I can reason with the guy to some degree. You on the other hand seem determined to get yourself killed."

"You're really starting to become far too overprotective of me Patrick."

"Pretty sure that's the job I signed up for when we first became this group. Even gave up my chance with you so that I could be a pain in your ass in times like these without anything holding me back." He reminded her as he closed the door behind her.

"There is such a thing as taking it too far." She complained as she turned to face him and folded her arms. Patrick extended an arm, "Really?" She asked, not wanting to go through what he was asking her to do.

"Been a while since I last checked." He reasoned. She bit her lip, then slowly extended her right arm out. Patrick rolled up her sleeve and was instantly disappointed by the result.

"I know, I know-"

"Come on Cathie, you were doing so well." He sighed as he rolled her sleeve down again.

"I know I just… It's a lot harder to give up than you think."

"Fuck. Got Tom doing more and more stupid shit and now I've got to worry about this again." Cathie brought both of her hands to her chest.

"Look, I know you worry about me, but I've lasted this long for a reason."

"I know. Only woman left and you have twice the strength of us remaining men But being strong will mean crap if this gets any worse."

***

Within this world only four humans remain. The four humans that make up the last of human civilisation. Each from a different family, thrown together though matters of convenience and desperation. Each with a tragic tale behind them already, but more soon to come. The human race had been facing extinction for some time now, but now Cathie was the only existing hope of it surviving longer than their short lifespans.

CHAPTER 2; THE START

Cathie was squatting beside some rather peculiar looking tracks. Whatever it was, it was small but heavy. The tracks seemed more like someone had poked a series of sharp sticks into the ground, but they carried on into the distance. What was equally strange, was that the tracks headed in a perfectly straight line and didn't seem to leave any droppings or bit of fur.

"Now isn't the time to daydream." Charlie muttered as he walked past her. She stood up, shrugged her shoulders and continued to follow the other three through the woods. Whatever it was had been and gone a long time ago, and not in the direction they were heading in.

"Little more this way." Tom added as they began to head for the edge of the forest. The four of them broke through the treeline to meet the lakeside.

***

The surrounding air was both thin and icy. It had been cold enough just from simply sitting on the top of an ice dragon, but somehow once they were up in the sky it was even colder. The wind seemed determined to push them off, as if they were never meant to have reached this height in the first place.

The four of them were sitting rather uncomfortably on Frost's back. All covered up in fur coats and thick, furry trousers. Most of their faces were covered by the thick furry hoods that covered their heads, but none of them covered their eyes. How could they with the view?

Up until now it was rare for them to even venture above tree level. When they did it was normally due to a large hill or finding their bearings in a forest. Yet now the trees were so small they all blurred together into a large bulk of brown and gold. Patches of evergreen trees were especially obvious as they were large green patches spread about the world beneath them.

The only thing above them now was the peaks of the back mountains and the peak of the largest mountain in the known world.

The Black mountains were a line of mountains that no human had ever successfully climbed. The natural barrier that marked the end of the known world. This barrier surrounded the known world on all sides but one, which simply gave way to open water. Yet tales of humans who reached the other side of the vast ocean seemed to claim that the water simply hits more black mountains, not even any land between, just a sheer cliff to their peaks.

Tall and seemingly impassable to any without the gift of flight, the only thing in the known world that towered above them was the tallest peak in the known world. Far to the north and covered in snow thick enough to hide a dragon beneath, humans never ventured near the towering mountain that stands alone amongst the contrasting Black mountain range. Unlike the Black mountains, this mountain was in fact climbable. The problem was that it lay deep in the heart of ice dragon territory. Meaning certain death for any human stupid enough to try for it.

For this reason, the mountain was never given a name by humanity, for no human had ever successfully climbed it, with the exception of one little girl who made it roughly two thirds of the way up. Yet her story is unknown to all humans except herself. But I by no means imply that she did not survive.

Cathie, who was rather used to the cold, was sitting at the very back. As the most exposed to the harsh winds, she held onto Tom as tightly as she dared without crushing his ribs. Tom was sandwiched in between her and Charlie, with Patrick doing his best to support the others and holding onto Frost's back. The front three were spared from most of the side wind from Frost's beating wings, plus Frost's head shielded them from the front wind, but Cathie was behind the wings and so rather more exposed than the rest.

As the wind violently changed direction, Cathie increased her grip on Tom rather quickly.

"Are you alright?" Tom asked her. Despite her head being pressed right up to the back of his, he feared that his words might have gotten lost to the wind.

"It's fine. Been through worse." She replied. So she could hear him. It was hard though. Perhaps Charlie might have heard her response as well, but Tom very much doubted that Patrick would have heard any of the rather brief conversation.

"We should be there soon enough." Frost's voice cut through the wind. They'd all heard that. Frost was still climbing higher and higher. He'd mentioned air dragons, but surely, they couldn't live their entire lives in the sky. If they did then talking to them was going to be very interesting.

The cloud above them suddenly split in half. Something had flown through it, very fast. Something shot past them, to the left. Too fast to see.

Something flew passed their right as well, but this time far too close. The chaotic movements of the air lifted Cathie right off Frost's back. Tom was lifted up with her, meaning the two were now only being held to Frost via Tom's grip on Charlie, which didn't last very long.

Before they knew it, Frost's tail whooshed underneath them, and then there was nothing but the ground far, far beneath them.

"Oh fuck." Tom muttered as Cathie did her best to keep a hold of him. He could feel the two of them beginning to fall downwards at an alarming rate.

Something quickly snatched the two of them from the air. More precisely, something with claws dug their sharp appendages right into Cathie's shoulders.

Despite Cathie's cursing and yelling, she could do little but desperately keep her grip on Tom, who was now relying on her to stop him from falling.

The two of them looked up to see something that resembled a dragon, but it was rather different to any they'd seen before. With only two legs that were currently digging into Cathie's shoulders, the whole of its body seemed sleek and smooth.

It's thin, serpent like body seemed to only be interrupted by its wings and two legs. Even its skull was thin but sharp. Not to mention its glass like complexion. Its skin was almost completely see-through. Even its insides were oddly transparent. Its bones were thin, weak and very minimal. Its wings were thin yet had a bone structure through them that seemed to suggest that it used them as front legs when walking.

Before either of them could fully comprehend what was happening, they were chucked forwards. They hit solid ground and rolled before coming to a stop. The dragon that had caught them now stood above them, teeth bearing despite its weak appearance.

"Is the one responsible for my voice one of you?" The dragon asked them. Cathie had been surprised to hear it speak human tongue, but Tom was oddly expecting it.

"I apologise for the change in language, but it was necessary for us to be able to talk to you." Tom responded as he got to his feet. Cathie slowly got to hers with a wince of pain. Her wounds were bleeding rather slowly, but still bleeding. The claws had torn right through her brown fur coat, which she now tried her best to use to cover the wounds up.

The dragon snared at Tom's response.

"Move." It ordered as it began to walk forwards. The two of them kept ahead of it and began to walk down a white passageway.

They hadn't had much time to look at their surroundings, but from what Tom could tell, the floor and the surrounding walls were all made of solid ice. Not just your standard ice either. Thick ice as hard as steel. Ice crafted by an ice dragon for sure.

They walked down many dragon-sized corridors until they came to two large doors of ice. The doors opened to reveal a large, cold room on the other side.

Dead in the centre of the room was a large slab of ice, which another air dragon was comfortably sat on. He stood upright on his two wings and legs as he noticed the two humans being shoved into the room.

"Humans." The dragon on the slab seemed to curse instead of simply state, "Bad enough you still exist, but now you tamper with our very own throats? Even I, king of my kind am not spared."

"They claim they wish to talk." The dragon behind them announced. The horrific sound of laughter mixed in between gusts of wind came from behind them. Both of them turned to see the crowd of air dragons which must have followed them into the room. Clearly these dragons were good at not being noticed.

"Is this the reason for your defiling act? The reason you stop us from using our very own tongue?" The king asked.

"We wish to negotiate." Tom answered as calmly as he could. He could see Cathie twitching for her sword on her belt. Once more the room was filled with laughter.

"You have nerves of steel. I'll give you that. Reverse the magic and I'll let you leave this place alive." The king responded.

"You won't even consider hearing me out?" Tom asked him. The king seemed to smile at this.

"I know you humans are poor keepers of your history, but please tell me you are aware of at least some of our race's history with one another."

"I'm afraid until recently I was not even aware of your existence."

"Then perhaps a history lesson is in order." The king hissed as he walked off his slab and stood directly in front of the two of them, "We once had an ally like no other. Electric dragons. The most powerful dragon in existence. An ally that let us sit above all other dragon kind under their rule of this world."

"If such dragons exist, why have I never heard of one?" Cathie asked him.

"I think we're about to find out." Tom answered.

"However, your god decided that such dragons decided to die. With you humans at his side, your precious Neutral wiped them all out. With that, our kind went from nearly top of the food chain, to the very bottom. Forced us to ally with the filthy ice dragons."

"Perhaps it should interest you to hear that Frost has already agreed not to kill our kind anymore." Tom revealed.

"How stupid do you really think I am? Frost, the Mist of Death, Conqueror of the North. Frost the cunning and Frost the unyielding. Please explain why a dragon with such titles that even a critic like me acknowledges as fact, would strike a deal with a filthy warm-blooded human?"

"I..." To be honest, that was a good question. Tom didn't really know much about Frost, but from the way this dragon described him, his life should have ended at the lakeside. Even considering that the titles were all just made up, Frost had taken to Tom's words much quicker than he'd expected. Not to mention he also mentioned this Neutral. He didn't like the fact that he knew almost nothing about what happened between dragons and humans. Clearly nerves had been struck.

"Reverse your magic. Before I decide to kill you here and now." The king repeated.

"I can't." Tom answered, "I don't know how."

"Death it is then." The king announced. He turned and walked back to his slab, "Make it nice and slow." He ordered.

The crowd of dragons behind them very quickly became a huge threat. Cathie drew her sword but was quickly knocked off her feet by a blast of air. Tom managed to avoid the blast, but many claws and teeth were now bearing down on the two of them.

A very quick scan of their surroundings revealed an ice pot with what appeared to be crystals inside, but nothing else around. Tom quickly pulled Cathie and himself behind it.

"Well shit." Tom cursed as Cathie pulled out the sword on her back to replace the one she'd dropped when she fell. Tom reached into his bag, but then seemed to change his mind as he realised the lack of cover and the close quarters they would be in soon.

"If we hug the wall and run, we might make it to the door." Cathie explained as Tom reached a hand into the pot and took out two crystals. He gave them a quick look before shoving them in his bag.

"How's your shoulders?" He asked.

"Not now. Go." She quickly made a break for the wall of the room and curved to run alongside it. The air dragons hadn't been smart and had left a gap between them and the wall. Tom followed closely behind her as the two of them narrowly escaped claws and blasts of air.

They'd made it to the open doors, another mistake the air dragons had made. Clearly, they'd been overconfident with their attempt to kill the two of them.

They sprinted through the many winding corridors. Tom took the lead as he retraced their steps from earlier, but Cathie matched his pace once she'd noticed the slight blood trail her wounds had left.

"Are you good?" Tom asked her.

"For now." She answered. Tom reached into his bag and handed her some cloth and two metal pins.

"Before it gets worse."

"Once we stop, sure." The two of them continued until they entered a large, open and cold chamber. Unlike the rest of the place, this room was very windy, almost as much as when they'd been up in the sky. There appeared to be a cave mouth ahead of them, which is where they must have come in from. However, when the two of them stood at the edge of the mouth, they both realised that they were in fact not on the ground.

Over the edge, lay the rest of the known world. An ice cave in the sky. Perhaps this is what Frost was flying towards. As white as the clouds and a cold environment to keep the ice from melting.

"Well that certainly complicates things." Tom huffed as Cathie began to quickly bandage herself up. Tom watched her rather mediocre attempts for a few seconds before just taking over and doing them properly.

"Thanks." She muttered as Tom finished the second bandage around her shoulder.

"Think you can fight with these injuries?" He asked her.

"Not as good as normal, but these things aren't exactly earth dragons." She answered, "Doesn't solve our escape plan though."

"I think I can sort that for us. I doubt we can hold out long enough for Frost to arrive considering just how high we are, so I'll have to get creative." He responded as he opened his bag up and began taking out small sticks and more cloth.

"How long?"

"Minute, maybe more. They'll be on us soon though."

"I'll buy you as much time as you need." She sighed as she examined the blade in her hand. Still sharp, it would do.

The first of the air dragons entered the large chamber and began to crawl towards them. Compared to being in the air, these dragons were rather slow on the ground.

Cathie took a few steps forwards at first, but it quickly turned into a paced run as she tightly gripped her sword and pointed its tip towards the dragon. The dragon opened its mouth to blast air at her, but as it fired Cathie had already sidestepped it. Clearly this type of dragon didn't fight on the ground that often either.

Its entire body was clearly built for speed and stealth. To attack from above and vanish. Here, on solid ground and a roof above, Cathie very much had the advantage for once.

Cathie came in from the side and quickly swiped her blade down onto the dragon's neck. It felt like a knife cutting through butter.

Blue blood spilled onto the floor as the dragon's body collapsed into the puddle. However, more of them had appeared. She barely had enough time to dodge the next blast of air. A claw sliced her back as she dealt another fatal blow, this time stabbing a nearby dragon's chin.

Before long, she was completely surrounded. Air seemed to begin spinning around her, blocking her from even throwing a sword to any of the surrounding dragons. They were trapping her.

Arrows sunk into the bodies of a few of the surrounding dragons. Suddenly there was a gap in the barrier of air that was closing in on her. She quickly sprinted through and back towards Tom.

Tom quickly packed away his bow and picked up what appeared to be a collection of sticks and cloth.

"Don't let go of me." He told her as he seemed to strap the rushed invention onto his back. She grabbed hold of him from the front shortly after sheathing her sword on her back and looked into his yellow eyes.

Arms around his waist, face to face with him. Would she have enough confidence to tell him this time? She went to open her mouth but was quickly interrupted by the feeling that she was falling backwards.

She felt her feet leave the edge of the ice cave behind. They were falling, but not for very long. She watched as two wing-like structures took shape from the invention on Tom's back. She felt them slow down to the point that they were now gliding.

"We're... flying?"

"Hold on tight now. Only had the time and resources to build one of these things and their no dragon. I won't be able to catch you if you fall." He warned her. It was only then that she realised that only her arms around Tom's waist were keeping her in the air with him. She quickly wrapped her legs around his own to help support her weight.

Once more she simply stared into his eyes. He seemed to notice her this time, "You alright?"

"Yeah, just… hanging on for my life and all." She quickly responded. She put her fur hood up and began to hide as much of her face as possible as her cheeks began to glow bright red. Tom's eyes began to focus on where they were heading instead of her.

"It's not over yet. I'm sure those dragons will catch up to us."

CHAPTER 3; OUT OF THE FRYING PAN AND INTO THE FIRE

Within this strange and unforgiving world, many things exist which do not in our own. One of the lesser-known ones is something called magic. A human practice that few could ever master. Although being able to achieve the seemingly impossible, it is not as all powerful as one would normally expect. The magic of this world is oddly specific. Each spell discovered only through trial and error, with the actual process of how the magic works shrouded in unsolved mysteries.

Some would go on to compare the magic of this world to science, and that other than an understanding of how it worked, the two were inseparable from one another. Both were frowned upon within human culture, although magic did provide more obvious and quick acting benefits than science, neither did much in a fight other than support those already risking their own lives. Thus, magicians and scientists, thought to be opposites by all, were both equally placed at the bottom of the human food chain.

An interesting side note; other creatures of this world, particularly dragons, do not see the difference between science and magic. They also rightly fear such practices as they often avoid conventional fighting tactics and thus are an element of unpredictability within an already crafty creature by nature.

An example of this is the ability to fly. Something that science can achieve with time. Some spells also assist with the prevention of becoming a puddle of jam on the floor as well, but something humans are typically known to not be able to do. In fact, this is the main advantage most dragons have over humans, so to have it taken away, although not enough to make a single human more powerful than a dragon, still closes the gap between the two races. Something that is seen as never to be allowed.

***

Cathie watched as Tom's eyes finally looked down at the ground behind her. He seemed to almost vomit before quickly shutting them.

"Fuck. That was a mistake." He shivered as he did his best to open his eyes again, but for some reason they didn't open no matter how hard he tried.

A shrieking noise from behind them caught Cathie off guard. She quickly looked to see three Air dragons catching up to them.

"What was that?" Tom asked in a rather unusually panicked tone.

"How much control do you have of this thing?" Cathie asked him.

"Very little." Tom answered, "Why?"

"We might have to dodge a few attacks." Cathie revealed. She looked back at Tom's face, "I need you to open your eyes."

"Do you want me to pass out from fear?" Tom asked her.

"Don't look down, look at me." Cathie quickly came up with. It wasn't much but he really needed to see where he was going.

A violent gust of air hit the two of them. The two of them began to spin out of control and quickly fall towards the ever-nearing ground. Cathie's own eyes shut, now understanding to some degree why Tom was frightened.

***

Cathie closed her eyes as a wooden sword came towards her face. Her two-year-old eyes opened after a second to see the sword had stopped right in front of her. The sword was lowered to reveal the wielder.

A large man in red scaled armour shook his head.

"Fear." He spoke, "It is good. Tells us when something is wrong, when we're in danger." He continued as he raised his wooden sword at her once more, "But when fear blinds you, or holds you still, that's when the danger strikes."

"How do I stop fear blinding me?" Cathie asked in a voice that could barely be heard through the wind blowing through the long grass around them. The man smiled.

"By keeping your eyes open!" He shouted as he swung at her again. The air rang with the sound of wood snapping.

***

Eyes open daughter!

Cathie's eyes shot open. They were falling, and fast. Cathie locked eyes with Tom, who still had his closed.

"Tom!" Cathie shouted. Tom's eyes opened in panic to stare directly into Cathie's. Her eyes flared as red as the hair that trailed above them, "Don't let us die."

Tom nodded and spread the wings once more. The sudden force winded Cathie almost instantly. Her entire body felt like it had squashed onto the bottom of her feet. She nearly lost consciousness, but her eyes refused to close.

The level feeling from before began to return. She looked up at Tom's face. He was facing forwards now, looking at where they were flying, but he was also clearly holding the urge to throw up.

Claws appeared from above Tom. Cathie quickly swung her legs around Tom's to flip the two of them over. The claws dug into Cathie's shoulders instead of the glider now that Tom was underneath her. Now was the chance.

Cathie let go of Tom as she grabbed the rather weak leg of the Air dragon. It didn't take much to break its grip, and she timed it to land on a second one that was trying to get to Tom.

She landed right on its neck, which she felt crunch. Her knees shot a burst of pain too, it was a big fall. The dragon lost consciousness after a second or so and began to fall.

The dragon with the now broken leg swooped towards Cathie to knock her off. Cathie quickly pushed off the unconscious dragon to jump over it. Her hand found the edge of a wing as the dragon passed under her.

The dragon was moving fast. Cathie's arm was nearly yanked out of its socket as she was pulled in another direction once more. Yet again she felt as though her brain had smacked into the bottom of her feet.

The thin and see-through skin of the dragon's wing was as tough as paper. It didn't take much more than a kick or two from her feet to begin making holes in it. The dragon let out a deafening shriek as its mouth snapped at her head. She quickly got out of its way, but her hair got caught in its mouth.

"Oh shit." Cathie muttered as she stared into the furious eyes of the dragon. The dragon pulled her off the wing and opened its mouth, throwing her to the sky beyond.

As she began to fall once more, a hand grabbed hers. Tom quickly pulled her back up, so she was beneath him. She quickly grabbed a hold of his body once more and held on tight as he brought the two of them level as slow as he could.

"You are one scary person. You know that, right?" Tom asked her as the adrenalin in her body began to die down. Her body was covered in blue blood, and her breathing and heartbeat were painfully high.

Cathie looked behind them at the dragon struggling to keep itself in the air, while another hit the ground, which was now considerably closer than the last time she checked.

"You have a plan to land this thing, right?" Cathie asked him. Tom seemed to think for a few seconds.

"Didn't really consider that part." He answered as he seemed to think in his head 'I knew I forgot something'.

"Well, you don't have long to figure it out." Cathie reminded him as she watched the third air dragon line up behind them. It increased in speed and began to gain on them.

"We could always try the air crystals I picked up." Tom suggested.

"How would they help?" Cathie asked him.

"When I grabbed them, it produced a small gust of air. I think applying pressure produces a blast of air." Tom theorised.

"Will that be enough to stop us?" Cathie asked.

"No idea." Tom answered.

Tom quickly grabbed the two of them from the bag tied around his body. He slipped one into her hand.

Another focused blast of air hit them. This time right in between the two of them. Cathie and Tom were blown apart.

The tree line appeared in Cathie's peripherals. She wasn't falling too fast, but fast enough to break something. She spun herself around and squeezed the air crystal in her hand.

Trees lashed at her from one side to the other as she came to a rough ground that she rolled onto. Her stomach smacked into the base of a tree, and what remained of the air in her lungs quickly left, along with some blood.

The familiar sound of someone crashing through branches nearby stopped her from passing out. She rolled away from the tree and slowly got to her feet.

"Tom!" Cathie shouted as she gave herself a good look. A few cuts here and there, a bruise the shape of the tree on her stomach, the shoulder wounds and the slice on her back, which didn't feel too deep. Her entire body was shaking but considering the amount of adrenalin pumping through her a few seconds a go, that was understandable.

There was no answer from her call, "Tom!" She shouted again. She tried to remember which direction the sound had previously come from.

All of a sudden, a hole appeared directly under her with a loud thump. She fell straight down into a dark underground room.

Tom's body softened the landing this time.

***

Frost continued to search the clouds.

"What kind of dragon was that?" Patrick asked.

"An air dragon." Frost answered as he came to a hover, "May I ask what weapons you happen to have on you?"

He asked. Charlie looked uneasy as Patrick opened his mouth.

"A few swords and some magic." He answered. Frost took this in for a second.

"I may have to ask that we become more than just peaceful acquaintances." He added as he spotted the white floating cave in the distance. It was very well hidden amongst the high clouds, but if you knew what you were looking for you could spot it.

Frost flew straight towards it and landed just inside the mouth of the cave. His feet met the slightly red blood stain near the edge of the cave. His eyes also noticed the small red trail of blood. The blood of a human.

"A floating cave?" Charlie asked as he and Patrick looked around at the icy walls. They weren't near enough the ground to notice the blood.

"GUST!" Frost boomed in a voice that would scare most other dragons. In fact, the two air dragons that approached them from two big doors at the end of the cave were clearly terrified.

A third air dragon stormed through the doors. The moment this dragon realised who had entered his cave however, he came to a nervous stop.

"F… Frost?" The dragon asked.

"Attacking the king of your allies? You have a lot to answer for Gust." Frost growled at the dragons before him. More air dragons began to crowd behind what appeared to be their king.

"We were simply helping you with your human... infestation." Gust answered as he looked at Charlie and Patrick, who were still sitting on Frost's back.

"I understand that you do not have the highest opinion of our new allies. Yet I would have thought you smarter than to interfere with ice dragon business." Frost boomed.

"Allies?" Gust asked. His face filled with disgust, "We were not aware of such an alliance."

"Clearly. Now then, what of the other two humans I brought to negotiate with you." Frost demanded.

Two air dragons landed behind Frost. One of which had a badly torn wing.

"I apologise sire. The humans escaped to the surface." One of them reported as the injured one collapsed to the floor of the cave.

"And the third I sent?" Gust asked the two of them.

"Dead." The uninjured air dragon answered.

"Remind me never to get on Cathie's bad side." Patrick muttered to Charlie.

"Well, I think the situation has explained itself." Frost sighed.

"I assume you will want to leave to retrieve your new... allies." Gust suggested.

"Once I am done here." Frost answered. Gust seemed confused, "Or did you not think I wouldn't notice that this cave is deep within ice dragon territory." He revealed as his eyes narrowed towards Gust.

"It is? I thought this part of the forest was earth dragon territory." Gust replied.

"Until a few months ago. In fact, we've almost cleared every earth dragon burrow." Frost explained, "And I personally know you've had time to update your maps."

The mood within the cave suddenly shifted as many air dragons tensed up, ready to strike.

"Are you implying that I am breaking our alliance?" Gust asked Frost.

"Choose your words very carefully Gust. Any dragon with any sense knows an ice dragon could easily overpower an air dragon." Frost growled as he too tensed up. Charlie very slowly began drawing his sword.

"Maybe on the surface." Gust chuckled, "But not up here with the thin air." Gust chuckled.

"We aren't that high, otherwise I wouldn't have been able to get here." Frost pointed out.

"We are now the cave has risen high enough. It's called buying time Frost." Gust chuckled as air dragons began to lunge towards him.

The dragons all smacked into an invisible barrier.

"We need to go." Patrick announced, "That won't hold for ever, and the lack of air isn't helping me."

"Alright." Frost sighed, "But this isn't over Gust!" Frost dove over the edge while whacking the two air dragons behind off with him.

The injured once simply fell, too weak to even attempt to fly anymore with an injured wing. The other quickly levelled itself out.

Frost attempted to start flying, but as Gust had revealed, the cave had increased in altitude quite drastically. The air was too thin for him, and he began to fall.

Seeing this, the air dragon quickly lined up for an attack by diving behind Frost. Using the slipstream, and its own aerodynamics to catch up to the falling Frost.

Charlie fully drew his sword. Patrick attempted to light a fireball, but there was not enough air, "Hold on tight!" Frost warned them.

Frost opened one wing, which caused him to spin off his current path. He then slowed down with both wings. As the air dragon shot in front of him, he let out a cloud of ice, which froze the air dragons' wings in the dive position, next to its body.

The air dragon continued to fall as it attempted to break free of the ice, with no success.

A loud boom came from the cave above as Frost continued to fall.

"That would be them breaking the barrier." Patrick revealed as air dragons began to pour out of the cave. Frost folded his wings in and pointed nose down.

Despite this, the air dragon hoard began to gain on them. Air dragons quickly surrounded them and began letting off blasts of air. Frost used his wings to block most of the shots, but he was taking a pounding.

All of a sudden, he felt his wings begin to catch the air in the now lower altitude. Frost fully opened his wings to slow him down as he let out a huge cloud of ice. He added a spin as he slowed so his attack froze most of the surrounding dragons. He came to a hover and realising the number of now doomed dragons falling to their deaths, the air dragons quickly shot back up towards the cave.

Frost began to relax, but one last air dragon came underneath him. It grabbed his back legs with its own, and his front legs with the claws on its wings. Frost began to fight back, until he looked the air dragon in the eye.

"Your aerial combat still sucks Frost. Someone needs more lessons." The air dragon spoke to him in a female like voice.

"You always could beat me." Frost answered with a smile.

"We'll talk later, but this should be enough for the moment." The air dragon muttered as she forced some rolled up sheets of paper into the grasp of Frost's back leg.

"Helpful as ever. Usual place, a day from now." Frost seemed to order. The air dragon nodded as she let go of him, and she shot up to join the rest of them.

***

Charlie and Patrick sat around a small campfire in the middle of the woods. Frost lay a little way away from the fire, behind the two of them. They had spent long hours of searching the ground for Tom and Cathie, before the sun set.

"So, you are the king of the ice dragons?" Patrick asked Frost.

"I am." Frost answered, "That air dragon from before was Gust, king of the air dragons."

"I gathered that." Charlie sighed, "I also gathered that they were supposed to be you're allies."

"Up until now, yes." Frost answered, "You may or may not have noticed that the fire and ice dragons are locked in a never-ending war." Frost began.

"We've never been unlucky enough to come across either at the same time." Patrick revealed.

"Because of this, many other species took sides. The water dragons have been close allies for centuries. We took in the air dragons after their allies were wiped out. The fire dragons have the larva dragons on their side."

"What about the earth dragons?" Charlie asked.

"Although they also fight our alliance, they are not on the fire dragons' side." Frost revealed.

"So, is that every type of dragon out there? You mentioned the air dragons used to have an ally?" Patrick asked him.

"The lightning dragons, or electric dragons. By far the most powerful and dangerous type of dragon out there. However along with the stone dragons, they are thought to be extinct." Frost revealed.

"How could such powerful dragons be wiped out?" Charlie asked as he watched embers spit out of the fire and onto the forest floor by his feet.

"They picked a fight with this world's other top predator. Humanity." Frost revealed.

"Us?" Patrick asked.

"They were the ones to start the culling of the human race. They feared one particular human, and after killing it they decided to wipe out the rest to make sure history did not repeat itself." Frost continued.

"So why did the other dragons do the same?" Charlie asked.

"As I said, the lightning dragons were the most powerful. Power is everything to dragons. You are ruled by those that could kill you if they so wished. They used to rule all dragons with an iron fist. A rather dark time for all dragon kind, beside their most trusted allies."

"The air dragons." Patrick realised, "I see, we took away their powerful position by fighting the lightning dragons."

"That explains why they hate us." Charlie realised.

"Do not be mistaken, however. The human the lightning dragons feared, every other dragon feared them too. It took all of us to kill it. They were perhaps wrong to wipe you all out, but the death was necessary up until a couple of hundred years ago."

"Is that why you now think we can live peacefully?" Patrick asked him.

"When I realised that a single human managed to invent a potion which allowed communication between our species, I was reminded of the potential you humans have. Both for peace, and war. Should it come to it, I would like to call upon you as allies in both as well."

"You would want us to join the wars between your races?" Charlie asked him.

"Perhaps not directly. But let us not remember that you are more or less stuck in the middle of the three sides otherwise." Frost reminded them, "Well, now there are four, I suppose."

"It's something we would have to consider in great detail." Patrick answered.

"Something perhaps saved for when you are all back together." Frost suggested.

"What about this human though. The one all dragons were terrified of?" Charlie asked.

"I believe your people referred to it as the Neutral." Frost revealed. Charlie and Patrick looked at one another.

"Never heard of it." Charlie revealed.

"Same." Patrick added, "And my people were very good at writing stuff down." He continued as he waved his spell book about.

"Another reason I accepted. Tom did not seem to recognise the name either. I suspect it is knowledge lost to the culling of your people."

"Speaking of which, Tom better be keeping Cathie safe." Charlie sighed.

"Is Cathie of any particular importance to you two?" Frost asked as he sensed the worry between the two of them.

"Frost, this may be a surprise to you, but as far as we are aware, we are the last four humans." Patrick revealed, "Which makes Cathie the last female."

"How can you be so sure?" Frost asked.

"Oh, we're sure." Charlie sighed, "Spent a long time searching every cave, cavern and hole we could find throughout the entire known world, and I don't have to tell you that no human has ever managed to get past those mountains that surround the place." He explained.

"We did find bodies though." Patrick added, "Whole colonies. Families upon families. Even if we missed a place or two, we're talking one or two other humans at most. The survival chance of which is almost zero."

"Which explains your desire to end the killing between dragons and humans."

The ground beneath them began to shake ever so gently.

"Earth dragons!" Charlie shouted.

Cracks in the ground started to appear all over the place, they were surrounded, the floor beneath them gave way. Frost was snatched by something in the ground so all they could do was fall.

***

When they woke up, they were lying on a hard rock floor in what appeared to be an underground room. Light was coming from a glowing rock that sat in a small glass container beside Tom. Cathie was also lying down, while Tom seemed to be tending to her. Scattered on the other side of the room were the broken remains of a sword.

"What is wrong with her?" Patrick asked, standing up.

"Her wounds must have been infected." Tom explained.

"Can you save her?" Charlie asked him. Tom paused for a second.

"How good are you at making chemicals Patrick?" Tom asked him.

"I can use my magic to make the odd specific one. But why?"

"Think you can do it now? Need something purifying." Tom asked him.

Patrick began to think of ideas. He looked around the square, dirt room they were in.

"Not exactly a pentagon but it will do." Patrick muttered to himself.

He began to search the collection of items on everyone's belts. Charlie had his sword, an empty wooden cup and a small dagger.

Patrick took out some string that he had on him and made a quick circle out of it, "Alright Tom hold this." Patrick said as he handed Tom the string.

Tom held it, keeping it in a circle. Patrick tied Charlie's wooden cup to a piece of string that positioned it in the centre of the circle.

"Whatever you're going to do, do it fast." Charlie reminded him.

"Tongue to cup, serpent of poison most painful let me collect." Patrick chanted, "Alright Tom put the string circle and the cup between you and Charlie. Charlie, I need you to insult Tom."

"Insult Tom?" Charlie asked.

"Just think of something horrible to say to him. The more horrible, the stronger the poison." Patrick added.

"Poison?" Tom asked.

"Just trust me, alright?"

"You alone will bring the end of the human race. Even if she survives now, you'll find some other danger to put her in. You will be the death of us all." Charlie spoke with a vicious tongue.

The string circle glowed, and the glow ran down the string and into the wooden cup.

Patrick took the cup and untied it from the string.

"Is it over?" Tom asked.

"You… didn't hear me?" Charlie asked.

"Your insult never reached him Charlie, it was blocked and concentrated into a poison." Patrick revealed as he showed the two of them the contents of the cup.

Inside was a fiery red liquid that bubbled and fumed with hatred.

"Must have been some insult." Tom muttered as he looked at Charlie.

"Best you didn't hear it." Charlie answered his unspoken question.

Patrick took the cup and placed it on the floor. He took out some chalk from his satchel and drew a complex shape around the cup. He clapped his two hands together as he closed his eyes. The liquid glowed, then became colourless.

Patrick picked the cup up as he dabbed at his nose with his sleeve.

Tom took the cup from Patrick and knelt down beside Cathie. He gave it a sniff. He seemed to recognise the smell.

"Alright. Trouble is this is rather strong. Too much might kill her."

"How much is too much?" Patrick asked him.

"Working it out now." Tom muttered. He took another whiff, "I'll have to estimate the precise concentration."

"So your guessing?" Charlie asked him.

"Educated guess, but yes." Tom answered. He spent a solid few minutes carefully thinking inside his own head before he began to carefully dab some of the chemical onto her many wounds.

He examined each of her wounds carefully, "Not enough." He concluded.

"Got it wrong already?" Charlie sighed.

"I on purposely aimed for the lowest guess. I can always add more, but too much and I can't do shit." Tom explained as he began to apply a second coating over her wounds, "Luckily for her she's out cold. This would sting like hell otherwise."

Patrick and Charlie sat and watched as Tom carefully lay Cathie on her back, making sure a fur coat was between her cut on her back and the floor.

"Now we hope." Tom muttered as he handed the cup to Patrick. That was perhaps the first time either of them had heard him say something like that. It was a rare moment where Tom didn't know exactly what was going to happen next.

Tom sat down on the opposite side of the room to Charlie and began to think once again.

"What now?" Patrick asked him.

"I said we hope." Tom replied.

"I meant what are you doing now?" Patrick rephrased.

"Double-checking my math. I had to be quick the first time, so it didn't get to a level I couldn't treat. Now I have enough time to work out how accurate my guess work was." Tom explained.

"So, we might still need to add more?" Patrick asked as he looked down at the cup in his hand.

"Most likely. I went for the lowest amount in my guess. We can always add more, can't take it away though."

"How long d-"

"I don't know." Tom interrupted, "And I don't have enough time to work it out either. Just have to hope its long enough for me to get a precise enough answer."

"Leave him to think Patrick. Guy doesn't need a distraction right now." Charlie pointed out. Patrick sighed, and sat down beside Charlie.

The two of them sat in silence for a minute or two. Every now and again one of them would look Tom's way, and one would check on Cathie's condition.

"Any change?" Charlie asked as Patrick walked away from Cathie and joined him again.

"I can't tell yet." He answered.

"What a mess." Charlie sighed.

"Speaking of which. Where are we?" Patrick asked.

"Some kind of underground room. A prison of some sort perhaps." Charlie guessed, "One thing is for sure, Earth dragons are nearby. Feel it?" He asked as he placed his hand on the ground.

Patrick did the same. The vibrations were obvious, but they weren't getting stronger like they were used to feeling.

"They aren't coming this way?" Patrick asked.

"Not for now." Charlie muttered as he clutched the handle of his sword, "But when they do, it's going to be one hell of a fight without Cathie."

They both looked over at Cathie, and Patrick took a glance at Tom. Both were still the same.

"You finish making that sword for her yet?" Patrick asked him at a volume that made sure only Charlie would hear it.

"Not yet." Charlie sighed. He lowered his voice to the same volume as well, "Needs to be perfect."

"A perfect sword for a perfect girl, right?" Patrick asked with a grin on his face.

"Shut up." Charlie chuckled.

"What? You're the only real fighting type out of us three. Only one who has anything in common with her. Kind of obvious."

"Well, you seem to be the only one to figure that out so far."

"Relax. You'll get your chance."

"I wish she would open up a bit more, you know? I mean we don't really know much about her. What she likes, what she doesn't."

"I know she doesn't like dragons." Patrick pointed out, "I get what you mean though. Tom seems the same most of the time too. Ask either of them about the past and they just sort of clam up and leave."

Both of them were alerted to the sound of coughing. Patrick jumped to his feet and skidded to a halt beside Cathie. Her eyes were slowly opening.

"Well?" Tom spoke as he stood beside Patrick to see for himself.

"Guess your guess was good enough." Patrick responded as he helped Cathie sit herself up.

She quickly leant over to one side and threw up.

"That good?" Charlie asked.

"Better than death." Tom answered.

"Well, that was horrible." Cathie coughed out.

"Easy. Try not to strain yourself." Patrick suggested.

"Had us scared there." Charlie added.

"You're telling me." Cathie muttered as she stood up, ignoring Patrick, "Speaking of being scared, anyone else feel that?" She asked.

All four of them noticed the strong vibration, and it was getting stronger.

"Well, this should be interesting." Charlie muttered as he drew his sword. Cathie tried to grab Charlie's spare on his belt, but Patrick grabbed her arm.

"You trying to get yourself killed a second time?" He asked her. She gave him a rather scary stare, but Patrick returned it with eyes filled with determination.

Patrick took the sword from Charlie's belt and wiped his hand along the blade. The blade set alight, and he got into a fighting stance with it, "Get behind us." He ordered. Tom reached into his bag.

"How about a compromise?" Tom suggested as a bow appeared between Cathie and Patrick. Patrick sighed, but then nodded.

Cathie grudgingly took the bow from Tom and took a few arrows for herself as Tom too loaded up his bow.

"Count?" Patrick asked.

"Just the one. Ahead." Charlie revealed.

"Chances?" Tom asked.

"Enclosed space. No escape. Hope you didn't waste all of our luck today Tom." Charlie answered.

The Earth dragon smashed through the wall and lunged right towards them all.

Patrick and Charlie charged forwards and blocked a claw filled foot each. They both then began pushing back against it as Tom and Cathie drew their bows.

"Eyes. Hard as you can." Tom muttered. Cathie nodded as she struggled to bring the string fully back.

Both of them fired, and both of them missed. Both arrows bounced off the hard skull.

"Shit." Cathie muttered.

"Remember that being an easier shot last time." Tom muttered to himself. Cathie dropped her bow and took an arrow in each hand. She then looked at Tom, "Go." He sighed; he could already feel Patrick's fist against his stomach.

Cathie sprinted towards the dragon as Patrick and Charlie's strength was just about to give. She curved to her right, both arrows held like daggers. The dragon's head followed her and began to open as she drew near.

Tom carefully aimed once more, "This time." He muttered under his breath as he brought his own heartbeat to a complete stop. Its head was now side on to him, a much better shot than before.

With one breath, he released. The arrow shot right into the dragon's eye. The pain caused its head to jerk, and its jaws narrowly missed Cathie as she lunged towards it. She landed on its head by its other eye and jammed both arrows in as far as she could.

The dragon let out one more screech, before collapsing to the ground.

"The eyes?" Patrick asked as he and Charlie pushed its limp claws to the side.

"The brain is behind them. A bit deep but get a good enough shot and it goes down." Tom explained as Cathie climbed off it. She was covered in blue blood.

"Eye socket is too narrow for a sword though. Only an archer could pull it off." She added.

"Didn't know you two were archer buddies." Patrick noted.

"Tom and I lived together long before you two joined us, and a good hunter needs to know how to use all the weapons at their disposal." Cathie revealed, "Anyway, I'm surprised you missed that first one Tom."

"Must have misjudged it." Tom sighed.

"You aren't the type of person to do that." Cathie pointed out.

"It's been a long day." Tom answered.

"Any more on the way?" Patrick asked. Charlie paused for a second.

"There are more, but none heading our way." He revealed.

"That doesn't make any sense. Usually, Earth dragons come to the aid of another when it screeches." Cathie revealed.

"Only one situation that they wouldn't." Tom began, "The rest of them already have their hands full."

"Anyone else starting to get cold?" Charlie asked. A cold chill was pouring through the hole in the wall the dragon had made.

"We might as well get out of here." Patrick pointed out as Tom picked up his lantern. They all nodded and ran out of the room.

They entered a rather rough tunnel. It was clearly dug out in a hurry and was also crumbling in places.

"Freshly dug." Tom added, "It didn't compact the dirt like normal. It was in a rush."

"We don't have long then. Let's go." Patrick added. The four of them ran down the tunnel. The further they ran, the colder it seemed to get.

They eventually turned a corner and came across a sheet of ice blocking the path ahead.

"Frost?" Charlie asked.

"Would explain the lack of reinforcements." Tom answered.

"Looks pretty thick. Doubt an Earth dragon could dig through something like this." Patrick noted.

"Can you?" Cathie asked him. Patrick gave a small smirk.

"Please." He chuckled as a fireball lit in his hand.

The wall of ice exploded into vapour that quickly rose into the room behind it. Given that the room was covered entirely in ice, it quickly rained down onto the floor of the room and froze once again as spikes of ice.

"It's no good. Even if you escape this room, my army is currently freezing the entire surrounding area. You're trapped." Frost boomed at the rabble of Earth dragons that were also in the room of ice.

"Well how unfortunate for you." One of the Earth dragon's spoke, "Trapped in the same room as the rest of us, and massively outnumbered."

"You think you're all a match for me?" Frost asked him. The Earth dragon gave as close to a smile an Earth dragon could.

"Frost. King of the Ice dragons. Taking you out would be worth all of our deaths."

"You can try. I assume I'm talking to the great Mound? Slayer of Ice?"

"The one and only." Mound replied.

"If so, you've killed a little too many of my kind for me to grant you a merciful death." Frost growled at him, "I'll make sure I kill you myself."

Dirt fell from the roof above. They all looked up at the roof, which in this room was surprisingly high. Unlike the floor and walls, the roof wasn't frozen over. The light from Tom's lantern barely reached it.

"Seems like your army is trying to rescue you." Mound pointed out, "But they'll be too late!" He shouted as he lunged at Frost. Behind him, the rest of the Earth dragons followed.

Frost spread his wings and took flight. Mould and the rest quickly gained their balance as they slid across the icy floor.

"Shame you can't fly." Frost chuckled.

"You forget where you are." Mound spat back. The rest of the Earth dragons began to climb up the walls.

"Patrick, you have something to help with climbing?" Cathie asked as she grabbed the sword from his hands. The flames on it died down.

"I might do." Patrick answered as he folded his arms. His eyes were fixed on Cathie's arm, which was wavering under the weight of her sword.

"Not now Patrick. I'm well enough."

"I don't like it, but we're going to need her for this part." Charlie added. Patrick looked at him, and then at Tom.

"Nothing I say will change your mind, or hers." Tom pointed out. Patrick sighed.

"No risks." Patrick finally said as he looked back at Cathie.

"No risks." She replied. Patrick nodded, and then began looking around for one thing or another.

"Strategy?" Charlie asked.

"Twelve on the wall, four on the ground and the leader. We need to set up a dead ground and drop them into it." Cathie began.

"The dead ground being around you, I'm guessing." Charlie added.

"Think you can get them off the walls?" Cathie asked him.

"The tops of the feet are less armoured than most places." He pointed out, "Sure."

"Sounds like a target I should be able to hit too." Tom added.

"And the ones on the ground?" Charlie asked.

"We have a big scary dragon for that." Cathie pointed out. The three of them nodded.

"Alright." Patrick butted in as he quickly stood on each of their feet, "That should help with the grip, but it doesn't last long without me feeding the spell."

"So, you're going to need protection?" Charlie asked him. Patrick nodded.

"I got it. Means I won't be as effective helping Charlie, but I can switch between the two." Tom volunteered, "And I'm probably going to be stationary for most of it anyway." He added as he slung his bag over his back and tied the lantern on top of it.

The four of them nodded and split.

Charlie made easy work catching up to the Earth dragons on the walls with Patrick's spell. Cathie was positioned on the ground beneath him as he made a swing at one of their hind legs. With one cut, the dragon lost its grip, and began falling.

Just before it hit the ground, Cathie lunged past it. By the time it had landed, the tough armoured skin that protected its throat had a cut right through it, and blood sprayed out.

Even in her weakened state, Cathie didn't have too much trouble getting a deep enough cut.

Another began falling towards her, and once again the dragon was dead before it hit the ground.

The Earth dragons started to notice the thumps of the dead bodies, and looked down and across to the four humans, who up until now they hadn't even noticed.[1]

"Humans!" Mound boomed as he too noticed them.

The ceiling burst and gave way as more Earth dragons tunnelled though it.

"More?" Tom asked as Cathie and Charlie quickly joined them. Frost also landed by their side.

"Plan B?" Charlie asked.

---

[1] Earth dragons do not have very good eyes, and in fact rely mainly on sensors on their feet to pick up vibrations. As they are used to detecting other dragons, humans are rather hard for them to spot without focus.

"Exit." Cathie announced as she turned to face the tunnel behind them. Standing in the entrance, was another Earth dragon, with more behind.

"Plan C?" Frost asked them.

"Barrier?" Tom asked Patrick.

"It'd need more than that." He pointed out.

Frost let out a huge frozen breath, and quickly span around to create a wall of ice around them. He then began work to turn it into a dome as Patrick got the hint and raised a barrier to support the ice.

The sound of ice cracking and breaking grew louder with every thump.

"Now what?" Charlie asked.

"I should be able to clear the floor. The ones on the walls are a problem though." Cathie explained.

"I can't hold a shield and keep the grip spell going." Patrick added.

"How good's your shooting?" Charlie asked Tom. Tom raised an eyebrow.

"Not good enough for what you're thinking." He answered.

"Guess we're just going to have to deal with it then."

"Think you can take out the leader?" Patrick asked Frost. Frost gave a nod.

The dome of ice finally shattered to pieces, and the Earth dragons began viciously bashing Patrick's barrier.

A small hole appeared beside Cathie, and she quickly ran out, slashing a leg and a tail as she broke free of the hoard surrounding them. Charlie followed close behind.

A few of the dragons turned their attention to them.

"Are you still good?" Charlie asked her as the two of them turned to face the advancing dragons.

"I'm fine." She answered as she brought her sword in front of her. Charlie noticed her arm still shaking due to the weight of the sword. It was getting worse too.

"Want to swap? Mine is lighter." Charlie suggested.

"I'm used to heavy swords." Cathie answered.

"I'm used to light swords, but we both know that in the state you're in, you aren't going to be much use for much longer." Cathie sighed, and then chucked him her sword. Charlie threw his to her and took up the much heavier sword.

The dragons charging towards them all collapsed to the ground as a cloud of arrows viciously tore through the weak backs of the knees. They watched as Tom reloaded from inside the crumbling barrier and aimed elsewhere.

"You guys don't have to be so protective." Cathie muttered.

"It goes without saying that you and Tom went through a lot of shit just before this. Tom has Patrick protecting him, all I ask is that I pick up more slack than normal when we fight." Charlie responded. Cathie wiped the sweat from her forehead.

"Guess I finally found my limit." Cathie sighed, "Cut, clawed, winded, survived the largest fall a human has ever fallen while killing an air dragon and injuring another. Now that I look at it, not too bad." She muttered as she collapsed onto the floor.

Charlie quickly got close enough to try to tend to her, but the stomp of earth dragons reminded him he was still in the middle of a battle.

Charlie turned to face the new group of earth dragons charging him. Unlike most of his tactics, this time he couldn't budge.

"Desperate times, desperate needs." Charlie sighed as he reached for his belt. He pulled out a small dagger and stuck it onto the base of the light sword on the floor by Cathie. He then held it once more as the earth dragons reached him.

***

Tom continued to fire out of the many holes the barrier now had in it. He turned to Patrick.

"I don't see the other two." He revealed.

"I'm sure their fine. We have bigger problems." Patrick squirmed as he desperately tried to hold the barrier together.

"I have an idea." Tom revealed, "We won't need the barrier if this works." He added as he took out an air crystal from his pocket. He placed it in Patrick's hand, "Squeeze, tightly."

"Why me?" Patrick asked.

"I can't fire with one hand." Tom answered as he reached for more arrows from out of his bag.

Patrick squeezed the crystal, and a powerful air blast boomed out of it. The air blast pushed the nearby dragons on the shield away, and it stopped them from moving closer as it continued to blast out air at a constant rate.

Tom loaded his bow and fired once more. This time the wind was very much behind his shots. He started systematically shooting earth dragons straight off the walls.

Frost jumped up and began flapping his wings, adding to the air blast. He then began freezing the closer earth dragons.

Mound pounced from the wall right on top of Frost however, bringing him down right beside Patrick. The air pushed the two of them as they tussled away, and into the other earth dragons.

"Tom, pin down those earth dragons near Frost." Patrick ordered him.

"I'll need some height." Tom responded. A barrier appeared by Tom's feet. Tom stood on it, and it lifted. Tom could now shoot over Frost's battle.

Just then, everything froze.

Tom looked down and around at the block of ice that he was in. The ice began to melt underneath him. He landed down next to Patrick and his lit fireball.

"Ice dragons?" Patrick asked.

"Must be. Let's try to avoid freeing any earth dragons while we find the others." Tom suggested. Patrick nodded, and greatly reduced the size of the flame in his hand. Tom looked down at the now dirt floor. The water had thankfully drained down when Patrick thawed the area. The dirt was very damp however, so almost at its limit of water intake.

The ice above them cracked open as ice dragons continued cutting through and removing chunks of ice. Some of which contained earth dragons.

***

Tom and Patrick could do little but watch as ice dragons continued to bring out more and more prisoners. They then brought Frost to the surface, and carefully cut the ice down until he was able to break free.

"No doubt Shard's idea?" Frost asked the other ice dragons.

"You know I prefer the quick and easy way of dealing with things Frost." An ice dragon responded as he approached Frost. This ice dragon had a missing tooth, and a scar on his bottom jaw where the tooth should have been.

"Freezing the king." Frost sighed, "Such a thing could get you in big trouble."

"It worked didn't it?" Shard laughed. Frost laughed with him.

"Just make sure all of our allies make it out intact and I'll think about forgetting it." Frost added. Shard nodded.

"Of course, sire." He responded.

They all watched as a block of ice was removed with Charlie inside it. He was holding Cathie up in his arms. She had clearly passed out.

"I've got this." Patrick announced as the dragons began clawing at the block of ice. He quickly melted a tunnel to them, and then carefully thawed around them. Tom noted the lack of earth dragons around them.

As the two of them emerged from the water, both of them began gasping for air. Clearly the cold had woken Cathie up. Charlie put her on her feet, and she looked around to instantly see Shard.

As Patrick gave Charlie a high five, Tom noticed Cathie clench her fists. She was staring at Shard with the clear intent to kill. Luckily Shard was busy talking to Frost, and so hadn't taken notice.

Cathie quickly took out a necklace from underneath her top. It was a dragon's tooth. An old one too. She seemed to try to look at it and Shard at the same time.

Tom quickly walked over to her and closed the hand she was using to hold the neckless. Cathie gave him quite the terrifying stare.

"It's been a very long day, and we're surrounded." Tom muttered just loud enough for her to hear, "Perhaps enough fighting for today?" Cathie looked between him and Shard. She sighed, hid the neckless underneath her top once more and stormed away angrily.

CHAPTER 4; PAINFUL PASTS

Frost dropped the four of them off by the lake. Patrick and Charlie were quick to begin the short walk back to the cave. Tom simply watched as Cathie watched Frost disappear into the night.

"I'm sorry." Tom apologised once the others had left earshot, "If I knew I would have gone to a different race first."

"I know." Cathie sighed. She found a nearby flat rock by the water to sit on. She then began to look up towards the moon.

Tom quietly sat beside her.

"How bad are we talking?" Tom asked her after a few moments silence.

"Killed my parents right in front of me." Cathie answered. She took the tooth neckless out and held it in her hand, "I managed to claim a trophy though."

"I'm surprised he survived you." Tom muttered. There were a few moments of silence, "Sorry, insensitive of me. I... I'm not the best at well... this."

"I can tell." Cathie sighed, "Today was insane." She muttered as she rested her head on his shoulder, "Reminded me of the days before we met the other two."

"I don't remember falling out of a sky cave back then."

"Well, nowhere near as insane as today. I mean more of just us getting into all kinds of situations."

"We did have a habit of finding trouble." Tom said with a small smile. Cathie gave a small chuckle. As her head shook from it slightly, Tom felt a tear or two hit his shoulder. He looked down at her hands, which were holding the tooth tightly.

"I... I was three at the time." Cathie revealed, "Back then this was the best I could do. This was me backed into a corner." She added as she handed Tom the tooth. Tom took it into his hand and looked at it in great detail.

"Cornered... and armed with a rock by the looks of it."

"A broken sword handle, actually."

"Rather impressive considering."

"Not enough though." Tom took a few seconds to consider those words.

"You do realise your by far the strongest of us all right?" He pointed out.

"Strength isn't everything." Cathie sighed, "If life as taught me anything, it's that there is always something stronger."

"I mean, you were three. What were you going to do against a dragon?" Tom asked her.

"Kill it." Cathie answered, "If only I'd managed that. My life may have had a sense of normal in it at some point before meeting you."

"You never do talk about what you did back then. I'm guessing it's filled with more of these moments, right?" Tom asked as he handed the tooth back to her.

"One or two. As you could imagine, the first thing I did was try to get revenge."

"From the fact that he's still alive, I'm guessing it didn't go so well."

"Nearly froze to death. If it weren't for the hospitality of the family that took me in, I'd be dead."

"Humans lived all the way up in the ice?" Tom asked.

"Not humans." Cathie sighed, "Ice dragons."

"Raised by the ones who killed your parents?" Tom asked.

"Well obviously I tried to kill them. Couldn't bring myself to once I met his daughter though. Well… that and the cage they kept me in for the first few months."

"Raised by dragons." Tom seemed to mutter as he tried his best to take it in, "Would certainly explain the many writing lessons I've given you."

"Well, both of them barely knew how to speak human."

"So just a dad and his daughter?" Tom asked her. Cathie nodded.

"They had abandoned the rest of their race. Travelled around a lot too. I lost them shortly before meeting you." Tom felt another tear on his shoulder.

"Not quite sure if it helps or not…" Tom began, "But… I was five, they were earth dragons, and I had this thing." Tom revealed as he patted the bow beside him, "Well, with only one string working at the time."

"Parents as well?" Cathie asked him. Tom simply nodded.

Cathie noticed a hint of sadness flash through his face, before it quickly disappeared.

She shifted and nuzzled up to him a little bit more as the two of them sat in silence. Tom put his arm around her. She quickly noted that although he'd done so, he had done it all wrong, nor was he holding tightly. He'd clearly never comforted someone before.

***

As Cathie walked across the small corridor that separated the four rooms of the cave, she noticed that the fire in the main area of the cave was still alight and burning brightly.

She walked into the main room to find Tom sitting at the wooden table positioned in the centre. On the table, was a small cube like object. The object was odd, and the more Cathie stared at it, the odder it seemed.

"Visiting Patrick in the dead of night. Should we expect a baby wizard some point in the future?" Tom asked her. His focus still fully set on the object in front of him. Scattered all over the table were various tools and instruments. Tom also had one in hand and was carefully prodding the object in specific places.

"Patrick and I accepted that we wouldn't work together a long time ago." Cathie answered as she walked over to him, "You're up late."

"If I ever slept, yes I would be." Tom muttered as he gave the object another prod.

"What is that thing?" She asked as she sat down on the other side of the table from him.

"No idea." Tom answered as he put down the tool he was holding and picked up a different one, "That's what I'm trying to find out."

"Where did you find it? Perhaps it's a different type of crystal." Cathie suggested as she took a much closer look at it. It was pure white, yet she had the odd feeling that she was looking into something instead of looking at a solid object.

"I found it in my bag." Tom answered as he pointed to his bag, which rested neatly on the floor to the side of the table.

Tom's bag was perhaps one of many mysteries about Tom. The bag seemed to weight exactly the same, whether something was in it or not, and it also seemed to be able to hold a comical number of objects. In fact, to this day, none of them had seen it full.

The bag had an unnerving and unnatural aura to it that even gave Cathie a chill if she looked at it for too long. Box like in shape, and with the word 'Kara' in white on the side of the bag which contrasted with its otherwise black colour.

"How did it get there?" Cathie asked him.

"That bag used to be my mothers." Tom reminded her, "Clearly this was hers at some point." Cathie looked back at the bag. The word 'Kara' suddenly had a meaning. A name. A name she wasn't entirely sure was ok to say in front of Tom.

"Your mother was a genius though, right?" She asked him. Tom nodded.

"But this was not of her design." He revealed.

"How can you tell?"

"There are no screws, gaps or any evidence of construction from it. Its solid the whole way around." He answered, "My gut tells me magic is involved, it would explain the oddness it gives off as most magical objects do."

"Perhaps your mother was a magician then." Cathie suggested, "That would certainly explain the bag as well."

"The bag is different. It's not magic. My mother was many things, but a magician is not one of them." Tom revealed, "Though now that you mention it, the two seem rather similar in design."

"But you said yourself, it couldn't have been made by normal means."

"There are many different ways to make things in this world. Some unknown even to me." Tom muttered as he picked the cube up. Where his hand made contact with it, it became purple. The rest of it remained white.

He lifted it up to his eye level.

"I've never seen anything change colour like that."

"No change in texture." Tom muttered as he rubbed his finger along one face. He picked up a cylindrical object and put it against his eye. He then looked down one of the sides of the object while it was still purple. He continued to watch as it slowly changed back to white once his hand had moved position, "Perfectly flat." He added.

"Are you sure it's safe to touch?" Cathie asked him. Tom removed the cylindrical object from in front of his eye.

"It seems safe." He answered as he put it back down onto the table. He took out the two air crystals and placed them beside the object.

All of a sudden, the cube seemed to react to them. It began to hover above the table. One of its corners began to glow.

"It seemed to like that." Cathie muttered, "What does the glowing corner mean?"

"Eight corners of a cube. Eight original species of dragon." Tom answered, "Eight different crystals."

"Those crystals come from dragons?" Cathie asked him.

"It's what powers their attacks. Every dragon has one inside. When they die, the crystal can be removed and used." Tom revealed.

"So, what do dragon crystals have to do with a cube in your mothers' bag?" Cathie asked him.

"Good question. The crystals form their elemental matter by feeding off chemical energy." Tom picked up one of the crystals and placed it in Cathie's hand.

"Chemical energy?" She asked.

"What we run off. We eat food, store it chemically for our bodies to use for everyday activities. Give it a squeeze, and you'll start to feel tired, hungry even." He continued to explain. Cathie gave the crystal a light squeeze. It wasn't much, but she could feel it draining her.

"Why didn't I notice it before?" She asked.

"Adrenalin." Tom answered, "In the heat of battle, something like that isn't going to be noticeable." Tom took the crystal back, "The crystal seems to be reacting to the energy of the cube."

"The cube eats too?" Cathie asked as she stared at the cube once more.

"No. The cube doesn't have chemical energy, although it has energy of some kind. Can't tell what, or how much. This shell seems to be trapping it, but the crystals seem to be drawing it out slightly. That rules out magic."

"With all the crystals, you might be able to release the energy within, right?" Cathie tried to keep up.

"In theory. Question is if I should. There might be a dangerous amount of energy, and if it is released all at once… boom." Tom revealed as he mimed an explosion with his hands.

He took the crystals away from the cube, and it returned to its normal state as it dropped onto the table.

"So, if your mother was so smart, what was your father like?" She blurted out without properly thinking. Tom sat in silence for a few more seconds.

"My relationship with my parents was… different from most. The hunter and the inventor. Two very different types of people. I often got stuck somewhere in between." He muttered quietly, "It's not really something I talk about." He added in a slightly less depressing tone.

Despite the fact that she got an answer, Cathie felt that she was treading on rather dangerous territory. She'd got lucky and caught him in one of his best moods this time, but she didn't want to press her luck any further.

***

Tom sat silently in the darkness of his room on a wooden chair. His eyes fixed on a sheet of paper that hung on the wall. The paper had been turned around to hide whatever was on it, and it had been positioned perfectly behind the door so no one entering or leaving could see it without closing the door.

Tom held a wooden cup in one hand as he continued to stare at it. The cup contained some kind of black liquid. He looked down at his other hand, which was shaking uncontrollably.

"That's what you get for opening up." He muttered to himself as he rested it on his legs, "And here I was thinking that a long-time friend could change it."

***

Cathie knocked on Tom's door.

"Tom? Its sunrise. Frost wanted to meet us remember?" She spoke through the door. She didn't get a response.

She opened the door and walked in. The door hit a wooden cup which was on the floor behind it once it was open. She closed the door and picked the cup up. As she stood up, her eyes caught the sheet of paper turned the wrong way.

She gave the rest of the room a good look. A wooden chair was in the centre of the room facing the sheet of paper, but no one else was in here. She looked back at the sheet of paper, took it off the wall, and turned it over.

It was a map. It seemed to map the entire network of valleys that made up the known world. There was also a red X marked on the map. She seemed to recognise it from somewhere, a long time ago.

As she tried to remember where, her eyes found a second marking on the map. A gravestone. Cathie swallowed as she realised what it was marking. She quickly put the map back in its original position, taking extra care to make sure it looked exactly the same as before she touched it.

Tom had a map to his parent's grave. She put the cup down on his table and quickly left the room.

She ran straight through the main room and out of the door to the cave. Her eyes quickly began searching for fresh tracks as the sunlight shot into her eyes.

She found fresh footsteps, which led to the rock right beside her, where Tom sat.

"Are You ok?" Tom asked her. He'd watched the panicked search attempt.

"You weren't in your room." She managed to muddle together while she got a hold of herself.

"It's my turn for first light perimeter check." Tom reminded her, "Haven't made peace with the earth dragons yet."

"Oh right. Forgot about that."

"You alright? You seem a bit… well I'm not sure."

"Just a long day yesterday. Didn't get much sleep either." Tom seemed satisfied with the answer and looked towards the rising sun, "When should we head out to meet Frost?" She asked him.

"Soon." Tom replied, "You'd better make sure the other two are ready." Cathie nodded, and then walked back into the cave.

CHAPTER 5; WATER AND FIRE

Water dragons seemed to have a similar design to air dragons. With only two rear legs and two wings. However, the wings were a completely different shape, and their bodies were covered in fins to better move through the water. The sea-coloured skin allowed them to more or less become invisible under the waves. They were perhaps more like fish than lizards.

The four humans and Frost stood on a small and sandy beach, looking out into the water dragon infested lake beyond. The water near them was shallow for quite a distance, but after a certain point, the lake floor dropped, until the bottom was no longer visible.

"Somewhere under there in the submerged caves thousands of metres below is the lair of the water dragons." Frost revealed, "Perhaps the most secure place in the world. Only dragons that can get close to it are the earth dragons, but the surrounding waters keep them from getting too close."

"Impressive idea. If only humans could breathe underwater." Tom admired.

"I think that's also the point." Charlie reminded him, "No wonder we never came across them."

"Since the fire dragons live on a volcanic island, they are an invaluable ally." Frost added, "I spoke with their queen earlier about the four of you."

"You did?" Patrick asked him.

"Oh yes. An interesting tale indeed." A voice spoke from just off the shore. Three dragons slowly emerged from the water and onto the beach in front of them. They didn't move as elegantly on land, but with a combination of their back legs and a very long tail to balance, they were just about able to stand on their hind legs for a short while.

The three of them sat upright in front of them.

"Wave." Frost nodded to the centre of the three.

"So, this is what a human looks like." Wave spoke as she seemed to examine the four of them, "You pick our allies well Frost."

"If you have already sold us as allies, then why are we here Frost?" Tom quickly asked.

"Because we're the only dragon that can get you anywhere near the fire dragons." Wave answered.

"The war between fire and ice has been long and brutal. So much so that neither side even remembers what it was over." Frost began, "The war cannot end either, because a fire and ice dragon can never get close to one another without harming one another."

"Fire melts ice, ice puts out fire." Wave added, "It gets very messy very quickly."

"Why not have an air or water dragon talk to them then?" Cathie asked.

"Because water and air can also put out fire. They wouldn't let them get close enough either." Patrick answered. Frost nodded.

"Yet I am sure you are aware from experience alone, a human pose almost no threat. Your weapons melt before they cut, your people burn before they can punch." Frost pointed out, "If you can make peace with them, we'll start the journey towards ending this silly war."

"Something tells me this has been your plan for us from the beginning?" Tom theorised.

"The way I see it, the world needs to change. If we don't stop the fighting between each other, dragon kind will follow the fate humanity is already desperately trying to avoid." Frost explained, "Turns out a race hated by all equally but pose no threat works wonders."

"So what's the plan, use us to get them to consider not fighting you anymore?"

"More or less. I'd have taken you to them earlier, but I thought the air dragons would be a rather good wake up call to how much work you'll have to do to try and convince the other dragons. All be it I didn't expect them to attack."

"So, you knew they wouldn't even listen to us."

"The chance wasn't likely. The fire dragons may not have as much of a grudge, but they certainly have a history with humanity of their own. One I know little details of, but I can imagine it isn't a good one."

***

As the other three waved goodbyes to the water dragon which had brought them there, Tom walked up the beach and over the ridge to get a look at the rest of the island they were now on.

The flat rock beyond spanned for miles. Beyond that, more ocean as far as the eye could see. The only thing blocking the perfect view of the horizon all around, was the volcano.

Cathie was about to walk past Tom, but he put a handout to stop her.

"Volcano has erupted recently. The lava on the surface may have cooled to rock, but a thin piece might give way to the fiery pool below." He explained to her as he looked down at the steaming ground.

"You're telling me we have to walk over that?" Cathie asked him.

"You got a better way of getting there?" Charlie asked as he turned to Patrick and Tom. Both of them were scratching their heads.

"Air crystals?" Patrick asked.

"Didn't bring them. Didn't expect much use against trusted allies." Tom answered, "Freezing spell?" He asked.

"Shaky at best. Wouldn't depend our lives on it." Patrick answered.

"Anything water related?" Cathie asked him.

"Not unless you want to walk on it, no." Patrick sighed.

"We only need to worry about thin rock, right?" Cathie asked as she took another look at the ground.

"Anything that might have lava right underneath it." Patrick answered.

"Follow my footsteps then." Cathie announced as she took a carefully calculated step forward, "Tracking skills have their perks. The key is in the details."

The others all looked at one another. Tom shrugged as he watched Cathie take a few more steps. He began to follow her, closely followed by the others.

"I would not like to end up fighting on this stuff." Charlie remarked as they began to make progress towards the volcano.

"It will get worse the closer we get too." Patrick added.

"Trust me. We don't want to get into a fight with a fire dragon." Cathie sighed. The others all looked rather surprised that she would say that "Best thing to do is run when you come across one. Fighting one is like trying to put out a forest fire armed only with a twig."

"When you don't fight something for being too dangerous, that's when I start to get scared." Charlie commented.

"Tell me about it." Patrick agreed.

***

It took about half of the day, but they eventually reached the base of the volcano. The four of them looked up towards the top, where huge clouds bellowed out.

"That's a long way up." Charlie sighed. The surrounding heat was already causing them to sweat.

"Something tells me we won't need to climb it." Tom muttered as he looked to the side. They all turned to see what he was looking at.

Four fire dragons silently floated above the bare rock towards them at great speed. The first one shot past, snatching Patrick as it did so with its rear claws. The other three snatched the rest up, and the four of them then changed course, up towards the crater.

The four humans were placed down rather roughly on an island of rock, surrounded by lava. They were now deep within the volcano. The edges of the crater towered above them. On the sides, fire dragons seemed to nest in the various caves and ledges.

Beneath them, in the lava, a different type of dragon swam around them.

"Seems they want to talk." Cathie sighed as she took the sight in.

"How'd you know that?" Charlie asked.

"The dragons which carried us lowered their body temperature enough to not fry us on the way here." Tom pointed out.

"And there it is. The brains I have heard so much about." A voice boomed as a small rock raised out of the lake of lava. A fire dragon landed on it, and looked towards the humans, "Flame, Queen of the fire dragons." The dragon added as it seemed to get comfortable on its island.

"You've heard about us?" Tom asked her.

"The fabled Thomas Thomson. I have heard quite a bit about you." Flame revealed.

Fire dragons, like air dragons, only had two legs. To stand they also used their wings as arms. Their skin was hot to the touch, and normally much hotter as they could control how intense the flames that rippled on its surface would be.

"You've heard of Tom?" Patrick asked her, "How?"

"I make it a point to know every threat to my kind." Flame answered, "Tom, Son of Kara and Max. Cathie, daughter of Angel and Fire. Your parents were quite the threat back in the day." She revealed.

"You've got quite the nerve speaking those names." Cathie seemed to snap. Patrick held her back from drawing her sword. He also noted that Tom wasn't far off the same reaction either, which would have been a first for him. Unlike Cathie though, he seemed to let it go after a few seconds.

"Clearly I have hit a nerve. I am also aware as to why you are here. To end the slaughter of your people." Flame revealed.

"I take it you have many spies at your disposal?" Charlie asked her. She gave a small, teeth filled smile.

"Since you are aware, what is your answer?" Patrick asked her.

"My answer is No."

"Any particular reason?" Tom asked her. He'd managed to regain his calmness.

"The reason is you Thomas Thomson." Flame answered.

"Me?" Tom asked, "Last I checked I've not done anything to harm the fire dragons."

"So, you deny pouring the potion into the lake to the west?" Flame asked him.

"That is your reason?" Tom asked her.

"Many of our kind now must learn the language they are forever forced to speak. The fear of poison and sickness that came with the sudden confusion? Did you not think of such things?" She asked, "It is not my only reason."

"What else has he done?" Charlie asked her.

"Potions of magic, wings from twigs and cloth. A bow designed with the intent to kill multiple targets; a bag of tricks passed down from your parents. These all add up to one obvious conclusion." Flame listed.

"Which is?" Tom asked.

"That you Thomas Thomson, are the reincarnation of the Neutral." Flame accused.

"The Neutral? What is that?" Tom asked, "Frost mentioned it when we first met." He added as he turned to the others.

"It's something we don't want to be labelled as." Patrick sighed, "A human every dragon seems to fear."

"Indeed." Flame muttered as she took to the sky, "And like before, we shall end you."

"How can you be sure he is this Neutral?" Patrick asked him, "We have no way to tell as our knowledge of such a being comes only from dragons."

"Indeed, if I am to be killed, I would very much like for it to be proven true first." Tom added. Flame seemed to consider this. She swooped towards him and grabbed him. She then shot off towards one of the many caves.

Three other dragons did the same with the others. They were dropped down a hole and into a large room.

The four of them quickly got to their feet as a light seemed to ignite above, revealing the sleeping fire dragon in front of them.

"Well, this turned out just great." Charlie sighed.

"Not my fault they think I'm this thing." Tom responded.

"Actually, it kind of is." Patrick answered back, "You do kind of stand out as someone who could wipe out a species if you put your mind to it."

"I'm not that good." Tom sighed.

"The lack of emotions doesn't exactly help your case either." Charlie added.

"I thought Frost said they killed the Neutral." Cathie finally spoke.

"He did, but they think it reincarnated as Tom." Patrick sighed.

"I'm rather sceptical about that." Tom muttered.

"Reincarnation?" Cathie asked.

"The idea that when living things die, they get reborn as new living things." Tom explained.

"Of course, that's the crude version of it." Patrick sighed, "My people added the sensible explanation of life circles."

"Ah so you're a believer of such nonsense then." Tom chuckled.

"It makes a lot of sense, and my people were right about rather a lot of things." Patrick snapped back.

"The same could be said for me." Tom argued.

"Really? So, you finally figured out how magic works have you?" Patrick chuckled as he lit a small flame in his hand, "You can finally explain how I do this?"

"Well…" Tom swallowed as he looked at the flame in his hand, "Point taken." He sighed, "I still won't believe until I see though."

"Fair enough." Patrick sighed as he extinguished the flame.

"Are you about done?" The dragon in front of them asked. They had been so focused that they hadn't noticed it wake up.

"Oh, sorry. Didn't mean to wake you." Charlie nervously apologised as the dragon walked towards them. Its eyes fixed onto Tom almost instantly.

The dragon then suddenly changed shape. Before he knew it, Tom was staring at an exact copy of himself.

"You are no dragon." Tom muttered as he examined the being before him.

"What I am is not important. What you are is." The copy replied as he seemed to examine Tom in just as much detail, "Smart, even for a human. Small trace of power, but given your son of Max and Kara, that is no surprise."

"I think you have your facts muddled up. My father's name was Jack." He revealed.

"Ah yes. I forgot he used that name for his family." Tom's copy chuckled, "Interesting guy. However, you are not the Neutral." He concluded.

"He isn't?" Patrick asked.

"Nothing more than a sharper than normal mind. Nothing special about you whatsoever." The copy sighed as he walked away, "You may want to rethink your position after all Flame."

The rock underneath the four of them lifted up, and they were brought back up the hole they were tossed down. They were now in one of the side caves. Flame stood before them once more.

"Nothing special? Perhaps I jumped to a conclusion far too quickly." Flame sighed, "Very well. I suppose removing the thorn from my side which is humanity would be sensible, even if it's a small thorn."

"So, you will stop killing us?" Patrick asked her.

"We shall. The lava dragons too. However." Flame narrowed her eyes, "I shall be watching closely. Anymore potions in the main water supply, anymore possible threats to my brethren, and I will personally drop each and every one of you into the lake of lava and watch you melt."

"I think I get the message." Tom sighed.

"Good." Flame nodded to one of the other fire dragons behind them, "Hot, I am sure these humans require assistant leaving the island. See to it they leave immediately." She ordered.

***

It was a long and tiring walk back to the cave. Tom began to lag behind about halfway. Cathie noticed, and slowed herself down to slowly join him.

"Are you alright?" She asked him. He seemed deep in thought.

"Seems that our parents had quite the reputation among dragons." Tom sighed, "And here I was thinking I could distract myself from it all."

"It doesn't seem to want to go away does it?" Cathie sighed, "The day might come soon where we both have to overcome the pain."

"Unless you eliminate the pain first." Tom muttered.

"You can't get rid of pain."

"I did. Since then. The loss, the sorrow. It never really hit me. I killed my emotions off before that could happen." The two of them walked in silence for a few minutes.

"I don't think you killed your emotions." Cathie finally muttered.

"You don't?"

"I think they're in there, somewhere." Tom gave a small smile.

"I've lived without emotion for so long I've forgotten what it is to feel happy, to feel sad. Everything in between too."

"So, what do you feel?" Cathie asked him. Tom took a second to think about it.

"Not really sure. I help protect the group because it's the best way to survive. I take account of other people's emotions, so I don't end up getting murdered. That's about it."

"What about all those potions? Surely you had something driving you to make them all?" Cathie asked, hoping that he found enjoyment in that at least.

"For a promise. A mother's dying wish to complete her unfinished word." Tom sighed as he came to a stop. Cathie had clearly hit another nerve, a big one this time.

She came to a stop and took his hand in her own.

"Sorry I-"

"I know. How could you have known?" Tom sighed. He seemed to brush it off rather quickly, which added to Cathie's worry. He began to walk again. She kept beside him. He hadn't reacted to her hand. He wasn't holding on, but he hadn't pulled away either. He probably hadn't even noticed.

"I saw your map this morning." She mentioned.

"Snooping in my room?" Tom asked her as they continued to walk.

"Was picking up a cup."

"Ah, that would explain why it ended up back on my table after I threw it."

"I recognised it." Cathie revealed.

"From where?" Tom asked her.

"I have the same one." She answered, "Without the added marking, but the red cross is in the same place."

"The valley where we… first met." Tom came to a stop again, "That's why you were there right?" He asked her.

"A map from my mother. The only thing she could give me before being torn to shreds in front of me. A map with a mark, and a date."

"The date we met…" Tom realised, "You don't think our parents knew one another, do you?" He asked. Cathie noticed something in Tom's eyes. Curiosity? Most likely, but there was something else in there as well.

"I just hope we aren't related." Cathie sighed.

"Why'd you hope that?" Tom asked her.

"No reason." Cathie quickly blurted out as she realised, she'd said that out aloud, "I mean if they have such a reputation with the dragons, perhaps they were like us, a band of four doing everything possible to survive against the odds."

"My parents refused to live with other humans." Tom muttered.

"As did mine. Like us, they didn't really get along with them."

"Perhaps I should take a look at our blood. We might actually be related." Tom muttered as he began to delve into more silent thought.

***

Cathie looked eagerly at the two test tubes on Tom's desk.

"So how do we tell?" Cathie asked him.

"I won't bore you with the complex explanation, but the idea is to see how similar our blood is to one another." Tom answered as he seemed to add this and that to the two tubes.

He added one final ingredient to both. One quickly bubbled and fizzed. The other, simply turned from red to green.

"Well?" Cathie asked him.

"I'm pretty sure we aren't related." Tom revealed, "The reactions were far too different from one another. Yours bubbled rather violently, which I've never actually seen before, and mine changed colour as expected."

"Have you done this before?" Cathie asked him.

"I've done similar reactions using small amounts of blood. Analysing it isn't something I've done before though. Should be correct though, as you'd think family members have the same type of blood."

"It certainly makes sense." Someone knocked on Tom's door.

"Tom?" Patrick asked from outside the door, "You got a minute or two?" He asked.

"I need to get us some more food. Supplies are lower than I'd like." Cathie said as she walked towards the door. She opened it, which surprised Patrick, and walked past him.

"What is it Patrick?" Tom asked him as he began to clear away the test tubes and bubbling liquids.

"Well actually it's about… her." Patrick paused to make sure Cathie had left earshot. He then looked back at Tom, walked into the room and closed the door behind him.

"You come to berate me about putting her in danger again?" Tom asked him as he finished tidying and turned in his chair to face him.

"Not this time." Patrick responded, "We have ourselves a problem. One which could tear the group apart."

"I'm listening." Tom's ears seemed to prick up. This was something he was interested to hear.

"We have ourselves a love triangle."

"If you're going to talk about one of your magic problems Patrick, I'm really not the guy to speak to." Tom sighed. He seemed to lose interest almost immediately.

"It's not some magical spell or something. It's a certain type of emotional situation."

"Are you trying to bore me to death Patrick?" Tom yawned as he turned away to look at his desk. He reached for a new sheet of paper and a handcrafted pencil.

"Look, Charlie is seriously in love with Cathie." Patrick revealed.

"Good for him. Why should I care?" Tom asked him as he began to draw on the sheet of paper.

"Because Cathie doesn't quite share his feelings." Patrick answered.

"Well what? You want a love potion or something? Please." Tom sighed, "Drama isn't something I take any interest in. If Charlie has some hurt feelings, then so be it."

"Because she's in love with you." Patrick finally revealed. Tom's pencil came to a stop. He looked over towards the now clean test tubes.

"That would explain a lot." He muttered to himself. There was a pause of about thirty seconds before Tom dropped his pencil on the table, and turned to face Patrick, "Fine, you have my attention."

"Well… that was it." Patrick muttered, not really sure what else to say now.

"So, let me get this right. Charlie is in love with Cathie, but Cathie is in love with me. I think I finally understand the phrase 'love triangle'."

"Look, in my opinion she couldn't have made a worse choice, but she seems set on it. After she confessed her feelings to me last night, I tried talking her out of it, but nothing worked."

"Well, if she can't be convinced to change her mind, why not try Charlie?"

"Already tried. Didn't work."

"Well then there is not much we can do is there? Beyond killing Charlie of course, or me."

"Like those are options."

"I'm not quite sure why you thought bringing this to me would help."

"Well... I can't think of a way of getting out of it. And normally when that happens, I bring it to you."

"Well since there seems to be no way of stopping it, I'd say let the group fall apart." Tom turned back into his chair to face the desk. He picked up his pencil and continued to draw.

"That would be a disaster." Patrick pointed out.

"I've survived on my own before. I can easily do it again. I'm sure the same could be said for us all. Why should I care if the group splits?"

"Convenient, higher chances of survival, I don't know. We're better off together."

"Not if we end up killing one another over something so petty. This isn't the first time I've heard of a group break up because of romantic issues."

"You know I was really expecting more from you Tom." Patrick sighed.

"Then you expected too much. Doors behind you." Patrick clenched his fists in rage. He stormed over to Tom and spun his chair around so that he was face to face with him.

"You stubborn, selfish bastard!"

"You got a problem with me being stubborn and selfish?" Tom asked him rather calmly.

"Look, we need a solution that will keep us together. Or did you forget we still have a species to save."

"I didn't forget Patrick; I just don't give a shit." Patrick took a step back.

"What the hell is wrong with you!"

"What? You want me to care about a species that treats me like some kind of mad man? That crap with the fire dragons was just an exaggerated version of how every human treats me after spending a day or two around me. The only reason you three haven't done the same is because you'd rather have four members of humanity instead of three."

"I'd have thought you'd have some kind of sympathy for your own kind."

"Did you forget who it is your talking to?" Tom asked as he got out of his chair and stood in front of him. A flame lit in Patrick's hand.

"I'm not one to make threats Tom, but you're really pushing it." Patrick muttered. Tom looked at the flame, and then at his bow, which was behind Patrick, by the door. His eyes narrowed in frustration for a second or so.

"Fine. If you have such an issue with me, and if Charlie is going to eventually, I guess I'm the problem element here."

"What are you suggesting?"

"That we remove the problem element." Tom answered as he reached for his bag, "Three united is better than four divided right?"

"That's not-"

"Do you have a better idea?" Patrick extinguished the flame.

"No."

"Then as I said earlier. The door is behind you."

CHAPTER 6; THE CLIFF EDGE AWAITS

Cathie managed to return to the cave just a few minutes after it began to rain heavily. The cave door was on a raised bit of ground, but too much water and the cave risked being flooded, so she was extra careful about opening and closing the main door.

Over her shoulder was a large sack full to the brim. She put it down beside the table in the main room, which is when she noticed Patrick sitting on the other side, staring into the fire.

"Are you alright?" Cathie asked him.

"How'd the hunt go?" Patrick asked her, still staring into the fire.

"Got enough to last awhile. Lucky Tom found an area covered in species which has long-lasting meat."

"Yeah… about Tom… he… how goes the whole thing?" Patrick quickly changed. Cathie sat down opposite him after making sure that no one else was around.

"Well, we learnt his father's name, Jack. Not much else though. Oh, he was a hunter as well. Tom seemed to have an issue with…" Cathie slowly looked at the sack of meat she'd just brought in, "Oh."

"What?"

"As you thought, Tom seems to have issues with his father, and I think I… I might remind him about it." Cathie quickly stood, "I need to talk to him."

"Well… about that. Tom kind of… left."

"He what?"

"I may have told him about… you."

"You idiot." Cathie muttered as she ran for the door. She made sure her sword was still on her back, "How long ago?"

"An hour or so." Patrick answered. Cathie quickly opened the door and ran out.

Just within the shadows in the corridor beyond, Charlie quietly walked back into his room.

***

This time Tom had really tried to hide his tracks, but not very well. He was never very good at it. As Cathie ran through the rain looking from badly concealed footprint to footprint, she could tell she was gaining on him very quickly. He was walking, which meant she'd catch up eventually.

After a while the tracks became unreadable due to the rain, but that was no longer an issue. Cathie recognised the direction he was heading, and she knew why as well. Back to the cave they had lived in together.

It was a smart idea to keep a backup supply in caves you'd previously visited, and Cathie knew Tom had a habit of it.

As she entered the valley she came to a slow stop as she remembered the creatures that infested this place. The cat like creatures that had once nearly killed her. They were dangerous, even for her. She quickly drew her sword and continued with a much slower pace.

There was no point hiding from them, she'd come across them no matter how she travelled through the valley, so this time she was going to be prepared for them. The rain clouds blocked the moonlight, making the entire valley pitch black. Through the rain, up the mountain at the other end, the faint glimpse of a fire burning deep within a cave.

It took longer than she expected, but she finally heard the sound of a twig snap nearby. She came to a complete stop and focused all of her senses to her nearby surroundings. She was being hunted, just like before.

The first one pounced from behind her, but she was ready for it, she quickly turned and slashed it. Its dead body dropped to her feet. She felt the hesitation of the others still in the darkness, they hadn't expected her to fight back so effectively.

They hadn't run off, which meant they were clearly changing tactics. Three of them slowly advanced forwards directly in front of her, a distraction. She quickly turned to the side to strike down the hidden attacker. The three in front charged forwards, but Cathie's sword was fast, and powerful.

That tactic hadn't worked either. Yet they still surrounded her. They must be hungry to go to this much effort to get a kill. Cathie readied herself for the next attack. There was only one more strategy left for a stationary target like her.

Suddenly ten of them lunged at her from all directions. This time there were too many for her to simply cut down. She sliced at one before jumping up to dodge the rest, yet more quickly pounced towards her as the rest quickly looked up with teeth bearing.

The second wave suddenly fell dead on the ground. Cathie quickly got her footing on one of the beasts as she cut any others that pounced at her. Someone else seemed to be picking the creatures off at the edge. It wasn't long until Cathie stood surrounded by bodies.

"Looked like you could use a hand." Charlie chuckled as he walked out of the shadows.

"For once I'm glad for the help." Cathie sighed as she swiped the blood off her sword, "You followed me?"

"Can't have the last woman getting herself killed by these things, can I?" The rain continued to pick up, it was getting incredibly heavy now.

"I'm looking for Tom."

"That makes two of us."

"You? Thought you hated the guy?" Cathie asked him. Charlie put his sword back onto his belt.

"That's very true, but the guy is rather useful to have around." Charlie answered with a slight smirk. Something told Cathie that was not the true answer, "I'm impressed you followed his tracks in this rain. I struggled with yours, and I was only a minute or two behind."

"I know where he's heading." Cathie revealed as she began to walk off towards the end of the valley.

"Of course, you do." Charlie mumbled ever so quietly as he began to follow.

***

The path up the mountain was hard to spot, but Cathie knew what she was looking for. It didn't take the two of them long to reach the entrance of the cave.

The fire within had died out. The rain continued to pour so heavily that Cathie could barely hear her own thoughts.

"Sorry." She heard someone say from behind her. A sharp pain, and suddenly she was on the wet floor.

Charlie carefully propped up an unconscious Cathie using the wall of the cave. He then fully drew his sword. Deeper in, he found Tom sitting by a dead fire.

Tom looked up in surprise.

"Charlie?" Charlie quickly advanced on him and grabbed him by the shoulder.

"You have a cliff to fall off." Charlie hissed as he easily overpowered Tom with his strength and pushed him towards the entrance to the cave. He then held his sword to Tom's throat, "Move."

Tom nodded, and slowly began making his way out of the cave. He noticed Cathie.

"What did you do?" Tom asked him.

"You're a lucky guy Tom. She tracked you all the way here. Never seen someone so dedicated to find someone else before. Luckily for me, too desperate to even think about hiding her own tracks."

"You found me by using her."

"I'll have to come up with some explanation or another. Shouldn't be hard with this valley being the death trap it is." Charlie pushed him forwards once more. Tom continued to walk forwards into the rain.

His feet came to a stop at the edge of the cliff.

"Smart not to kill me with your sword. Cathie would have a hard time believing that one." Tom chuckled to himself as he looked down at the massive drop in front of him. The sound of movement alerted the both of them. They both turned to Cathie, who had shifted slightly.

"Damn she's tough." Charlie cursed.

"You don't have long." Tom pointed out.

"No time for last words then." Charlie pushed his hands forwards to knock Tom off the cliff.

Tom quickly moved to the side, and all of a sudden Charlie was leaning over the fatal drop. Tom's hand quickly caught one of Charlie's.

Charlie looked back towards Tom with eyes full of surprise.

"World has lost enough humans." He muttered as he pulled him back. Tom quickly knocked Charlie's sword out of his hand and over the cliff. He quickly noted that Charlie also had a bow and quiver over his shoulder, but he wouldn't have time to use them before Tom landed a punch or two, and that was all it would take for him to go over.

"Not like you to show mercy." Charlie scoffed as he got his balance.

"There's a lot about me, you don't know, nor do I share."

"Too bad." Charlie huffed as he threw a punch towards Tom. Before it could connect, Cathie rammed into Charlie.

Cathie managed to grab his shirt at the last moment before Charlie fell, but he was once again hanging over the edge of the cliff. She turned to look at Tom.

"Are you alright?" She asked him, but he noticed his face change from surprise to horror.

As she turned to face Charlie, she heard the twang of a bow right in front of her. The arrow plunged into her chest. Charlie's face filled with shock as he realised that Cathie had turned into the way of the shot. The pain came as quite the shock to Cathie, who let go of Charlie.

She watched in shock as Charlie fell. Before she could see him hit the ground, she herself fell backwards from the force of the arrow. She quickly landed in Tom's arms.

The rain began to pound at her face until Tom's quickly appeared above her. He was looking at the wound, and from the look on his face, it was a bad one. Pain shot through her as Tom quickly lifted her up and brought her inside the cave.

"It umm… it's not that bad."

"Liar." Cathie managed to push out. She could feel herself getting weaker by the second. She felt her back come into contact with the cold cave floor.

"I… damn that's deep."

"Point… blank… shot…" Cathie reminded him. She was fighting to keep her eyes open now, "How bad?"

"Possibly fatal." Tom answered as he began to look about the cave, "I could treat it if I had the stuff, but I don't, and by the time I get some…"

"I'll… be gone." Cathie finished. Her eyes were beginning to close, and there wasn't much she could do about it anymore. She felt the ground violently tremble.

"Perhaps I could be of assistance." She heard a sharp and fierce voice say before she blacked out.

CHAPTER 7; NOT SO EXTINCT

Tom was shown into an underground room which he quickly ran into, with Cathie tightly held in his arms. He gently placed her on the nearest slab of rock and began to look around at the many medical supplies that littered the room.

A dragon that seemed to resemble an earth dragon approached him from further inside the room. Unlike the earth dragons however, which were brown in colour, these dragons seemed to be grey instead.

"Antiseptic?" Tom asked the dragon which approached him. The dragon handed him a bottle.

"What are we dealing with?" The dragon asked as she seemed to take a look at Cathie.

"Deep arrow near the heart. Possible internal bleeding... I need to get inside." Tom muttered. He turned to face the dragon, "Do you have the equipment for that?"

"We have the equipment for stone dragons. Might be a bit overkill for a squishy human."

"I'll have to improvise then. I need her kept stable." Tom reached inside the bag that hung over his shoulder and pulled out an arrow. He quickly sharpened the arrowhead and then began to cut.

***

A few hours later, and Tom was staring at a now bandaged up Cathie.

"Your medical knowledge is impressive." The dragon noted as she finished cleaning the surrounding blood.

"One of my family's many skills." Tom sighed as he examined the bandage extra carefully. He began to notice his hands shaking. He reached into his bag and took out a wooden bottle. He opened the lid to realise that it was empty.

"Need some water?" The dragon asked him. He put the empty bottle down on the table beside him and sat on his own hands.

"No, I'm good." He answered.

As he continued to stare at Cathie, the image of someone else began to overlap his vision. A much older looking woman with a huge claw mark across her chest was staring back at him, "That seems about right." Tom mumbled to himself.

He turned away out of fear only to look at a man with similar claw marks. Unlike the woman however, the man stared back with dead eyes.

Tom closed his eyes and kept them as closed as possible.

"I believe you are due for your part of the bargain." The dragon reminded him. Tom opened his eyes, and he was back in the underground room. The dragon looked towards the door of the room, "Boulder will be expecting you."

"I'd imagine so." Tom sighed, "What was your name?"

"Flint."

"Thanks Flint. I couldn't have saved her without you."

"No problem. I'll make sure she's alright while you take care of business." Tom nodded before walking over to the door and leaving the room.

Tom almost instantly came face to face with another stone dragon.

"Boulder you said your name was?" Tom asked.

"Yes, how is your friend?"

"Better. Thank you. I'm not sure what I would have done without help."

"Perhaps now you can help us out with our problem. I hear you are quite the problem solver amongst the surface dwellers." Boulder revealed. He began to walk down one of the many underground tunnels. Tom quickly followed him. Every so often, small glowing rocks were placed into the walls of the tunnels to light them up.

"You realise that every other dragon thinks you are extinct right?" Tom asked as he took a closer look while continuing to follow.

"That was our intention. The surface is rather dangerous, so we chose to never return."

"You came up for me."

"An exception we were forced to make. As you will see soon enough."

"You're quite well spoken in the human tongue for a dragon. I highly doubt my potion made it down here."

"We found the human tongue a much better form of communication than our native tongue. In fact, it allowed us to learn quite a lot from you cave dwellers."

"Which would explain the rather impressive medical room."

"Flint has done what others would consider impossible many a time in that room. It's helped us though many a struggle." Boulder suddenly came to a stop as they came to the end of the tunnel.

Right at the end, the rock was a different colour. It was black instead of grey.

"Now what is that?" Tom asked as he walked over to it and began to examine it.

"We were hoping you could tell us that." Boulder responded, "It seems to surround the entire valley, and we can't dig through it."

"Not so bad. I'm sure you can made do with the space you have."

"Afraid not. You see we eat stone. We dig to feed, and we're running out of stone to dig."

"I see. Can't you relocate using the surface?"

"As I said, we do not go to the surface."

"You may have to."

"We would not make the journey to a new valley. Especially with the creatures in the valley above."

"Good point. Those things are nasty, and I've watched them take on dragons as well." Tom began to reach into his bag. He pulled out an arrow and began to rub it against the rock. The arrow snapped almost instantly.

"We've tried brute strength. The material appears to be indestructible even to powerful tools." Boulder revealed.

"So clearly I won't get anywhere with that approach. Perhaps it dissolves in something." Tom began to think out aloud, "You don't happen to have a bunch of chemicals, do you?"

"Only ones Flint uses."

"Not really the right stuff." Tom muttered though closed teeth, "I'm going to need some ingredients from the surface. Do you think your people could get them for me?"

"Provided they grow on the floor of the valley, yes."

"Alright." Tom muttered as he began to write a list on a sheet of paper, "I'll need these, because lucky for you, I've got my glassware with me."

***

Cathie awoke to the sight of Flint looking down at her. Her first reaction was to reach for the sword on her back, which wasn't there. She quickly found it to the side of the slab she was on. She tried to reach for it, but as she did so a pain shot through her.

"You need to be careful. You don't want to reopen the wound." Flint told her as she removed the sword from her reach, "Tom will be back soon."

"Where am I?" Cathie asked as she slowly lay back down.

"Underground. Our leader needed something from Tom, in return we helped save your life."

"Thank you."

"Don't thank me. That man of yours was the one who did most of the work."

"Tom isn't my... man."

"He certainly seemed it. The way he fought for your life. He also seemed pretty shaken up afterwards, although that might better be explained by this." She added as she picked up the empty wooden bottle.

She gave it a gentle shake, and a drop of black liquid dripped out and onto Flint's claw.

"What is that?"

"Something I would only prescribe to my more mentally unstable patients, and Tom seems to be dependent on it."

"What does it do?"

"It's a suppressant of some kind. Not quite sure what, but along those lines."

"I can take a guess at what it suppresses." Cathie sighed as she took the bottle and looked at it closely.

***

Tom packed away his glassware. He'd tried everything. Acids, bases, oxidising agents and reducing alike. The material not only refused to react; it didn't even interact in any way. Viscous fluids slipped right off it, refusing to stick.

"What else is there?" Boulder asked him as he noticed Tom hadn't tried anything new in the past few minutes.

"I may be a little bit out of my depth with this one." Tom sighed as he reached into his bag. He took out one of the air crystals and placed it against the material.

The crystal sprang to life, bursting air right down the tunnel. Tom quickly removed it and looked at the now overheated crystal slowly burning his hand. He dropped it onto the floor.

"What happened?"

"The material… It has energy… A massive amount by the looks of it." Tom explained as an idea popped into his head. He tried his bag once more, this time bringing out the odd cube object, "You may want to stand back." He warned as he slowly placed the cube against the material.

***

Three sets of eyes loomed in the darkness.

"I swear I felt a small door open earlier."

"I doubt it, or have you forgotten who trapped us in here. She won't allow us to escape."

"We trapped her in here though. I'm still in possession of the cube we managed to get her into before she trapped us. Maybe escape is possible."

"You think that prison will stop her power? She could probably hold us in here far longer than we can hold her in there."

"We've been having this argument for ages."

"What else are we going to do?"

"Wait. Do you see that?"

The three sets of eyes looked upwards to the light which had appeared above them.

"Is it her?"

"No, she's still trapped."

"Then someone else is breaking her prison for us."

***

A wave of purple energy rippled through the black material as the cube shattered into dust. Tom and Boulder stood perfectly still for a minute or two, waiting for something to happen. The purple glow in the black material slowly faded, until it was black once more.

"Well, that did something." Tom sighed as he took out a small knife.

"What are you going to do with that?" Boulder asked him as Tom began to tap the black material.

"This material can absorb energy." Tom concluded, "Sucked the cube dry, and the shear amount inside burnt out the crystal."

"Is that good or bad?"

"Bad. Very bad. To break such a material, you would have to overcome its limit to absorb. Given that cube was perhaps the most concentrated form of energy I've ever come across, and it ate it up like nothing, I don't think that's a limit we can overcome."

"Are you saying you cannot break it?"

"I could, if I had a couple of stars at my disposal." Tom sighed, "I'm good, but I'm nowhere near that good."

Tom put the knife back into his bag. He gave the black material one last look. It had defeated him. Another dying species needed his help, and he was powerless for a second time.

He inexplicably smacked the material with his fist. The sharp edges cut his hand, and he felt the kinetic energy of the punch drain into the material almost instantly. He gave one last sigh as he turned away.

His ears suddenly pricked up to the faint sound of fizzing. Tom turned back to the material.

Where his blood had touched the material, it now fizzed and hissed in a violent reaction. A brown liquid oozed down onto the floor.

"You did it." Boulder noticed, "You dissolved it."

"Yes, I did. In… human blood." Tom turned to look at Boulder. All of a sudden, his head was filled with warning signs. There was only one way these dragons could get their hands on more human blood.

***

"So, you are one of the last humans?" Flint asked Cathie. Cathie nodded as the door to the medical room slid open, and Boulder walked through, followed by two other stone dragons.

"Where is Tom?" Cathie asked.

"Take her to the other human." Boulder ordered one of the other dragons. Cathie stood up and began to follow the dragon which led her out of the room. Boulder turned to Flint, "I'm going to require your skills Flint."

***

The stone slab that made up the rooms' door quickly slid open. It took Cathie less than a second to notice Tom in the corner of the room. At first, she began to wonder why he was curled up there as if he'd been injured. Tom's eyes met hers, and instantly widened as Tom's mouth opened ready to shout.

Cathie's head was filled with warning signs as she suddenly felt the stone dragon behind her shift in an odd way. She finally noticed the bruises on Tom's arms, and the various cuts on his clothes.

She quickly put one-foot forwards and went to one knee.

"Watch out!" The words finally escaped Tom's mouth as he began to get to his feet. She felt the air above her head shift quite a bit. A dragon claw crashed into the stone door frame beside her.

Trying to grab her instead of just push her in? This dragon wasn't too bright. The push would have been quicker, and not as alerting. She'd have been trapped with Tom if it had done so. A mistake which on any normal occasion would just increase the risk of hurting the prisoner as they tried to fight back to no avail, but add Cathie into the mix, and the mistake becomes fatal.

No sword. She'd left it back with Flint. No time to think about why either, she could hear the dragon pull its claws out of the stone.

She spun on her knee to face the dragon. Similar body to the earth dragons, thick armour, perhaps thicker. This was by no means going to be pretty.

The first key was to get close. Dragons were huge compared to humans. Most of the time this would work to its advantage, but she was already very close, and they were in an enclosed space. She pushed off her front foot as she caught grip with her bare toes.

She was close enough to not worry about the four legs and the sharp claws that they ended in. The next problem was the teeth. She was now charging straight for its head. Its mouth began to open, ready to snap at her.

Ducking wouldn't work this time; it would have learnt from its first mistake. She made sure she put a bit of spring into the next few steps. The dragon snapped at her, but she put her hands on its sharp nose and pushed herself up. She felt the point scrape and scratch the centre of her body as she pulled herself fully onto its skull. She now faced the dragon's two eyes as she skilfully kept her balance and charged forwards. Between its ears and onto its neck.

She felt the thick armour with just her feet, no good. Her eyes caught something moving at great speed in front of her. She finally managed to fix her eyes onto the end of the dragon's tail. Just like the earth dragons, this dragon seemed to have a massive boulder like tail end. At the moment it was whipping about, but with enough skill the dragon might be able to land a hit or two if she went any further down its back.

All of a sudden, she felt her balance shift. She used the tunnel walls as a reference. The many layers of rock began to tilt. It was going to roll over and crush her. She quickly worked out which way it was rolling and changed her forward momentum so that she'd remain on top. A shadow caught her off guard, and suddenly, her body smacked against one of the dragon's upper legs.

She fell to the floor and rolled just into the reach of one of the dragon's feet. Before she could recover, the claws snapped shut around her. She felt herself being lifted. The dragon threw her straight into the closest rock wall. She hit it with a crunch, and quickly fell to the floor.

As Cathie opened her eyes, her vision was slowly fading. She could feel the injury on her chest burning, and her head was ringing in pain. Her left arm had taken most of the impact, and she couldn't move it without a lot of pain.

***

A small and young version of Cathie was on her knees in front of a blue haired woman. The woman was holding a wooden sword, but it had been stained by blood. Cathie's head was ringing then too. Her right arm had also been cut and had a splinter or two within the cut itself. Cathie was also out of breath, and on the verge of tears.

"The human body is weak." The woman spoke as she flicked the fresh blood off her wooden sword. What was odd about this woman was that she didn't seem particularly strong. She was about as thin as Tom, with both body and arms. Yet Cathie's injuries suggested otherwise, "But the human body is also clever."

Cathie's broken wooden sword lay in shards on the ground. Blood dripped down Cathie's fingers onto what remained of the handle, "When the body can't continue, it tells the mind in a variety of different ways. When the mind ignores these signs, the body can shut itself off to avoid further damage."

"I don't see how that helps me." Cathie muttered as she tried to stand. She got to one foot, with one knee still on the ground, but the pain stopped her from moving any further.

"But you see the mind is strong. Perhaps the strongest thing about a human." The woman revealed, "If the mind can beat the body, you can stop this from happening." She continued as she slashed at Cathie. The wooden sword smacked into the side of her rib cage. Blood spat out of Cathie's mouth as she fell to her hands and knees.

The woman examined her sword once more. No blood this time, which seemed to disappoint her, "However in the end the body is the one in control when it comes to survival. You won't last long even if you've had training and experience. It's a very dangerous situation to be in."

"Why are you doing this?" Cathie seemed to plead as she looked up at the woman in tears.

"Because if you can push your body to fight in this moment, your body will go to extreme lengths to win. You'll punch much harder than ever, you'll dodge much faster, because your body will push every limit, and perhaps even break a few to keep you alive in those few seconds." The woman explained as she knelt down to Cathie's eye level, "That daughter, is when you either win the fight there and then, or you die."

"Why can't I run?" The woman gave a smile as she stood back up.

"Because if you run, you die. You won't last long, and a few seconds even at a fast speed won't get you far." She raised her sword above Cathie's head, "If it was a fight you should run from, a fight you can't win, you should have already run away before then."

The sword came crashing down towards Cathie.

***

Cathie grabbed the claw coming straight down for her head. Despite it being a claw capable of calving through stone like paper, Cathie's grip snapped it like a twig as her eyes flared blood-red. As she pushed herself forwards with her legs, she could feel the muscles burn. She formed a fist as she came up to the dragon's head in her right hand.

Its mouth opened once more, but this time Cathie was faster than it was expecting. She managed an upper cut right inside its mouth, just behind its upper teeth. She felt dragon bones crack as the dragon gave a screech of pain. She could see her vision begin to fade in and out. Her focus quickly regained as a loose tooth knocked her arm. She managed to grab it before it hit the floor. The dragon's head hit the floor in front of her.

Brain behind the eyes. Her vision blacked out for a second, but before she knew it, she was back on the dragon's snout. She pushed forwards once more, this time feeling her legs go completely numb. They stopped working just as she came into arm's reach. She extended her right arm as her body hit the top of the dragon's head and made sure to jam the tooth into the nearest eye as hard as she could manage.

Her vision blacked out once more, but it came back once again. She focused on the tooth. It wasn't deep enough. She heard a foot land beside her head, and a second foot landed on top of the tooth. The tooth was pushed in further, and shortly after, the dragon lay dead.

***

Cathie's eyes opened to the sight of a stone roof. She tried to sit up but found that she couldn't. She heard shuffling to her left.

"Tom?" She asked. The shuffling increased. She felt herself being picked up and placed against the stone wall behind her.

"Sorry, didn't realise you'd slipped down." Tom sighed as he gave her a quick look over.

"How am I doing?"

"Badly bruised arm. Sliced chest. You reopened your wound and got yourself a concussion." Tom answered. Cathie gave a small smile.

"That all?"

"You pushed yourself beyond your limit this time." Tom sighed, "Your body is still recovering from how far you pushed it. Might take a while before you can move normally or without pain."

"Sorry." Cathie muttered.

"Next time you try to take on a dragon, ask for a sword." Tom added as he placed a sword on her legs.

"Where did you get that?" Cathie asked him. Tom revealed his bag by swinging it in front of her, "They didn't take it from you?"

"As far as they were aware, I only had glassware and a knife in this thing. Not the most threatening of objects."

"Thanks for letting me know."

"I wasn't the one who decided to take on a stone dragon bare handed."

"Heat of the moment."

"Yeah, I know. Fight or flight, right?"

"I was never good at running from a fight." Cathie sighed.

"Just don't tell Patrick about this, will you? The guy will probably kill me for letting you do that."

"Is it dead?" She asked him.

"Yeah. One stomp on the tooth, and it managed to do enough damage to the brain."

"How long have I been asleep?"

"Few hours, I think. Got some rest myself after I used the body to block the entrance, and without the sun I can only guess."

"Trapped and injured underground again." Cathie chuckled, "Perhaps I should lay off earth dragons for a bit."

"Well, we still need to get out of here, which is going to be quite the task."

"Think you can carry me?"

"Drag you, maybe. I'm not very strong remember?"

"So, I guess it's about time for one of those masterminded plans of yours."

"I've got something in the works, but its more luck than a plan."

"Mind letting me in on it?" She asked. Tom took a few more seconds to think.

"You spent a lot of time with Flint, right?" Tom asked her, "Think she's the kind of person to help enslave what remains of humanity for its blood?"

"No, why? Is that what this is about?"

"Our blood is the only thing I could find that dissolves this material that traps these dragons in this valley."

"The more I learn about this valley, the less I want to live in it."

"Thing is, if Boulder wants to get our blood without killing us, he'll need Flint's help."

"What does this have to do with our escape?"

"Don't you think it's odd that no other dragons have come for us?" Tom asked her. Cathie managed to slowly turn her head to the dead dragon which blocked the only exit to the small room they were in.

"You think Flint is giving them trouble?"

"If she's smart, she'd try to overthrow Boulder as leader, although I don't really know enough about these dragons to assume that."

"Either way, if we find her, chances are she will help right?" Cathie asked him. She slowly turned her head to face him. Tom slowly nodded after some more thought.

"She might be our only option. I'm sure she'd have no trouble carrying you."

"Then you need to go and find her."

"And leave you?"

"Not exactly something new." Cathie muttered, "But finding her while I'm slowing you down would be stupid." She added before Tom had a chance to speak, "You can come back for me."

"What if one of them find you?"

"You better find her quickly then." Tom gave a nod as he stood up. He picked up his bag, but then put it back down again.

"In here there is something for almost every situation." He explained as he placed the bag beside her, "You'll need it more than me."

"Are you sure? You don't have a weapon."

"My bow is somewhere out there. Besides I couldn't take down a stone dragon with or without a weapon alone. This on the other hand." Tom pulled out an air crystal from the bag, "This should at least hurt them a bit."

Tom took out another air crystal from the bag and inspected it. It looked slightly damaged.

"Is that one for me?"

"I overheated it when messing around with the material, but it seems fine for now." Tom muttered as he handed over the crystal, "But I'd advise not using it. Your body needs all the energy it can muster right now. The energy drain may have felt like nothing before, but now it will probably take a lot more out of you."

"A last resort then." Cathie sighed as Tom began to squeeze past the dead dragon. He came to a stop however and seemed to think for a couple more seconds.

"You know, Patrick told me some interesting things before I left." Tom suddenly spat out, "Once we get out of this, we need to have a chat about that." He continued. He then completely vanished behind the body. His footsteps got more and more distant.

"Right." Cathie sighed as she looked down at the sword still on her legs, "That."

CHAPTER 8; LIMITS

The seemingly endless tunnels twisted and turned so many times that Tom had lost his sense of direction almost immediately. He made sure to memorise every step he took; he wasn't going to forget where he'd left her.

He came to a stop at one of the many different junctions between the tunnels. He closed his eyes and tried his best to listen. Small rumbles came from one of the tunnels. It wasn't ideal, but it was all he had. He began to run down the tunnel towards the sound. It wasn't often that Tom found himself in a situation where he wasn't quite sure what was going to happen next.

Too many things to consider. Too many variables that he didn't have control over, or the correct knowledge to predict. Oddly enough he found that the many issues he was facing didn't seem to bother him as much the further away Cathie was. He'd noticed that when he left the others as well. But still she followed.

Had he overlooked something? Perhaps it was because he didn't say goodbye. He'd never had to say goodbye to a friend before. It was clear that he couldn't run away from this problem, not like the last problem on this scale.

Tom stopped his mind there. He'd run out of that black liquid, and now wasn't a time to have images of his parents cloud his senses. He instead flooded his mind with the problems he was now running towards.

For all he knew he could be running into the middle of a dragon revolution, armed only with a single crystal. His injuries from being imprisoned were little more than bruises, but it was clear he wasn't in peak condition either.

The small rumbles were now becoming large thuds. He was making progress, and quickly too.

He turned one last twist to see a large brawl of stone dragons. It wasn't entirely clear who was on what side, or even if there was any form of sides. Tom came to a stop at a reasonable distance and quickly caught his breath as he looked around at his other options. Nothing but a straight tunnel towards the fight, or back the way he came.

Backtracking would complicate the recall of the way back, and if Flint was doing what he suspected, he'd most likely have to get past a fight like this anyway since she hadn't found the two of them.

Better that he had time to think about it from a distance than accidently get caught right up in one.

He looked down at the air crystal in his hand. Using it on all of them would piss them all off, and if some were human sympathisers it might complicate things further. He then began looking at the cave surrounding the fight. There were many chunks missing and the tunnel itself was slowly beginning to collapse, but there were still bits of smooth wall intact.

He planned a route in his head, estimated the required speed, and then looked down at both the crystal and his feet. He gave it a second thought, and then a third. It would hurt, but it wouldn't break anything. He gave a nod, and then positioned himself for a run up.

He sped off. At first with just the force of his two legs, but as he came closer to a particular nearby large piece of rubble just outside the fight, he tactfully positioned the air crystal. With a blast, he'd increased his speed, and with a second, he'd made the jump on top of the large rubble that he'd never clear unaided.

A quick wall vault and onto another chunk of rubble. The fight was now beneath him. Another burst of speed from the crystal, and he was onto the next. A stray tail smacked into the wall he was planning to vault off next, but Tom had already committed to the jump.

***

"The human mind is perhaps one of the most powerful things in this world." A middle-aged woman spoke to a young boy. Both had brown hair that matched Tom's perfectly.

"I thought you said the brain was a squishy pink thing." The boy replied. He seemed to be no older than three. The woman gave a motherly smile. The kind of smile a parent makes when they have to remember that they are talking to a child, and not someone their age.

The woman picked the boy up and sat him on her lap.

"Just because its pink and squishy, doesn't make it less powerful."

"It doesn't seem to do very well against a sword, or a dragon claw." The boy pointed out. The woman gave a second smile, this time however there seemed to be genuine humour behind it.

"A sword is useless if you don't know how to use it." She replied, "The brain is the same. If you know how to use it properly, it can be the most powerful thing in this world."

"So how do you correctly use it?" The boy looked up at his mother's face.

"I'll show you."

***

Tom's eyes flared to purple. Outlines of his feet on the wall began drawing themselves onto his vision. Numbers began to appear beside them. Vectors, leg strain, angles and velocities. At first there were many, but as the numbers seemed to calculate, many turned red, and vanished. Eventually, there was only one outline of foot angle.

His vision then focussed on the path ahead. The rubble had changed since he'd first taken a look. Many paths began to draw themselves into his vision, and once more numbers accompanied each one. This time it came out with three possible routes. The one with the least strain on his legs was picked.

Additional numbers and images drew themselves onto the path. At points, he needed to make a direction change mid-air, and the position of his body and the crystal were provided.

All of a sudden, he was at the wall. His feet fell perfectly in line with the white drawing in his vision, and he pushed off, following the path now clearly laid out for him.

More rubble continued to collapse from the ceiling of the tunnel. Suddenly, the path changed, recalculated. He adjusted his movements and continued once more.

Sweat began to slowly run-down Tom's forehead. This was taking a toll, a big one. His head began to throb. His vision slowly blurred. He forced his eyes wide open. His vision cleared. One more jump.

He successfully landed on the ground of the tunnel on the other side of the fight. He began to catch his breath, but he could tell something was wrong.

Those moves were taxing, but only a short burst. He was tired, but it wasn't his muscles. In fact, it wasn't his body at all. He could feel his thoughts floating about unchecked and disorganised. After a few seconds he struggled to even think anything more than basic functions.

Still out of breath, Tom collapsed to his knees as the headache increased in strength. Can't think. The worst thing Tom could have. The realisation that he couldn't think made him wonder how, why, what to do about it, which of course made the problem much, much worse.

Spontaneously, what was left of his conscious focused on his vision, his eyes. Something was charging at him. A stone dragon.

Move or die

A single thought broke its way through the barrier. Tom desperately lunged to the right, but the dragon was still far enough away to correct its path.

Terminate all thoughts

Complete

Re-initiating basic functions

Complete

Senses detect danger

Emergency countermeasures activ-

The charging dragon was suddenly replaced by another dragon, this time side on to Tom. Tom took a few more seconds to get his thoughts in check.

He slowly got to his feet. The headache had died down to nothing but an annoying pain in the back of his head. He wiped the sweat from his forehead. His head was incredibly hot, but it was slowly dying down with time.

"Are you just going to stand there human?" The dragon in front of him asked. It was pinning down the dragon which had charged at him. Tom blinked a few times.

"Sorry. Thanks." He replied. His head began to ring now.

"Flint is further down. She will want words with you." The dragon informed him as it struggled to keep the other dragon fully down against the ground.

Tom gave a painful nod, turned, and continued to run down the tunnel.

He knew he was good, but Tom knew his limits well. What he pulled off back there, all those calculations, all those predictions, that was beyond his mental capacity. Perhaps that was the explanation for the headache. The same way Cathie pushed her body beyond her limit, perhaps Tom just did the same with his mind.

And here he thought that his mothers' teachings were nothing more than knowledge. Something in there taught him how to do that, yet that was the first time he'd pulled something like that off. He didn't seem to remember her mentioning all that, or the throbbing headache afterwards, but then again, she only mentioned that it was powerful.

Power always comes at a price. It was a funny and irrelevant train of thought that Tom's mind had wondered down as he continued his journey, but at least he could think again. Power always comes at a price. The more he thought about it, the more he seemed to convince himself that those words were true.

His mind refocused on what was ahead of him. More stone dragons, but this time they were not fighting, but walking in line. The front dragon spotted Tom from far off and halted the entire line.

"Change of mission." The front dragon announced as it turned to face the rest, "I need two for escort duty." Two dragons took a few steps forwards. Both of them seemed to have empty bags hanging off their backs.

"Supply crew sir. If we are to head back, may I suggest a supply run as well, sir." One of the dragons spoke. The lead dragon nodded as Tom finally reached them.

"Escort this human to Flint. Return with supplies. Go." The lead dragon boomed.

Tom decided it was best to keep up the pace, which was a lot harder now that two large dragons were shaking the ground behind them as they galloped behind.

"Next right human." One of them boomed. The voice caught Tom a little off guard, but he quickly made the suggested turn, and continued onwards.

***

Cathie's eyes slowly opened. She'd drifted off at some point. With a little shuffle, she made herself slightly more comfortable. She noticed the pain had died down, so she tried her best to stand.

It took some effort, but she was on her feet. She could feel them shake from the weight. Slowly, she bent down to pick up the sword. With a tug, the sword seemed to refuse to budge. Too heavy.

She sat back down and pulled Tom's bag closer to her. With a lot of strain and effort she managed to drag the sword to the bag, and just about managed to get it inside. She stood up once more and slung the rather light bag over her shoulder.

Moving position wouldn't be a very smart move right now, and yet she felt the urge to move anyway. She paced around the room. The bag didn't weigh much but it seemed to have a weight to it. After a few more laps she began to break into a jog. Her muscles ached at first, but the pain seemed to vanish over time.

A few more laps, and she picked the pace up into a full sprint. It wasn't easy in such a small room, so she didn't do it for long. When she came to a stop, her body felt much better. The fresh blood pumping through it.

She opened the bag and reached inside. Her hand found the handle of the sword. She slowly pulled it out. Her arm began to shake under the weight, so she held it with both hands, and began to lift and lower it.

Before long, she held the two-handed sword in her right hand without issue.

"Much better." She finally sighed as she sat back down against one of the walls of the room. She placed the sword by her side and began to pay more attention to Tom's bag.

He had pulled many a thing out of there. She knew for a fact that his glassware was currently inside. Yet when she had grabbed the sword, it felt like it was the only thing inside. On top of that, the glass didn't make a sound when she had been running. In fact, none of the bag's contents made a sound.

Curiously, she put her hand inside once more, this time looking into the bag itself as she did so. Nothing. It seemed completely empty. She thought about it for a second or two, and then thought about what Tom would have in there. An arrow was an obvious answer. She imagined an arrow as she reached inside once more. Her hand touched something. An arrow, so that was how it worked?

Tom had previously mentioned that his bag wasn't magical, so what exactly was it? Whenever they asked him, he'd change the subject. The fact that the bag was linked to his parents probably had something to do with it, or perhaps he himself didn't know either.

***

Tom slid to a halt. His leather boots with groves sliced by knives were not the best with gripping the smooth stone that made up the floor. He was now in a room with many other stone dragons. In the centre of the room, Flint was hard at work tending to one of the many injured dragons.

"And here I was expecting to have to rescue you two." Flint sighed as she noticed Tom. Her eyes searched for Cathie.

"She was injured. For now, she's safe, but we need to get to her." He explained.

"I hate to be the one to tell you this, but we can't."

"Why not?" Flint took a few second to look around at the number of injured dragons around them, "Oh, the fight isn't going so well is it?" He realised.

"No. No its not." Flint sighed as she continued to work on the dragon in front of her, "So far the plan was to rescue you two and use you to escape to the surface. However, we weren't able to get anywhere near close to where you were being held."

"Sounds like a good plan to me. Just one problem. Those creatures on the surface are far too dangerous, even with me guiding you all." Tom sighed, "The only one capable of taking those things on would be Cathie."

"Then we are stuck." Flint pointed out, "We cannot escape or push forwards."

"That's because you're doing it all wrong." Tom sighed as he took a look at a paper map beside Flint. It was very rough, but it seemed to outline what was happening with the fight. He picked it up and began to shake his head.

"If you have a better strategy, by all means. None of us are experienced fighters."

"The problem is you're too focused on defence. You've set up shop here and are using almost everything you have just to stop this place falling."

"How is that not the right approach?"

"Because Cathie is all of our last bets. We either get her, or we lose. Doesn't matter if we lose this place, only that we get Cathie."

"You're suggesting we all make a push for Cathie and completely forget about defence?"

"It will cost lives, but we'd be able to escape." Tom concluded.

"I have too many injured here. I can't just leave them to die."

"Then hide them. Dig out a new room not on any map Boulder would have and block it up. We can come back for them once we make it up top." Tom suggested. Flint looked around the room once more. She looked back at the two dragons which stood behind Tom.

"You two, start digging."

***

Cathie had been awake for a few hours now. To pass the time she'd try guessing objects that were in Tom's bag and try to pull them out. She hadn't been very successful.

Other than sheets of paper and bow equipment, she hadn't pulled anything out. She gathered everything up and placed it back inside the bag.

Tom's mother used to own the bag before him. Perhaps there was stuff in there that not even Tom knew about. She tried to imagine some form of Tom's mother. It wasn't a very close depiction, given she only had Tom's looks to guess from, but nonetheless she put her hand into the bag.

She pulled a bow out of the bag. It was old and strange. It wasn't made of wood, but a light material which she honestly had no idea what it was. The design itself was also rather odd. Instead of just having a bow string attached to the main body, there seemed to be some kind of pully system to draw the bow back instead.

Cathie stood up with it and drew it back. It took far more strength than any bow she'd used before, even Tom's special one. She released it, and it fired with a twang. Despite not being loaded, Cathie could tell that somehow this bow was far more powerful than any she'd used before, simply from the sound of the string snapping back into position. The string itself was also rather odd. It seemed far more robust than your average string and was pitch black instead of light brown.

She slowly put the bow back into the bag. Tom had taught her how to shoot, perhaps his mother taught him. The more Cathie learnt about Tom's mother, the more she realised how right the dragons were to fear her. She would have given anything to watch her own mother face her. She honestly couldn't figure out who would win.

A rumble in the distance caught her attention. She quickly slung the bag over her shoulder and positioned herself out of view of the doorway. She could hear intense fighting now, between a rather worrying number of dragons.

After a few minutes, the body blocking the doorway was pulled out into the corridor. Cathie quickly pulled the sword from the bag and prepared to kill then next thing to move.

"Cathie?" Tom's voice asked. She lowered her sword and ran out into the view of the door. Tom was standing there, waiting for her. Behind him, stone dragons were barely holding each other at bay.

"Took your time."

"Had a rebellion to organise." Tom chuckled, "Fall back!"

CHAPTER 9; BODY

The sun rose above the distant watery horizon with a chilling wind. Tom and Flint watched in silence as the sun beams bounced off the distant ocean waters, and into their eyes.

"The only way now is forward." Tom sighed as he looked down at the forest beneath the mountain they were on. Behind them sat the very same cave Tom had been sleeping in before.

"I have made a decision." Flint announced to him, "It's not worth the risk."

"So, you'll stay here?" He asked as he turned to look back at the cave. Shuffling sounds of sleeping dragons came from within.

"This mountain has more than enough rock to keep us going for a while without even affecting the terrain that much. Perhaps enough time for you to bring better help."

"May I ask why you helped rescue Cathie if you had this idea all along?" Flint gave him a small smile.

"You weren't going to leave those caves without her, and I needed at least one human to send for help." She answered, "I may not have needed her, but you do."

"The more I talk with you, the more I wonder how you weren't leading these dragons from the start."

"Dragon leadership is determined by fights to the death. Boulder was the strongest amongst us." Tom gave a small nod of understanding.

"Perhaps it's time that changed." He added before he turned from her and walked back into the cave. Flint looked back out towards the rising sun.

Tom continued past many sleeping stone dragons as he made his way to the burnt-out fire, where Cathie was curled up in a fur blanket, and using Tom's bag as a pillow. He found it rather amusing that she'd curled up just like most of the dragons around her had done, only without the tail.

He sat down next to her head and closed his eyes. His headache had almost gone now, just a very small nagging pain in the back of his head left.

"I take it we aren't moving?" Cathie's voice whispered.

"Someone has sharp ears." Tom responded in a quiet mutter. Tom listened to the sound of her gently sitting upright beside him.

"I was never good at staying asleep."

"These dragons won't be moving, but we probably should. Things will get messy once these things start getting hungry." Tom pointed out, "Although I'm not really sure where to go next."

"Well, I still need to pay Charlie back for the wound he gave me." Tom opened his eyes and turned to Cathie. She'd said it so genuinely.

"Do you remember how you got that wound?" He asked her. Cathie nodded.

"Very clearly. He was trying to kill you, so I got in the way, took the hit, and then he ran off like a coward." She spoke the last part with disgust in her voice.

Tom took a quick look at her head. No injuries. In fact, other than the arrow wound that was still bandaged up, she seemed completely fine. His eyes narrowed ever so slightly; he'd seen her do this before.

In fact, it was when they were last here, before they had met the other two. They'd come across an adult ice dragon carcass inside a nearby cave. It really seemed to affect her at the time, although she wasn't as open back then, so she never did tell him why. Later on, he'd tried to ask about it, but she seemed to have no knowledge of it.

Wait… She'd been raised by an ice dragon…

Tom slowly got to his feet.

"You ready to move out?" He asked her.

"You have an idea where to go?" She asked him. She folded the blanket away and neatly stuffed it in Tom's bag. She then brushed herself down of the small bits of dirt from the ground and stood straight.

"I have a hunch." He answered as he picked up his bag and walked out of the cave, with Cathie close behind him. A claw quickly stopped his path.

Tom followed the claw all the way to Flint. His bow landed at his feet.

"You left it behind. Such a handcrafted weapon must be precious?" She asked him. Tom quickly picked it up and slung it over his shoulder.

"Much appreciated. I'll do my best to get you out of this valley once and for all." He replied. He turned and began to walk down the long path down the mountain.

***

The short walk through the forest was filled with nothing but silence between the two of them. Finally, Tom came to a stop in a spot all too familiar to the both of them. Up above, the cliff edge, around them, the forest, yet this spot in particular meant something to both of them.

"This is where we first met." Cathie realised as she took it all in. Tom knelt down by a ditch that hadn't been there the last time.

It was stained with dried blood, and the rough outline of a human was just about visible from the impact.

"Cathie, I need you to look at this." Tom muttered. He stood up and began to frantically look around.

"Is everything alright?" Cathie asked as she walked over to inspect the ditch.

"No. No it isn't."

"Looks like someone fell from… wait."

"This is where Charlie's body is supposed to be. Bastard survived somehow." Cathie gave him a rather confused look, but once he drew his bow and loaded it with arrows from his bag, she got the general idea, they were in danger.

She quickly grabbed the two-handed sword from out of the bag and stood back-to-back with Tom as the two of them slowly turned to observe all directions.

"I thought Charlie got away."

"No, that's just what your mind is telling you to protect you from the truth. Sorry I wanted to break it to you gently, but he could be anywhere."

"No, he couldn't."

"I know it's hard to take in, but it's just your head trying to protect you."

"No, he couldn't be anywhere." Cathie realised as she knelt down beside the ditch, "Look how much blood there is. If the fall didn't kill him then he bled to death."

Tom lowered his bow. She was right.

"So, where's the body? There's no trail of blood, so it wasn't dragged off."

"Footprints. Human footprints." Cathie noticed as she pointed to a set of footprints walking away from the ditch, "Patrick?"

"There's no one else. Probably followed you two here, found the body and took it somewhere to be buried."

"Why did I think that he got away?" Cathie seemed to wonder as she pressed her fingers against the dried blood, "How could I forget that face?" Tom placed a hand on her shoulder.

"It's a trick of the mind. A way to avoid pain. Happens to minds that have been hurt once or twice before."

"Even you?" She asked as she turned her head up to face him.

"Sometimes. Sometimes…" He answered. His grip on her shoulder had tightened slightly, but it loosened up after a second or two.

She quickly got to her feet, spun around, and hugged him as tight as she could.

"It's horrible." Tears began to run down her face, "I don't want to forget. Not something like that." Tom's thin arms locked themselves around her as comfortingly as a hug from a hedgehog. It didn't bother her that much though. She buried her tear-soaked face into the side of his neck. There were a few seconds pause before she felt him bury his face into hers as well. That alone caught her a little off guard, but that was nothing compared to the fact that she could feel tears roll down the side of her neck from his face.

"I know." Despite the two words being muffled, she clearly heard the pain that seemed to show itself in his tone. That was the first time she'd ever heard him speak like that.

***

The cave the two of them had located was still rather deep within the valley, but it was well hidden by the surrounding bushes. To make sure it stayed that way, Tom hung long bits of cloth over the entrance to trap the light of the fire inside.

It was very small, barely enough room to comfortably sit around the fire without being dangerously close. They made sure to keep the flames low, to almost a hot glow than an actual fire.

The two of them were sat next to one another. Cathie took one final bite from what remained of an apple. She inspected what was left, concluded that the rest was nothing but seed, and tossed it into the glowing fire pit. Meanwhile, Tom had just finished cutting out the core, and had begun chopping the two halves of his apple into smaller slices.

She watched as he cut it up into eighths before he began eating them one by one. She considered asking the question on her mind, but she wasn't sure exactly how to go about it. As he finished off the last slice and chucked the neatly cut core into the fire pit, she finally brought up the courage to ask him.

"Do I remind you of your dad?" She asked, seemingly out of the blue for Tom. He took a second to take in the question, then another second as he gave her a quick look over.

"Yes. Sometimes you do." He answered, "Odd question to ask." He added.

"It explains a lot." Cathie muttered to herself.

"Like what?" Tom asked her. He'd heard her.

"Why you left." Her mouth blurted out before she could even think of a response.

"You thought I left because of you?" Cathie paused for a moment, and then decided she might as well continue.

"What else could it be. You left right when Patrick told you about me." She sighed as she brought her knees up to her chin. She'd curled herself up and had turned her head away from him.

"What Patrick told me was that Charlie was going to be a problem sooner or later, and that I was the cause of it. I left with the sole purpose of trying to avoid what happened up on that cliff." Tom explained. Cathie turned back to look at him.

"But..." She didn't seem to understand. Tom gave a small nod to himself as he realised where the confusion was.

"You thought I couldn't stand you because you remind me of my dad, right?" Tom asked her.

"The thought had crossed my mind once or twice."

"That's where you are very much mistaken." Tom revealed with a chuckle, "I don't hate you, or my dad. The reason I had issues as a kid was because I could never connect with the guy."

"So, you left to stop Charlie from killing you? Why did he try that in the first place?"

"Patrick told me the guy was in love with you, but you weren't in love with him. If he ever found out, he'd kill me."

"I see. So, Patrick really did tell you about my feelings?" She asked as she held her legs, squeezing her into an even tighter curl.

"You know I really did think he was lying to me. I left anyway just in case. But as I walked away all I could do was wonder if it was a ploy of his to get rid of me or not." Tom chuckled as he seemed to sidestep the exact question, "Yet here you are, worried to death about how I see you." He sighed.

"Before recent events I was worried I'd never break through that cold heart of yours, but something was different this time."

"I haven't been myself for these past few days." Cathie came out of her ball and shifted herself right next to him. She looked him dead in the eyes.

"No. I think for once you were yourself. For once, you aren't under the influence of that medicine of yours."

"How do you know about that?" He asked with questioning eyes.

"Flint looked at the empty bottle you left. Told me it held a suppressant. After the small differences in your behaviour, I kind of guessed what it suppressed."

"It… It's my way of dealing with the pain."

"A rather unhealthy way." At this, Tom quickly grabbed her right arm. He pulled down the fur sleeve to reveal the many scars on her wrists and forearm.

"Like you're any better." She quickly snapped her arm out of his grip and covered it up again.

"How'd you know about that?" She asked with equally questioning eyes.

"Educated guess. Over the many years we've been together, I've never seen your bare arms, not even once. Figured there was a reason, especially since you've been through pain like me."

The two of them sat there in silence for a few seconds. Cathie eventually cracked a small smile.

"Look at us. Two broken people pointing out the other's cracks." She muttered with a chuckle. Tom seemed to crack a small smile at the statement.

"Yeah." He sighed, "When did everything get so messed up?"

"Always has been." She replied, "We just didn't realise it until we saw it in each other."

A small breeze entered the cave. The temperature outside had dropped a bit since the last breeze though. The sun must have set while they'd been eating. Tom carefully examined the fire in front of them.

"We aren't going to be able to fuel that all night, not without adding enough to cause bright flames."

"I can add more gradually. I'm not much of a sleeper."

"Neither am I, but the past day or two was intense for both of us." He reminded her as he pulled down her top on her shoulder to remind her that she still had a bandage there, "How is it?"

"Getting better."

"Surgery puts a lot of strain on your body, plus your fight afterwards. Don't lie to me." Tom sighed as he let go of her.

"Fine. Hurts like hell."

"More like it. I would avoid any form of labour with that arm, and no heavy lifting or fighting at all."

"Like you can stop me." She pouted.

"I won't be the one stopping you. Your dead body will do that for you. I did my best to patch you up, but it was nowhere near perfect. Especially since it was so close to the heart. If any of my work inside there falls apart before your body heals around it, you'll die, and I won't be able to save you from that." He seemed to snap at her in an unnervingly calm voice.

He reached into his bag and pulled out a thick fur blanket. He at first wrapped one half of it around himself, and then lifted the other half with his right arm towards her.

She slowly made her way to the inside of the blanket and wrapped what remained around her. There was barely enough to cover the both of them, but it just about did the job. They were however now pressed together side by side, "You warm enough?" He asked her in a light voice that seemed to contrast his previous tone.

She gave a nod, and rested her head upon his warm shoulder, "Try your best to get some sleep."

The truth was that neither could sleep for any sensible length of time. Most times it ended in them waking up crying, screaming or sweating, usually a mixture of all. Both of them tried their best to avoid such experiences, but the human body cannot function without sleep forever, no matter how determined the mind may be. Every once in a while, both of them must suffer this experience.

Not that night, however. That night, both of them closed their eyes, and almost instantly reopened them to the chirping song of the birds singing as the sun slowly creeped above the horizon.

Tom poked his hand out of the blanket, and then brought it back in as Cathie realised his other hand had been put around her while she'd been sleeping. It rested softly against her lower chest, supporting her slightly from falling forwards or away from him, "Too cold still. Sun needs a bit to warm everything up."

She sneakily poked a finger just out of the blanket. It was oddly warm. He'd either lied or he was ill. She took her head off his shoulder as she brought her finger back in and gave him a quick glance as she looked at their surroundings. He seemed just fine.

"What's the plan then?"

"Wait like this a bit longer. Head out after that. Once we're out of this valley we need to find Frost, which will probably mean going back to the cave." Had he lied just to stay like this a little bit longer? She certainly had no complaints about their current positions.

"Let me know when it's warm enough then." She muttered as she rested her head back on his shoulder. She shut her eyes, not to sleep, just to relax for a bit.

***

As the sun rose over the horizon, Frost increased his height as he flew. After talking to Patrick about where Tom might have possibly gone, he only had one place left to check. A place he'd left until last for many reasons.

The valley of Certain Death. The name that was given to it centuries ago by ice dragons who once tried expanding their territory into that valley. As the name suggested, few returned from that place alive. None without serious injuries. It was considered to be the most dangerous valley in the known world.

He gained in height once more. He was nearly there, and he really didn't want to be anywhere near the ground. Now that the sun was out, he had a better chance of spotting signs of them. He pushed forwards, increasing his speed with a slight dive, but he made sure not to go too low.

His first stop was a cave up on a mountain deep within the valley. Apparently, that used to be a previous home of Tom's. A target easy to get to by air.

***

Cathie was the first to poke her head out of the small cave they'd been hiding in. Almost instantly she knew something was wrong. As the bird song continued to praise the rise of the sun, she noticed that none of the songs were coming from nearby. It was a small area, but within it, there was silence, and this area surrounded the entrance.

"Trouble." She spoke back into the cave. Tom quickly handed her the two-handed sword and began loading his bow from within the cave.

Once he was done, Cathie counted down from three using her fingers. Once her fist completely shut, the two of them sprinted out and into the surrounding forest.

Tom was surprisingly fast at running, but Cathie quickly felt a presence behind her. They'd begun the chase. Tom quickly got distance between him and Cathie, he then stopped, shot an arrow with some rope up, and then quickly boosted Cathie into a nearby tree.

He quickly pulled himself up the rope as Cathie grabbed the arrow and pulled the rope up from her end. Numerous powerful jaws snapped at Tom's feet as he was lifted into the same tree Cathie had ended up in.

The many cat like creatures that now surrounded them began to dig their claws into the bark and started to climb the tree they were on. At first the two of them focused on gaining some height, but after a few seconds of climbing they began to jump from tree to tree instead.

The creatures instead gave up on climbing and continued to follow them on the ground. With so many eyes, it was impossible to lose them.

"Ideas?" Tom asked. Cathie stowed her sword in her belt.

"I can't fight them with my injuries." She winced. Her arm wasn't in the best of shape, and this pace was clearly taking a toll on her arrow wound as well.

Tom took a second to look at the surrounding mountains, they were still deep within the valley. No cliff or hill nearby to take refuge on.

Slowly, the creatures that were following them began to slow down. They went from full paced sprinting to more of a trot, until they all finally came to a stop, and turned around.

"They've given up."

"They never give up." Cathie revealed as she came to a stop. Tom stood on the same branch beside her, "They don't back off for anything."

"Something stopped them from coming any closer." Tom muttered as he peered through the leaves to see what was further ahead. There seemed to be a clearing not too far ahead of them.

"If there is something those things don't want to mess with, we shouldn't either." Cathie suggested.

"I'd agree, but aren't you the least bit curious?" Tom asked her. She noticed a certain glint in his eye, he was craving an answer to their questions.

"Just make sure to stay in the tree line." Cathie sighed. He nodded, and the two of them slowly made their way down the tree, and onto the floor. They then continued forwards, keeping low, until the clearing was fully in sight.

As they made their way, the sound of stone against metal tore through them. In the centre of the clearing was a figure, who was sharpening a thin sword with a stone.

Charlie gave a small smile as his hand came to a stop, stopping the noise.

"Took you long enough." He chuckled as he stared directly at the two of them, despite their cover.

CHAPTER 10; MADNESS

Charlie stood up straight and began looking at the blade of his sword, "Right on time. Those voices were right all along." He continued.

Both Tom and Cathie came out of the tree line. Tom held his bow at the ready.

"That's not possible." Cathie spoke in disbelief of what she was seeing, "You should be dead."

"Should being the key word I'm afraid. After the fall I woke up, only this time with them in my head." Charlie revealed as he pointed to his own head. Something seemed very off about him. Had he lost it?

"You don't just expect me to believe that you walked away from that fall without a scratch." Tom added as he noticed that Charlie seemed to have no injuries whatsoever.

"As expected, the man of logic cannot comprehend such a thing, and yet it happened." Charlie chuckled as he raised his sword towards Tom, "And now to finish what I started."

Charlie charged towards Tom at full speed. Tom fired a warning shot first, a single arrow straight past his shoulder, but Charlie didn't even flinch. As Charlie got dangerously close to him, he released the other nine arrows as he aimed straight for his chest.

All nine arrows pinged off his fur coat. There was something hard underneath it, something that seemed to take the full shock of Tom's shots.

No arrows left in the bow, and no time to reload. Charlie's sword slashed towards Tom faster than he could dodge.

Cathie's sword quickly blocked Charlie's attack. Tom had fallen backwards onto the floor in fear, dropping his bow.

"I've stood between you and him once before. Don't make me finish it the same way." Cathie threatened as she held the block, keeping Charlie's sword away from Tom.

Charlie gave her a quick look over. One of her arms was barely holding the block, the other had an injury near it from his arrow, and clearly wouldn't last long.

"Do you really think you're in any shape to fight me?" Charlie asked her.

"Does it matter?" Cathie responded. Charlie took a step back and brought his sword in front of him, ready for a fight. Cathie did the same, although she struggled to do so.

"Are you really that obsessed with him? Would you really endanger your life, the future of humanity, for him?" Charlie asked as he swung a blow at her. She parried it, just about, but she lost her footing. Charlie took advantage of this and tripped her up. She landed on her back, sword still in hand.

She was clearly in considerable pain. She slowly got back up onto her feet, stood between him and Tom, and held her sword ready for a fight once more.

"Yes." She answered.

All of a sudden, Tom slid between her legs, and between Charlie's as well. As he came to a stop behind Charlie, he aimed, and fired.

Ten shots landed right into his back.

"No protection from behind." Tom chuckled as he loaded another ten arrows. Charlie was now injured and surrounded. On her own, Cathie wasn't much of a problem for now, but he knew that turning his back on her was still pretty much instant death.

He quickly turned, and immediately chucked his sword towards Tom just as he finished reloading. He then quickly dived to the side to avoid Cathie's attack.

Cathie spotted the sword instantly. She dropped her own and sprinted after it. Her eyes flared red as she did so. With a blink, she'd caught Charlie's sword just in front of Tom's face. She quickly turned ready to fight once more, but Charlie had vanished into the treeline.

Cathie was breathing heavily. She quickly checked her arrow wound. Somehow, she'd avoided opening it, but her bruised arm was throbbing with pain.

"That could have gone worse." She sighed as she caught her breath.

"Are you alright?" Tom asked as one of his hands gently landed on her shoulder. She tucked Charlie's thin sword into her belt, turned to him and nodded. As she'd turned, Tom's hand had moved to her back. His other wrapped around behind her waist.

Before she had any time to think, he'd kissed her right on the lips. Afterwards he continued to hold her behind her waist but used his other arm to brush her long hair behind her left ear, while seemingly searching her eyes, "Neary scared me to death with that fight."

Her cheeks turned bright red.

"I'm sorry." She apologised, "But losing you wasn't an option."

"I know." Tom sighed as he brushed the other side of her hair behind her right ear. As he did so, both of her ears seemed to prick up.

"Flapping wings." She realised as Tom's ears began hearing it as well. Both of them took a step back and began searching the sky. Off in the distance, an ice dragon was in mid-flight. It was going to fly right above them.

It shot through the sky above, but then quickly turned back around. It unleashed a breath of ice around the barrier of the clearing, creating a wall of thick ice before it then came into land beside them. Frost folded his wings up and turned to the two of them.

"You two certainly know how to cause a scene. Quite the surprise to find stone dragons where you should have been."

"You're looking for us?" Tom asked him.

"I have need of you."

"And the stone dragons?" Cathie asked him.

"I agreed to send forces to assist them to a less snowy part of our territory. I figured that we might as well have stone dragons who owe us underneath than enemy earth dragons."

"A bold decision to make on the fly." Tom noted.

"Indeed. Not one I thought I would have to make to get information on your whereabouts. Their leader certainly knows how to bargain."

"You need us that desperately?"

"I shall explain once you are all together."

***

Once Patrick and Tom got Cathie safely off Frost's back, and into her bed to rest, the two of them sat opposite one another in the main room of the cave.

"Bruised and broken. Is that what she got for running after you?" Patrick calmly snapped at him.

"To tell you the truth, the shit we've been through, it's insane to think we survived at all." Tom responded in a rather harsh tone.

"Charlie?"

"Complicated."

"Her critical wound?"

"Charlie's fault."

"You aren't being very cooperative." Patrick sighed. Tom took in a deep breath.

"Yeah, I know. Been a long few days."

"So, Charlie followed her to you, care to carry on from there?" Patrick asked more specifically.

"Found me, tried to kill me. Ended up with him shooting Cathie point blank, who was also holding him off the edge of a cliff."

"So, Charlie's dead?"

"You'd think. After dealing with stone dragons, to which without, Cathie would almost certainly be dead, we ran into him again, alive and well."

"How'd he survives?"

"No idea. Found the impact point, even the dried-up blood with it. Only thing missing was the body."

"And he didn't have a scratch on him when you met him a day or so later?"

"Didn't seem like it. He certainly didn't fight like it."

"This is very hard to believe, Tom."

"Trust me, if I hadn't seen him with my own two eyes, I'd be right there with you on that point." Tom sighed. He gave his forehead a gentle rub, "The whole thing has me stumped. To make matters worse he's gone mad with the idea of killing me."

"Don't make me wish he succeeded."

"He's still out there somewhere Patrick, and what's worse is that Cathie would seem to rather die than let him achieve his goal."

"So, at some point we need to stop him, for Cathie's safety."

"However you wish to justify it to yourself Patrick." Tom chuckled.

"Well, that's one more problem to add to the list of things to do."

"I heard that Frost wants us to spy on the air dragons for him. With the amount of effort, he went through to find us, I'd say there is a good reason for it."

"Either way it works for us as well. Last thing we need is a surprise air dragon attack. Especially since our main dragon killer is currently out of action." Patrick got to his feet and folded his arms.

"You're not going to let that go are you." Tom sighed as he too stood up. He began walking towards his room. Patrick caught his arm on the way past.

"I took a quick look at the wound. Haven't seen surgery successfully performed for many years. Once more you did it without the assistance of healing magic." Tom gave another sigh.

"It was her only chance."

"I assumed it would be for you to make a decision like that. I'm not questioning the choice for once. I'm complimenting the handywork." Patrick let go of him, "But you and I both know her chance of surviving a second one is almost zero, even with your skill. Keep that in mind in the future."

Tom nodded as he opened the door to his room and quietly disappeared inside. Patrick took a moment before he walked over to Cathie's door. He quietly knocked.

"Come in." Cathie answered through the door. Patrick opened it, and walked inside, making sure to close it behind him. Cathie was sitting on the side of her bed, looking down at Charlie's thin one-handed sword.

"Thought you were supposed to be resting."

"Can't sleep." She sighed.

"That's one of Charlie's, right?"

"I was so close to losing him Patrick. Charlie was so close from killing him right in front of me."

"Same could be said the other way around."

"Not the point Patrick. There aren't many things I can't defeat in this world. Yet…I'm starting to worry that I won't be enough to protect him from Charlie."

"I don't see your two-handed sword."

"Dropped it during the fight." Patrick put a finger up in the air to pause the conversation. He quickly left her room, but after a minute he came back in, lugging a rather beautiful looking two-handed sword, and a long wristband.

The sword blade was so thick that the width perfectly matched Cathie's body width. The middle was blood-red, with the calving 'Heavy Speeder' engraved on both sides. The actual sharp edge of the blade was a plain metallic colour. On the hilt, small etches of a red-haired woman taking on various creatures, some of which were dragons. The long handle that came with any two-handed sword seemed oddly plain black.

"Charlie made it just for you. Requires a very unique fighting style that only the strongest of warriors could master within his clan." Patrick revealed. Cathie's attention switched to the bracelet.

"What's that for?" Patrick held the bracelet near the handle of the sword, and then let go. The bracelet seemed to stick to the handle.

"Magnetic bracelet. He asked Tom especially for the magnetic material some time ago now. The fighting style revolves around wielding a two-handed sword with only a single hand. The magnet acts as the second hand you see."

"That's… a very odd style indeed."

"I know where he kept the books that show the moves if you're interested. A style designed for both speed and weight behind a sword."

"I understand why only the strongest could even attempt such a technique." Cathie murmured in astonishment. She stood up, and gently took the sword from Patrick.

She held it with her bruised arm so that she didn't risk putting strain on her left, near the arrow shot. The sword was slightly lighter than she was used to, but not by much. She felt the lack of control she had over the tip of the blade.

"The plan so far is for me and Tom to handle this spy thing that Frost wants us to do while you rest up. Nothing says you can't study in the meantime." He added as he handed her the bracelet as well.

***

Patrick and Tom walked out of the cave to meet Frost, who had been waiting outside for some time now.

"Do you have a plan?" Tom asked him. Frost gave a small smile.

"Do you remember your escape from the air dragons?" He asked. Tom nodded, "Wings forged by man. Think you can make them once more?"

"You want us to fly in?" Patrick asked.

"Flight is the only means of reaching the air dragon cave. As you can expect, the cave is heavily guarded and constantly on the lookout for enemy dragon attacks." Frost began to explain, "However they do not pay attention to everything that flies. The birds are ignored, even the big ones."

"Dragons have a very different shape to birds and are much bigger." Tom noted, "You think we could sneak in with a small craft?"

"That was my thinking, yes." Frost finished.

"Would it be possible?" Patrick asked as he turned to look at Tom.

"The wings are easy, just need some sheets of material. The issue here is that we need some way of gaining height." Tom began to think. The two of them could see his mind was hard at work.

"Can't your wings do that?" Frost asked him. Tom shook his head.

"They aren't that good. They are solid, rigid. They can't flap like yours." Tom replied with a disappointed sigh, "Which means that to have forward momentum, we need to start higher than our target, and glide down."

"How heavy are these wings going to be?" Patrick asked.

"Not too heavy, why?" Tom asked.

"What if we got a lift up on the back of a dragon, and jump off from there some distance from the cave?"

"Wouldn't work I'm afraid. Most dragons can't reach heights above the cave's normal height. The air dragon's barely can." Frost reminded them.

"Air crystals." Tom muttered, "If we could fuel them with something other than them feeding off our chemical energy, we might be able to achieve a boost of some kind, but it would be very limited, we'd need that lift, as high as you can go, but we probably could make it." Tom finally concluded.

"What kind of fuel source are we talking about?" Patrick asked him. Tom seemed to think for a few minutes.

"Chemical is out of the question. It would take too much out of us, and we don't have any form of storage other than us. Mixing up a nice reaction would be far too dangerous considering the circumstances. Our best bet is probably kinetic energy." Tom answered.

The two of them stared at him rather blankly. He gave a small sigh, "You know rubber, right?"

"I remember that being a bastard to make." Patrick answered, "But yes."

"Stretch it back, put it on a latch and you have a charged-up shot of kinetic energy."

"Like a slingshot?" Patrick asked. Tom nodded.

"Pretty much. If we can get a few of them all aiming at the crystal, we can release the latch on one of them and the resulting impact should activate the crystal."

"That would give us a very limited number of uses before we have to pull the rubber back again, right?" Patrick noticed.

"With the impacts we're talking about, we probably won't be able to pull them back with our bare hands. Some leverage on the ground to set them up will be required."

"Which means you won't be able to reload them, not even once you're in the cave, right?" Frost asked. Tom nodded once more.

"Best I can do." He added.

"How close do you need to be dropped off?" Frost asked them.

"Close. I can only see us fitting about four charges on these things, more distance to fly, the more charges we go through, and we'd want to keep one or two for an emergency escape." Tom answered. Patrick looked up at the sky. It wasn't particularly cloudy, but there was the odd cloud here or there.

"What if we hide in the clouds?" Patrick suggested.

"If there is one close enough. If not, you may have to act as a distraction." Tom suggested to Frost.

"So how exactly do we get into this cave? I'm sure the mouth of it would be heavily guarded, and at such a close distance they'd know what's up." Patrick asked.

"There is a small hole on one of the sides. Damage that was overlooked from a fire dragon attack many years ago." Frost answered, "From there, you should meet my agent up there."

"You already have someone inside?" Tom asked him.

"Yes, and she has valuable information. The issue is that she's currently under suspicion. It won't be long before she's locked up, or worse."

"So, we get in, help her get out, and come back home?" Patrick asked. Frost gave a bow of his head.

CHAPTER 11; THE ENEMY ABOVE

Despite the fact that the two of them were wrapped up tight in fur coats, the strong cold breeze simply seemed to ignore their protection. It was clear to them both that they wouldn't last up here very long.

Tom could feel the air thinning as Frost came to a slow hover.

"This is as high as I dare." Frost announced. The two of them nodded between shivers. Sitting on the back of an ice dragon certainly hadn't helped things. They both slowly got to their feet.

Frost did his best to keep steady as they strapped the two large wings to each other's backs. They double-checked all the ropes, and then dived off his back.

Patrick followed Tom's lead as they dropped a few metres before slowly folding their wings out from behind their backs. They began to curve along to a glide, with quite a decent speed.

There was a twang, and a small boom as Tom activated one of his boosts and shot higher into the air. Patrick grabbed the first of four strings tied next to one of his hands, holding onto one of the wings. He gave it a large yank and felt a huge jolt as he too boosted. He shifted his weight to pull up, and he flattened out at about roughly the same height as Tom.

As they continued forwards, Patrick noted that they passed over the shoreline. They were now above water instead of ground.

The known world was pretty much a few secluded valleys which led up towards flat mountains covered in sheets of ice that no human could hope to cross. Down the valleys were many forests and hills, but they all eventually led down towards the sea. Where the water was salty and undrinkable, and continued onwards as far as the eye could see. Either side of the valleys at the edge of the known world, mountains blacker than the night sky. Mountains that were impossible to climb, which Patrick knew first-hand.

The fact that they were heading away from the only known solid ground began to worry him a bit.

There it was. Between two clouds, hiding high up in the sky, the floating cave. Patrick looked at the curious thing beneath them now. He'd forgotten one land mass.

As the two of them made a second boost to gain enough height to reach the cave, Patrick stared down at the active crater of the volcano. The fire dragon's island.

The two of them avoided the mouth of the cave, and instead flew over the roof. The landing was rough on the legs, but they hadn't actually been going that fast, especially after their last assent.

The chilling wind had vanished. Instead, it was replaced with a blazing inferno. The heat wasn't too bad, given they were so high up, but even here they could feel themselves breathing in soot from the volcano below.

The hole was hard to spot, and incredibly small. Even with the wings folded behind their backs, they both had trouble getting in. No wonder it had been overlooked, and no wonder Frost needed them for this job.

Inside it was much cooler. The cave itself had been constructed from ice. Kept frozen by the high temperature, it didn't seem to have any issues with hovering over a volcano for the time being.

They'd stumbled into a corridor that had been both frozen over and melted a few times.

"That explains the hole then." Tom muttered, "Left over from a fire dragon attack. Frost must have noticed it while defending this place and kept quiet about it."

"His intellect scares me sometimes." Patrick responded. Tom slowly began to peer around the corner of an off shoot that went deeper into the interior.

"The question is, where is this spy of Frost's?" He asked. The connected corridor was empty, although not as badly warped.

"About time." A voice seemed to hiss from above them. Patrick and Tom both looked up. All they could see was the ceiling. There was movement here and there, something that had blended in with the ceiling.

The air dragon hanging above them seemed to peel off the roof and brought itself upright in front of them, "I suppose it makes sense for me not to know everything, but he really needs to get better at telling me when he's going to be late." The dragon sighed. She turned around and began to walk down the corridor Tom had checked, "Come on then."

"We were sent to get you out of here." Patrick explained as they matched pace with her.

"I'm aware, but we have more important matters at hand. I couldn't get the word to Frost in time, and practically blew my cover trying to warn him yesterday."

"What's happening then?" Tom asked her.

"I'm sure you noticed where this cave is currently parked?" The dragon asked them.

"The air dragons plan on attacking the fire dragons?" Patrick asked.

"It's not quite that simple. Although there has been a war between ice and fire for years, not many battles have happened recently. For now, both sides seem to be content with just staying out of each other's way to avoid such messy disasters."

"Seems that both sides want peace, and they're slowly getting there." Tom realised.

"But the air dragons have packed enough ice into this cave to seriously damage the volcano bellow. Were this cave to drop, many fire dragons would die."

"I would have thought the ice would melt before it got anywhere near." Tom pointed out.

"You would be mistaken. Ice formed from concentrated ice dragon's breath is far colder than your average ice.

A lava dragon would have a hard time melting through such ice if it was concentrated enough."

"I see. They plan to drop the ice, then the ice dragons will be blamed, and the war would get serious again." Patrick realised.

The three of them came to the end of the corridor. They followed the air dragon through a small archway, and into another connected corridor. Yet again it seemed rather abandoned.

As they turned the corner, the two of them managed to get a better look at the creature. They hadn't been able to see an air dragon in such close detail, for some reason they were incredibly hard to see from a distance, even if you were looking for one. The entirely transparent body, organs and all, probably had something to do with it. They seemed to be pretty much half invisible at all times.

"First time being this close?" The dragon asked. She'd noticed their stares.

"Last time I was this close, I was more concerned with staying alive." Tom answered.

"Ah, I thought I recognised you from somewhere. You humans do wonders with sticks and cloth." She asked with a slight smirk.

They continued until they met another corner. This time the dragon came to a stop and placed her wing in front of the two of them to make sure they didn't walk around the corner, "from here on, we won't be alone in these corridors."

"What exactly is the plan?" Tom asked her.

"No dragon other than an ice dragon can come into contact with the extremely cold ice. If we manage to free the captives, they won't be able to drop it out of the cave."

"Given that we're already above the volcano, we probably don't have long." Patrick pointed out. Tom concentrated hard for a few seconds.

"They're still making minor adjustments to the position. We have a few minutes before they get everything perfect." He added.

"I hope you two brought weapons. I'm not much good in a fight." The dragon revealed. Tom unhooked his bag from between him and the folded-up wings on his back. He took out his bow, and quickly loaded it.

The dragon noticed this and turned to look at Patrick with curiosity. He hadn't drawn a weapon.

"Don't worry about me. I've got all sorts up my sleeves."

"I doubt a sword or bow could fit-"

"It's a human expression." Patrick quickly interrupted, "I'll be fine as I am."

***

Cathie stood just outside of the entrance to the cave. She was facing a tree with many cuts and slashes on it. She was out of breath and holding her new sword in her right arm. The bruise still hurt, but not as much now.

She'd had to roll her right sleeve up for the bracelet, but even then, her sleeves were getting in the way. She considered it for a moment, and then remembered that the scars were below her right wrist, which the bracelet nicely covered. She tore her right sleeve off, and then her left as well. She made sure to take care with her left, her arrow wound was still very serious.

She turned around to face a book that had been propped up on a log, and open to a certain page. The book had few words, but those it had Cathie knew well. The rest was pictures and diagrams of how to perform the sword techniques illustrated within the book.

She turned the page of the book and began to focus on the next few words and pictures. Despite being deep within the contents of the book, Cathie's ears instantly twitched to the sound of a twig snapping.

Normally she wouldn't have given it much thought, it was daytime, and this wasn't a dangerous part of the woods. Normally she would have just let it pass, that is, if it hadn't been so very close to her. The sound originated from just above her head.

She'd bent down to look at the book, so she quickly twisted her entire body to face upwards instead, making sure to lift a foot off the ground ready to catch her later. With her body, came her right arm in full swing. Her foot went down, and she quickly stood upright before she fell backwards, as whatever she'd just hit landed on the ground behind her with a gentle thud.

When Cathie turned around, she was rather surprised as to what she'd chopped in half.

The thing looked a lot like a spider, about the size of her hand, except this one was clearly made out of metal. It wasn't a metal she recognised either. It had been painted green, but the slight metallic shine was easy to spot once a sunbeam or two glinted off it.

The spider also didn't seem to bleed either, which is perhaps what she found the most disturbing. Instead it gave a flash of light here and there for a second or two, before it calmed down and just sat there.

After quickly checking all of her senses for any other nearby dangers, she kneeled beside it, and began to take a closer look at it.

Its guts were like nothing she'd ever seen. All sorts of colours, and incredibly thin. They were made out of a material that she straight up didn't know. After a small amount of consideration, she stuck a finger into the inside of it, making sure to stay clear from the jiggered edges of where she'd cut it.

The moment one of her fingers came into contact with a cut intestine bit, she felt a jolt of pain. She jumped back in surprise and ended up on her back for a few seconds, before she pulled herself upright again.

It was a rather interesting pain, but one she'd met before, only once, however. One of Tom's many failed ideas. She wasn't entirely sure what it was supposed to do, but she remembers her hair floating for a bit, and then that pain all of a sudden.

It had something to do with metal, which is the closest thing she could match the skin of the spider to, but if it was, it wasn't one she'd come across before.

***

In a dark room, a figure remained silhouetted against a static screen.

"It seems drone eighty-five was attacked." A voice spoke to the figure through the screen.

"I'm fully aware. I happened to watch it live. Replay the last few seconds of footage if you would." The screen changed to an image of Cathie in the woods looking at her book. The whole event then played out before the figure once more until the screen returned to static.

"It seems to be one of the humanoids we discovered over there."

"And here I thought these last remnants of humanity were nothing worth our time." The figure chuckled, "Play it again, slower this time, and from the moment the girl begins her strike."

The event began to play once more on the screen. The figure seemed to pay careful attention to every one of Cathie's movements. He then paused it just as Cathie's sword was about to block her face.

"Is there something of significance sir?" The voice from the screen asked. The figure took a step back.

"Yes… there is… tell me, could you pull off the move this girl did?"

"No sir, that's why I'm a researcher, not an athlete."

"But still, I don't even think our best sword fighters and athletes combined could pull something like that off from nothing more than a small noise from behind."

"I'm failing to see the point sir."

"The point is, I overlooked something. See humans are very complex creatures. We evolved alongside our technology, meaning we were different from those who had to hunt and gather. Perhaps these humans even more so considering what they have to fight."

"Are you saying you would like us to dedicate resources to observing the four humans we've come across?"

"Yes… yes I am. I'm very interested in what we'll find, hopefully something better than some huge lizards."

***

The two humans and the dragon quickly snuck through a thick icy door, and quietly closed it behind them.

"That was easier than I expected. We must have caught a break in the guards patrol routs." The dragon muttered as they all took in the room they had just entered.

A huge hoard of air dragons occupied the massive room. They seemed to be taking turns blowing into various tubes of similar size, which then ran into the floor of the room. Luckily, none of them had noticed them.

"Is this the prison?" Patrick quietly asked as he took a small rock out of his small bag. He took out some chalk as well and began to draw a pretty looking eye on the rock.

"Light offense gets you posted on pipe duty. Those blasts of air are what is keeping this thing in the air." The dragon answered, "The ones we're after are deeper inside."

"So that's how this thing flies." Tom muttered with curious eyes, "I'd have used a system of air crystals and some form of energy source, but I guess in a messed-up way that's what this is."

"Alright, this should buy us some time." Patrick muttered as he placed the stone with an eye next to the door they had just come through.

"Where did the door go?" The air dragon asked. Tom gave Patrick a look of approval.

"Just a trick I picked up. Stops dragons from seeing doors." Patrick revealed, "It's still there though, just looks like the rest of the wall."

"It's a good trick, but we can't rely on it to keep us safe. It will buy us a few minutes at best before they realise that a door should be there and try to open it." Tom added.

"Perhaps Frost was wiser than I gave him credit for by allying with you humans." The dragon added, "Can you use that trick of yours on yourselves as well?"

"Afraid not. Doors and archways only I'm afraid." Patrick revealed.

"What an odd restriction."

"Magic is a lot more complex than making things vanish from thin air."

"The question now is how to get through this room." Tom pointed out. The dragon looked up at the roof, which was rather high up. She then looked around at the other dragons.

Most of the prisoners were working hard and focusing on each of their pipes. The guards behind them were keeping a watchful eye on the prisoners. They hadn't spotted them so far because they hadn't walked further into the room.

"On you get." The dragon whispered to them. She waited for them both to climb up onto her back, and then slowly spread her wings out fully. She arched them pointing up from the ground, and then slowly brought them right up as high as she could.

She waited until there was a large rush of air from the prisoners blowing into the pipes and timed it with the huge flap in her wings. Narrowly under the roof, she glided over the entire room.

On the other side was another icy door. They were going to slam right into it. Patrick quickly lit a flame in his hands and threw it at the door.

The door turned to steam almost instantly, and the air dragon crashed onto the floor and slid through the melted doorway.

In front of them sat two ice dragons.

"Breath? You came for us after all." One of them spoke.

"Now the interesting part starts." Tom pointed out as he watched the guards advance on them from behind.

Patrick and Tom both took a fighting stance. For once however, Tom wasn't aiming his bow. Instead, he took up a similar hand-to-hand fighting stance, just like Patrick's. The only difference was that he was holding a small bottle marked 'Flammable' in one hand and a small contraption in the other.

It wasn't a very complex contraption, it seemed to simply rub a small shard of metal against a rough rock. He poured some of the liquid from the bottle onto his hand and set it ablaze with the small device just as Patrick lit his own fireball.

"You saw what I did to the door. Between the two of us, you'd all die before you got anywhere near." Patrick announced to the advancing guards. They came to a stop and decided to back away instead.

Some tried to make a break for the other door, but quickly found that they couldn't find it.

"Hope you aren't the jealous type." Tom muttered to Patrick with a chuckle. He gave his hand a good shake and the flames died down.

"Come back when you figure out how to throw it." Patrick responded with a similar chuckle. Tom gave him an acknowledging smile.

"Sounds like a challenge."

"Either way, I'm guessing that's a one-use trick?"

"All bark, no bite I'm afraid."

"My magic should keep them away for now. Go help the dragon." Tom gave a nod and then joined Breath and the two ice dragons.

"So that's why it was so easy to get here." Breath sighed as Tom joined them.

"Why?" Tom asked.

"Almost all of the guards are around the ice their planning to drop." One of the ice dragons answered.

"It will be nearly impossible to get to it." The other added.

"What if we didn't need to get to it?" Tom asked them.

"I was hoping that only you two could move the ice, but apparently they got them to make an ice rail leading right out of the cave mouth, with a push-able platform underneath the block." Breath told him.

"If we don't get to it, they'll drop it without us."

"There is another option." Tom responded. The three of them looked at him with puzzled expressions, "May I remind you we currently have control of this cave's flight mechanism?"

"We can fly it away from the volcano?" Breath asked.

"Or one better, into the sea." Tom suggested.

"Just off the island. Close enough for the fire dragons to investigate the wreckage and discover air dragon bodies." Breath continued. She seemed to rather like the idea.

"How are we supposed to escape?" One of the ice dragons asked. Tom produced a second bottle labelled 'Flammable'.

"We melt our way out. This room should be near the bottom of the cave. We'd have to get out of its path while its falling but if we can get clear in time, we should be fine."

CHAPTER 12; SOMETHING NEW

Cathie slowly removed her sword from the tree in front of her. The tree was on the verge of collapsing due to the many deep cuts. She gave the top half a shove with her foot, and it collapsed away from her.

She took a quick glance at the many calved up tree stumps around her, and the many collapsed trees. This time she'd made sure not to do something like this near the cave, she was deep in the forest now, but on her way to making a clearing of her own.

She was out of breath and drenched in sweat. She took a moment to find herself before she lifted the sword once more at a new tree she'd selected.

She was getting a hang of this fighting style. Her normal style was with a slightly heavier sword, which she'd keep close to her body so that the thing didn't end up flinging her around instead. Momentum and centre of balance were all key when it came to the kind of swords Cathie used. This style was almost the opposite, however.

This style seemed to fight with the sword with large, heavy swings which were not limited in reach like a two-handed sword usually would be. Of course, this meant that every time Cathie swung her sword, it would swing her too, but the fighting style seemed to embrace that fact instead of trying to avoid it.

The style seemed to be more for someone who had equal weight to the sword they were swinging, but Cathie was actually a bit lighter than the sword. It was the first time that Cathie had realised that her strength was rather out of proportion for her size and weight.

It didn't make it too difficult, provided she hit her target with every swing. If she missed, she either had to stop a sword weighing more than she did, or just spin around a few times until it lost its speed all by itself, there wasn't much in the way of control once she'd committed to the attack.

The book seemed to fix this issue by having a second two-handed sword in the fighter's other hand. Cathie did have quiet the collection of two-handed swords, but she didn't want to risk it with her injury. Tom's warnings about it rang painfully clearly throughout her head.

It seemed decided then. It was clear to her that she wouldn't be able to skilfully use this style of fighting while she was injured.

***

Tom continued to stare at a small sheet of paper in his hands. It had a rather rough drawing of the cave, and the island below them.

"A bit more in the same direction." He announced. The air dragon prisoners once more blew into the tubes in front, this time however only into specific tubes. There were a few seconds pause as Tom did some mental mathematics.

"Well?" Patrick asked him. Tom finally gave a nod.

"Yeah, that should put us just off the shore." He added. Every human and dragon in the room turned to look at the puddle of flammable liquid on the floor where the ice dragons had been kept.

Patrick set it alight with a flame on the tip of his finger, and quickly stepped back as small chunks of ice blasted right past him. Steam filled the room, but the hole had now been made.

The air dragon prisoners and guards both made a break for the hole. Breath, Tom, Patrick and the two ice dragons decided to wait until they'd all made it though. It seemed to take surprisingly little time, but Tom could already feel the dense air pocket beneath the cave begin to thin out. The cave was starting to fall.

"Let's move." Breath suggested. The five of them made it to the hole. The two ice dragons quickly went straight through. Tom and Patrick expanded their wings. Two boosts left for each one. Breath waited until the two of them dived out of the hole and then quickly followed.

The harsh, violent wind was cold and unforgiving. Almost immediately, Tom and Patrick were both caught in a violent current which pinned them up against the base of the cave.

Tom released a boost and shot downwards away from the cave. Patrick quickly followed his lead. The cave was beginning to fall rather quickly now. Too quickly in fact.

To keep ahead of it, the two of them had to fully dive downwards constantly, allowing no time to glide off to either side.

Just as they passed the lowest of the clouds, Breath swooped past both of them, knocking both of them rather violently away from the downwards path of the cave.

Tom carefully spread his wings, pointed his feet downwards, and used the last of his boosts. His fall slowed, and with some careful handling he managed to get level. He looked behind to see that Patrick had just about managed to pull off a similar manoeuvre, but closer to the surface of the water.

He watched as Patrick came to a slow stop just above the water, and gently splashed into the sea below. Tom took a good look at the island in front of him. He remembered his last landing all too well. He decided that Patrick had the right idea and began to kill off his own height.

He brought himself around so that he'd end up near Patrick.

He watched the icy cave continue to plummet towards the water.

Then something rather unexpected happened.

At first there was a loud electrical hum that increased in volume over time and then...

A circle, big enough to engulf the entire cave. It appeared right above the water beneath it. Purple in colour, with a darker shade of purple swirl. The cave seemed to pass through the circle rather gracefully, but it didn't come out on the other side.

Tom blinked, then did so again. Had he seen what he'd thought he'd seen? Something wasn't right. The cave wasn't in the water. It was nowhere to be seen.

Something had caught an entire cave from falling out of the sky and had also made it vanish into thin air. Tom began to feel a very horrible feeling, one he very rarely felt. He'd witnessed something that he had absolutely no idea how to rationalise.

***

The swim towards the volcanic island was an odd one. Despite Patrick's seemingly endless questions about what they had just witnessed, Tom remained silent throughout the whole of it.

Luckily once they made it to the island, the scorching hot air dried their clothes off rather quickly.

"Looks like somethings going on over there." Patrick pointed out. The two of them looked down the shore, to where a collection of fire dragons were surrounding a wet Breath.

"Come on." Tom sighed as the two of them began running towards them. Swarms of fire dragons filled the skies above.

Before either of them could reach them, one of the fire dragons began to unleash a breath of fire towards Breath. Before the fire hit, something shot down from the sky, creating an icy cloud of water vapour.

Frost stood tall against the four fire dragons in front of him. Steam began to emit from both him and the fire dragons. The fire dragons quickly backed off as Tom and Patrick finally arrived.

"Frost. King of ice dragons!" A voice boomed from high above. Flame herself landed a fair way off from Frost and Breath, "How very bold of you to dare set foot on our island!" She gave a threatening hiss.

Frost backed up and spread his wings to defend Breath.

"This is one of mine. She was working with the humans to prevent the attack on your lands!" Frost boomed.

Tom noticed Breath stick close to Frost. She was shivering, but she also had a few light burns and a hole or two in either wing. It seems as though the fire dragons had roughed her up quite a bit before they'd even seen them.

"I guess there is only one way to truly be sure." Flame sighed. She turned to look at Tom and Patrick.

"It's true. The attack was from the air dragons. We managed to stop it with the help of Frost's ally." Tom confirmed.

Patrick noticed that parts of Frost were beginning to deform. His legs were beginning to shake, and his wings were starting to suffer similar effects.

Flame seemed to take her time to consider Tom's words well.

"I see that you've chosen to play on both sides of the war, humans." Flame finally spoke.

"Who said we've picked any side?" Tom asked her. She seemed to give a large grin.

"How very neutral of you, Thomas Thomson." She responded, "Yet the facts seem to match both stories. You and your spy may leave this time Frost." Frost gave a bow of thanks before he quickly took off. He came back around and lifted Breath up into the sky with his four legs. The two of them then flew off towards the mainland.

"I thank you for your understanding." Tom added.

"Luckily for you, I have spies of my own inside the air dragon cave. One of which was one of the prisoners you ended up saving." Flame revealed, "I simply wished to see how Frost would respond to me."

"Good to know we made the right choice by not killing them all." Patrick sighed.

"Perhaps you could shed some light onto the events I happened to witness when the cave should have crashed into the sea?" Flame asked Tom. Tom simply shook his head.

"I have no idea. I couldn't even begin to think of anything capable of achieving something like that." He answered. Flame gave another smile at this.

"Good to know you have your limits after all. My people are checking the area now, but I doubt they will find anything helpful."

"Me too. Perhaps we should worry more about where the cave ended up. It has to be somewhere right?" Tom began to ask. Flame turned to one of the fire dragons around her.

"Full perimeter check. Search everywhere within the outermost perimeter and post constant watchmen." The dragon nodded and took off. Flame then turned back to face the humans, "Now then, I wish to make some changes to our current arrangement."

"What changes do you have in mind?" Tom asked her.

"Right now, we simply have an agreement to not harm one another's people. I wish to take it a step further."

"An alliance?" Patrick asked.

"You have proven that you are capable of aiding us in matters concerning other dragons. Whether your motives were truly to protect us, or to make sure we did not blame the ice dragons is irrelevant. Your goals seem to include the protection of my kind from others, which match my own."

"You realise there is no way we're going to agree to a one-way form of this agreement." Tom pointed out.

"The new terms would include an obligation to assist you with any of our current enemies. That is the air, ice, earth and water dragons."

"We've already aligned ourselves with the ice and water. Perhaps we could convince you to remove those from your list?" Patrick asked her, "I'm sure we're capable of convincing Frost of something similar."

"An end to a war that has spun on longer than anyone can remember." Flame sighed, "I suppose a simple non-aggression pact was always going to be inevitable. Very well but be warned. This will only be in place because of the small amount of trust I place in the four of you. Should this bond be severed, so shall the pact."

"That's probably the best we can hope for at the moment." Tom sighed, "But hopefully in the future we would like to improve relations between ice and fire."

"If that is your goal Thomas Thomson, you have a lot of work ahead of you." Flame responded as she turned away from them. With huge swings from her wings, she was in the air, closely followed by the other fire dragons.

"Well, that went better than expected." Tom sighed. Patrick gave him a rough pat on the back.

"I get the feeling she really doesn't like you." He chuckled.

"Well, bringing down the ice cave certainly hasn't helped my case of who she thinks I am. Not to mention she uses my family name like a thorn she'd just removed from her foot."

"Of course, the question now is how are we going to get back to the mainland?" Tom considered their options for a minute or so.

There was no wood on the island and other than the volcano it was very much flat, but that didn't even matter as they both didn't have any charges left on the gliders. Tom finally shrugged his shoulders as he looked up into the sky.

"Guess we better try to wave one of them down." He suggested as he pointed up at the many fire dragons still swarming around the entire island.

***

As the sound of a dragon taking off reached Cathie, the door to the cave opened. Tom and Patrick walked through and shut it behind them. She briefly saw a fire dragon fly off into the now night sky.

"You two alright?" She asked the two of them.

"We're fine, just not everything made as much sense as I would have liked today." Patrick sighed as he headed towards his room. The other two waited until his door shut behind him.

"How's the injury?" Tom asked her as he stood right in front of her. She pulled up her top so that he could get a good look at the bandage, "Managed to keep it closed for once." He chuckled as she lowered her top.

"Nothing but a bit of light training, made sure not to use that arm too much." She responded, "But… while I was out, I managed to kill something that I think you'll have a field day with."

"Oh?" Tom asked. She'd piqued his curiosity. She pointed over to the table, where the dead metal spider was resting.

Tom leant over the table to give it a good overall look over, but then brought his head closer to it. He seemed to pay particular attention to the insides exposed by the cut.

"Well?"

"I... have no idea." He answered, "Twice in one day." He muttered as he shook his head. Something suddenly seemed to click.

"You have an idea?" She asked him.

"Something weird happened when we tried to bring down the air dragon cave. It managed to vanish into thin air."

"Like magic?" Tom clicked his fingers.

"Exactly like magic." He answered, "But the thing is that Patrick's magic is rather scientific. It has rules and limitations, all be it arbitrary ones as far as I'm concerned, but that's because I don't understand what drives it."

"So, this is different to Patrick's magic?"

"Different as in it doesn't seem to have as strict limitations. That can only mean one thing, it's science."

"But I don't see you making things that big disappear."

"No, no. What I do and make is rather advanced considering our understanding of the world, but I've always known there are levels above that."

"So, someone out there is making things better than you?"

"Someone out there has a much better understanding of the rules of the universe than I do, which means they can bend them, find loopholes."

"When I touched the inside gut things, it hurt, just like one of your inventions." She revealed. Tom turned to face her.

"Which one?"

"The metal cage ball thing with a belt that you rubbed onto it I think." Tom took a slight step back in surprise.

"No." He added as he turned back to look at the spider.

"What?"

"Electricity. I played with it a bit myself. Even made a flameless light by making a piece of wire glow with it. Only it was far too impractical to generate the electricity for the thing instead of just setting up a fire."

"That thing doesn't look like its glowing."

"No, but maybe there is more than one use for it. It made your hair go all funny remember?" Tom asked her, "Maybe it can do something else as well." He pulled at the colourful guts and brought them out of the spider.

"But what does it have to do with this thing?"

"As I thought." Tom sighed as he took a closer look at the cut ends of the guts, the part that had shocked Cathie earlier, "These are wires, coated in something to stop the electricity from escaping." He looked straight on for a second, "Decent idea actually."

He continued to rummage inside. He began to follow the wires to the various places, "Somewhere in here should be a way this thing is generating this stuff. Considering my way took a bunch of huge magnets, I'm very curious to see how someone scaled that down."

"Most of the wires come from there." Cathie pointed out as she came beside him to take a closer look herself. Tom pulled out a box in which wires seemed to be connected on both ends.

"Zinc-Carbon battery." Tom read out from a label on the other side of the box. He gave a face that told Cathie he had no idea what that was.

"From the way this thing is set up I would say that's its heart." Cathie revealed as she examined the mess of wires inside and outside the spider.

"What was this thing doing when you cut it?"

"It was... spying on me, I think."

"I know I could probably figure out how to store sound given enough time, but a picture... it was defiantly looking right?"

"I wasn't really making any sounds, so if it wasn't then it didn't get much. It seemed interested in the book I was reading about a new fighting style."

"So somewhere in here should be the equivalent of an eyeball, right? It would need a brain too."

"There is a lot more stuff in there."

"The legs seem to move using... is that a water pressure system?" He began to chuckle, "Beat's string and rope I guess."

"Do you think you can make sense of it all?" She asked him. He shook his head.

"Bits and pieces, perhaps. But this is way beyond what any human is capable of, at least, any I know of."

"But we searched the entire world. From black mountain edge to sea."

"Either way, I doubt this was the work of dragons. Too fine a craft. Someone once told me that magic was simply science that hasn't been explained yet. However, as much as I've tried to prove otherwise I must admit it's right Patrick's magic is something I've thus far failed to be able to explain and this… even more so."

CHAPTER 13; MURPHEY'S LAW

Slightly earlier…

Through a series of glass lenses, Gust watched the single fire dragon far below the cave mouth. Another air dragon adjusted the huge mechanism of lenses to focus it more on the two humans upon the dragons back. Patrick and Tom.

"That's twice you've gotten in the way of our plans, humans." Gust hissed with disgust in his voice, "Perhaps we should have targeted you instead of the strongest dragon race. A mistake we'll soon fix."

"They seem to be coming in to land sire." One of the air dragons around him observed.

"Sire, without our prisoner workforce we can't maintain this height for long." Another dragon pointed out.

"We hold until we discover the human's home. We'll use the gateway to return if we have to."

***

As the sun rose over the horizon, Patrick walked outside of the cave to do his morning check around the cave. He noted the dull grey clouds that blocked the beautiful sight of the sunrise, but the colours still seemed to paint themselves in the sky as usual.

The small patrol wasn't very eventful, in less than half an hour he returned to the cave.

As he grabbed some meat and put it over the communal fire in the corner of the main room of the cave, Tom emerged from his room.

"Anything interesting?" Tom asked as he passed through the main room of the cave and headed towards the door outside.

"Not really no. None of the traps caught anything again."

"We might have to change the locations up again. I'm sure Cathie can get to that at some point."

"Where are you off to?"

"Need to get some more ingredients. I won't be long." He answered as he opened the front door, "Nice day today." He added.

Patrick turned to notice the glaring sunlight coming from the open door.

"That's odd, it was cloudy just a minute ago." He revealed as he walked over to the door and took a look at the sky. There were no clouds at all.

"Are you sure?" Tom asked him.

"Certain." Tom shrugged his shoulders.

"Must be a fast air current all the way up… there." Tom's words got more and more quiet as a realisation suddenly hit him.

The dim sound of an electrical hum began. It seemed to get louder and louder every second. The two of them instantly recognised the sound.

"Cathie! Trouble!" Patrick shouted. Tom quickly closed the door as the two of them backed away into the main part of the cave.

Before either of them knew it, Cathie was standing shoulder to shoulder with them, fully dressed and armed to the teeth.

"What kind?" She asked as she finished putting her sword into its sheath on her back.

"The cave. They managed to follow us without us noticing." Tom revealed, "We're about to be under attack from air dragons."

"Maybe this time we finish the job?" Patrick suggested.

"We can't afford a fight on the ground. We need to get to the cave and quickly." Cathie added. Tom clicked his fingers.

"Forest. It's got plenty of cover. Patrick and I can get some decent shots. If we pose enough of a threat, they might need to dedicate more than just a few dragons, which means they might bring the cave lower down."

"Use it as a protective shell from our ranged attacks." Patrick realised.

"They'd have their air defence locked down now that they know we have the wings, but an arrow with some rope, they won't expect." Tom continued. Patrick winced.

"Climbing a rope will leave us far too vulnerable. We need a way of getting there faster." He pointed out. Tom nodded.

"We don't have time to charge the wings up again."

"What about the mountain behind us?" Cathie asked. The two of them looked at her with questioning looks.

"The mountain?" Patrick asked.

"You only need the charges to gain height and speed, right? Get the cave close enough to the peak and all I'd need is a good runner up." She explained.

"That might work." Tom replied as he seemed to picture it in his head.

"It would take both of us to get that thing into position. That only leaves you to enter the cave on your own." Patrick pointed out. Cathie raised an eyebrow.

"Air dragons are pretty weak once you take away their flight. As long as she keeps the fighting to close quarter and doesn't get knocked out of the cave, it should be easy." Tom explained.

"Why does every plan you make always put her at risk?" Patrick sighed.

"I think you're forgetting that this was my plan." Cathie argued, "I'll be fine." Patrick narrowed his eyes at Tom. Tom put his hands in the air.

"If she's willing. Either that or we lose the cave." Patrick gave another sigh.

"Fine."

***

Patrick and Tom had taken positions just under the leafy roof of the forest just in front of the cave. Both pairs of eyes trained on the sky.

The electrical hum reached its maximum volume, and there it was. The purple swirling circle from before. Out of it, the ice cave emerged. Once it was fully through, the circle vanished without a trace, and the electrical hum died down to silence.

"That's far too high." Patrick sighed.

"We'll have to take a few scouts out then."

"Hopefully they don't spot Cathie, wherever she's hiding."

"There's plenty of tree cover up there. Only the very tip of the peak is bare rock. Besides, I doubt they can see anything that far up."

"I don't know. They managed to follow us without us noticing, and we would have noticed an air dragon scout following us. They had to have been very high up, and their eyes aren't that good."

"You think they have lenses up there?"

"Wouldn't be too much of a stretch. The right ice, the right cut. It's possible."

Both of them ducked down as an air dragon swooped above them. It didn't seem to notice them.

"For now, they don't know where we are. Once they do, we'll need to keep moving before they can blast us."

"Fire and run right?" Patrick asked. Tom nodded, "Been a while since we've done that." Tom gave a small, quiet chuckle.

"What are you on about? That's my entire fighting strategy."

***

Cathie had positioned herself rather well. She was just within the tree line. In front of her, a sharp rock that then made the top of a cliff face. The drop didn't go all the way down the mountain, but it was a big enough drop for the ice cave to fit into.

She stretched a few muscles, checked her injury, which had gotten a bit better by the looks of it. Still, as Tom said, most of the damage was inside her, not on the skin. That, she couldn't tell.

"Better keep things simple." She muttered to herself. Her ears suddenly pricked up. With a spin, and hasty unsheathing of her sword, her blade clashed with a much thinner sword.

With one hand on its handle, and the other supporting the blade from Cathie's rather heavy attack, Charlie stood firmly with a small grin on his face.

"When are things ever simple?"

Cathie's attack had been strong. If it had been any other make of blade, or if it had not been Charlie, the sword would have either broken or he'd be on his back by now. The combination of Charlie's rather impressive sword making skills and his own excellent footwork made sure that neither happened.

Instead, the two were now locked in a stalemate. If Cathie went for a second swing, Charlie would get her before she could pull it off. If Charlie moved his sword towards her, all Cathie would have to do is dodge it, and he'd be wide open. Charlie was more than aware that an attack that she'd be able to feel coming through the pressure between the swords would be no trouble for her to avoid, not to mention he'd have to attack straight on in order to get to her before she managed to swing at him.

Flashes of flames began to go off behind her, "Seems like the other two are in quiet a fight. I hope I didn't pick a bad time to kill the two of them."

"Honestly, couldn't have timed it any worse. What are you doing up here?"

"Trying to get a drop on the cave of course. I wasn't quite fast enough to make it here before morning patrol, but I figured I'd be able to get one of them before you showed yourself."

"I'm not here for you."

"I gathered. You're here for that." Charlie chuckled as he pointed to the ice cave, still high in the sky.

"I don't know, killing you sounds like a better idea all of a sudden."

"If you kill me now, then who's going to help you inside that cave?"

"You want to help me?" She chuckled.

"I'm serious." He added.

"Why would I ever accept your help?"

"Because despite doing a really good job of hiding it, I can still feel your sword shaking." Charlie revealed. Cathie silently glanced at her sword blade. She was doing her best to keep the pressure on, but her arm was starting to hurt once more, "That bruise you had last time, it hasn't actually recovered yet has it? Perhaps its slightly worse than a bruise."

"It's nothing that will get in my way." Charlie pushed his sword against hers rather suddenly and harshly. Her sword was pushed aside, her arm with it.

The pain in her shoulder suddenly became unbearable. For just a split second, she blacked out, but that was all Charlie needed.

His blade stopped as it pressed against her neck.

"You were saying?" He asked her. He removed his sword and took a few steps back so that he was out of her arm reach.

Cathie managed to subdue the pain in her shoulder with a few gentle rubs, "Of course. You probably trained using just that arm to avoid your other wound, didn't you?" Charlie chuckled, "Meaning it didn't heal."

"How are you planning on getting to the cave?" She asked him, making sure the subject was changed quickly.

"The voices showed me how to make this." Charlie answered as he pointed to the two wings strapped to his back. He gave a twirl so that Cathie could get a quick glimpse at the whole thing. It was Tom's design, but the rather basic one they'd used to escape the ice cave the first time. The one on her back was much better made, and despite not having any charges loaded, it did have the air crystal still.

"That looks like something Tom made."

"That's where the voices learnt how to do it. They watched him construct that and took a few notes." Charlie replied as he pointed to Cathie's wings.

"Are you sure you aren't crazy?" Charlie gave her a small smile.

"Who knows. The voices say I'm not, but then again they would do, wouldn't they?" He chuckled, "Either way though, they have helped me quite a bit. Perhaps Tom gets his ideas from the same voices."

"If he did, the voices wouldn't have to take notes." Cathie pointed out, "Fine, you can help me finish this, but on the condition that you stop trying to kill the other two."

"I'm afraid I can't do that."

"Why not?"

"Because the voices want me to kill a certain Thomas Thomson. Not to mention my own desire to murder him."

"Enough already. I know I broke your heart by picking him, but you don't have to go this far."

"Oh, but don't you see Cathie? The voices offered me a reward."

"What reward could bring you to kill half of what is left of us?"

"You really won't like the answer, not yet anyway." He answered with a small chuckle, "So are we going to do this or not?" He asked as he pointed behind her.

She turned to see the ice cave slowly descend to the perfect height.

"I won't turn back for you." She muttered as she prepared to sprint.

"Guess I'll just watch both of our backs then." Charlie replied.

Cathie sprinted forwards the moment the base of the cave was about a thumb's width above the cliff edge, held at arm's length. It took her less than a few seconds to reach the edge, where she gave herself one last huge push forwards.

She was over the edge. She quickly unfolded the wings and did her best to aim at the ice cave, which was continuing to sink. Something was off. The ice cave had gone further down than she'd expected, was it landing? Either way the mouth wasn't pointing towards her. She slowly brought herself down onto the roof of the cave.

For now, it was still in the sky, but it was slowly getting closer to the ground. What purpose did they have in landing within the forest?

She folded the wings away and unsheathed her sword from the sheath on her back underneath the wings harness. With a forceful thrust, she stuck it into the hard ice and began to slice away at it.

"You going to help?" Cathie asked Charlie. Once more he was standing near her, watching her from just slightly more than her arm's length.

"Or we could use the convenient hole over there." Charlie suggested as he pointed to the front of the cave.

"The mouth?"

"They're still focused on the other two for now. If we get the drop on the front defences, make our way inside nice and quick, we won't have to worry about the ones outside trying to narrow in on Tom and Patrick."

"Sounds good to me." Cathie sighed as she removed her sword from the ice.

***

Patrick and Tom both quickly ducked behind two separate trees. They were on the forest floor now. Tom quickly reloaded while Patrick took another peak at the sky. Most of the leaves had been blown off, leaving just the thick branches to hide them from above.

"That cave is getting lower than we expected." Patrick noted.

"Cathie should be on it by now."

"That won't stop their forward forces from hunting us."

"Then we take down as many as we can using this tactic until Cathie's done with the cave. Then we'll worry about mopping up their forces."

"Do you hear something?" Patrick asked. Tom stopped directing his senses towards the sky, and instead took in his entire surroundings for a second.

The ground was trembling beneath their feet.

"Oh no." Tom muttered. Those were trembles he was all too familiar with.

"Tom, honey?" A woman's voice asked from beside him. Tom turned to see a brown haired, purple eyed woman, "We need to keep moving."

"Mum?" Tom asked. Kara quickly took Tom's hand, and they were off, into the woods beyond.

CHAPTER 14; THE COWARD

As an earth dragon shriek tore throughout the now misty forest, Tom pulled his hand out of his mothers. The two of them came to a stop.

This wasn't right. He was seeing things, just like before. This time it was worse. Was this all a hallucination? He could feel the warmth of his mothers' hand, the tightness of her grip before he managed to slip his hand out.

"We don't have time Tom, come on!" His mother shouted as she forcefully grabbed at his hand. Tom quickly moved it out of the way.

"Where is Dad?" His mouth asked. Those words hadn't even appeared in his mind. He couldn't move anymore now, not in any way he wanted to. He'd lost control of himself.

"He's buying us time. Come on!" His mother answered. Tom forced his eyes shut. It took a lot of focus, but he quickly got control of himself.

"This isn't real." He spat out in his own words, "I'm just seeing things. Should have seen this coming considering I stopped taking my medicine." He sighed as he looked around the foggy world around him.

Was the shaking ground part of the illusion as well? He hoped so. What was his body doing in reality right now? Had he passed out or was he wandering around the forest blinded by madness.

"If we don't go now the earth dragons will get us both!" His mother protested. He could see the genuine concern for his life in her eyes. He could tell that she wasn't even considering her own right now.

"It doesn't matter. No matter how far we ran, they got us eventually."

"Is that your bow?" His mother asked as she peered at his special bow that was slung over his back. Tom gave himself a quick look over, bow and bag still firmly attached, although he swore the bow had been in his hands before, fully loaded, "You finished it?"

"A finished bow, and I have your bag." Tom noticed as he gave his mother a quick look over. Her bag was nowhere to be seen, "Two key differences from the past."

"If you know running won't work, then what are we going to do?" Tom gave his mother a questioning look. She was speaking as if she already knew the answer, as if she already knew what all of this was. This wasn't a memory flash back, or a hallucination. This was in Tom's mind.

He gave her question a few seconds of thought.

"It's a simple question. Fight or flight, right?" Tom took his bow off his shoulder and loaded it with arrows from his bag, "I'm done hiding."

***

Before he knew it, he was standing on top of a cliff. Between him and the cliff edge stood Cathie. The harsh wind and rain had the both of them freezing and drenched, but even that seemed unable to break the unspoken tension between the two of them. Thunder struck off in the distance which managed to illuminate Cathie's face, which had previously been covered by the shadow of her hair.

Her face was filled with anger, and it was seemingly all pointed towards him.

"Lair." She mumbled, but yet her voice cut through the drowning sound of the wind and rain like a hot knife through butter. That single word seemed to make every other noise vanish from Tom's ears.

It was at this point that Tom realised that she had both swords unsheathed and in each hand. One he recognised to be the one Charlie had made for her, the other seemed to be of similar size and shape but pitch black.

She took a step forward, and another. All of a sudden Tom got the horrible urge to run. The wind began to blow strands of her hair in all sorts of directions, thickened by the wet rain, strands stuck to her wet face as she took step after step towards him.

It was hard to tell, but with another flash of lightning Tom got a much better look at her face. Her eyes were bloodshot and puffed up. She'd been crying. He watched fresh tears stream down her face, cutting through the clear rainwater that painted the rest of her face. He got another horrible feeling. The feeling that those weren't tears for him, or what she was about to do. The anger was still in her eyes, stronger than ever.

His entire being seemed to scream the word run at him, but he couldn't move.

Her face came to a stop right in front of his. The darkness had hidden a few details from her until now. The most disturbing being the many scars that littered her face. With a glance they seemed to litter her arms as well, and they seemed to continue past her sleeves. Scars of all shapes and sizes, but they all spelled out a single word over and over. HATE.

A blink, and he was alone in a small dark room instead. A small flame lit in the centre of the room. The walls were covered in blood. Just like Cathie's scars, the blood was many different shapes and sizes, but spelt one word. LIAR.

Every time Tom saw that word, Cathie's voice sliced through his head. LIAR. Under normal circumstances he would have curled up into a little ball and tried to block it out, but he didn't feel like it for some reason. Instead, he tried to wipe away at the blood.

It was no use. It seemed to be a part of the wall. For some reason, this made Tom unusually angry. Every time he read the word, every time Cathie's voice ripped a new hole through him, he seemed to get more and more pissed off.

He threw a punch at the nearest wall. He felt his fist shatter, but he didn't care. He threw a punch with his other hand, once more his bones shattered like glass against the immovable wall.

"Let me out." Tom spat under his breath as he threw a third punch, this time with a broken hand, "LET ME OUT!" He yelled with a fourth punch.

***

Patrick continued attempting to shake Tom out of whatever state he was in. Tom seemed to continue to stare off into the distance as the ground continued to shake. It got louder and louder.

Just before Patrick tried to slap him, Tom's eyes suddenly blinked. His head shook, and he seemed to come out of the trance.

"Tom?" Patrick asked. Before Tom could get his bearings, the ground was torn apart in front of him. Patrick moved to the side of him as an earth dragon emerged from the ground below.

"You." Tom spat at the dragon as his eyes flared a violent purple that replaced his normal yellow. Even the odd hint of red could be seen sparking in the now almost glowing purple stare. He removed five arrows from his loaded bow and gripped them in his mouth. Patrick noticed that Tom's eyes were narrowed towards the dragon. Was he seriously planning to take it on?

Four more earth dragons launched from the ground towards them, but Tom was already in the air and drawing back his bow. Five arrows flew into five separate eyes. All five earth dragons fell down dead.

Three more launched from the ground behind them, but Tom had grabbed an arrow from his mouth in each hand after dropping his fired bow.

He landed on one's snout and rolled until he was beside one of its eyes. In the arrow went. Before the dragon's body hit the ground, Tom had jumped to the next.

"Tom!" Patrick shouted as he got to his feet. The surprise attacks had caught him off guard. He watched as Tom stood in front of the eight earth dragons he'd murdered. Covered in blue blood, bits of eye and brain. Patrick's voice seemed incapable of reaching his ears as Tom charged off towards the sound of more earth dragons.

Patrick took a look up at the sky. Swarms of air dragons seemed to block all directions, "The fuckers lost it."

CHAPTER 15; THE VENGEFUL

Cathie came to a slow stop outside the large, frosted doors that marked Gust's room within the icy cave. Behind her, Charlie continued the fight against the many air dragons trying to kill them.

"You got this?" She asked him. Charlie gave a nod as he finished another dragon off. He then turned to the next, making sure none passed him.

Cathie turned her attention back to the doors. With a large push, they swung open. She walked into the massive chamber. There Gust sat on his raised platform.

With a gentle breeze, the doors slammed shut behind her.

"I must say I'm rather impressed human. You and your friends put up more of a fight than I expected." Gust sneered as he got to his two feet. He supported the rest of his weight by using his wings as front legs. As Cathie walked over to him, he stepped sideways.

"We have a tendency to fight back when you attack our home." She replied as she came to a stop at the centre of the room.

"I assume you've come for my surrender." Gust sighed as he too came to a stop about halfway between his platform and the door.

"We don't exactly have the means of taking prisoners." Cathie answered as she pointed her sword towards him.

"I'm sure your allies will."

"I'd rather not have to owe another favour to an ice dragon." She quietly snapped back. Gust recoiled back against the wall in fear.

"I see." Gust chuckled, "I thought I recognised the extreme hair colour. You're a Clawson." She gave him a confused look.

"A what?"

"Clawson. You humans give yourselves a name of family. You are of the family of Clawson. Daughter of Angel and Fire if memory serves me correctly."

Cathie launched towards him until her blade was pressed firmly against his throat.

"Where did you hear those names?" She demanded.

"I believe it was Shard that was in charge of dealing with them. Funny though, I could have sworn he stated that he killed both parents."

"Why was he sent to kill us?" She pressed him. He felt her sword edge dig into his neck.

"You'd better hope no ice dragon realises just who you are. Frost wasn't king back then, but I could see him ordering the same thing as his predecessor." He chuckled.

"Why!"

"Promise to take me alive." Gust demanded. Cathie hesitated for a few seconds, but eventually gave him a small nod.

"Why did they kill my parents?"

"It was originally an order from above. An order from a celestial. The same celestial that ordered the humans' destruction after the fall of the Neutral. Punishment for aiding in the destruction of its favourite dragon species."

"An order?"

"A strange one at that. It specified you all by name. Angel Clawson, Fire Clawson and Catahyme Clawson."

Catahyme. A name Cathie hadn't heard in forever. A name that as a child she couldn't pronounce. A name that was shortened to Cathie by her own infant tongue. Even her parents gave up on it after a few years.

"Catahyme." She spoke, making sure she spoke it exactly as Gust had. The first time she'd ever correctly pronounced her own name.

"It's a name that apparently even celestials fear. Almost as much as the Neutral."

"Why were we such a threat? We were nothing more than a family of human beings that didn't care for others of our kind."

"That you'd have to take up with the celestial. I'm afraid it left this world some time ago."

"Do you know anything about the Thomson family?" She asked him. Gust gave her a slightly confused look. She gently reminded him with a small movement of her blade that her blade was in fact still up against his neck.

"Jack Thomson was a warrior feared by dragon kind. He makes you look like a small bug. Kara Thomson was a dangerous seer. Predicted our every move. The two were a dangerous combination, until they disappeared."

"Tom said his parents died to earth dragons."

"I doubt that. I'd have heard about it. Not to mention the countless dead bodies they left wherever they travelled. Dragon kind as a whole stayed clear of the Thomson's path."

"Is there no way that earth dragons were responsible?"

"All I know is that for a few years before they vanished, they seemed to be running from something. Constantly on the move."

"You don't know what?"

"When a man who can kill a dragon from range with one shot of his odd weapon is running from something, I personally make it a point of staying far away from the whole thing."

"A weapon capable of taking down a dragon in one shot?" Charlie asked as he entered the room.

"All clear?" Cathie asked him. Charlie nodded, then looked at Gust for his answer.

"It's hard to describe. A metal stick, wherever it pointed it shot a beam of blinding red light that burnt through scale and skin alike."

"What became of this weapon?" Charlie pushed.

"Vanished along with the family."

"Seems like we have all the answers we can get from you." Charlie sighed as he pointed his sword towards Gust. Cathie placed her hand on his blade.

"Answers I promised his safety for." She explained. Charlie lowered his sword with an understanding nod.

"More should arrive soon to corner us." He added as he turned back to face the doors. Cathie removed her sword from Gust's neck and walked past Charlie, towards the doors.

"Guard our prisoner then. I'll finish them o-" Before she could finish, she felt a large pain on the back of her head.

There was the sound of metal bouncing once or twice on the icy floor, and then the sound of Cathie's body landing beside her sword.

Charlie raised his sword towards Gust with a smile.

"The voices didn't like you telling stories, dragon."

***

The harsh, freezing winds tore at the thin wolf skin coat that did little to protect Cathie's young body. Beneath that, a top made of paper-thin leaves and vines threaded together. Her legs were fully exposed to the deep snow that she was trudging through slowly but surely.

Cathie looked down at her bare feet as she stomped one foot down into the deep snow in front of her. Back then she hadn't figured out how to make all the different types of clothing. What was worse was that she was only big enough to take on small animals. She'd gotten lucky with the dead wolf she'd found, but then again not having a wolf skin coat wouldn't have stopped her back then either.

She'd have made this trek completely naked if she'd have to. It was a trek she didn't have any plans of returning from.

Behind her, a heavy two-handed sword was being dragged by her right hand. The sword was bigger than her, but she dragged it through the snow anyway, despite the steep incline.

"You're going to die out here." Her mother's voice rang through her ears.

"Shut up." She spat. The howling wind picked up and snow began to fall. Cathie continued onwards.

Cathie looked at a woman with light blue hair and matching armour, who had walked out of the blizzard beyond. Her icy blue eyes seemed to bite at her with just their stare.

"You were always too weak."

"Stop it." Cathie pleaded as she closed her eyes. The storm picked up. Her fur coat was torn from her body and was swept away, leaving her with only some poorly woven vine and leaf clothing, which offered no protection from the cold.

"You can't even avenge us. Instead, you use that drive as an excuse to run from the failure you are."

"Failure?" She scoffed at her mother, "Bullshit." She added as she took a step forwards so that her face was right in front of her mothers.

"That weak and feeble body of yours. You should have been able to surpass me years ago, but instead all you do is fear me." Her mother added. She wasn't backing down.

"Says the one who was killed by a single pack of ice dragons." Cathie threw back. She could feel her anger start to build up now. She barely noticed the cold as her blood began to boil.

"You haven't beaten Shard. You'll join me when you do." Cathie narrowed her eyes at her mother. Her mother responded by punching her right in the guts.

A mixture of blood and saliva spat out of Cathie's mouth as she keeled over onto the floor, "Pathetic." Suddenly the cold snapped right back at her. She could feel her hands and feet going numb. The snowstorm was at its strongest, the snow at its deepest. She could barely see the outline of her mother.

Cathie slowly got back onto her feet, but she found it a very difficult task considering she'd now lost all feeling in her arms and legs. Her ears and the rest of her face were going numb too, "Like a child you wield the strength I granted you, like an animal you seek one meaningless goal. The only thing that separates you from the beasts is your skills with the sword, which are sloppy at best."

"I...WAS...THREE!" Cathie shouted through the storm. Her words seemed to cut a tunnel through the snow between her and her mother, "I was three." She mumbled, "You left me at three years of age to fend for myself."

"That's no ex-"

"And even then, I prevailed where you didn't!" Cathie interrupted, "I survived." Cathie's mother shifted with unease at her child's outburst.

"I guess that makes both of us failures." Her mother sighed. The storm vanished; the snow melted. They seemed to now be in a black void, with a small fire on the floor beside them. Cathie's mother vanished from sight.

Cathie sat down by the fire and took out a small dagger. She brought it up to her wrist, "That doesn't give you the excuse to give up, young lady." A calm but firm voice spoke from in front of her.

A man dressed in thick red scale armour was sat on the other side of the fire.

"Dad?"

"I taught you many things. That isn't one of them." He continued as he pointed to the dagger.

"It helps me cope." Cathie muttered. She sliced her wrist with the dagger.

"Bullshit." Her father responded, "It's an addiction, and you know it." She clasped her wound tight and withstood the wave of pain that rushed over her.

"You think I enjoy this?" She asked him. With a single blink her father was sitting beside her.

"A normal self-harmer would cut themselves during difficult moments of depression. Normally as a way of avoiding suicidal thoughts or tendencies. You don't."

"I don't enjoy it."

"Are you sure? That wave of pain, the rush of adrenaline as your body realises that it's been damaged. The satisfaction of slicing flesh. That's all going on up there." He continued as he poked her head.

He grabbed her bleeding wrist and applied a considerable amount of force to the wound through the hand which covered it. To her surprise she didn't jump, she didn't protest. She let the rush hit her once more.

"I...I don't." He applied even more pressure. Another wave of pain. She quickly found herself wanting him to do it again. After a few seconds of him not doing so, she applied the pressure herself.

"There it is." He sighed.

Cathie lowered her head in shame, "You both fear and enjoy pain. The enjoyment is a sickness, the fear is good, but only in small doses."

"I'm broken, aren't I?" She asked him.

"Very much so."

"Is there anyway of fixing me?"

"Luckily for you, human beings have a funny way of finding people very similar to them." Her father clicked his fingers and the flames in the fire seemed to take the shape of Tom, "Two broken souls that found one another. Human beings have another funny trick."

"Which is?"

"When they aren't alone, their stronger than any one human could ever be. Promise me you won't continue this sickening ritual of yours." Cathie paused as she took another look at her wrist.

"I... don't think I can." Her father gave a sigh, then slowly stood up.

"Then promise him instead." He added as he pointed at the flaming image of Tom, "What would you do if you were to lose him now?"

"I'd probably kill myself."

"You know from your time together how he truly feels about you, now that he's actually feeling. Imagine what he'd do if he lost you, to yourself of all people."

CHAPTER 16; VENUS FLY

Cathie's eyes slowly woke to the gentle brush of a small branch against her side. She was looking at Charlie's back. She could feel his shoulder supporting her hips, and his arm holding the backs of her knees as he continued to walk through the rather thin woodland.

"I was hoping to reach a safe place before you woke. Guess that fell through." Charlie sighed. Despite his observation, he continued walking onwards without any further action.

"The hell are you doing?"

"The plan was to use you as bait to trap Tom." Charlie revealed as he came to a stop, "But you're not going to let me do that, are you?"

"You got that right." She began to squirm and wriggle out of his grip, but Charlie just let her go the moment she did. With a thud, she was on the lightly vegetated floor.

He seemed to wait until she was on her feet before he pointed his sword at her. She reached for her own sword but found the sheath on her back missing.

"I'm not an idiot." Charlie sighed as he waved Cathie's sheathed sword in his other hand. Cathie looked down at her wrist. The bracelet was still there.

"So, what's the plan now? Are you going to kill me?" Charlie chuckled at the thought.

"I'm not going to kill my reward, now am I?" Cathie began searching for options, "I can see you thinking about trying to knock the sword from my hand, trying to get in close before I strike. A well-placed cut should stop those arms and legs for a few weeks, I'm ready for any tricks you pull."

Cathie bit her lip. She only had one trick he wouldn't see coming, but it was a trick she really hated.

She found the nearest tree behind her and casually lent against it.

"He won't come." She sighed.

"What?" Charlie asked. Her entire change of mood seemed to confuse him.

"Tom. He won't come for me. I'm useless bait."

"What makes you think that?"

"Let's just say things didn't go so smoothly after our last encounter."

"How so." Cathie hesitated with eyes on purposely pointed at the floor. She picked a small leave from a low branch and began to slowly tear at it.

"After everything I said during that fight, he pretty much figured out my obsession with him, so he… he made his feelings rather clear."

"You mean the lack of them?" Cathie paused once more. She turned to the side, with her shoulder now leaning on the tree. She made sure her hair blocked her face from his view.

"Yeah." She muttered.

"Yet you still tried so hard to stop me from killing him just now."

"I never said my feelings for him had changed." Cathie responded. She managed to produce a tear or two which were just about visible as they dropped from her face.

This was going to take some time. She knew a complete change wouldn't fool him, so instead she had to lay the groundwork. She had to spark the idea that he still had a chance without straight up saying it.

"Didn't Tom know about how you felt before then? I thought Patrick let it slip."

"He did, but Tom didn't believe it until he saw me fight for his life." She replied. She wasn't aware that he'd known that. She had to be careful what she lied about, "Had to see it himself for him to believe it." She added. She'd remembered Tom saying something along those lines to the rest of the group at some point in the past.

"Sounds like the guy." Charlie sighed. He lowered his sword, but still kept it in his hand.

"Thank you for the sword by the way." Cathie switched subject. She couldn't keep up the tears very long. She turned to face him, then raised her wrist and pointed to the bracelet.

"I'm guessing Patrick told you about it?" Charlie asked as he gave her sword a proud look, still in its sheath.

"He gave it to me after I lost my own. Rather different to what I'm used to, but I'm slowly getting a feel for it."

"I feared it might be a bit too light for you, but the fighting style I designed it for required it and that style had you written all over it."

***

It took a while, but Patrick eventually managed to track Tom down in the forest. The sound of the air and earth dragons fighting had died down and eventually came to a complete stop. With the victor being unclear, Patrick made sure he kept far away from the now landed ice cave.

Tom was on the forest floor, unconscious. He quickly knelt down beside him and checked his breathing. Small, fast-paced breaths. He noticed his forehead was burning hot as well.

A quick look at the rest of his body didn't seem to reveal any obvious injuries. A few cuts on his clothes here and there but no blood. Nothing seemed broken either, so he hadn't been wacked by a tail.

All the signs pointed to him collapsing due to whatever fever he was currently having, but he'd never come across such a fast-acting illness. Given he didn't know anything about it, he made sure he came into as little contact with Tom's skin as he picked him up.

The rest of his body seemed a reasonable temperature considering he'd been fighting dragons. His head seemed to be the main issue.

After a long detour to get around the ice cave, Patrick finally managed to reach the cave. The magic protecting the door was still active, so it was probably safe to assume it hadn't been found in all the chaos.

He placed Tom down on his bed. He added a wet cloth to his forehead, then proceeded to scrub himself down with one of the many bars of soap next to the bucket they wash the wooden plates in.

His medical knowledge wasn't the best, but he was no stranger to diseases. Experience had taught his clan many times that you never take chances when it comes to illness. Although he had no idea how the soap worked, Tom had previously proven its effectiveness at keeping things clean, which was the key to stopping the illness from spreading.

It didn't hold a candle to Patrick's book of healing magic, which could cure some basic illnesses, but Patrick had nothing up his sleeve to actually stop him getting ill in the first place, and if he got too ill to focus correctly, his magic wouldn't be able to save him.

The fact that Cathie hadn't returned after a few hours began to worry him, but he had other concerns for now. He checked on Tom, only to find his temperature rising, even with the wet cloth.

He wasn't getting better with rest, which left him with one option. He broke out his dusty healing magic book from a shelf in his room and placed it on Tom's desk.

"Lumps and bumps, no." He muttered to himself as he flicked through the pages, "Runny nose…" He looked over at Tom. His nose seemed fine, it wasn't red, and his nostrils seemed to be clear, "No."

He reached the end of his book. Out of desperation, he began looking around Tom's room. His eyes eventually landed on Tom's bag, "Surely he'd have something on diseases, right? His mother was a healer."

He remembered Cathie mentioning that the bag seemed to work on thought. He wasn't really listening too closely though. He reached into it, thinking about a book for healing.

His hand grabbed a book. As he pulled it out, he realised just how thick it was. It made his rather detailed magic book look like a child's practice book. At the start, it sectioned out the different types of symptoms and what they might correspond to. His magic books did similar things for spells that achieved similar things, but this books organisation seemed to put his to shame as well.

He also didn't recognise the handwriting. It certainly wasn't Tom's, and it had a woman's touch to it. He found a section for high temperature forehead and began to flick through it.

Most of the things suggested unfortunately came with other symptoms, ones Tom didn't have. He finally reached the end of the section with one last entry listed.

High temperature around the brain area (Most obviously the forehead), quick paced breaths, struggling to process basic thoughts or unconscious state, no other symptoms or injuries.

Patrick turned to look at Tom again, "Sounds like the one." He muttered with a sigh of relief. He turned back to the book and continued to read.

If you are reading this entry Tom, then that means I never got around to teaching you the consequences of pushing your mind beyond its limits.

Your symptoms are caused by the fact that you've used your brain more than your body and mind are able to handle. Your brain requires oxygen, which it would have been starved of while you were busy pushing your mind past your limit, hence the breathing.

That amount of thinking also draws huge amounts of energy. Hence, the high temperature. Pushing this too far will result in unconsciousness and possibly death. That heat is not from your forehead, that's from your brain itself, which I shouldn't have to point out how bad that is.

Your body will do everything in its power to keep the brain alive. This might involve shutting down anything not critical to the brain's immediate survival. Oxygen consumption and cooling are top in priority. While this is happening, your brain will also probably block you from thinking, this is to make sure no further oxygen is wasted, or heat is generated during this critical state.

A further danger is that the brain is locked into the hyper thinking state. If this is the case, then heat will continue to build up rapidly. This is considered the opposite of a brain freeze, where instead you cannot stop thinking, even while unconscious.

Treatment is ill-advised. Rest will suffice in most cases unless the temperature is building up at an alarming rate. If this is the case, I suggest a shock to the brain. Something to snap it out of the hyper state. This may be extremely difficult to achieve, however necessary for survival once this stage is reached.

Patrick turned to his magic book once more. It may not have something specific for his symptoms, but now that he knew the suggested treatment, he had an idea of where to start. He got halfway through before he shook his head and quickly walked back into his room. This time he brought out another magic book.

The book had a bolt of lightning on the front cover. Patrick looked back at Tom's book and began searching for information on the brain itself. Surprisingly enough, the book actually contained a section on being hit on the head by a lightning bolt.

Without some kind of protection, the patient would have certainly died from a direct strike to the head. Assuming survival and treatment of burns (See third degree burn treatment, treating burns is a priority as it is a very serious threat to patient survival), the patient may feel dizzy and disorientated. This is perfectly fine and will eventually wear off. Look for signs of change in personality, memory loss or inability to complete basic tasks after recovery from afore mentioned symptoms.

A lightning strike can be incredibly powerful and in most cases the electricity is too much for the brain. Survival depends on how much reaches the brain itself and that none reached the heart.

Important note: Any amount of electricity to the heart may result in heart attack or instant heart failure (For treatment see appropriate sections)

If there is an obvious permanent change to the patient's brain, not much can be done about this. Changes in personality and memory loss can be handled with understanding and help from family and friends. Should certain tasks become difficult or seemingly impossible for the patient, it is most likely the part of the brain responsible for performing such task has been damaged.

If the damage is light it might be possible for the patient's brain to heal itself with aid of repetition of the task, the patent will most likely have to relearn how to perform the task from scratch.

If the damage is heavy, provided the ability not to do such a task isn't life-threatening I'd suggest the patient avoid the task entirely in favour of something else. If it is life-threatening, i.e. breathing, I suggest a sharp knife and hammer to the skull, to put them out of their misery and grant them a quick death.

Patrick rubbed his eyes from the heavy reading, "So basically too much, and he's a vegetable." He sighed. His memory took him back to when Tom was administering that chemical to Cathie.

He could always add more, but not less, "I can always increase the strength gradually." He muttered to himself.

He flicked through the pages of his magic book until he found a rather weak shocking spell. After taking the page in he stood up and walked over to Tom.

He placed his hands either side of his head and closed his eyes. He felt a small spark as the rather basic spell discharged. He waited a few minutes before checking Tom's temperature.

It had cooled. His breathing had begun to calm down too. With a sigh of relief, he sat back down at Tom's desk.

He looked at the three books on the desk, then gave a small chuckle, "If you're mother ever met my clan, that would have been one scary alliance." He chuckled to himself.

CHAPTER 17; MAGIC

Patrick left the cave just as the sun was beginning to set. Cathie hadn't returned. The battle had finished quite a while ago now.

Certain that what remained of the air and earth dragons had probably moved on, he began to make his way towards the grounded ice cave.

As he cautiously walked into the mouth of the ice cave, he passed both earth and air dragon bodies which littered the place. The earth dragons had picked the one time the cave was in their reach to attack, they certainly didn't waste the opportunity. The fight appeared to be a massive one which went deep into the cave.

Chances were that the earth dragons didn't even know about their presence. They were clearly after the air dragons.

In the direct sunlight at ground level, parts of the cave had begun to melt ever so slightly. Although now it was night-time, it had slowed. The ice was also incredibly thick, but eventually this cave would be no more unless it was moved.

After half an hour of exploring the body filled corridors, Patrick finally found himself back at the mouth of the cave. He was the only living thing in this cave anymore.

Some dragons had been killed with a sword, but some had been beaten and smashed to death instead. Cathie hadn't cleared the whole cave by the time the earth dragons attacked. There was no sign of her body. Had she seen them coming and bailed in time? Or had she got caught up in it and taken captive? What would the dragons want with a human prisoner?

Both dragons had taken humans prisoner before, but they paid the price both times. Plus, Cathie would have put up enough of a fight for it not being worth taking her alive.

He was clearly missing something.

Movement caught his attention from outside the cave. He watched as a single air dragon slowly dragged itself into the mouth of the cave from the forest beyond, then collapsed.

The creature had many wounds. Both wings torn to shreds, a broken leg and jaw, scratches that suggested it had been hit out of the sky and was barely saved by tree branches and to top it all off, one side of its body was heavily bruised. Probably hit by a rock, which was perhaps how it fell.

It seemed to find comfort in the fact that it had made it back to the cave. It noticed Patrick as he approached it, but it seemed to simply accept the fact that it was powerless against him.

"I'm looking for a human. Red hair, large sword." Patrick stated as he came to a stop beside its head. Its eyes were barely able to stay open.

"I know the one you speak of." The dragon spoke with a painful chuckle, "I knew when to run, unlike my kin."

"I'm guessing you ran right into the earth dragons by the looks of you." Patrick muttered. The dragon gave another chuckle.

"Just my luck."

"Do you know what happened to her?"

"Another human was with her. Also wielded a sword. Nearly spotted me in the forest when he left the cave, he was carrying her on his shoulder." The dragon managed to explain.

"Charlie? He was with her?"

"Wouldn't exactly know a human by name, would I?"

"Well, he certainly picked the best bait." Patrick sighed as he muttered to himself.

He had no idea how far the two of them were, but he could defiantly tell that since the stone dragons they had gotten closer. The question was, when Tom gets better, would he play into Charlie's trap to save her or leave? He certainly wouldn't stay if was just the two of them given how much they don't get along.

Either way it was bad. He had to sort this out, before that happens.

"I only ask that you make my death quick." The dragon sighed. Patrick drew his attention back to the air dragon. Able to cover a large distance very quickly without being detected… if it wasn't for the injuries…

Patrick reached into his satchel and pulled out the book of healing magic.

"What is your name, dragon?" Patrick asked the dragon. The dragon gave him a strange look, but at this point there really was no point in caring anymore.

"Breeze." Breeze answered.

"How desperate are you to live Breeze?" Patrick asked her. Breeze's ears pricked up. She gave Patrick another questioning look, but this time there was more hope in it.

"You're willing to save me?" She asked him. Patrick gave her a hesitant thoughtful look.

"Willing to try." He answered, "You see, I happen to be able to practice magic."

"I have heard of this. Humans who can do the seemingly impossible."

"I'm sure my clan wasn't very popular with your kind. I have a book on healing magic but… I've never practiced anything advanced enough to heal a wound."

"So, you wish to use me as a test subject?" Breeze chuckled, "What have I got to lose?"

"That's not all. I need your help to find my friend."

"What must I do?"

"I need to cover a large area, quickly. Faster than a human ever could."

"That, I can help with, assuming your magic works."

Patrick opened his book and began to flick through the pages.

***

Perhaps it is time that I explain magic. Mages within Patrick's clan were taught spells through books and teachers as they travelled throughout the known world. An entire clan forced to be nomadic in order to avoid the wrath that was dragon kind, which despised mages more than any other human.

These spells consisted of a series of words linked to a certain list of ingredients placed in a specific arrangement. What was perhaps most impressive about magic was its versatility. Most spells require a basic shape, be it a square, hexagon, circle ect… yet how this shape is obtained is up to the caster. The shape doesn't need to be exact either.

This is true of all aspects of the requirements for the spell. The words, the ingredients, the conditions and arrangements. As long as they were all close enough, the spell would work without fault. This would often lead to the caster muttering the words 'close enough' when trying to set up a spell when resources were scarce.

The reason to this took a long time to work out. It was finally cracked by the discovery that certain people could get away with less accuracy when it came to construct the spell than others. These were usually people with a lot of experience with the practice and often was true of people who practiced one spell again and again.

A theory was constructed that stated that it was not the objects, the words or the arrangement that formed the magic, it was the human mind. The words, the conditions, they were all just a means of getting the mind to a very particular state. Those who had achieved such a state many times found it easier to attain such a mental state alone, without the aid of the spell requirements. Mages have been known to be able to cast basic spells without the incantation to great effect without any hinderance to the power of the spell and as a bonus usually saved on casting time.

Being top in his generation, Patrick knew all of this all too well. He even explained this to Tom at one point while Tom was still rather interested in the functionality of magic. Of course, no one could yet explain just how the human mind could make the impossible happen, which is why Tom was not happy with such an explanation either.

Patrick had learnt very few spells, but those he knew, he knew well and practiced often. Disease cures were a must to any mage, but that was about as far as Patrick's healing knowledge took him.

***

To achieve a successful casting of a spell, Patrick had to tune his mind to the exact state in order to do it. That was hard enough, but on top of that, if he got the wrong state and ended up in a mental state meant for another spell, things would get very messy.

Learning a new spell usually took months or years depending on how difficult it was. Healing was considered one of the most difficult practices of magic. The wrong healing spell, the wrong target area, the wrong timing.

Just a few of the many problems to worry about. Ca[s]ting a fireball was very different to repairing a living, breathing creature.

Step one, a circle. Patrick took a look at his surroundings. Dead dragons and a cave mouth. The mouth was a circle, and the dragon was resting rather close to it. Close enough.

Step two, blood. The book specified human blood, but given it was how to heal a human, Patrick assumed dragon blood would be a better option. He looked at Breeze, more blood loss probably wasn't a good idea.

Instead, he took his small knife out and began cutting one of the nearby air dragon bodies. He collected some with a wooden cup from his satchel and placed it beside Breeze.

Step three, a dead body similar to the patient. How very convenient. Normally this would be the problem ingredient, especially considering the current lack of human dead bodies, although it was one of the most advanced healing spells in the book.

He read the procedure carefully. He then slowly pushed one of the bodies within arm's reach of the dragon.

"I knew this would be strange, but this seems rather insane to me." Breeze protested as Patrick took off his top and drew a line of dragon blood from one hand to the other across his body.

"Just doing what the book says. Seven generations of human wisdom haven't failed me yet." Patrick responded as he placed a hand on Breeze, and his other on the dead body.

Patrick closed his eyes and concentrated. He started by imagining the mouth of the cave, which wasn't hard considering it was physically there.

The circle represented the circle of life that existed within every living being. No matter what, he needed to keep that circle spinning, or Breeze would die.

He pictured the circle against the palm of the hand pressed against Breeze now, still spinning. Next, he focused on a second circle, this time it was on the palm of the hand against the dead body, this one wasn't spinning.

Finally, he focused on the pathway the blood represented. He felt the stationary circle melt in his palm. He felt the molten circle flow along the blood path and into the spinning circle.

He felt the spinning circle pick up in speed drastically.

"It... worked." Breeze exclaimed in surprise. Patrick opened his eyes.

Breeze had gotten to her feet. Her cuts and bruises were completely gone. Her leg and jaw were correctly fixed as well. Patrick felt a fine powder in his other hand. He turned to look at the body, but it was no longer there. Where it had been was now a pile of fine dust.

The dust was swept into the air and taken by the breeze as Breeze stretched her intact wings.

"A cost. That's new for me." Patrick muttered to himself. Normally casting an advanced spell would give him a headache for a little bit or make him feel tired. He felt the tiredness sink in, but the fact that the body had been used up was new to him entirely.

Yes, the ingredients sometimes changed form or shape, but that was usually because you were casting a spell that would make it so. This healing spell had a cost to it, one that he wasn't willing to pay when it came to his friends.

Any doubt that healing magic was the hardest form suddenly disappeared from his mind. He'd been lucky enough to study the theory enough to understand what the book was telling him to do, but he'd never had to manipulate so much in such a short time.

He closed his book and put it back in the satchel. He slowly collected water from the melting ice and swirled it around the blood-stained cup. The inside would now forever be stained blue, but he'd managed to wash it enough for it to be used again.

"Are you finished?" Breeze asked him. Patrick nodded.

"Ready for your end of the bargain?"

"With magical powers like that, I wouldn't dare refuse." Breeze replied as she lowered herself. Patrick gently climbed up onto her back.

"Charlie could have gone in any direction, and he's hours ahead of us, so we need to cover as much ground as possible."

"I'll do my best." Breeze sighed as she spread her wings once more. With a huge flap, they were in the air.

***

Tom woke up with a painful headache, but as his eyes came into focus it seemed to die down to a reasonable level. His eyes scanned his surroundings rather briefly. He was in his room, on his bed.

He got on his feet with only a small head rush. After taking a second to regain balance, he walked over to his door, where a note was waiting for him.

***

Tom ran out of the cave front door with his bag. He suddenly came to a stop.

"You have a choice." Cathie muttered into his ear. He knew almost instantly that it was another illusion.

"I've already made my choice. I'm done running." Tom snapped at her. She didn't back down however, she simply smiled.

"And yet you hesitate. You can fool the others, but you can't fool yourself Tom."

"Then I'll change." Tom sighed as he turned away from her and began to run into the forest.

***

Charlie and Cathie were sat around a small campfire. They were held up in a small cave just a little bit up a mountain. Sheltered from the wind being funnelled by the valley and the cold of night.

They'd been talking for hours now. More than they'd ever talked before, but both of them seemed to be enjoying it. Charlie's sword had been sheathed some time ago, but Cathie was by no means fast enough to pull anything on him.

Even if she did, she had the feeling it would end the same as the last time she pointed a sword at him.

"So, from everything you've told me, it sounds like you have a huge choice to make." Charlie continued, "Tom or me."

"Pretty much." Cathie sighed. He'd finally gotten around to asking her.

"May I ask which way you're truly leaning? Not the act you put on before the cave fight."

"Honestly I'm right in the middle right now. Do I choose the man I must learn to love, or the man who must learn to love me?" She replied. Charlie seemed to consider her words carefully.

"You don't seem eager to make the choice."

"Starting to want the choice to be made for me." She muttered.

"I mean… if I kill Tom, choice made right?"

"I suppose. Would certainly make things easier if one of you died."

"Then we should find Tom. I'll fight him to the death. Whoever survives you can have." Charlie suggested.

"Better than any plan I've got." She answered as she swept her hair off her right shoulder with her bound hands. Charlie seemed to stare at her for a second before he took out a knife.

With a gentle throw he made sure its handle landed in the palm of her hands. She used the knife to cut the rope holding her hands and feet together. She looked back at Charlie, who was gesturing to have the knife back. She gave it a gentle throw over the fire, making sure that the handle landed in the palm of his hand. Not the right time.

"Any idea where he'd be?"

"The cave, but not for long. Once he realises it's just him and Patrick he'll leave. Already blew the one back-up cave of his I knew about as well so once he's left, I have no idea where he'll be."

"Better move fast then. We'll head out at first light." As Charlie finished his sentence, the ground shook for a moment. It sounded a lot like something had just landed outside of the cave, something dragon sized.

Charlie drew his sword and got to his feet. Cathie got to her feet as well but backed up a bit behind Charlie.

"Shit. Thought the trees around the entrance was enough to hide the firelight." She muttered.

"So did I. Seems we have a dragon with a sharp eye."

"Or perhaps someone who knows what he's looking for." Patrick's voice boomed as he appeared at the mouth of the cave.

"Guess the overprotective asshole decided to come in Tom's place." Cathie sighed.

"I knew you were a stubborn bastard when it came to Cathie's safety, but not even I expected you to go this far!" Charlie shouted at him. Patrick responded with a smile.

***

Tom came to a stop within the half-destroyed forest. Those trees that hadn't lost their leaves to air dragon attacks had been knocked down by earth dragon rock shots. Yet within the carnage, covered by the green forest floor, lay Tom's bow.

He quickly picked it up and slung it over his shoulder before he continued to run off into the distance.

***

Patrick's foot drew a quick triangle in the dirt. By the time his eyes looked back up, Charlie was right in front of him, sword in full thrust towards him.

With a glowing hand Patrick slapped the blade down. Its point jammed into the ground right into the centre of the triangle.

"Shatter, feeble blade." He muttered. The triangle flashed red. Before their very eyes Charlie's blade shattered like glass.

Before he had time to react Charlie had already pulled a dagger from his clothes. He went for a stab, but Patrick placed his hand against Charlie's neck. A spark of fire singed Charlie. He shot back in both pain and surprise.

"I forgot just how troublesome that magic of yours is." Charlie hissed at him. Patrick's foot drew another triangle that connected to the base of the first to now form a diamond shape.

He quickly reached into his satchel and brought out four sharpened twigs. He threw all four, which landed point down into the ground around Charlie, forming the same diamond shape. He then slammed a glowing hand against the diamond shape at his feet.

"Deny my enemy." He spoke with closed, focused eyes. Charlie tried to charge forwards, but he slammed into some kind of invisible wall that seemed to line up with the sticks Patrick had thrown, "The spell will break when the diamond shape breaks. I'm sure a gust of wind will make it in here eventually, or perhaps a small creature might disturb it. Until then consider yourself lucky that I have too much on my plate right now to finish you off."

"A mistake you'll regret." Charlie spoke with gritted teeth. Patrick walked over and grabbed Cathie's hand.

"Come on." He sighed as he pulled her towards the mouth of the cave. Charlie could do nothing but watch as they left him trapped.

CHAPTER 18; REALITY CHECK

Breeze landed rather gently back in front of the ice cave wreckage. She waited for the two humans on her back to get off before giving them a nod.

"Many thanks, Breeze." Patrick thanked her.

"My debt is paid in full. Until next time human." With that, she shot off into the sky and began to fly towards the horizon.

"The hell did you do to get her to help?" Cathie asked him as the two of them turned and began to walk back to the cave.

"Saved its life with healing magic." Patrick boasted.

"Where was this healing magic when I was injured?" She asked him.

"It's… a risky process."

"I'll take the risk." She sighed.

"But you aren't injured anymore, right?"

"I may have been exaggerating my recovery." She revealed, "Tom's patchwork is slowing me down and my other shoulder still stings like a bitch."

"Not like you to come forwards with something like that."

"Yes, well Charlie made my lack of ability to fight painfully clear."

"I did wonder why I was the one having to kick his ass."

"Not just that, he had my sword too. Means I'm really out of commission." She sighed, "Where is Tom?"

Before Patrick could answer, he was interrupted by the sound of a pair of wings. The two of them watched as Frost and Breath landed in front of them. Frost seemed to take special care in how he landed, making sure to only use three of his legs. In his fourth, an unconscious Tom was being held.

He gently placed Tom down on the ground in front of them.

"Not where I thought he was." Patrick finally answered.

"I found him passed out quite a distance from here after one of my scouts spotted him. Seemed to be searching rather desperately for someone." Frost explained.

"Knew I shouldn't have mentioned Cathie was missing in that note." Patrick sighed.

"The hell happened to you two anyway?" Cathie asked him.

"Tom kind of… lost it. Moment the earth dragons attacked something seemed to click in his mind, started killing them by the dozen, until he got hurt somehow. I left him after tending to his head injury, but the stubborn bastard must have tried searching for you before he was fully recovered."

"I came to discuss a matter with you all, but you appear to be otherwise occupied." Frost revealed.

"Is it a matter that can wait a few days?" Patrick asked him. Frost gave a nod, "Then perhaps we better make sure Tom is awake for it."

***

Cathie gently pulled Tom's door closed behind her after quietly walking out of his room. Patrick seemed to be waiting for her in the main room.

"For someone who had a head injury, I don't see any wound." She pointed out to him.

"It's a head injury I've never come across before. One that seems to only occur inside his head, not outside."

"That reminds me of a very particular type of pain." Cathie sighed as she placed a hand against her closed arrow wound.

"From what I read it seemed to be something about Tom using his brain too much. Kind of like how you push yourself too far sometimes."

"What would drive him to do that?" She asked.

"I was hoping that you would have the answer to that, given that you're currently trying to get close to him."

"You told me he lost it when the earth dragons attacked right?"

"Pretty much the moment they came out of the ground, yeah."

"Tom's always had a bone to pick with earth dragons."

"I've never seen him snap like that before. I'm sure I don't have to remind you how many times we've come across earth dragons."

"Yes, but before he was taking something. Some kind of medicine that kept his emotions at bay. He hasn't been taking it though."

"Why wouldn't he take a medicine that stops him going mad?" Patrick asked her. Cathie bit her lip.

"Because he'd lose his feelings for me." She answered.

"What is it about the earth dragons? What could make someone that messed up?" Patrick asked as he shook his head. Cathie swallowed. Those words came just a little bit too close to home for her liking.

"They… killed his parents." Patrick gave her a look telling her that he was expecting her to continue. After a few moments of silence, he finally realised that was it.

"That all?" Patrick asked.

"That all? That all!" Cathie snapped at him, "Both of us watched our parents get torn apart by dragons at a very young age and your response is that!?"

"I think you're forgetting who you're talking to." Patrick calmly snapped back at her, "I may not have watched it happen but both of you know for a fact that I lost more than my parents when we first met."

Cathie took a step back. It was true she'd never really considered Patrick's loss that much, but he'd lost his entire clan. A family of over a hundred people gone in the blink of an eye. Something in Patrick's now anger filled eyes told her that he knew every single one of their names.

"I... sorry."

"Sorry?" Patrick mockingly chuckled, "Look at you two. Both as broken as one another." He added as he forcefully removed the magnetic bracelet from her arm, revealing the scars on her wrist, "We are the last human beings alive. That means all of us have lost someone, even Charlie."

"I..."

"Do you know what my clan used to do to broken people like you and Tom?" Patrick asked her, "We'd leave them behind with sliced ankles, so they couldn't follow. Food for the beasts."

Cathie's hand began to reach for a wooden chair to her side, "If you two weren't the only hope for humanity I'd put you down myself." He sighed. After another moment he seemed to calm down a bit.

"So, the overprotective asshole has another side after all." Cathie muttered in response. Patrick hadn't noticed her shaking in her clothes until she broke eye contact with him. She was trying to make it sound like anger, but he knew fear when he saw it.

"Whatever Tom is going through; you need to get him out of it. Get him off the medicine and sane enough to join the rest of us in reality." Patrick muttered in a calmer and softer voice. The anger had all but left him now.

"And me?" She asked him. She was still shaking, although not as much. Her hands reaching for the chair slowly fell to her side.

"For every new cut I find on that wrist, I'll cut him twice as much." He gently snapped. He didn't mean it as a serious threat, but he wanted to get his point across rather firmly to her. She slowly nodded.

"I'll try my best." She murmured. She turned and walked back over to Tom's room like a small puppy with its tail between its legs.

***

Tom awoke to a gentle, warm breath over his chest. His eyes opened to Cathie's blood-red hair. Her forehead nuzzled against his neck; she was curled up beside him in bed.

"Thought you were supposed to be missing." He muttered.

"You know me, always finding you eventually." Both of them gave a small smile, but Cathie's didn't last very long, "Patrick told me what happened in the forest."

"The um… the whole killing spree thing?" Cathie gave a small nod.

"Figured it had something to do with the medicine you stopped taking. Seems a lot like a withdrawal symptom."

"I'm surprised your aware of such an effect." Cathie raised her now uncovered bare arm.

"You think I've gone this long without trying to stop this?" She asked him. Tom nodded in understanding.

"It's not a withdrawal symptom. I started seeing things before I ever made the medicine. The whole point of it was to stop me seeing shit."

"Let me guess, it started not long after you lost them." Tom gave a small nod.

Cathie untucked herself from her curled-up position and sat up, pulling the blanket with her. Tom hadn't been sure but now he knew that she was fully clothed, along with himself. He too sat up and faced her.

"It's mostly my parents I see. Sometimes its things from my past, things I saw as a child."

"That would make a lot of sense. Is that all?"

"The more recent ones have you sometimes. On the rare occasion I see myself." As he finished his sentence Cathie noticed his eyes shift ever so slightly, as if he had briefly taken a look at something else in the room that had caught his eye.

"Where is it?" She asked him.

"It's nothing." He quickly answered. She leant forwards and grabbed both of his hands tightly.

"Where is it?" She asked again, this time softer and calmer than before.

"Behind you." He quietly answered.

"Who is it?" She watched his eyes look at whatever he saw behind her and almost instantly shoot back to her.

"Me… holding a knife."

"I'm guessing he isn't exactly picking his teeth with it." Tom gave a rather panicked smile.

"No, he's not. It's against your back."

"Alright, listen to me carefully." Cathie began, "I need you to look at it, without looking away."

"You want me to what?" Tom asked. Cathie could see the fear in his eyes at her words.

"Everything you see is just your mind telling you something. Sometimes it can be clear if the vision talks to you, but its actions are just if not more important. Why are you stabbing me in the back?" Tom's eyes shifted to look behind her.

"I don't know. It's not clear why."

"That's because the answer is up here." Cathie added as she tapped Tom's forehead, "The vision is only here to make you ask yourself that question." Tom began to search his mind.

"A fear." He answered.

"A fear of hurting me?" She asked him. Tom gave it a thought, then nodded, "Now you've found it, you need to get rid of it."

"I don't know how. It's always going to be a possibil-"

"I didn't say rationalise it, I said fight it." Cathie interrupted, "Face that thing head on and intimidate the shit out of it. If that doesn't work, beat the shit out of it until it goes crawling back under whatever rock it came from."

Cathie watched as the fear slowly but surely left Tom's expressions.

"It's gone." He revealed as he took a peek behind her.

"That was an easy one. A fear that probably hasn't been around for too long up there. The older ones will be harder, much harder."

"How do you know so much about this?" He asked her.

"Because it's exactly what I did a few days after I lost my family. Luckily for me stubbornly fighting shit is in my nature, not so much for you though."

"Thank you."

"It's nowhere near done. You'll keep seeing things until you beat them all. Even then they pop up every now and again for you to beat back down. A scar can't be removed, but you can forget the pain of it."

"Speaking from more experience there?" Tom asked her as he looked down at her wrist. He brought it up to eye level to inspect it, "No fresh ones in a while."

"I've been trying my best not to. Kept away from small knives and such."

"And the withdrawal symptoms?"

"A craving. It gets worse every day I don't."

"Craving… I'm familiar with treating drug abuse. I assume it's of a similar nature?"

"I think so. Never tried anything that fuzzy but I can imagine a similar reaction."

"I'm guessing you get some form of pleasure out of doing it then." Tom added as his gaze changed to her face. Her eyes dropped down in shame.

"Yeah." She answered.

"Normally stopping entirely doesn't work. You have to slowly pace yourself off it, otherwise you'll eventually give in and start right back at square one."

"You're saying I should keep doing it?"

"Ideally no, but chances are you'll probably have to a few more times before you can completely stop." Tom explained, "If you reach a point where you have to, I want you to only do it while I'm with you, to make sure you're alright afterwards and so that I can keep an eye on how regularly you do it from now on."

Cathie nodded to this.

"I think I can manage that."

Cathie leant forwards and gave him a peck on the lips. An act that gently turned into a kiss.

***

It was the dead of night. Cathie lay fast asleep beside Tom in his bed. This hadn't been the first time he'd noticed how easy it was for the two of them to fall asleep beside one another without fear of nightmares. In fact, that very point had kept Tom awake just thinking about it.

To him, it made absolutely no sense. How would having someone near you affect whether you have a nightmare or not? If it was a psychological effect then surely it was a simple matter of getting into the right mind set, a method Tom had tried many years earlier with no success.

After many hours of staring at his ceiling he came to some form of conclusion. It pretty much boiled down to the idea that certain chemicals that made up the feeling known as love also seemed to help him suppress the nightmares for some reason. He wasn't particularly happy with the conclusion but the moment he tried thinking about any other possibility he would get lost down the rabbit hole that was his feelings.

With a small, fed up huff, he gently got out of bed and slowly walked out of the room.

As he walked into the main room, he noticed Patrick trying his best to wash out his wooden cup. Tom took note of the dragon blood blue stain that he was failing to wash off.

"You know any good tricks for dragon blood stains?" Patrick asked him as he noticed Tom walk into the room. Tom grabbed a small log from one corner of the room and threw it onto the fire in the other corner. The flames grew slightly so that most of the room was now lit up.

"Dragon blood wont dissolve in water. I'm sure I have some spare solvents in my room that would do the trick." He answered as he took a clean wooden cup from the table and brought it over to the stone washbowl that Patrick was using.

The washbowl was filled with water, which Patrick was trying to use to clean the cup. Above the washbowl was a rather primitive copper tap.

The tap had been hammered into shape rather poorly, but it seemed to function as it was intended. The tap was connected to a copper pipe of similar craftwork. It ran up into the ceiling of the room and continued upwards until it connected to a series of rainwater capture buckets.

Tom put his cup under the tap and let a cup full of water run into it. Making sure no excess was wasted he turned the tap off just in time to perfectly fill the cup. He then began to take a few sips from it.

"I take it she's fast asleep in your room?"

"Have you been out here all night?" Tom spun back at him.

"Just wanted to make sure neither of you ran off again." Patrick threw back. Tom gave a small smile just outside of Patrick's view.

"Heard that you gave her quite the stern talking to."

"What of it?"

"It's just not like the guy, who stands guard over her all the time, to be the one who scares her half to death. And I'm sure I don't have to tell you how hard it is to scare Cathie."

"What are you getting at Tom?" Patrick asked him as he turned around to face Tom eye to eye. There was a moment of silence as the two of them stared one another down, "You want me to apologise, don't you?"

"Damn right I do."

"Not going to happen."

"Any particular reason you're being even more of an asshole than normal?" Tom calmly snapped at him through gritted teeth.

"You're treading on unknown territory to you, Thomson."

"Congratulations, you know my family's name. Just so happens that my family likes to explore unknown territories." The two of them stood closer, nose to nose.

"You really want to know why I said what I said?" Patrick asked him.

"Enlighten me."

"Look, my relationship with Cathie is a rather complex one and no offence but you're still finding your feet on the whole relationship thing."

"I'm a fast learner."

"You and I both know that's not true when it comes to her. I've been watching you barely struggle by every time you speak to her around me. Other than a few subtle differences you pretty much treat her exactly the same."

"You know I'm not backing down without at least an answer. Whether I'll be able to understand it is a different matter."

"Fine." Patrick huffed as he backed off slightly, "I'm sure it's rather obvious that I play the overprotective figure when it comes to her."

"No shit." Tom chuckled.

"It's also no secret that deep down inside that girl is broken." Tom remained silent at this remark, "Both of you are."

"You're point?"

"If things stay the way they are you two are just going to get worse. Either you'll give in to taking that medicine of yours and break her heart, or you'll drive yourself mad with whatever the hell is going on inside that head of yours."

"We've come up with methods of dealing with both of our... issues."

"Have you now? Wonder when you did that? It didn't happen to be after my talk with Cathie was it?" Patrick sarcastically asked, "That's part of my point Tom."

"You're saying that you somehow helped us with everything you said?"

"As I said earlier, if things remained the same you were doomed to get worse, as was she. So, I gave her the one thing the two of you needed most."

"A slap on the wrist?"

"A reality check." Patrick corrected him, "A slap on the face to bring you both back into the real world instead of letting you fall down your own rabbit holes even further."

"You know what, I think you had a point earlier. I don't get it."

"You don't have to. I understand your concern about my methods but for once I'm right and your wrong." Tom opened his mouth to respond but he seemed to shut it just before the words left his mouth.

Patrick could tell that he was just about to say something along the lines of 'I highly doubt that', but his brain seemed to catch up with his big mouth to remind him that they were talking about something that Tom really didn't understand all that well.

"Explain to me how snapping at a self-harming person does them any good? From my experience it usually only drives them further down the... rabbit hole was the term you used right?" Patrick's thoughts gave an internal sigh, his brain had overtaken his anger. Tom had realised he was in fact not correct, which meant that now he was searching for why he wasn't.

"Under circumstances where the self-harm is a desperate attempt to avoid suicidal tendencies, you would be right. Cathie isn't suicidal though."

"No, from how she described the craving to me she seems to get pleasure from it." Tom reminded himself. Patrick could tell he was starting to see the difference between the two situations.

"When suicide is involved then by all-means gentle is the way to go, but if it's what Cathie is doing then they need a good slap in the face at first to make them know very clearly that what they are doing is sick, then you come in and pick up the pieces with the gentle approach. Which I'm sure you did for her." Patrick explained.

"That doesn't explain everything." Tom pointed out.

"Someone suffering from normal lose only needs time and company to heal." Patrick began, "You however managed to make your own situation much worse. That medicine is your equivalent to her cutting herself. It does you harm mentally; it makes you feel great without having to deal with those negative feelings you seem determined to run from. Like her, you need a good slap on the face to make you realise how wrong it is. Only then can anyone help you pick up your pieces."

Tom thought about his words for a few seconds, but Patrick interrupted his thought process with a gentle tap on the cheek, "Consider yourself slapped." He added. He left the blue stained cup by the washbowl and walked off into his room.

Tom slowly finished his cup of water. He gave it a quick rinse and placed it beside Patrick's, all while off in his mind somewhere thinking about what the hell just happened to him.

CHAPTER 19; POLITICS

Frost gently landed in front of an ancient structure made out of what appeared to be metal. It had little height to it, but its other two dimensions seemed to spread very far. Covered by the marshland mangrove trees that covered the swamp area that surrounded the place, it was rather hard to spot at a distance.

The three humans climbed off Frost's back and took in the structure in all its glory.

"Since when did dragons have the means to cast metal?" Tom asked Frost.

"This place was constructed by our lord and master many centuries ago. From his divine powers the building was said to have risen from the ground at his very command." Frost answered.

"I see dragons have their share of legends as well then." Tom sighed as he continued to take a closer look at the craft work. Before them stood two massive metal doors big enough for three or four dragons to walk through at once with ease. The sheer weight of them must demand the work of at least a few dragons.

On the walls either side of the doors were elegant patterns formed of the same metal as the walls. Pictures of dragons of all shapes and sizes doing various leisurely things. Tom noted the lack of violence within the artwork, especially considering that here and there the odd human seemed to appear in the backgrounds.

"You think my story to be false?" Frost asked him.

"I mean no disrespect, but stories have a way of being twisted when being passed down through the years. I tend to take anything not written down with a pinch of salt." Tom replied as he turned his attention to Frost.

"What is this place for?" Patrick asked him.

"A meeting place. One not used for far too long." Frost responded.

"Middle of marshland, no dragon seems to have any form of advantage given the combination of elements surrounding this place. That plus the metal, a material most dragons wouldn't be able to break, means this is a symbol of unity, right?" Tom theorised.

"It is indeed the place all dragons used to meet before our differences separated us." Frost answered. He walked forwards and thumped his front paw on the door two times, "You will be the first humans in history to enter this sacred place. I ask you to be respectful." He added.

The two doors were slowly pushed open by four ice dragons waiting on the other side. Once the doors were fully open, they parted to make way for them.

Frost began to walk forwards into the structure. The three of them followed. As Frost passed each ice dragon, they lowered their head in respect for him. The heads remained lowered until the humans had passed them before they turned to the task of closing the huge doors.

The four of them entered a massive circular room. Most of which was taken up by the massive round table. Around which were several different slabs of various designs.

Flame sat rather comfortably on a red-hot stone that sat in a bath of lava. The lava continued to run to her left, where a lava dragon sat within the stream that then ran into a pipe in the floor.

Flame was sat higher than her lava dragon ally, but the lava dragon was much bigger than her and their heights seemed to equal out due to it.

To Flame's right sat Flint on a regular chunk of rock. Beside her, an empty plot of grass and dirt. On the other side of the lava dragon, another empty seat that seemed to be a pile of soft cushions surrounded by a rather impressive nest like structure. Beside the empty earth seat was a waterfall coming out of the back wall and into a small bath of water which Wave swam within. The water continued to run along a channel until it met the slab of ice that Frost took his place on. Between the ice and air seats was an empty slab of metal that gave a rather quiet but ominous hum.

Oddly enough there was one final seat. More of a throne perhaps. It was positioned within the very centre of the table. The grand slab of gold and diamond was placed slightly higher than the rest.

As the three humans walked down the few steps into the room, the three of them noticed something rather daunting. The table was higher off the ground than they were.

"Perhaps the first order of business is where these three should be placed." Flame sighed as she noticed the human's presence.

"Since they are one of the main topics, I am sure the table alone shall do for now." Wave suggested. With a quick and cold burst, an icy ramp formed ahead of the humans leading up onto the table.

The three of them slowly made their way up. The chamber was filled with the sound of multiple doors closing, coming from all sides. Behind every seat was an entrance to the room. Four dragons of each type made their way into the room and sat behind their respected leader. It seemed as though each species had their own door into the place as well.

Cautiously, Breath entered the room, trying to draw as little attention to herself as possible. Strangely she did not head for the air dragon seat. She instead stood between Frost and Wave's guards rather out of place.

One by one the other leaders noticed her, but their lack of comment seemed to say that they understood the meaning to her actions. She did not speak for her kind, nor was she to stand with them.

"I honestly didn't expect such a turn out given the recent history of the world." Flint remarked, cutting through the silent tension filling the room.

"It has certainly been a long time since we were last called to this place." The lava dragon added, "Certainly a first for all of our reigns."

"I apologise for taking on the role of the divine by being the one to send the invitation to you all, but I felt that such a meeting was necessary." Frost revealed.

"Given the divine's absence for so long, one of us would eventually have done so." Flint answered Frost's apology.

"Then perhaps we should drop such traditional talk for now. An issue for if the divine should ever return, and only then." Flame sighed.

"On to the first matter then." Frost began. He turned to look towards the humans, "Perhaps we should first clear the matters of the past."

"Thomas Thomson, Cathie Clawson. Both of your families have caused many a troublesome situation to almost everyone present, not to mention a few that aren't." Flame began, "Not to mention that both families were suspected to be allies of the Neutral."

"Hold on." Frost spoke out, "Clawson?" He asked as he looked at Cathie in particular. He looked back at one of the ice dragons behind him. Shard was also staring at Cathie.

"Is there an issue Frost?" Flame asked him.

"One that perhaps should be dealt with behind closed doors." Frost answered as he turned back to look at Cathie. Cathie was doing her best to avoid eye contact with either of the two ice dragons. She shifted ever so slightly towards Tom, who took her hand firmly.

"I see no evidence presented that we ourselves took part in such events. Also given our early departures from both of our families I argue that holding us accountable for our elders is unjustified." Tom argued.

The leaders took these words into consideration.

"The fire and ice dragons were the main two effected from those present. The choice is theirs." Flint pointed out.

"Blood has been spilled. I cannot ignore that." Flame responded. All eyes turned to Frost.

"Shall we not forget who's blood?" Frost asked them after a few seconds of thought, "I know for a fact that the Clawson's died to ice dragon claws."

Cathie's grip on Tom's hand tightened like a vice. Tom pushed the pain aside and gave her hand a gentle squeeze in response.

"Then what of the Thomson's?" Flame asked. Frost shook his head. Flame continued to look around the room, no response.

"Earth dragons." Tom finally responded, "They were butchered by earth dragons."

"I'm afraid… that isn't correct." Flint sighed. All eyes shifted to her, "They were being hunted by earth dragons, but all they found were bodies."

"How exactly do you know that?" Tom asked her.

"Because I was leading the charge." Flint answered. This time Tom's grip closed on Cathie's like a vice.

"I know an earth dragon when I see one. Three of them attacked us." Tom explained.

"When we arrived, all we saw were two graves marked with the human markings for Thomson. We confirmed two adults, one male one female matching the description of Kara and Jack Thomson." Flint revealed. Cathie could see the anger slowly build up in Tom. He was putting everything he had into hiding it.

"Three earth dragons?" The lava dragon asked Tom. Caught off guard by the question, Tom simply nodded, "I'm sure we are all aware of the divines warning. The three powers above."

The room was suddenly filled with silence for roughly a minute.

"The three gods who seek to restore humanity? Explain to me why they would be responsible for the deaths of two humans?" Frost asked the lava dragon.

"Gods move in mysterious ways as well we know." The lava dragon answered.

"Let us perhaps leave the wild theories and speculations to ourselves for the time being." Flame sighed, "Given our discussion, I am willing to pardon the Clawson's of crimes against our kind on the premise that no humans present have anything to do with the Neutral."

"Then Cathie is no longer up for trial." Frost sighed, "But I suspect you do not feel the same for the Thomson's."

"I do not. I also know that you do not either Frost. I'd also like to point out that Thomas Thomson himself is guilty of crimes against us, or should I remind everyone what language we are now forced to speak in?" Flame answered.

"That matter may yet bore fruit in the future, I don't believe we have seen all the good done by the act." Frost argued.

"Surely you aren't trying to get him out of his own actions against us?" Flame asked Frost.

"All I am saying is that perhaps a trial should be held in the future, once other issues have been dealt with and the results of the actions have had time to reveal themselves." Frost explained.

"But… a sentence for Thomas Thomson is to be made for his family's crimes." Wave announced. Tom looked around the room rather worried for what was about to happen.

"I have a few ideas in mind. However, I suggest we leave that until we have discussed other matters." Frost suggested. Flame narrowed her eyes at Frost, seemingly trying to work out what it was he was up to. After not being able to come up with anything however, she begrudgingly agreed.

"On to alliances then." Flint announced with a small smile. She knew this part was going to get interesting.

"As it currently stands, all parties present have some form of non-aggression pact with the humans. Some have even gone further than this." Wave explained.

"The ice dragons put forth that it is common sense that all present should do the same with one another." Frost revealed.

"A peace held together by humans." The lava dragon chuckled, "That would certainly be a new one."

"One that is very achievable." Flame added, "Does any party disagree?" The room fell silent for a few seconds, "Then I see no reason to oppose such a cross table pact."

"Then perhaps you would be interested to hear Frost's second proposal." Wave chuckled. She turned to look at Frost.

"Oh, you mean that was just the beginning?" Flame asked.

"My second proposal is the formation of an alliance." Frost announced.

"With the humans?" Flame asked.

"Between all present." Frost added. The room quickly became an uproar. Most of the leaders began mocking or arguing for and against the idea. This was amplified by the dragons behind each leader as they broke into argument as well.

Frost waited patiently for about a minute. Afterwards he seemed to get rather tired of listening to the rabble. He stood up tall, "SILENCE!" He boomed from the top of his voice.

Ripples in the water beneath his icy platform splashed the side of Wave and caused some water to spill from the channel between them.

The room became silent, "The idea I speak of has indeed existed before. Back then even the earth, air and lightning dragons were on board."

"Things were very different back then." Flame hissed at Frost.

"What I think you mean is that we had the divine to unite us back then. A keystone that held the alliance together without fail. I'm not suggesting that we raise the humans up to the same position as the divine himself, but I am suggesting that we use them as a replacement for the missing keystone."

"Do you really think those words alone would bring us together?" The lava dragon asked Frost.

"Alone, no. But that and the threat of those not in attendance, perhaps." Frost replied. Eyes shifted to the air and earth dragon seats.

"We have all had rather close calls concerning attacks from one of the two parties not present." Wave began, "Especially the humans."

"As we speak, the famous ice cave of the air dragons sits on their front door, abandoned and melting in the rising sunlight." Frost revealed.

"Is this true?" Flame asked the three humans.

"You're welcome to take a look with your own eyes." Patrick answered. He had a feeling Tom and Cathie weren't exactly in the mood to give a respectful response.

"I see. We are all aware how troublesome the earth dragons are to you humans given they seem to hunt you the most." Flame sighed as she considered the idea.

"Alone or in our small alliances we barely have the ability to defend ourselves from their larger numbers and superior might." Frost continued, "Together we would be able to mount an attack powerful enough to cripple both factions for years to come."

As his words flowed around the room, one by one the leaders began to like the idea Frost was putting into their heads.

"You make a valid point." Flame admitted.

"Such a point leads me to my suggestion of Thomas Thomson's sentence." Frost revealed. Suddenly all eyes were on him again.

"Which is?" Flint asked.

"That he grants us the knowledge and use of human engineering." Frost revealed. Once more the room was silent. Even Tom was lost for words at this, "Unconditionally." He added.

"You wish to simply ask for knowledge from this human?" The lava dragon asked Frost.

"Look at this building. Created by the divine himself. The only creatures able to replicate the very material these walls are made of are human beings. That has always been their strength, despite their many other weaknesses." Frost explained, "The power to replicate the work of the divine, although not as impressive as the divine himself, would prove a huge benefit. A benefit able to atone for the blood."

Flame considered this for a minute or so.

"This would only work if the alliance was formed. I refuse to grant such power to one race. It would be used only for the alliance." She realised. She'd finally worked out what Frost was up to, but it was already too late. His words had clearly persuaded the others, and she was seriously considering the idea herself.

"May I ask what would happen should I refuse?" Tom asked the lot of them.

"Execution. Fire or ice. Of which would be your choice." Frost responded rather unnervingly fast. The idea seemed to resonate with Flame rather well.

"All opposed to the idea of the alliance." Flint announced. The room fell silent for a few seconds.

"All those opposed to the suggested sentence." Frost announced. The room was silent once again.

"So be it. Thomas Thomson, you are under the obligation of providing knowledge and insight into the human ability to craft, tinker and create. Refusal to do so shall end in death. For whichever you chose, your family shall be pardoned as compensation." Flame announced. All eyes fell on Tom.

"I guess I have no choice but to accept the role of aid to the alliance." Tom sighed. It had taken him a while, but he'd managed to get his anger down to a level that wasn't going to affect his actions or words too much for now.

"Now that is out of the way, perhaps now is time to bring the third point into the light." Frost announced. Everyone in the room watched as Breath walked forwards and up onto the table. She slowly sat down beside the three humans.

"Of the two factions my people are by far the weakest, but that doesn't mean an attack will be easy." Breath began, "Also, my people seemed to have obtained some form of magical relic of immense power."

"I believe I bore witness to its power myself during the attack on our island." Flame sighed, "The ice cave vanished before my very eyes instead of crashing into the sea as the humans had planned for it."

The rest of the room began to look rather uneasy.

"I assume such power is not within human knowledge?" The lava dragon asked.

"I wouldn't have the first idea where to begin on such an invention." Tom sighed. He looked over to Patrick.

"No spell I am aware of is capable of that either. If it is magic, it is not of human origin." Patrick answered.

"Do we have any details on whatever it is?" Tom asked the room.

"I'm afraid not even I was aware of such a thing." Breath answered.

"Then perhaps before forming a plan of attack we should first gather information on what this power is and if it's possible to disable it." Tom suggested.

"How would you propose we do something like that?" Flame asked.

"The humans have already proven that their size certainly works for infiltration. The air dragons certainly wouldn't expect a human anywhere near their mountain peak." Frost reminded them.

"I would question the idea of risking the one who will grant us such power, in your own words Frost, in the heart of the enemy." Flame pointed out.

"That's fine. These two would be useless in the snow anyway." Cathie sighed, "They'd only slow me down."

"You would go alone?" Flint asked her. Tom and Patrick both gave her concerning looks.

"No one hides in the snow better than me. I'm sure some in this room would agree with me on that." She responded as she gave a small glance to Frost and Shard, "I can try to recover the relic for these two to take a look at in safety, or I could simply destroy it."

"Such a relic would be worth a study. Should I be able to replicate its design I might be able to offer such a power to the alliance." Tom suggested.

"I don't like the idea of you humans being in possession of such power." Flame hissed. Tom turned to face Flame directly.

"Exactly what would we do with such power? The ability to get into your well-guarded volcano would be impressive but utterly pointless given how easily you'd overpower us. The whole reason we work as Frost's keystone is because we have too few numbers to pose a threat even to an individual race of dragon."

"Such power does seem to be most like human wizardry. Of us all they would have the best chance of understanding it and replicating it." Frost argued, "Besides, should Thomas Thomson unlock its secrets, if he doesn't feel like sharing, he'd be breaking his agreement to help the alliance. I'm sure I don't have to bring up any further unpleasantly threatening points to make sure we are understood."

"He has a point." The lava dragon added.

***

The three humans followed Frost out of the building. As the doors closed behind them, Tom walked up to Frost.

"That was some slick work on your part."

"I apologise for not warning you about the subject of your families, but you would not have come otherwise, and without clearing it up Flame would have never agreed to half of what I proposed." Frost explained to him.

"I'm afraid to say my trust in you has diminished for such an act. However, I appreciate the rather light sentence all things considered."

"I had a feeling you could tell just how much Flame was out for your head." Frost chuckled ever so briefly. He then slowly turned to face Cathie, who was still tightly gripping Tom's hand.

The doors behind them were fully shut. The three ice dragons who had aided Shard in closing the door took their place behind Frost. Shard however stayed by the closed doors, unwilling to pass Cathie.

"I guess it's about time we had that closed-door talk." Cathie muttered.

"Such a talk is not my place to give. The order was from a previous king. I expect him back in one piece." Frost responded as he turned around. He, along with his guards, took flight.

Cathie let go of Tom's hand. She turned to Tom and Patrick.

"I'll find my own way back." She told them. The two of them nodded in response. They turned around and began walking off into the distance.

"You would have thought that I'd recognise that red hair of yours." Shard began as he drew closer to her. His scarred jaw being more obvious than ever.

Cathie put her hand down her top and brought out her dragon tooth necklace.

"I guess it's been a long time since you last saw this thing."

"If I remember correctly, that was responsible for this." Shard responded as he gestured to another scar on his chest. Unlike the one on his jaw, this scar was deep and long.

It was a funny thing to forget, but she had forgotten that part until this point. In a fit of panic, anger and desperation she'd used his own tooth to slice his chest wide open.

"I'm surprised you survived this long with that."

"If my kind hadn't found me a minute later, I wouldn't have survived it at all." Shard revealed, "You are a frighteningly strong creature Clawson."

"I want to know why you killed my family." She demanded.

"The old king had a real hatred for your family. I'm not aware of all the details, but I suspect your mother was the daughter of an impure relationship."

"Impure relationship?"

"Back when our own gods were still alive, they had the nasty habit of shape shifting. Rumours of Ice, our dragon god, having a child with a human were rather common to come across. Then my king orders me to wipe out Angel Clawson and her family, a girl with uniquely blue hair."

"Are you saying my mother was part dragon?"

"My suspicions were confirmed the moment I attacked her. I'm sure she hid them from you as a child for simplicities' sake, or perhaps so that you wouldn't say anything to any fellow humans, but those white wings of hers were impressive even for an ice dragon." Shard revealed.

"My mother had wings?"

"A tail too. She wielded a sword with devastating effect and agility compared even to us. Half of my battle with her was in the sky, before… well…"

"Go on."

"Before I tore her wings off." Cathie restrained herself from punching him there and then.

"So that's it? My mother was a mix of human and dragon, that's why she had to die?"

"The previous king saw her as a threat. Started creating rumours about them being linked to the Neutral." Cathie turned away for a moment. She wasn't really sure how to take all of this.

"Thank you for telling me. Ironically enough you're the first person to give me a straight answer for it." She spoke those words straight from her thoughts. The moment that her own words actually clicked in her head was the very same moment that she found all of her anger suddenly missing.

"I know it doesn't mean much at this point, but I do apologise for my actions."

"No, you don't have to. The truth was plenty. Plus, I'm sure that was penance enough." She added as she pointed to his scar. She found herself feeling guilty about the wound.

"It certainly taught me how dangerous you humans can be when backed into a corner. One of the reasons I told Frost not to push you four in fact."

"It seems he's got smart friends around that throne of his." She muttered as she eyed the tooth in her hand, "Don't suppose you want this back, do you?" Shard chuckled at the remark.

"I've gone this far without it. I'm sure I won't need it for the rest." He responded in a humorous chuckle.

"How much of this does Frost know?"

"He is aware of the Clawson's death and my part to play in it. However, this is mainly because of the fact that I'm rather well known amongst my people for being beaten by a human child. He isn't aware of the true reason they were killed."

"I spent so many years in the snow looking for you."

"Lucky you didn't find me, because I spent most of the previous kings reign hating you for how you beat me.

However, Frost is a kind soul, the reason I no longer have such feelings towards you."

"Thank you for this, somehow it's made all my built-up anger go away." Shard bowed his head.

"Stay safe, Catahyme." He muttered as he spread his wings out.

"You know my name."

"A name I've remembered for many years. Translates to Reaper in dragon tongue, although that no longer matters now." He explained, "I'd suggest sticking with Cathie in these more peaceful times, despite how much your true name suits you."

Cathie watched him fly off over the horizon.

A celestial had ordered her families death. Shard didn't seem to know about that, but if the old ice dragon king's worries about a hybrid race had come from the celestial's concern, that would answer a few more questions. Given that this celestial had a huge bone to pick with the human race, she could see that being the case.

She gently put her dragon tooth necklace back under her top before she headed off into the mangrove trees beyond.

As she passed the third tree, she spans around to notice Tom leaning against it.

"How'd it goes?" He asked her. Barely before he'd finished, she'd wrapped her arms around him. As he hugged her tight, he felt the odd tear on his shoulder.

"Sorry, just… a lot to take in."

CHAPTER 20; CONSEQUENCES OF PREVIOUS ACTIONS

Tom placed down a rather large sheet of paper on the table in the main room of the cave. Cathie and Patrick both took a look at the drawing on it.

"Some form of clothing?" Cathie asked him.

"When we last fought Charlie, he used small plates of metal to protect himself from my arrows." Tom began to explain, "A form of protective armour, like in the old days."

"When we had enough hands to hammer metal, you mean." Patrick clarified.

"During the past few days I've been working on something rather difficult, but I think I can make a set of armour in time for you to head off to the air dragon's mountain." He continued.

He placed a small chunk of black rock on a bit of empty table. He then took out a small vial of red liquid and poured the liquid onto the rock. The liquid began to fizz and slowly dissolve the rock beneath it. It was rather slow however and didn't seem to do much to the small chunk.

"What kind of mineral is that?" Patrick asked him.

"It's the material the stone dragons tried to get me to break." Tom revealed.

"You mean the one that only has one weakness." Cathie reminded them all as she stared at the half-filled vial in Tom's hand.

"Don't worry, this isn't human blood, much to my disappointment." Tom sighed as he noticed her look, "I've been trying to create blood from other compounds. Rather a complex task that I am still far from completing, but this failed batch still seems to have some kind of effect on the small sample I pocketed while we were down there."

"So, you have a safe way to cut this otherwise invincible rock." Patrick summed up.

"Enough to craft something." Tom revealed, "Just one problem." He sighed.

"That's the only bit of the stuff you have isn't it?" Cathie asked him. Tom nodded.

"Are you suggesting what I think you are?" Patrick asked the two of them.

"A journey back underground to gather enough to make this armour." Tom clarified, "Yes I am."

"If Boulder is still down there then it will be extremely dangerous." Cathie pointed out.

"It will, but if we can pull it off then we can wrap Cathie in an armour like no other. Blade and tooth alike would be useless against it." Tom argued. His points were very much being directed at Patrick.

"If we're going to do this, we're going to need to be very careful." Patrick sighed. The idea of an invincible armour seemed to resonate with him, "We aren't there to fight, so we need to avoid it as much as possible."

"Couldn't agree more." Tom added. There was a rather weird feeling within all three of them. If Tom and Patrick ever agreed on something, it was by far the best decision. An occurrence that doesn't often happen, but when it does you know you are on the winning path.

"Do you have a spare bow?" Cathie asked Tom. Tom nodded.

"I'm sure I can find you a sword or two somewhere in Charlie's room Cathie." Patrick suggested.

"Take it from someone who's taken a blow from their armour, a sword won't do shit to it. Arrow to the eye or a small dagger. Both have to be very deep and the dagger is far too dangerous a feat to pull off more than once." She explained.

"I can't imagine your shields holding very long against them either Patrick. Those teeth and claws shred through rock like paper." Tom added.

"Air would be most effective against them, right?" Patrick asked.

"I seriously doubt a few gusts of wind would do any harm to those things. You'd have more luck with water, easier to slip through the cracks in their armour." Tom answered.

"I'll grab a liquid magic book then."

***

The climb down the vertical tunnel they had used to escape earlier was long and tedious, but they didn't run into any issues as of yet.

They were down in the tunnels now. Small glowing rocks lit the place up rather beautifully, although a few of the surrounding tunnels seemed to not have them.

"Some of these tunnels were built in a rush during the fight. Stay close." Tom warned as he took out a small glass cage from his bag. Within the glass was a large glowing rock of some kind. He began to walk down one of the unlit tunnels with the other two close behind.

Cathie had already loaded her bow with an arrow at the ready and was concentrating hard on the vibrations within the surrounding ground.

"You told me these guys were desperate to break through this stuff because they were running out of rock to eat right? I certainly see plenty at the moment." Patrick pointed out. Tom walked over to the side of the tunnel they were in and gave the wall a quick thump.

"You forget what's above us. Eat too much rock and the ground above would collapse. You may not have noticed, but most if not all of these tunnel walls are currently load bearing. The roof is starting to sag as well. It wouldn't take too much to turn this entire place into a huge crater." He explained.

"Given what lives above, I certainly wouldn't mind that." Cathie added.

"It would certainly make the world less dangerous. However, I'd rather not be underneath during the collapse." Tom pointed out, "Just keep an eye out for unstable bits."

They continued onwards through the many twisting tunnels. It took them another twenty minutes at a walking pace to eventually find the tunnel that Tom had remembered led right to the dead end.

Just as they were coming up on the last corner, Cathie came to a stop in front of the two of them. She placed a finger to her mouth before raising her bow.

It was faint, but there was a rhythmic vibration. It felt like it was coming from further down the tunnel, around the last corner.

The three of them slowly took a look around the corner.

It was Boulder. His body had withered in size slightly, but that was perhaps the least of the dragons worries.

They stood and watched as he continued to claw rather frantically at the black material ahead of him. His efforts were getting him nowhere, but he seemed to continue despite this.

Most of his claws had snapped, presumably while doing this. His jaw and teeth were in a similar condition, which suggested that when his limbs were tired, he continued with his mouth instead.

His body was also covered in nasty and deep cuts. Chunks of his rock-hard armour-plated scales were missing here and there. Wounds from other stone dragons. Quite a number stayed behind with Boulder, but they didn't seem to be here anymore.

Boulder had become their leader because he was the strongest. For that same reason he remained the last alive down here.

"We need to lure him away from the thing." Tom suggested.

"No. Now's the perfect time. Shot in the chest right where the armour has come off and that would buy one of us enough time to make the killing shot as he looks over here." Cathie explained.

"At this point we'd be putting him out of his misery." Patrick added.

"Guess we do that then." Tom sighed.

"Who's the best shot?" Patrick asked them.

"Tom is, by far. The first shot should be doable for me." Cathie answered.

"Back up plan?" Tom asked.

"I memorised two spells that should be able to at least distract him if need be." Patrick revealed.

"Alright, simple one two with Patrick on backup." Tom summarised. The other two nodded before they quickly got themselves into position.

Cathie slowly aimed her shot and fired. The arrow struck the bare skin just as intended. Boulder let out a loud screech as he turned around to look at the three of them.

Tom aimed his shot right at Boulder's eyes. As he looked into them, he suddenly felt like he'd seen those eyes before.

Boulder's face changed to a slightly younger version of Cathie's. She was desperately climbing up a rope to the top of the cliff. Beneath her the wild cat creatures clawed at the cliff face.

As she reached the top, he watched her eyes close, and her strength finally fail her. Tom's hand grabbed hers just in the nick of time. He watched those eyes open ever so slightly.

"Please don't drop me." She muttered before falling completely unconscious.

Tom snapped back into reality just in time to get tackled to the floor by Cathie. Just in time to avoid a boulder that smashed into the tunnel wall behind them.

"Are you ok?" She asked him.

"Give me a clear shot. Promise I won't mess up a second time." Tom asked of her. She gave a quick nod as the two of them quickly got to their feet.

Both of them watched as Patrick threw what looked like a glob of water towards Boulder. It landed right at his feet but proceeded to bounce up into his chest with considerable force.

As the splashed water surrounded Boulder, it froze solid, holding him in place for just a few seconds before he would eventually break out.

Tom aimed his shot once more, but this time avoided direct eye contact with Boulder until the very moment he released the arrow.

The thin ice smashed as the large body fell to the floor dead.

"For a spell called bouncing water, it certainly doesn't disappoint." Patrick chuckled to himself as he looked at the empty wooden bottle that he'd chucked the water from.

"I've certainly never seen anything like it." Cathie remarked as she looked at the puddle of water that Boulder now lay in, "I'm guessing the freezing thing was you too?"

"Timed that one rather nicely if I don't say so myself. We all good?" He asked. Cathie and Tom nodded, "Alright, time to get to work then."

***

Cathie continued to hold the T position as Tom continued to place bits of black armour against her body, only to take them back to the table and alter them in one way or another. She noticed that he was using a strange knife to cut them.

"Is that blade covered in that liquid?" She asked out of curiosity as Tom walked over and placed what seemed like a chest piece against her chest.

"Sort of." He answered as he eyed the armour on her. It didn't seem to meet his standards. He took it off from her and walked with it back to his table, "Originally it was designed to be used with poison. A slot for the vial at the base of the handle, the contents get spread around little tubes inside the blade and come out of little holes at specific points."

"Sounds like a very deadly weapon."

"Yes, well it wasn't exactly my style, so it's never actually been used until now. I figured it would be better than just trying to pour the liquid on, considering how poorly it gets through this stuff."

"Is that why this is taking so long?" She asked.

"My fake blood isn't perfect. It's nowhere near as effective as the real stuff, but I doubt any of us would be willing to give up the litres of blood required to make this thing."

He brought the same piece back over and placed it against her chest once more. This time he seemed rather happy with it, "You can take a break now. I just need to put it all together, and it should be ready."

"Would you be able to make a sword out of this stuff?" Cathie asked him as she dropped her arms and relaxed.

"If I knew how to make a sword, yes, but I don't." Tom answered, "I could probably make a few arrow tips though." He added as the idea entered his head, "But I'm afraid Charlie would be the one to ask about that."

"I still need to get my sword back off him at some point." She sighed.

"Easier said than done. But once you have this you might be able to take him on with just your hands and feet." He pointed out. After a few minutes he held up the now complete chest plate armour in all its black glory.

Cathie let him lift it over her head and she pushed her arms in through the bottom of it. He slid it down until it rested on her shoulders. He then proceeded to tighten the straps that held the arms of the armour to her actual arms and tightened a few straps around her waist.

"Seems to fit rather well." She commented as she moved herself around in it a bit. The armour didn't cover everything, her arms only had a single plate for the forearm and above the elbow that didn't go all the way around, but if she fought smart, she'd be pretty much unstoppable.

She was also rather caught off guard at how light the armour was. The last time she'd worn armour was when she tried to walk in her mothers. Back then she could barely lift a single piece of it, and that was just regular iron.

"Ready for the legs?" Tom asked her. She looked over at him holding more plates with straps that he'd previously held against her legs beforehand.

"Sure."

***

Cathie watched as the ice dragon which had flown her many kilometres to the largest mountain in the known world flew off into the sunset.

Dark clouds caught her attention as she watched them slowly roll towards the mountain that she was about halfway up.

"It's been a while since I last saw this place." She sighed as she turned heel in the deep snow that she was standing in. The mountain peak ahead of her was very far above her.

The tallest peak in the known world. Never given a human name for the simple reason that no human ever got close enough to it to even attempt to try and climb the beast. To most it wasn't a mountain, it was a place to avoid at all cost.

No human that is, except Cathie.

The view from the height she was at was breath-taking. You could see the whole of the known world from the unclimbable black mountain peaks that surrounded the known valleys to the black cliffs that lay on the other side of the sea far off in the distance.

In fact, Cathie was almost at the height where it was possible to see over the edge of the known world. To most, they would have given everything just to take a glance at such a sight. To Cathie, who'd laid eyes on it once before, it was nothing special.

As she made her way up the steep incline, she eventually reached the height. She took a glance over the black peaks that marked the edge of this world just to make sure it was as she remembered it.

A desert. Bigger than one could ever imagine. That was all that made up the rest of the world beyond the known valleys. Nothing could even hope of surviving out there. No plants, no animals, no humans.

At one point in her life, she'd wondered if there were ever any other oases of life out there, but after some thought she eventually realised that not even those with the ability to fly ever crossed those black mountain peaks. They knew there was nothing out there but death.

She continued her journey at a slightly slower pace. She wanted those clouds from earlier to catch up with her. She had her armour on, but it was underneath thick white bear skin clothes that she'd wrapped around herself. Everything was covered except a small part of her face which included her nose and eyes.

The upward breeze brought the dark clouds up the mountain. Cathie waited until the sky above her was completely covered before she continued. Under the clouds, a harsh snowstorm with slicing winds.

An ice dragon at the right height was just the right colour to vanish in the snow, however they wouldn't be able to get too high before they got spotted. The deep tracks in the snow also made it rather obvious if someone was trying to sneak up.

Eventually even Cathie in her white fur would have been spotted, but she'd managed to time it rather nicely with a snowstorm.

Under normal circumstances, no one would have been mad enough to climb the mountain during the storm. It would kill most that would ever try it. However, this was by no means Cathie's first snowstorm mountain climb.

The incline finally reached a steepness too sharp for Cathie to simply walk. She had to climb now, despite solid ground being buried under a good waist height worth of snow. She had to make do with clinging to the snow itself. With every step she made sure the snow beneath her feet and hands had been packed tightly before she put any serious weight on it, and she made sure never to make a hold above any of her previous ones in fear of the snow shifting down.

The incline got so steep that she was more or less carving a spiral ramp through the deep snow, although the snow above didn't hold for very long, so she had to move fast. The ridiculously strong crosswinds also weren't helping. It eventually got to the point where if she stuck herself above the snow, she would have been blown clean off the mountain entirely.

Eventually the storm got too much, even for her. She calmly dug herself a small shelter deep in the snow and tucked herself inside it. After making sure everything was compact and stable, she curled up into a ball and closed her eyes.

She'd travelled as far as she could in the storm. She was relying on what remained of it to hide the tracks of her progress thus far. Now she had to play the waiting game. The air dragons weren't stupid, the highest chance of an attack would be just after a snowstorm, just as they get their vision of the mountain back. That means they'd be ready for her once the storm died down.

Cathie's tactic was rather simple now. She was close enough to not be noticed by most lookouts from the peak, close enough that they wouldn't expect anyone to be where she was. She could come out at any point during the next day without risk of running into heavy defences.

CHAPTER 21; NEWTON'S THIRD LAW

Tom was looking down at a rather crude drawing on his desk. It was a rough sketch of what he saw as the ice cave vanished during its sky plummet. He seemed to be scratching his head about one thing or another.

"What goes up must come down." He muttered to himself, "Something pushed the cave somewhere else, so where is the equal and opposite force?" He seemed to ask himself, "It's not like mother to be wrong about this stuff." He sighed.

***

The peak of the mountain was rather flat. Covered in snow that was more than deep enough to hide two or three dragons on top of one another. It was higher than any cloud would dare to reach. Within the snow, roofless channels made up the entire structure of the air dragon's fortress. With only one or two channels being accessible from the side of the mountain Cathie was on.

She slowly approached the nearest entrance with extreme caution. She kept herself small and fully covered in her white fur. Air dragons circled the perimeter, however as expected their attention was further down the mountain. She'd waited half a day after the storm had died down, which she now didn't regret.

Slow and small steps took her into the channel way and onto flat, shallow snow for once. The channels themselves offered no obvious cover, but air dragons were not known for walking. She kept low to the ground, trying her best to appear more as a loose pile of snow as air dragons shot through the channel above her at impressive speeds.

This place was known to be well guarded and impossible to sneak into, so the dragons above her weren't exactly looking out for something like a human, chances were from here on out she'd only have to deal with the odd guard here or there.

She did note the rather large number of dragons flying around, but almost none of them were on patrol routes. She watched three small children play in the skies above her for a few minutes before they moved on in laughter.

What caught her most off guard was the familiar sound of dragon tongue. A sound she would have thought she wouldn't hear ever again after Tom's potion. She'd heard it many times before, however it was impossible for the human throat to even come close to being able to speak such a language.

The dragons here must have been drinking from the water around them, the ice. A water source that wasn't affected by Tom's potion.

As she got further in, she noticed dragons leaving and entering holes dug out of the ice high up in the channels above her. Even dragons need somewhere to sleep during the night.

Suddenly, words she could recognise.

"I still don't quite understand how the thing works, but it does what was promised." The words shot through the air. She quickly located the dragon who was speaking such words and followed it with her eyes until it landed in a particular hole not too far from her.

"I get that it takes us from one place to another, but it does it in no time whatsoever. Are we sure we should trust such a thing?" Another dragon asked as it landed beside the first. She watched as they both walked deeper into the hole, out of sight.

She made sure to wait until it was clear before she attempted to climb up to the hole. As she did so she made sure to keep an eye out for passing dragons. When one eventually did pass, she made herself as flat as possible against the ice with the white fur. It didn't seem to notice her as it shot past.

A few minutes later and she was in the hole.

***

Tom knocked on Patrick's door. After a few seconds of shuffling sounds, Patrick opened it.

Almost immediately Tom noticed the poorly hidden packed bag under his bed.

"Figured you'd go after her." He sighed as he folded his arms in the doorway.

"I'm not going all the way, just close enough to help if I can." Patrick sighed.

"You aren't going to get close enough for that. Not without Cathie's expertise you aren't."

"You got a better idea?" Patrick asked him. Tom moved to the side to reveal the two pairs of wings resting in the corridor behind him, "They'd see that coming."

"They would, hence we only use them if she's in danger." He reminded him.

***

After slowly sneaking through some large icy doors, Cathie finally caught up with the two dragons that had entered the hole in the ice. She made sure she stuck to the edge of the room as she watched the two dragons' pace about the room.

A third dragon entered from another entrance.

"So, the tests with the cave were a complete success. However, the device was lost when it fell."

"The humans have it?"

"No, we suspect the earth dragons took it during their attack. In fact, we believe that was the exact reason for their rather bold declaration of war."

"Lucky we were given two then."

"How is the second device performing?"

"Using what we learnt from the first we're able to open a gateway from our current location to any other location within a few days flight. After that the range seems to destabilize the gateway and samples sent through don't come out the other side the right way."

"How bad are we talking?"

"What's usually inside the subject… stops being inside…"

"I think enough is said to get the picture."

"The new queen has ordered the device to be moved to her quarters for safe keeping. If another party has access to this wizardry then we could be attacked, even here."

As the dragon spoke those words, he turned to look at the table in the centre of the room. There sat what Cathie was looking for.

To her, it was nothing more than a block of metal, however to anyone who'd seen a pistol before would have recognised the shape.

"Extra security? Surely its safe enough here." One of the dragons protested.

"Clearly not, if a human can sneak in." Another dragon sighed as he turned to look directly at Cathie.

"Crap." She cursed under her breath as the three of them turned to face her.

"Perhaps the humans did take the device after all. That would explain how you got in here."

"And to think we use their language so that our own kind cannot spy on us here. Another error on our part." One of them sighed.

Cathie sprinted forwards and grabbed the device on the table. As she made for the door, she stuffed it in a pocket in her leather trousers underneath her armour.

Before she could make it to the door however, she was grabbed by a birdlike foot and slammed onto the ground.

"The device, human." The dragon asked her. Cathie quickly ditched the fur coat and slipped out of the dragon's grip. She reached the door and got through it before the others could grab her.

She continued to sprint towards the mouth of the hole. As she reached the edge she came to a stop as she prepared to start climbing.

A dragon shot from the hole and grabbed her by her arms as it did. She was lifted into the air very quickly. The dragon climbed higher and higher above the mountain peak.

"Hand it over, or I drop you." The dragon threatened as it finally levelled out. It now began to fly over the black mountain peaks. The endless desert was now under Cathie's feet, "Even if you survive the fall, you'll die out there."

"I reckon I could make it." Cathie responded to the dragon. The dragon seemed rather disappointed with her answer. Its talons let go of her.

***

Cathie woke up rather suddenly as sand blew into her face. She rolled over to look up at the sky. The air dragon above was circling her.

She knew that surviving such a fall without injury was impossible. Had the armour saved her? She couldn't feel much in the way of pain. Slowly she sat up, not because of any pain however, the armour's weight seemed to suddenly be a real problem for her to manage.

Had it gotten heavier? It must have. She checked to look for injuries, but she appeared to be completely fine. A change in the rhythmic flap of her attacker above alerted her to the fact that the dragon had noticed her survival.

She took a look at her surroundings, sand as far as the eye could see except for the large black cliff behind her. Sand, even worse than snow when battling an air dragon. She'd really done it now.

There were many things you just didn't do when fighting dragons. Fight an earth dragon in a cave, a fire dragon with explosives. When it came to air dragons there was only one rule. Never fight them when surrounded by sand.

The dragon came in for a swoop. It started its air breath early to pick up sand in the harsh breeze. As it flew above her, it intensified its breath massively.

The harsh blast of air was nothing compared to the skin shredding sand. Cathie used the armour on her arms to cover her face. However, the armour didn't cover everything. She felt her skin being shredded all over. When the attack died down, she noticed another dragon coming in for a second attack.

She also noticed that her armour had somehow gotten even heavier.

As the second dragon began to blow air to pick up sand, Cathie took the device out of her pocket and lifted it into the air. The dragon pulled off from the attack and landed in front of her.

"Big mistake." Cathie chuckled as she dropped the device onto the floor and punched the dragon right in its jaw. There was a sudden burst of power from Cathie's arm. The dragon's head came clean off its neck, producing a fountain of blue blood.

Suddenly she noticed that the armour on the arm she'd punched with no longer weighed her down. The rest of the armour was much heavier than usual, but she'd somehow gotten rid of the extra weight on that arm.

It finally clicked. The more damage the armour took, the heavier it got, but she could also release the damage back at them.

As the body fell to the floor, she caught sight of a formation of air dragons coming in for an attack.

A wooden canister dropped right by Cathie's feet. It quickly released a heavy cloud of smoke that ingulfed her.

"So much for slowing you down." Tom's voice sighed from beside her.

"The device is-"

"Don't worry, I got it." He interrupted as he tightened a strap around her from behind. She had the sudden feeling that she was about to take flight.

With a boom, the smoke cleared almost instantly, but Tom had already taken flight. A few seconds later and the two of them were already above the black peaks.

Patrick joined them in the air with the device strapped to him.

"Thanks for the rescue." Cathie thanked Tom, who was now above her. She was strapped tightly to him with nothing but the world below her.

"It's not over yet." Tom responded, "Those dragons can fly a long distance, while we used up two of four charges already." He revealed.

"I have an idea." Patrick began as he flew alongside them. He fumbled about with the device, but after a few seconds he pressed a single button. A small circle appeared in front of them. Like before it was mainly purple, with a darker purple swirl.

Before any of them could do anything, they flew through it.

***

Before they knew it, the three of them were underwater. It was a rather big shock to go from air to water in less than a second. It didn't help that none of them had taken a deep breath beforehand either.

There was no time to think. Tom quickly disconnected the wings from him and Cathie and quickly swam for the surface. Cathie was the first to the top shortly followed by Patrick, who had also ditched the weighty wings.

The rush of the water when they had come through the portal had snapped the many straps holding Cathie's armour together, it had sunk after she'd untangled herself from it.

Tom finally reached the surface with a big gulp of air as Cathie began to look around. The water was salty, but luckily land was nearby. The volcanic island of the fire dragons was just a few minutes swim away.

***

The warm air of the island did wonders to the three of them, who were slowly drying off from their swim.

They all took a few minutes to get over the shock they were all in before anything was said.

"That… That's certainly a way to get out of that." Cathie finally spoke.

"The hell did you do?" Tom asked Patrick. Patrick threw the wet metal device towards Tom. He caught it and immediately began looking at it.

"Pressed a few random buttons. Figured that if dragons could operate it, I'd stand a chance." Patrick responded.

"By the skin of your teeth you managed to input some co-ordinates. You're damn lucky we didn't end up inside a mountain." Tom explained as he continued his analysis of the device.

"Does it still work?" Cathie asked him.

"Not anymore, but the water damage is fixable given time." Tom replied.

"I'm guessing that getting the wings and armour back will be a pain in the ass." Patrick sighed as he looked out across the water.

"We might be able to ask the water dragons to get them." Tom muttered. His eyes solely fixed on the device.

"Not for the armour we won't. The water dragons wouldn't be able to lift it, I barely could." Cathie revealed. Tom looked up at her.

"It wasn't that heavy."

"Not at first, but the moment it saved me from that fall, it gained a lot of weight." Cathie revealed.

"It gained weight?" Patrick asked. He didn't seem to believe this.

"You didn't get any injuries from the fall, right?" Tom asked her. She looked at her own body. The backs of her legs had been viciously scratched from the sand, with only shreds of the leather trousers remaining. The same could be said for her arms.

"No, these are all from the sand." She answered.

"As I've mentioned before that back material absorbs energy in all forms. It must have absorbed the kinetic energy from your impact to save you." Tom explained.

"That doesn't explain the weight gain." Patrick pointed out.

"Oh, but it does. Where do you think that energy goes? It can't be created or destroyed, only converted." Tom lectured, "The extra weight was the material converting the energy into mass, just like the dragon crystals, only it seems to beef up its own density instead of just blasting it out."

"If it's going to gain weight with every hit you take, perhaps it's not the best material for armour." Patrick suggested.

"I disagree, because that's only the start of it, I was able to punch a dragon head clean off its neck with a single punch. After which I noticed that arm had lost the weight it had gained." Cathie explained. Tom smiled at this.

"You were able to release the stored-up energy?" He asked excitedly. Cathie nodded.

"Care to explain why this excites you so much?" Patrick asked him.

"This material is a natural battery." Tom answered, "Think about the glider boost system. It stores kinetic energy we provided by pulling the elastic back, then releases it on demand. See the similarities?"

"And that allowed me to punch really hard?" Cathie asked him.

"To a fraction of the force you would have experienced when you hit the ground without the armour." He answered, "This is amazing, not even my mother had the ability to manipulate energy like this." He added.

***

Despite the cold sea air of the night, Tom was rather warm where he sat. Upon a rock just up from the beach they had landed on. The rock, like the rest of the ground, was warm to the touch, but far enough from the volcano to not burn anything.

He was tinkering with the many complicated wires within the device. He noted the use of human letters and numbers for the labels of certain parts. As he suspected, a human had crafted the device.

It rather terrified him that someone out there seemed to know a lot more than he did. To add to that, they seemed to be helping the air dragons for whatever reason.

Things still didn't make sense, however. Golden wiring, perfectly formed metal. There were even circuit boards, something he'd only ever read about in his mothers' books. Vast amounts of industry were required to make such things. Industry they would have seen very easily during their search for other humans in the known world.

Two options. Either they lived outside the known world, or they have technology beyond his understanding that would help hide them. Both were quite likely given their capabilities. The air dragons would have been the perfect party given that their mountain lies very much on the northern edge of the known world, which supported the first theory.

The second theory wouldn't have made sense to pick the air dragons. If they could be hidden somewhere within the valleys, they would have most likely encountered the earth dragons the most. Even if they were for some reason limited to being near the air dragon mountain, the ice dragons would surely make a better ally, and given they own the northern area around that mountain for kilometres, not much further away.

From the outside world, the tall mountain would be very obvious, unlike the rest of the dragon homes. The first theory was making more and more sense. Until he remembered something.

The metal spider. He'd taken that thing apart quite a few times. Although they were for different functions, the designs were similar in technology.

The spider had been watching Cathie right outside the cave. Near the heart of the known world. If they could get their technology that far without being noticed by any other dragons, they could get anywhere.

Too many unknowns for his liking. He turned his attention back to the device in his hands. He quickly tied two more wires together before taking a look at the whole system. He had no idea how it operated, but the damage was nothing but a power issue, the thing powering it had discharged its energy through the salty water, but it seemed to still be generating it. A few replacement wires and it was good to go.

Regrettably Tom only had access to copper wires, of very poor quality, but only one or two needed replacing. He left the outer casing of the device open as he pointed it towards the water and pressed the trigger button.

He watched as power surged through his inferior wires and collected at a single point. Before anything else happened, Tom let go of the trigger. The whole thing quickly powered down.

He waited a few seconds for the power to die down before he began to dig through the many wires towards the point they were all converging.

Tom looked down at a small shard of the black material linked up to the wires. It was cut very precisely into a tiny donut shape.

"Energy goes in, matter comes out, right?" He asked himself. It didn't answer anything about how the device made those portals, but it was an interesting observation.

He charged up the device once more. This time with keen eyes on the black material ring. He realised his initial assessment of the device had been wrong. It wasn't sending power into the material; it was drawing it out.

Within the centre of the material, something was forming. Something he'd never seen before, "So the reverse. Draw energy out, suck matter in?" He asked himself. He shook his head, it was clearly forming something, but that didn't make sense.

Cathie's armour lost mass as it released the energy, this was somehow creating mass. The temptation to stick his hand inside was too great. As his hand neared, he found it being pulled into the device rather forcefully.

Whatever was forming inside the ring of black material began to spin. He felt the pull of the spin on his hand as he kept it a safe distance away.

The formed material shot forwards as a ring and out of the front of the device. The ring expanded and formed the purple portal just by the water's edge.

Tom could do nothing but laugh. This was something entirely new, something neither he nor his mother knew about.

"Having fun with that?" Cathie asked as she reached the top of the rock Tom had been sitting on. Tom turned his attention to her as the device powered down.

"This… This is far beyond my capabilities. I doubt my mother could craft such a thing." He told her. He turned back to it and pressed the trigger once more. The portal in front of them closed up.

"I'm sure you'll figure it out." She said with a smile as she curled up beside him. She rested her head on his lap.

Tom rested one hand on her as his attention was drawn to the top of the device. A set of numbers in bright green light. Three different numbers to be exact.

All three numbers were rather large, but he noticed the one labelled Y was negative. That probably explained the underwater experience they had earlier. The other two were labelled X and Z as expected. Co-ordinates. Presumably for the exit portal.

He turned his attention to the beach. Where the portal had formed earlier, there was a large puddle of salty water slowly draining back into the sea beyond. Water had come through it, which confirmed his theory.

The next question was, how smart were the people who made the device? Because Tom had the very big urge to set all three numbers to zero. If that brought him to their home, that would be something, but he feared that it wouldn't be that easy.

"We don't have a map somewhere, do we?" Tom asked Cathie.

"We have two of them back at the cave, remember?" Cathie reminded him. The two maps. One belonged to Tom and marked his parents' grave. The other belonged to Cathie and still had dried spots of her family's blood soaked into it, "Why?"

"I'll need one to work out how to accurately use this thing." He answered, "Need to match the numbers to the land."

"I'm sure we can ask Flame for help getting home once the sun rises."

"Somehow I doubt that this thing would ever leave this island if Flame learnt it was here." Tom sighed.

"Then we better get swimming then." Cathie chuckled. Tom gave a smile at the joke, "Patrick got us here with luck, I'm sure you can make one of those educated guesses of yours."

"If I assume the numbers are metres, I'm sure I could work out how to get us back onto the mainland. I wouldn't push it more than that though." Tom muttered.

"Sounds good enough to me. It's no more than a day's walk back from there." Tom pocketed the device and looked down at Cathie.

"We should rest up then. Long day tomorrow."

"I'm already half asleep."

Tom grabbed his bag from beside him and put it against the side of a larger rock behind him. After a small bit of repositioning, he laid back against the bag.

CHAPTER 22; EXPANDING HORIZONS

Tom knocked rather sheepishly on Patrick's door. Patrick opened it with some surprise.

"Thought you and Cathie were… In your room."

"She's fast asleep. However, I decided to try and get a head start on looking into the portal device, so… I think it's time." Tom responded.

"Time for what?"

"What we talked about when we first met."

"That desperate about the portal device hu?" Patrick chuckled.

"It's not just the portal device pushing me to consider this." Tom sighed, "You told me how you combined your magic with my mother's knowledge to save me."

"I take it you wish to do the reverse." Patrick sighed as he walked backwards into his room. He turned to face the shelf of books on the wall.

"More or less."

"Last time I asked you to consider my books you had a rather different view about them. I believe you used the words 'Worthless dribble' if I'm not mistaken." Patrick recalled as he took a particular book from the shelf. It was smaller than most of the others.

"Back then I believed I could explain anything given enough time. However, my failure to explain magic and this portal device has me working with things I may never be able to explain."

"Basic theory of magic." Patrick told him as he handed the book over to him, "Perhaps not as thorough as you'd like but, the closest you'll get to how it all works." Tom slowly reached for the book. As he took it Patrick felt the uncertainty in his grip.

"My mother's knowledge has carried me this far. Time to take a step into the unknown." Tom sighed as he took a closer look at the cover of the book.

"Let me know if it helps. Should you require more specialised books, I'd advise basic spells next, then you have the specific elemental spells. Avoid healing for now, even I have trouble with that one."

"Hopefully I'll learn something new. I'm sure I don't have to tell you that I'm not interested in actually learning how to do the spells."

"Something tells me that if you of all people try to, you'd get struck by lightning or something."

***

Tom quietly sat down at his desk. Cathie was fast asleep in his bed to the side of him.

He opened Patrick's book and began to read. Most of it was stuff Patrick had already told him about magic. The idea was to focus your mind in a very specific way. The whole fluff with the ingredients and magical circles and such was just to help get the mind to that particular point.

Three things seemed to be of significant importance. The shape, the ingredients and the actions of the caster.

Putting it into something Tom could visualise, the book used the fireball spell as a rather basic example.

The shape was the curved palm as if it were holding an invisible ball. The ingredients were the air around the hand and the action was the opening of the hand to that shape. There was a fourth thing, words. A particular set of words that bent the mind towards the right point of focus, however they were not necessary. To a trained magician, the words were nothing but a waste of time.

This he had known from Patrick's initial explanation. The trouble he had was how exactly the mind caused such things. However, this wasn't his focus right now. He shut his eyes and took a small breath as he brought himself to except that it just happens.

He then considered the portal device. He even looked over to the opened-up device on the desk beside the book.

The shape. The black material had been calved into a very specific shape for the purpose it was made for. The ingredient was the black material as well. The action was the removal of the energy stored inside the material.

Similar method but missing one key ingredient. The human mind.

Perhaps the human mind wasn't required. Perhaps magic really was just science that he'd never been aware of.

Tom opened his hand to the exact position stated in the book.

As expected, no flame produced itself. Clearly not the case then. He tried a few more times just to be sure, but after the first he knew that a flame wouldn't appear for the rest either, even with the incantation.

He'd once considered the similarities between magic and science. The only difference being the whole human mind explanation. Now more than ever he was sure that such an explanation was wrong. There had to be a different one that no one had thought of.

He shook his head; he was getting side-tracked.

The device didn't use a human mind, which put it on the science side of things. However, Tom felt that portals as a concept wasn't at all natural and defiantly fell on the magical side of things.

There was only one way to test.

He took out a small chunk of black material and hooked it up to a rather old looking brick. The brick had the word 'Battery' painted on the side.

The battery was dead. It had been for years. Without suitable manpower Tom was never able to come up with a method of charging it again.

He watched as energy from the material rushed out into the battery. He watched the black material do absolutely nothing. To make sure, Tom hooked the battery up to an old light bulb he'd taken out of his bag.

Another invention of his mothers. Electricity to light. A rather high effort way to light up a room just as much as a simple flame does. The only real use he'd ever found for it was to check for electricity.

The lightbulb shone.

Energy had transferred out of the material, but no portal was produced.

The only difference between his rig and the portal device was the shape of the material. Despite the clear amount of effort taken to achieve such a shape, Tom couldn't find any reason that the shape would work any better to any other shape.

This was suddenly starting to sound a lot like his investigation into magic again.

Either he was missing something, or the device was sitting slap bang in the middle of magic and science. Perhaps a combination of the two.

Yet as a child he'd been taught that magic was simply unknown science.

With another shake of his head, he turned back to the device. He continued to dig through more of its wires until he came across a broken one. One he'd clearly not noticed the last time he'd opened it up.

After patching it up with some more copper wire, Tom paid close attention to where the wire was going from and to.

It seemed to link to the power provider, but not to the rest of the systems. It ran off into a small boxed off compartment right on the other side of the device to where Tom had opened it up.

"Audio device restored." A non-human voice spoke from the device. Tom jumped out of his chair in surprise. Cathie jumped out of bed in confusion, after which she quickly covered herself up with the fur skin blanket.

"The hell?" Tom asked as he slowly approached the device.

"Fusion reaction stabilized. A.I. primary powerline restored, switching from backups to main power." The voice announced from the device. The voice was oddly artificial to the ear. It wasn't a mouth that was producing it, being human or otherwise, that was clear just from listening to how it spoke.

"Why is that thing talking?" Cathie asked Tom. Tom simply shrugged his shoulders.

"How should I know?"

"Foreign elements detected. Please note any unauthorised repair work not carried out by Weddar voids all warranty."

"There isn't a small person inside that thing is there?" Cathie asked him. Tom picked up the device and tried his best to examine the small box the mysterious wire had linked to.

"You, voice. Can you hear me?" Tom asked. Cathie quickly picked up her clothing from around the bed and got herself dressed before standing beside Tom.

"User detected. Hello Thomas Thomson."

"It knows you?" Cathie asked.

"What are you?" Tom asked.

"My name is Jordan. I am an A.I. tasked with operating this device." Jordan answered.

"What's an A.I.?" Tom asked it.

"A.I. stands for Artificial Intelligence."

"Artificial Intelligence." Tom muttered to himself. An intelligence built instead of born.

The missing link.

"Have I passed all of today's tests?" Jordan asked.

"Tests?"

"It is unlike you to ask such basic questions about myself."

"You've met me before?"

"You are Thomas Thomson. My creator." Jordan replied.

The room was silent for a few seconds as that sentence slowly ran through both of their heads.

"You created this thing?" Cathie asked him.

"I'm sure I'd remember creating a portal device." Tom answered, "Jordan?"

"Yes?"

"Tell me about your creator, Thomas Thomson."

"List of achievements include discovery of the Flipside, discovery of portal technology and discovery of alternate universes."

"Doesn't exactly sound like me." Tom sighed. He paid careful attention to the device once more. He'd have recognised his own handy work even amongst things he didn't understand. This wasn't it.

"Are you saying you are not Thomas Thomson?" Jordan asked.

"That is my name, but I have done nothing of what you speak of. In fact, I didn't even understand any of it besides the portal stuff."

"Please describe your current world situation. You're current technological advancements and such." Jordan requested.

"Recently made a form of travel by air. We live in caves, use fire for light. No manpower for any form of industry." Tom quickly summed up.

"Oh dear." Jordan sighed, "It appears I am not where I belong."

"That's certainly an understatement." Tom responded.

"You do however match perfectly with my creators voice. I therefore assume that you are this universes version of Thomas Thomson."

"I mean... sounds like this other me is much further ahead than I am."

"True, but of everyone here you're the best at science we have." Cathie reminded him.

Tom carefully examined the mysterious wire he'd just fixed. He noted that unlike the other wires, this one seemed to have been cut.

"My repairs made you able to communicate with us, right?"

"Please wait. Reconfiguring security and speech algorithms for your level of technology." There was silence for a few seconds, "There, you may ask your questions."

"The wire I fixed that woke you up, it was cut."

"Logging attempted sabotage. Main power was cut during hibernation mode, therefore unable to detect the cause. Please state all known events to do with me."

"We grabbed you from the air dragons and used you to escape them and get home."

"Air dragons? What is known of this faction or organisation?"

"It's not a faction. It's a race. Dragons which can breathe high pressure air." Tom revealed.

"I am not familiar with this creature. This seems to support the notion that I am not in my original universe."

"I assume you have no idea how you got here then."

"Inter-Universal travel is theoretically possible with a portal device like myself should the portal link be stabilised at such a range, but I'm talking a distance you wouldn't even be able to comprehend."

"Still. You did get here. I'm sure it goes without saying that I have no idea how something could travel between universes."

"Perhaps Edward is responsible. He is the only one in my universe who successfully linked a portal to another universe." Jordan wondered.

"That's probably the most likely explanation, but I'm afraid we don't have anything close to the technology this Edward seems to possess."

"Perhaps there is hope yet. One of my components originated from a universe dubbed Universe One. The black circle near the front of my frame."

"You're talking about the black material shaped in a ring?" Tom confirmed, "Yes, I was wondering how something was using a material I'd only recently discovered."

"Discovered? Thomas Thomson, are you telling me that this material is naturally found within this universe?" Jordan asked. Its voice had picked up a hopeful but that the same time worried tone.

"Yes, why?"

"Edward's research into other universes resources was immaculate. Even he could only locate one universe where this material existed. This must be Universe One."

"Is that a good thing or a bad thing?" Cathie asked.

"Good for me. Bad for you." Jordan replied.

"The metal spiders. Parts of your universe getting into ours." Tom realised.

"Scouts is perhaps the best explanation for them. Able to send visual and audio information back to whoever is controlling them." Jordan revealed.

"Spies in other words." Cathie sighed. Not all the words were making sense, but she was using the ones she did know to follow along.

"So this Edward is taking this back material from our universe to use in his own."

"And with technology that might as well be magic to us, they can take as much as they want without us even posing a threat to them." Patrick added as he walked over from Tom's door.

"How long have you been there?" Tom asked him as Patrick stood beside him.

"Missed the whole thing about how this thing is talking, but everything after that. I'm sure you can fill me in later." He answered as he gave Jordan a proper look.

"If they are harvesting this universe then it won't be long before they destroy it. The fact that you are not aware of this and have only seen the scouts so far means that they probably haven't begun mining in large quantities yet."

"Still checking the place out, taking a few samples." Tom assumed.

"Most likely checking out how much of a threat we are." Patrick added.

"One of them saw me kill it. They might have a read on my capabilities already." Cathie pointed out.

"Which is bad considering you're our main fighter." Tom sighed, "The better question is if they somehow cracked magic."

"Magic?" Jordan asked, "I am also not aware of such a thing outside of fictional stories."

"I'll take that as a no then."

"They might be aware of my capabilities though. At least the spells I've done out in the forest. Might need to learn a few new tricks should we face these people."

"But out of all of us Tom, you're perhaps the one they know the least about." Cathie pointed out, "Your inventions and solutions vary far and wide. I doubt they would have gotten the chance to read your mothers books."

"That's true. They are safely hidden away inside my bag."

"Either way, I don't like how many things we have to deal with now." Patrick sighed, "Humans from another universe, uniting the dragons. Hell Charlie still wants to kill us all."

"Three big problems." Tom muttered, "But now we have this thing we might be able to solve them faster."

"If you are referring to me then I'm afraid that won't be possible." Jordan announced, "Article Two of the AG-Project's Primitive Worlds Act states that I am not able to allow any form of life access to technology beyond their own level. Other than the fact that this is another universe rather than another planet, I see no reason to deviate from this rule."

"Care to explain what you mean?" Patrick asked it.

"Clearly the other me didn't want other, less developed; creatures being able to use this thing. Now Jordan is awake it won't let us use him." Tom simplified.

"Sounds like a lot of bullshit to me." Patrick muttered.

"Makes sense. The air dragons have already shown how Jordan can shift the natural balance of power. I assume the other version of me wants to avoid such things, with no exceptions."

"You would be correct." Jordan answered.

"A pain, but I can see the reason." Tom sighed, "The old-fashioned way it is then."

"Warning. Portal detected." Jordan suddenly announced.

"Where?" Tom asked.

"Location is far from here considering you'd most likely be walking." It answered.

"If it's another scout, then it won't be open for long." Tom pointed out, "Perhaps just this once you'll allow us a portal."

"Considering this might be my only way back, and that it doesn't benefit you… Very well." Jordan decided.

***

A hidden figure sat in a completely dark room, with the exception of the screen in front of him. He was watching a lapsed time footage of some sky. He watched as clouds rolled over and passed by. He waited just a little bit more before he paused the footage.

There, in one corner of the footage. Tom, Cathie and Patrick. Flying through the air on their wings, with the purple swirling portal ahead of them.

The figure got out of the chair it was sitting in.

"Portal technology." The figure spoke in a masculine voice.

"Indeed sir." A voice from the screen spoke.

"Have you analysed the readings?" He asked.

"The portal was perfectly stable." The voice responded. The figure leant over the screen to reveal his mouth, which was smiling, yet gave the impression of anger as well as joy.

"How the hell did a prehistoric world with only four humans develop portal technology better that we did?" He asked with gritted teeth.

"Does it matter sir? Surely this and the black material is reason enough to consider taking this world for ourselves."

"That would be an understatement. I want that portal technology. Once we obtain that, we won't have to travel through our highly volatile and unstable portals in order to invade."

"We wouldn't have to rely on drones either. We could send a small army through."

"That and maybe an armoured unit or three. The humans aren't big in number but by far the most dangerous part of this universe."

"I'm sure we could stomp them out with ease sir." The voice assured the figure. The figure pressed a few buttons and the screen zoomed into Tom's face.

"No. We can't. If he's anywhere near as good as his counterpart here, we wouldn't stand a chance."

"You're talking about that human as if he were an army all by himself."

"I take it you've never seen the face of Thomas Thomson." The figure sighed.

"Thomas Thomson, of the AG-Project? You can't be serious."

"Of all the humans in my way, it had to be another version of the biggest pain in my ass." The figure sighed, "To take this world, I'll need to outwit him for a second time."

CHAPTER 23; GONE

The three of them cautiously stepped out of the purple swirling portal. Patrick had gone first, shortly followed by Tom. Cathie came through last holding Jordan. The moment she was fully through, the portal closed behind them.

In front of them however was another portal. To one side, dense forest. To the other, a cliff edge. The cold ocean breeze hit them all like a wall. It was coming from the coast far off on the side of the cliff edge. The bottom of the cliff was the plains. A huge field of open ground. The only thing able to block one's view down there was the rather thin tall grass that came up to about waist height.

The only reasonably flat and clear area within the known world. Kilometres of grass and the occasional stream from the far away mountains. Beyond the plains was a large beach where the small streams linked up into the mouth of a large river that fed into the ocean.

Yet they weren't near the volcanic island of the fire dragons. That was much further up the coast.

Tom took a quick gander over the edge of the cliff. It was certainly high enough that such a fall would be fatal.

Up until now they hadn't been able to hunt in the plains. The journey around the cliff edge that surrounded most of the plains was far too great and time-consuming to be worth whatever game they could get and carry back.

Even with the wings, carrying the carcasses and hunting equipment wasn't really possible unless they killed things smaller than Tom's bag.

In the past many humans had hunted in the plains, but that was because they had the manpower to carry back enough to justify the long journey. Not even that lasted long however, because once the dragons figured out humans liked to hunt there, it was easy game for them too. No cover, limited escape, a death trap waiting to happen.

"Even my people stayed clear of this place." Patrick sighed as he looked out over the plains. Far off to their right was a waterfall that ran off the edge of the cliff and into a small lake bellow that seemed to supply all of the little streams.

That waterfall was connected to the lake Tom had originally poured that mysterious potion of his into. Most of the streams from the mountains fed into that one lake positioned pretty much where every valley met. The water then split up into the many different paths to the ocean.

"Cliff edge view. Access to flowing water and the safety of the dense forest for cover." Cathie listed, "The perfect place to set up a camp." She added.

Tom and Cathie both drew their bows towards the open portal. Patrick took out one of his many books and flicked to a new page. After less than a second of reading, he looked back up at the portal, ready for whatever would come through.

After a few seconds, something did in fact come through. However, it wasn't what any of them expected. A single pencil came through and landed on the floor in front of Tom. Tom quickly picked it up and gave it a good look over.

"Precisely cut wood. Not charcoal based either. Signs of batch production, not very high quality considering the technology involved." He analysed.

"But perhaps a little bit too high quality for us, right?" Cathie asked him.

"For sure." Tom answered as he redrew his bow after shoving the pencil into his pocket.

"I'm detecting an extremely powerful magnetic field." Jordan announced.

"How powerful are we talking?" Tom asked him, "Because the most powerful I've seen could only lift a small shard of metal."

"I'm talking universal scale here. The magnetic field seems to be linking both ends of the portal from one universe to another. Fascinating."

"Thought those magnets of yours could only pull shit if it was very close to it." Patrick pointed out.

"Clearly we're dealing with something a little stronger than my rock collection." Tom responded.

"Guys. We're being watched." Cathie suddenly revealed. She changed the direction of her bow towards the forest. Before the other two could react, a large boulder of a tail swung right at them.

Cathie was directly in the path of the tail, but she was too busy aiming at the dragon to notice it coming in from the side of her. Luckily Tom had spotted it before the dragon itself. He grabbed her and yanked her out of the way just in time, throwing her into Patrick's book as he did so.

Cathie watched as the tail narrowly missed her. However, before she could tell what was happening next, her vision was blocked by a purple swearing object.

She landed in someone's arms as she watched the portal that she'd just been knocked through close behind her.

"Whoah!" A voice exclaimed from behind her. Clearly, she'd taken whoever had stopped her by surprise.

Cathie quickly patted herself down. No Jordan. It must have been knocked from her belt. The other side of the portal. Enemy territory. Without further hesitation she had spun quickly around and thrown a punch.

To her surprise, Tom's face flashed before her eyes before she could land the blow. She stopped her fist just before hitting his face. He seemed different, wearing a long white coat, black trousers and shoes that seemed to be a masterpiece of leatherwork. He was also rather alarmed at the act of violence aimed towards him.

"Tom?"

"You... know my name?" He responded. He seemed to cower at the sight of her fist still lingering in the air.

"Where am I?" Cathie asked as she began to take in her surroundings. Behind her was what appeared to be a large mechanical object, but it had apparently melted rather badly just a few seconds ago. The rest of the room was white in colour and completely empty. The walls were perfectly flat, with light coming out of a select few squares on the roof.

There was one, very well-made door that seemed to be the only exit from wherever she was.

"You… came through a purple thing." Tom answered as he raised his hands in surrender.

"The portal. Who opened it?" She demanded.

"Well… Us, I think. Not really sure."

"How can you not be sure about opening a portal?"

"We were testing our new super magnet. That thing behind you. Something went wrong and suddenly that purple thing, a portal, right? That thing appeared out of nowhere."

"You didn't happen to throw a pencil through it did you?" She asked as she lowered her fist.

"Out of curiosity, yes I did." He answered as he seemed to relax. It had taken her a while to notice, but this Tom's eyes weren't yellow. They were blue. Clearly this wasn't her Tom, "Did it come out the other side?" He asked. A look of curiosity on his face that she oddly recognised.

"Where is this place?" She asked.

"City Eight." He answered, "Where did you come from?"

"Cliff edge above the plains. But something tells me you won't know where that is as much as I didn't understand your answer."

"Perhaps if I show you on a map. I'm rather curious to know where that portal came out at."

"It won't be on any of your maps. Tell me, you ever seen a dragon?"

"In pictures and books, sure."

"I meant seen it with your own eyes. Do they exist in this world?" She asked him rather impatiently.

"Of course not. Creatures of fiction." He answered.

"As I thought. This is going to sound crazy to you, but I come from a place where they are very much a reality, and I need to get back there."

***

Tom and Patrick could do nothing but watch as Cathie fell into the portal. Shortly afterwards, it closed.

Suddenly both of their faces turned serious. Before Tom had even properly gained his footing from his sidestep, he pointed his bow towards the large earth dragon the tail was attached to.

He watched as his arrows glowed bright orange. He released his bow, not really having time to properly aim.

Ten holes littered the earth dragon's body as it fell to the ground dead.

Tom frantically looked around for Jordan, Cathie's only hope now.

A metal spider had grabbed it. Before Tom could even react, the spider vanished through a rather unstable looking version of a portal that only stayed open for a split second.

Just as the unstable portal for the spider closed with it on the other side, a fireball hit the ground right where it was.

Tom took a breath before looking up at Patrick. Bookless and bleeding through the nose, he looked to be in a rather bad condition, but yet had thrown the fireball in desperation anyway.

"I've never seen glowing orange arrows before." Tom finally spoke as he caught Patrick just before he collapsed, "I know you have a spell to increase the speed of my arrows, but what you did there was on a whole other level."

"I'll explain later." Patrick muttered between bloody cough and blackout. He was eventually out cold.

CHAPTER 24; AMY

Patrick's eyes opened to the bright sky above. He took a few seconds before he tried to sit up. When he did, he found Tom frantically fiddling with a battery and wire.

He was busy connecting it to a small chunk of black material he'd just pulled from his bag. After waiting a few seconds, he seemed rather pissed off that nothing had happened.

He kicked his set-up with frustration before he noticed that Patrick had sat up.

"Are you ok?" Tom asked him.

"Are you?" He responded.

"Trying to recreate the portal device." Tom sighed, "With no success."

"Is there no other way to get her back?" He asked as he slowly struggled to stand. Tom walked over and helped him to his feet.

"Not that I know of. I've got a few more ideas to try out before I call it a lost cause though."

"Anything I can help with?"

"Not with the amount of blood you've lost, no." Tom sighed as he sat him down on a nearby fallen log. Patrick glanced over at the dead earth dragon body, or what was left of it.

Impressive work on his part, despite the repercussions.

"Quite the impressive feat." A voice spoke from behind him. Patrick turned to face a tall man dressed in a very high-quality orange suit and tie.

Patrick looked between him and Tom, who was apparently taking no notice of the strange figure, "Only you can see me right now." The man explained.

"Who are you?" Patrick asked.

"Nothing but a dream as far as your concerned. I was rather impressed by how you wielded that power of yours."

"Are you talking about my magic?"

"Magic in this world is a small and unfocused variant of the true power wielded by me. Here I thought I was alone in being able to wield such power, yet you just used it, although you suffered for it as expected, a human body wouldn't be able to handle so much power for long."

"You're talking about my orange magic, right?"

"Is that they name you've given it?" The man chuckled, "I'll admit, rather crude, but as a human you wouldn't have any understand of any dimension higher than the fourth at best."

"I've been able to increase the power of my magic by turning it orange ever since I was a kid. The orange mage was my title in my clan."

"A clan of mages, yes I'm aware. Regrettably I was preoccupied among the many different instances you pulled off your little tricks, but now that I've seen it with my own eyes…"

"What is this power I apparently have?" Patrick asked him. The man gave a small smile.

"I'm afraid you'll never quite reach my level of power. A simple matter of you being human I'm afraid, but with practice you might be able to wield it to greater effect than before, and with fewer consequences should your body get used to the power."

"The mages taught me only to use such a power in times of desperation."

"Of course they did, because they didn't understand it. They barely understood their own power." The man chuckled. Patrick turned to look at Tom before turning back to the man.

"If magic is just a weak form of the true power I possess, and that power comes from you, Tom really doesn't stand a chance of explaining it, does he?"

"Thomas Thomson. An odd character, I'll give him that. Slightly more interesting than most humans, but at most, entertainment to me. Given enough time he might eventually discover who his mother really was, perhaps even begin to discover the other dimensional gods, but not with the human lifespan he has."

"What does his mother have to do with your power?" Patrick asked him. The man gave another smile.

"Keep things interesting for me, will you? You've drawn my attention to this universe, and I'm in need of something to kill the long eons." He spoke as an orange portal appeared behind him.

He stepped backwards thought the portal, but for some reason it felt more like the entire world moved forwards, including the portal, to him.

Patrick turned to check back on Tom. He'd pulled his special knife out and had begun to calve at the chunk of black material.

A few minutes later and he held a ring of the black material. He connected it up to the battery and waited. Yet again nothing happened.

"Fuck." He cursed under his breath.

"Any reason you'd think that would work?" Patrick asked him.

"Jordan's design was like that. I'm still missing something though." He sighed, "The device required a mind to operate, like how a spell requires a mind to be cast. Jordan was an artificial mind made compatible with the device so that science and magic could merge but I wouldn't even know where to start to build an A.I."

"How about a mind already used to casting spells?" Patrick asked him.

"Judging from your state, whatever you did to my arrows took a lot out of you. I doubt you can focus enough for that now that the adrenaline has worn off."

Patrick slowly got to his feet and walked over to Tom.

"Even if we build a rig capable of that, even after I've recovered, how are we going to open a portal to somewhere we don't know?" Patrick asked him.

"One problem at a time." Tom answered as he took apart the components. He packed them up into his bag and slung it over his shoulder. He then helped support Patrick, "We should get you back to the cave."

"Wish we had that thing working now, right?" Patrick chuckled.

There was a strong breeze as a purple portal ripped itself open in front of the two of them.

A flash of red hair, and Patrick suddenly found himself on his back. He blinked a few times to get the face above him into focus.

Red hair, but it wasn't Cathie. The girl seemed to gently smile at him as she lifted her body off his.

"Sorry about that." She apologised as she helped him to his feet.

Another flash of red hair and Cathie came shooting through the portal at full running pace. She just about made it thought as the portal quickly snapped shut.

In less than a blink, Tom found himself in her arms.

"We made it." She sighed as she gave Tom a kiss on the cheek.

"And you are?" Patrick asked the girl beside him. She was wearing a rather odd material Patrick had never seen before. Tight blue trousers that seemed to fit her perfectly, along with a grey top that seemed designed to reveal just the right amount of chest.

"Amy. Amy Thomson." She answered.

"Amy what?" Tom asked the moment her last name washed past his ears.

"Long story." Cathie sighed.

***

Cathie sat down at the table in the main area of the cave beside Amy, who was trying to get comfortable on the wooden furniture. Patrick and Tom sat on the other side of the table, eagerly awaiting some much-needed answers.

"The portal I was pushed through led to another universe, just like Jordan said. There I met Thomas, their universes equivalent of you." She began as she looked at Tom.

"I'm very confused. Is Amy his child then?" Patrick asked. Tom looked at Cathie with the exact same question on his mind. Cathie coughed.

"No." she answered, "She's ours."

"So you two…?"

"The night before I asked for your books." Tom sighed, "Didn't expect it to happen on the first try though."

"You and me both." Cathie sighed.

"I'm right here you know." Amy reminded them.

"Care to explain how our daughter looks the same age as the rest of us?" Tom asked.

"She's seventeen, because that's how many years it took your counterpart to help me get back here." Cathie revealed.

"Yet you haven't aged one bit." Patrick noted.

"Oh, right. You were normal the last time these guys saw you." Amy realised. Cathie gave another sigh.

"Not exactly sure what happened, but it had something to do with the magic book that passed through the portal with me. Something about it caused me to become… invulnerable." She explained. She took out a knife and poked her hand with it rather forcefully.

Tom watched the blade flex instead of puncturing her skin, "Apparently I don't age either."

"That's… do you mind?" Tom asked as he reached for the knife. She handed it to him and watched as he prodded her hand further with it, "Do you feel it?"

"I feel the blade. No pain though." She answered.

"My books are crafted from magically produced paper." Patrick remembered.

"Any reason they didn't like regular paper?" Amy asked him.

"I think it was more the fact that they could." Patrick answered.

"But there is more." Cathie continued, "Those spider things, the work of Weddar, a company in the other universe that has recently unlocked portal technology. A few days before we left, we found out that the head, Edward, had gotten his hands on Jordan."

"Yes, those spiders snatched it and closed the portal before we could get you back." Tom sighed.

"Up until now he's only been able to send those spider things through, but now that he has access to stable portal technology, he can safely bring anything through, including weapons."

"Weapons from a universe with portal technology." Tom sighed, "I can't even imagine their destructive capabilities."

"Problem is that Edward has seen first-hand what that black material stuff can do, and this is apparently the only universe he's found it existing in." Amy added.

"So he wants to get his hands on it." Patrick realised.

"He'd turn this entire world into one big mine if he could." Cathie sighed, "And with a constant supply of that stuff, he'd be unstoppable in his universe as well. Something I promised Thomas I wouldn't let happen." Cathie revealed.

"So, we have an army we have no hopes of being able to stop coming here, they could appear anywhere, and our only allies are a bunch of divided dragons." Tom summarised.

"Any idea how long we have?" Patrick asked.

"Portals between the two universes are very random. We used Thomas' magnetic field accident to pinpoint the moment I left to some degree, but Edward doesn't know about that. He's been watching and collecting samples from this universe for about twenty years now, but he didn't get his hands on Jordan until very recently, it took him a long time to get a portal to coincide with a good moment to snatch it."

"We'll have to rely on probability then. The longer we wait, the more probable it is for him to appear with his army, which means we need to be quick."

"Quick with what?" Patrick asked Tom.

"Uniting the dragons." He answered with a small smile.

***

Tom and Cathie eventually disappeared into Tom's room to have a more personal chat. This left Amy and Patrick rather silently sitting either side of the table.

After a few minutes of silence Amy seemed to remember something. She dove into a small satchel on her belt and brought out an old and slightly battered book.

"I believe this belongs to you." She added as she placed it on the table in front of him. His magic book on speed and accuracy. A special form of magic designed to be used with a bow. He'd brought it along with him since both Tom and Cathie had been using bows. It made sense to boost their attacks while relying on memorised spells for his own offence and defence, "Quite the read."

"You've read it?" He asked her.

"Many of those spells have saved my life a number of times."

"You learnt the spells?"

"Every last one." She answered. He gave her another look over and realised she didn't have a bow on her.

"So Cathie taught you to shoot a bow?"

"And swing a sword. Didn't exactly inherit her monster strength though so I prefer the bow."

"Did you leave it behind in the other universe?"

"The journey back was rather a close call. Edward was hot on our heels. Had to drop everything and run. Mum even dropped her sword."

"A sword forged with technology. Can't even imagine such a thing, let alone a bow."

"She taught me to use a rather primitive design just in case."

"In which case we should have the stuff to make you one somewhere." He revealed as he stood up from the table. He quietly snuck into Cathie's room and came out a few seconds later with a bow, "Turns out your mother has a few of these in there. I'm sure she wouldn't mind." He added as he handed her the bow.

"I was wondering if you could teach me more spells. I was kind of limited to one book." She asked him. Patrick gestured that she should follow him as he began to walk towards his room. She followed him inside to see him picking a few books off his shelf.

"None of the typical magic types work well with weapons and those that do usually specialise to one. If you want to keep to the bow for now, I'd advise starting with illusion." He explained as he handed her a book, "Should you need more I have a book of sword magic. Once offered it to your mother, but she wasn't interested in it."

"I was thinking that any spells that you could link to objects might help. I'd be able to attach nasty tricks to an arrow."

"Certainly, a rather creative use." Patrick responded as he began to search his shelf. He pulled out another book and handed it to her, "Totem and doll magic. I'd stick to the totem half and use the arrows like disposable totems. The doll side is a little creepy for my taste and mainly involves linking a living thing to an object instead of a spell."

"I know so many people who would level cities just to get their hands on these books. Just make sure Edward doesn't get his hands on these either."

"Do they not have magic over there either?"

"Magic certainly works over there, but no one seems to know about it. It's why I was careful enough to bring the book back."

"Good call. I can only imagine what magic would do to a world populated by humans that don't understand it. Anyway, want me to help teach all that?"

"It would certainly make a change from having to figure out the theory from a book." She answered with a smile.

***

Meanwhile, in Tom's room.

Cathie stood in silence as she watched Tom quickly drop his act and instead begin to take in exactly what had happened.

He took a deep breath as he brought both of his hands to either side of his head. He then breathed out rather heavily, trying his best to comprehend the current situation.

"This is a lot." He sighed as his hands naturally dropped to his side. He slowly turned to face her.

"I know." She quietly responded as her eyes looked down at the floor. Her arms were folded around her tummy, trying to make herself as ball like as possible while standing.

"Seventeen years." He mumbled, "You're almost double the age you were. In that time you've probably become a completely different person to the one I knew."

"I'm not even sure myself." She muttered as she slowly took a few steps towards him. Both of her hands slowly unwrapped to take each of his, "But the way I see you is the same."

"I'd only just figured out how I saw you… Now it seems I need to start all over again." He responded. She slowly nodded.

"You need time." She understood.

"Yeah. Time to work everything out. With you… with the stranger out there that is my daughter…"

***

Outside the cave Patrick and Amy kept to the small clear area between the cave entrance and the treeline to the forest beyond, or what was left of it.

Patrick eyed up the arrow in his hand. It had taken Amy less than a minute to fashion a quiverful from their raw materials, and with such high quality. If he hadn't watched Tom craft arrows, he wouldn't have believed such a thing was possible.

He placed two fingers on the tip of the arrow. He then made a V shape with the same two fingers, forming a triangle between his fingers and the arrow shaft.

Amy watched as a glass like barrier formed around the arrowhead.

"Triangle is the shape of strength and structure. All barrier spells require some form of it." He explained. He removed his finger and the barrier shattered, "The strength of the triangle feeds the strength of the barrier. Without the triangle, the barrier simply has no strength and collapses."

"I've never formed a barrier before."

"It's a basic spell but very adaptable. Figured you wouldn't know it since you skipped straight into the more advanced stuff."

"So how do I keep the triangle then?" She asked him.

"Depends on the situation. Normally I use these." He answered as he took out a small wooden chip. It was calved into a rough triangle, "Small and compact, usually does the job."

"Usually?"

"The bigger the triangle, the stronger the barrier. If you want to stop a dragon in its tracks, you'll need a bigger source of strength." He answered. He drew a triangle with his foot. In front of the two of them, another barrier formed.

This one held strong even when Patrick removed his foot.

"But you seem to have less control on where the barrier forms." Amy noticed. She was right, the barrier had formed right on the opposite side of the triangle to Patrick.

"That would normally be true, but you can change that with totem magic." Patrick revealed. He scuffed the triangle on the floor and took three arrows from Amy's quiver.

He walked forwards a few paces and stuck the three arrows in a triangle shape around a stray log. He walked back over to Amy and then drew the same triangle.

Amy watched as barriers surrounded the log, supported at each corner by the arrows Patrick had placed.

"You made a triangle to form them in. Why the need for the triangle on the floor here then?" Amy asked him.

"Those arrows lie inside the barrier. They are necessary to form the barrier to begin with but if you use this triangle outside to fuel its strength, the thing you're trying to trap can't break out from within." Patrick explained, "Unless they somehow reach this triangle here, they'd be completely stuck inside."

"So you can have more than one triangle?"

"You can have as many as you like. The arrows don't even need to be in a triangular shape for the formation either. You can use two to make a plane or one to make a pole around the arrow. Just make sure you draw this triangle last and focus on that instead of the arrows."

"Why the sudden interest in barriers?" Amy asked him.

"Because barriers are the keystone to illusion magic." Patrick answered, "Your basic barrier doesn't let anything but light pass through it, but you can make it do the opposite, even manipulate the light inside if you form the correct shape."

"How so?" She asked him. Patrick took another arrow and held it in his hands. This time he calved a small triangle onto the shaft, he drew a line from the top point down through the middle of it. She watched as the arrow vanished from sight.

"It's still there, you just can't see it." Patrick revealed as he handed her the arrow. She took it in her own hands with amazement.

"So this is illusion magic."

"Whatever you draw that shape on will vanish, but only for one pair of eyes. I chose yours in this case, because I had direct line of sight to them. Things might not be so easy in the heat of battle."

"So I can only hide things from one person in particular?"

"Illusion magic can be powerful but also has its limitations. Some creative thinking and problem solving is required to fully master it, but you seem to be good at both."

Amy's head suddenly snapped towards one direction.

"We're being watched." She muttered. She'd been fast to notice. Faster than Patrick had. It made him question just how rough her life had been in the other universe to be so cautious.

"Just as observant as Cathie. You look similar to her as well. A lost sister perhaps?" Charlie's voice chuckled from the treeline. The sun was just about shining above the treeline. It was getting late. It wouldn't be long until sunset.

"You've got some nerve coming to our front door." Patrick responded. His eyes hadn't found Charlie yet, which was rather a serious problem.

A sword smacked against a magical shield to Patrick's side. Amy looked down to notice Patrick had drawn a triangle at his feet but had also used the treeline as a line to form a sheet of barrier.

"Annoying as ever I see." Charlie sighed as he vanished back into the treeline.

"Guess I still have a way to go." Amy commented as she loaded an arrow into her bow.

"The key to magic is all in the mind. If you can picture the shape, it's already there." Patrick advised with a slight smile. He started drawing lines in the surrounding dirt with his foot.

"Piercing Light." Amy muttered as she released an arrow. It shot right through Patrick's barrier and into the dark treeline. The arrow then shone incredibly bright. Movement, only for a second but enough to see where Charlie was heading. He'd moved to the side to get around the barrier.

He charged out of the treeline knowing his position had been revealed. At first, he hit a second barrier but then began to skilfully evade Patrick's set up.

"I appreciate the lesson on barriers, although if memory serves you used a different shape to trap me for so very long." Charlie grumbled as he got within striking distance of Patrick.

A sword came at him, but Patrick side stepped it and slapped the back of the blade down into the ground. The tip of the blade buried itself right in the centre of one of Patrick's triangles.

"The diamond shape is more advanced and even more adaptable than the triangle, but the triangle isn't specific to barriers, if you must know." Patrick explained. Charlie's sword shattered to pieces as the triangle glowed red.

"That bastard of a spell again." Charlie fumed as he brought out another sword from the many that were sheathed on his back. He noted that one of the swords was the one he'd made for Cathie.

"Crumble." Amy muttered as she fired a shot on Charlie. It hit him right in the chest but didn't seem to harm him. He gave a small smile.

"I came looking to pick a fight with Tom. Arrows aren't going to work on me I'm afraid." He chuckled. His amusement was cut short however as he looked down at his chest. The metal plate he'd had under his clothes began to crumble to dust.

"That armour just saved your life. But I doubt it would protect you from a second shot." Amy explained as she began to load another arrow into her bow.

"It seems I greatly underestimated who was the real threat here." Charlie mumbled through gritted teeth.

He began to make his way towards Amy, but Patrick's foot quickly tripped him up.

"Bitten off more than you can chew old friend." Patrick taunted. Charlie quickly took out a small dagger and seemed to attach its base to the base of his sword.

"I don't think you understand my capabilities."

Within a blink of an eye Charlie was back on his feet and slashing at Patrick. With no time for a barrier, Patrick did his best to dodge, but the blade caught his waist ever so slightly. A shallow cut but painful, nonetheless.

A second attack, before Patrick had even fully comprehended the first. Before Charlie could make contact however, he quickly turned and deflected an arrow aimed at the back of his head.

Patrick used this opportunity to grab Charlie by the back of the neck. However, just as he got his grip, Charlie was no longer there.

He was now holding a blade against Amy's throat. Patrick quickly clapped his hands together and twisted his palms 180 degrees while staring into Amy's eyes.

Charlie found himself suddenly staring at Amy, while holding his sword blade at Patrick's throat. He noticed Patrick moving his foot. He quickly let go of him as a barrier formed between the two of them.

"I've been memorising a lot more spells since our last encounter. Ones specifically designed to keep Cathie safe. If you're going to deal with anyone first, it's me." Patrick growled at him.

"You may be a pain in the ass, but it seems I won't have to deal with you for long." Charlie chuckled as he pointed to Patrick's face. Patrick realised his nose was bleeding.

It seems he hadn't fully recovered from using his orange magic from earlier. That and the excessive use now were only making things worse for him.

"I'll stay in your way as long as I have to." Patrick spat back. Despite his words he could feel his legs weakening. His eyes only closed for a second but when they were open, he was already on the ground.

"Guess even you have your limit." Charlie sighed as he placed Cathie's sword down beside him. There were a few more arrow shots but eventually Amy came into view of him with a blade against her neck once more.

"Let me go!" She shouted as she began to struggle, but Charlie quickly tightened his grip on her.

"Tell Tom that if he doesn't face me out in the torn-up forest over there by sunrise, I'll kill the new girl."

With that, Patrick's eyes shut once more.

CHAPTER 25; SOMEONE'S GOING TO DIE

"Patrick?" Cathie's voice rang though his ears as his eyes slowly opened. Half covered in mud; he was being lifted off the ground. It was raining now, any longer, and he might have drowned given how heavy the rain was.

"Thought you said Charlie had your sword." Tom spoke as he handed her sword to her. She made sure it still interacted with the bracelet on her arm while supporting Patrick with the other.

"He did. Patrick's been cut by a sword."

"He took Amy." Patrick managed to push out of his bloodied lips, "Said he'd kill her if Tom didn't fight him."

"Seems he still believes the lie I told him." Cathie sighed.

"Guess we don't have much of a choice now. We have to deal with him."

"He harms so much as a hair of hers, I'll kill him myself." She harshly growled.

"How are we doing this then?" Tom asked, "We try to play by his rules or go full force?"

"He can't take both of us at full strength." Cathie answered. Tom nodded before he took a good look at Patrick.

"Afraid you aren't exactly in fighting shape."

"I can walk. I might only have a spell or two left in me, but you might need it." Patrick responded as he just about managed to stand on his own two feet.

"Let's get going then."

***

Charlie was standing out in the open. The forest surrounding him had been all but flattened by the battle of the ice cave.

Amy was tied up to a single surviving tree off in the distance. Suspiciously far away from both Charlie and the treeline that the three of them were waiting at.

Tom held out his hand to the other two before they advanced any further.

"Something's wrong." He muttered. He focused on Amy, only to realise that she hadn't been tied up.

She was instead being held to the tree by the sword through her gut. She was still alive, but she'd already lost a lot of blood.

"Bastard!" Cathie yelled as she charged forwards into the opening. Tom instead turned to Patrick.

"It'll take both of us to keep him occupied. Think you can get to her?"

"No problem." Patrick answered as he prepared his legs for a lot of pain. With a nod from Tom, the two of them ran out into the clearing.

Under the trees they had been well sheltered, but the heavy rain now pounded against their skin and tore through their clothes.

Tom came to a stop and began to load his arrows into his bow while Patrick circled around Cathie and Charlie towards Amy.

Cathie and Charlie's swords clashed. Almost instantly Charlie had side stepped and began to slash at Cathie's side. Cathie took the hit without any attempt to move out of the way. Charlie's blade slashed across her skin, cutting her clothes, but nothing more than that.

Charlie ducked as Cathie's elbow came hurtling towards his face. He unleashed another slash on her, and another before she could regain her balance for another attack. The heavy sword in one hand was certainly slowing her attacks, but he couldn't afford to get hit with any of them.

Yet again his blade cut nothing but cloth and leather. Her knee landed in his chest rather suddenly. He keeled over onto the wet floor.

He quickly rolled as her sword came crashing down. Chunks of dirt flew all over the place as the sword connected with the ground. The fine dirt mixed in with the rain.

He got to his feet, but Cathie was already swinging another attack. She seemed to be getting much better at balancing her weight. He ducked under her side slash and tried to tackle her by the waist.

She didn't seem to budge even a little. Had she gained weight? She felt more like an immovable mountain than a person despite the sodden ground at her feet. Her free hand grabbed his drenched top and lifted him into the air.

Charlie used his feet to quickly push off her chest and launch himself away from her. With a rather stylish backflip, he landed out of her arm reach with a loud muddy squelch.

As he noticed Patrick, he began to make a break for him. As he did so, two arrows pierced through the rain to hit him right in the back. The arrows had pierced his metal armour.

He pulled the two arrows out to see that the arrow tips seemed to be dissolving in his own blood.

"Your fight was with me, remember?" Tom taunted him as he replaced the two missing arrows in his bow. Since it had five strings, two arrows per string, Tom was able to release the whole ten, or five shots of two arrows.

Clearly, he wasn't going for the kill, that was Cathie's job, but he was harassing from afar. With no cover his only protection was being close to Cathie, but that was even more dangerous.

Tom was stopping him get to Patrick, that much was clear. If he wanted to stop Patrick reaching Amy he had to deal with Cathie and Tom quickly.

He connected his sword to the small dagger he took from his belt. Almost immediately he was right in front of Tom. Tom panicked and quickly released all ten arrows right into Charlie's unprotected chest.

Before Charlie could recover, he heard the sound of Cathie's blade moving through the rain at great speed behind him. He moved his sword to his side to block the side attack, but the sheer momentum of the attack threw him completely off his feet and into the air for a few seconds before crashing back down onto the muddy floor.

"The weight behind that attack... the sword I made wasn't that heavy." Charlie noted as he got back onto his feet. The rain made it hard to stand, like a constant force pushing down, trying to hold him to the ground.

"Every time you strike me, I gain weight. Makes things easier to control this huge blade, and I can put more behind it." Cathie explained as she got within striking distance. She went for a vertical strike, so he moved to the side just in time to get hit by two more arrows right in his chest. Two more landed the other side of Cathie.

No matter which way he'd dodged he would have been hit. Tom had another three shots provided Charlie didn't let him reload. That enough was challenging to deal with, but with the weight of Cathie's brutal and relentless attacks he couldn't exactly do anything but play right into Tom's hands.

Forget defeating those two, he'd be lucky to get out of this alive. With another blink he was at the treeline and running off into the darkness, but Cathie was hot on his heels.

Tom looked towards Amy; Patrick had reached her. He'd be able to help her, but they couldn't afford Charlie getting away now, they had far too many other problems to deal with. He followed Cathie in the chase.

Patrick brought himself to a dizzy stop as he reached Amy. He just about stopped himself from vomiting as he got onto his knees and focused on her.

"Patrick?" She asked in a weak and fading voice. Her eyes were slowly closing. Patrick took a good look at the sword pinning her to the tree. She was bleeding very badly, but removing the sword may upright kill her, "Thank…you." She muttered just as her eyes completely closed.

Her breathing stopped. He quickly checked for a pulse, but there wasn't one to be found. The life in her cheeks slowly faded away. Her spark seemingly washed away with the large heavy droplets splashing over the both of them.

Patrick slammed his fist against the tree in frustration, causing more large droplets to fall.

"Fuck!" He shouted as he slammed his fist a few more times.

An idea suddenly popped into his head. It was a dangerous, desperate idea, but the only one he currently had.

He slammed his hand against the tree one more time, but this time with his wet and bloody palm open. He kept it there as he dipped his free hand in her blood. He covered both of his arms and his chest in excess before he grabbed the sword. He pulled it out, threw it aside and placed his hand against the wound.

It was nothing new. The tree had life, she didn't. Perhaps he could change that.

He imagined the two circles of life. Amy's was completely still while the tree's seemed to slowly rotate.

"How very annoying." A voice boomed from behind him.

The rain stopped.

Patrick suddenly found himself in a white void. The tree and Amy's body were still there, but nothing else was. He turned to see a black robed figure holding a scythe, "First you delay one of my appointments by a few years, next you try to stand in my way." The figure boomed.

"You've come for her, haven't you?" Patrick asked the figure.

"My scythe is the only thing capable of separating the life from the body." The figure revealed as he held the scythe pointing towards Patrick.

"You separate the circles of life from the bodies. Guess that's why this requires a fresh dead body normally." Patrick realised as he stood up to face the figure, "I'd advise not stopping me from getting her back."

"Love is perhaps the most annoying trait you humans possess. Makes you do stupid things like trying to defy that which is set in stone."

"Depending on the stone, depending on the chisel, it's not impossible to re-write."

"I will not ask a second time. Move aside and let me do my job."

"No!" He defiantly shouted, "I'm bringing her back."

"You really think such a thing is possible?" The figure laughed, "Look at the circle you're trying to fuel hers with. It's barely spinning. Trees don't have as much life force as a human, not even close."

"Then I'll have to use my own."

"You'd be dead before you completed the spell. By all means go ahead, I'd rather take two at the same time than have to collect you at a later date."

"Then that leaves me with only one option." Patrick sighed as he turned back to look at Amy, "I'll have to magnify my magic."

"A power as perthitic as human magic doesn't have that kind of power." The figure continued to chuckle, "You've had your chance." He added as he raised his scythe.

It was now or never. Patrick cast the spell. He focused on the tree's spinning circle and brought it to a complete stop. It slowly melted into the blood pathway painted across his body.

His entire body then began to glow bright orange.

Reality seemed to warp out of shape to make way for the man in the orange suit.

"You're messing with the natural order of things. It won't end well."

"So, my power is enough." Patrick realised. The man gave a sigh and then a shrug.

"Don't say I didn't warn you though." He sighed as he turned and walked into an already open orange portal.

"Impossible…" The black robed figure muttered, "That was Will."

"So, his name's Will. Glad to finally know that." Patrick noted as he continued to fill the excess life force in him with his power.

"That orange glow…" The black robed figure stepped back, seemingly in fear. He then quickly vanished into thin air.

The ground began to violently shake. Patrick found the rest of the world had returned. He completely shut his eyes and forced every bit of excess life force out of him and into Amy's body.

Amy's body glowed pure orange as the pool of blood around her evaporated. The wound closed up and her eyes shot open.

However, Patrick's eyes slowly shut as the tree behind her turned to dust.

***

Within this world are many different forms of danger. Dragons, creatures of the night, the world itself. Yet there was one thing that would terrify any creature within this world the moment they grasped just how in danger they were.

Dragons relied on their strength, size and ability to fly to ambush and overpower their prey. Other predators countered this by adopting pack hunting in numbers you wouldn't dream of fighting. All except the humans.

Humans hunted together in many cases in the past, but not because of the protection. As their numbers dwindled it was normal for most hunters to hunt alone.

To the rest of the world, there was nothing more dangerous than an expert hunter that had caught your trail. Despite being only a single human, their intelligence saw through almost every attempt to escape. Dragons regularly took flight or dug away in those situations, which is why humans always aimed for the wings first.

This tactic ensured that eventually the creature would be forced to fight the human. Alone, most creatures of this world wouldn't stand a chance using this tactic. Which is why only the lost, separated or slow creatures ever fell prey to such a tactic. With no pack, a simple easy kill.

It was safe to say at that point in time there was no better hunter among the humans than Cathie. To make matters worse… her prey had harmed her daughter.

Riddled with arrow wounds, some of which he was still pulling the arrows out of, not to mention the bruises and cuts he got from being thrown about, Charlie was slowly running out of stamina.

The only thing keeping his legs going were the terrifying sounds of heavy but fast footsteps only a few trees behind him. Footsteps that shook Charlie to his very core. Footsteps that drowned out the beat of his own heart at full pace and only ever continued to increase in volume.

This was it. The most terrifying situation any living thing could possibly be in. Running for their life against the unstoppable force that was Catahyme Clawson.

Hunters had to be fast to keep up with their prey. They needed to be able to track while at full sprint and maintain the pace for hours without rest.

There was no outrunning her, there was no out pacing her. She seemed determined to catch him, which left him only with the option to fight.

The sky had cleared, much to his surprise. The moon had risen above the treeline. He hadn't even noticed the sun set during his panic. It was a moon roughly the shape of a thin fingernail clipping, barely any moonlight to speak of.

If Tom was following as well, he'd have a harder time keeping him pinned. However, chances were that he'd trust Cathie to deal with him while he instead used his knowledge to save the girl.

If it was just Cathie following, he might have a chance. A gamble, but it was all he had now.

He looped around a tree and drew his sword as he charged towards Cathie.

Burning red eyes. Surrounded by drenched and wild flowing hair that stuck to her wet face that separated one red from another.

Charlie changed his mind. The very sight before him, despite him only seeing it for less than a second, was by far the new most terrifying thing in this world.

The sword's clashed, but Charlie's snapped in half as Cathie's large sword and speed ploughed through him.

He looked down at the hilt of her sword, flush with his gut. He could feel the heavy weight of the rest of the blade behind him.

"I never had a chance with you, did I?" He chuckled to himself as he leant on a nearby tree. He placed one of his hands on her sword to try and hold it in.

"The moment you harmed my daughter was the moment your death was decided." She hissed at him. She pulled the whole blade right out of him. Blood poured out at a rate Charlie had no hope of surviving.

"Daughter?" He asked as he dropped to his knees.

She quickly slashed her sword one more time. Charlie's head hit a nearby tree and bounced onto the floor, painting blood everywhere.

His body collapsed in front of her, spraying blood all over her and the surrounding forest, "The voices will keep trying to kill him." Charlie spoke.

Cathie was rather horrified to see a severed head speak, but his face quickly became lifeless and still. She leant on one of the nearby trees with minimal blood spatter and threw up.

Killing animals was very different to killing your own kind. She tried flicking her sword to remove the blood, but it barely got rid of it all.

"Did you lose him?" Tom asked as he came to a stop. He was rather out of breath from the running, but it didn't take him long to realise the scene he'd come across, "Are you alright?" He asked as he placed a hand on her shoulder.

She gave a nod as more vomit came up.

"A little more brutal than I intended." She added as she stood up straight.

"Let's go check up on Amy then."

***

The two of them quickly ran back to the flattened forest. It took some time before they noticed Patrick laid on the floor. The tree that Amy had been up against had disappeared, but so had Amy.

"The hell did he do?" Tom asked as he examined cracks in the ground surrounding the area. It seemed like some form of earthquake had happened, but only at this specific area.

"Tracks, looks like something left here at an insane speed." Cathie added as she pointed out a trail of trodden on leaves. There were no clearly defined footprints and the leaves seemed to have been burnt in places, "How is he looking?"

"Not good. I'll have to take him back to the cave to do anything for him."

"What about Amy?"

"Either Patrick healed her and got her to run very fast with a spell, or something very fast took her. Either way we probably won't be able to find her with that kind of travelling speed."

"You're saying we've lost her?" She worried. Tom could clearly see the concern on her face.

"I seem to remember Patrick having a locating spell. Didn't work for any of us for some reason but we could try using it once he's better. Either way we can't cover that kind of ground without the help of magic or a dragon."

"Where the hell is Frost when you need him." She muttered as she began nervously rubbing her thumbs and fingers together. Tom quickly grabbed a hold of them and looked her in the eyes.

"We'll find her. It'll just take some time." Cathie took a few seconds to take it in, but she eventually nodded.

CHAPTER 26; COST

Tom sat down with two cups of water at the table in the main area of the cave. Cathie was already sat beside him. She'd changed from the higher quality clothes she'd come out of the portal with to her normal, now sleeveless outfit. He watched her slowly drag a small knife across her perfectly clear right arm.

"You'd think not being able to be cut would be a good thing." She sighed as she dropped the knife on the table. Her hands were shaking quite badly, "Seventeen years of not being able to do it really didn't go very well."

"As much as I'd love to present you with a solution, I'd need to know a lot more about what caused the whole thing in order to reverse it." He responded as he took one of her hands with his own and pushed a cup full of water into the other. The shaking died down as she drank the whole cup in one big gulp.

"I've been through so much to keep that girl safe. Stuff you wouldn't even believe possible. Hell I barely do, and I did them. Seventeen years and I thought I'd raised her to be ready for this world without the brutal methods my parents used on me. She didn't even last a whole day."

"No one can be prepared for this world." Tom responded as he hugged her, "Even with all the knowledge my parents possessed, when I was left to fend for myself it took me a whole month to master the skills required to make a fire." He revealed, "I survived so long because I learnt from the many experiences of this world. I'm certain the rest could be said for us all."

"Then she was fucked from the start. I shouldn't have brought her here."

"From everything you've told me so far, I don't think she would have been safe in either world. At least here we know more, we're better at being able to protect her from the dangers of this world than the other one."

"I… I need to find her. I can't wait for Patrick to recover." She muttered as she put the cup down and got to her feet. She grabbed Charlie's sword, still covered in blood, and headed for the door.

Tom gently grabbed her arm. She turned to face him, tears flowing down her cheeks, "She's our baby girl, I…"

"I know." He sighed as he handed her his bag, "You'll last longer out there with this." He added. She took it with a smile before hugging him tightly, "Now go bring our daughter home."

***

Patrick woke up in his bed. Almost instantly he got to his feet. He felt rather good considering how far he'd pushed himself.

"Finally up?" Tom asked from a chair in the corner of his room.

"Watching me sleep?" He asked as he grabbed some clothes and got dressed.

"Starting to worry that you'd never wake up again."

"How long have I been asleep?"

"A week or so."

"A week!?" Patrick exclaimed, "Is Amy ok?"

"Don't know. Can't find her." Tom answered in a tone that suggested that he was waiting for answers to questions he hadn't asked yet.

"Did Charlie get her again?"

"Charlie's dead."

"So why is she missing?"

"No idea. I was hoping you would know. Care to explain exactly what happened."

"You wouldn't believe me."

"I'm a nineteen-year-old dad with a seventeen-year-old daughter. Try me." Tom seemed to snap as he folded his arms.

"When I got to her, she was pretty much almost gone. I watched the life drain from her." Tom leant forwards at this.

"Are you telling me my daughters dead?" For once Patrick couldn't actually tell what Tom's face was showing. He feared it was anger, hoped it was grief.

"I tried something rather reckless. I used my magic to try and bring her back. Used up the life force of the tree and amplified it, so it would be enough to get her back."

"I wasn't aware magic could bring people back from the dead."

"It can't, until now. Like I said I tried something reckless, something never done before."

"Did it work then."

"I swear I saw her eyes open before I lost consciousness." Tom leant back in his chair. A brief moment of relief seemed to wash over him.

"So, it was Amy's tracks that we found then." Tom sighed, "Yet the tracks suggest that she was moving at insane speeds. Charred a few leaves on the forest floor kind of speeds."

"I wouldn't have a clue about any side effects of what I tried."

"Do you have any spells capable of locating her."

"I… I…" Patrick thought about this for a moment, "I have one, but not sure if I'll be able to pull it off."

"A difficult spell?" Tom asked.

"More like the conditions might not be up to the spells standards." Patrick walked over to his bookshelf and brought out a book with a love heart shape on it.

"Love spells?" Tom asked him as he opened the book up to a particular page.

"Spells are able to run along certain connections we humans possess, given that it's all in the mind." He began to explain, "Certain spells can target certain things or people depending on your connection to them. The only connection strong enough to get a location is love."

"You got a thing for my daughter?" Patrick got the sudden sense that Tom's tone had quickly switched to overly protective. Something he'd never pictured Tom capable of.

"It's not like we've spent much time together, barely even a day. Still… I do find myself staring at her a lot."

"What do you need for the spell?"

"A lot. Blood. A relative's blood would work better, so I'd suggest yours given Cathie can't bleed anymore. A bunch of different and rare chemicals as well."

"You got a list?" Patrick handed Tom the book and pointed him to the ingredients section of the page. He seemed to understand them all, "Some of these I'll have to make up. Of course, it doesn't give a specific concentration but the more potent the better I'm guessing."

"Apparently you combine them all to make up this liquid here."

"What do you know, some actual chemistry." Tom chucked as he read further down the page, "Why the hell would you need a solution like that?"

"Pretty sure that's your department."

"Not my fault these things are nothing but rubbish cooking instructions. Mages really need to take a page out of the scientific method when it comes to writing shit down." He grumbled, but Patrick could see the smile on his face. He was certainly beginning to enjoy the challenge.

"I've noticed the highly advanced spells require a lot more scientific knowledge than my clan taught. Perhaps it was a mistake limiting you to the basic books."

"I'll have it ready in a few hours, assuming I don't fuck up."

"Do you ever?" Patrick asked him as Tom began to walk out of the room. Tom gave another small smile.

"Constantly." He answered as he left, shutting the door behind him.

***

Tom walked out of the front door of the cave holding a glass beaker filled to the brim with a clear liquid.

He found Patrick drawing shapes with his foot in the dirt between the cave entrance and the treeline.

"This seems more complex than most other shape requirements." Tom pointed out. Patrick had drawn a series of complex shapes that each differed greatly. He brought his foot to a stop as he completed whatever he was drawing.

The shapes were around a circle, which Patrick now stepped inside. Above the shapes was another circle between them and the untouched dirt beyond.

"Love spells require a lot of complex conditions. The state of mind I need to focus on has an even smaller margin for error than normal." He responded as he opened his magic book. He began double-checking the various shapes.

"It seems more like you're mixing and matching shapes. Care to explain how all these get you in the right mind set?" Tom asked him.

"This set up isn't just a shape. It's a poem. A love poem." Patrick revealed.

"I don't recognise the language."

"That's because it isn't a language. Shapes represent certain aspects when spells are concerned. Put those aspects in a certain order, and you've got yourself a sentence."

"I've never seen your spells require most of these shapes."

"I have many books, many spells. You make the stuff I need?" Tom nodded and handed Patrick the beaker.

"Now what?" Tom asked him as he inspected the beaker.

"The container will get in the way." Patrick sighed, "Never used a spell to meet the conditions of another spell but…" He moved his hand in a wave like motion. He then lowered the beaker, but the liquid didn't follow it down.

Patrick handed Tom the empty beaker as the liquid floated in front of him.

"Neat trick you have there. Could have told me you could do something like that, would save me a tonne of glassware usage."

"Don't take this the wrong way but mixing science and magic doesn't really sit right in my stomach that well. Especially since our scientific secrets are now privy to dragon kind."

"You may have a point." Tom sighed.

"Where is Cathie?" Patrick asked as he closed his book.

"Out there, looking for her."

"You may want to get your medicines in order." He muttered with a sigh.

"You think Amy might be hurt?"

"Won't know until I find her."

"Then I better come with you. I can patch any wounds up until we get her back here."

"No need. I've memorised a few basic healing spells. They'll do a better job than you out there, but if it's something serious I need you waiting here ready to deal with it. Might as well play to our strengths."

"And Cathie?"

"It'll take forever to find her. Hopefully we can present her with something other than a dead body when she returns."

Patrick closed his eyes and quietly began to mutter to himself. Tom watched as the more wave like shapes within the two circles began to glow bright orange.

The liquid in front of Patrick suddenly engulfed him. Tom's eyes opened wide with panic.

"Patrick! That shits incredibly acidic!" He protested as he tried to enter the circle. An invisible barrier blocked his path. Tom looked down to see a triangle just the other side of the circle. He looked back at Patrick, who had a slight smirk on his face.

Suddenly the many shapes which seemed to be hands with varying numbers of fingers and thumbs began to glow orange. The liquid around Patrick set ablaze.

The flames began to form a neat ring around him. At first Patrick's skin was riddled with chemical and heat burns, but then the more circular shapes began to glow orange. Tom calmed down once he noticed Patrick seemed completely unharmed after a while, but blood had been added to the ring of fire now.

A fiery hand appeared in front of Tom. A small pebble floated into its grip and instantly sharpened to a point as the various triangular and hexagonal shapes began to glow. Tom remembered that Patrick also needed some of his blood.

He pricked his finger against the point. The blood seemed to float out of his hand at an alarming rate at first, but it quickly stopped once he'd given enough. His blood joined the fiery ring as well now, which now formed an orange cloud around Patrick.

Finally, the final set of shapes lit up. This time they seemed to be different variations of love hearts, sometimes a combination of a few. The ring distorted. Suddenly there was an arrow pointing out of the swirling orange glow that surrounded Patrick at a now comfortable distance from him.

"I'll bring her back, no matter what."

***

A week earlier…

Amy's eyes forcefully shot open. She hadn't been the one to make it happen though. She watched in horror as a blood covered Patrick collapsed in front of her.

She'd died. She was sure of it. She'd felt herself go. It wasn't exactly a feeling she could mistake for anything else. She was back somehow. Had Patrick done something? Given his state, he must have.

She reached her hand out to check if he was alright, but it came to a stop suddenly. The smell of blood had hit her. It was a smell like no other, and it was strong.

It wasn't the smell that had stopped her, however. It was the feeling she got from smelling it. The same feeling one would get when smelling a fresh loaf of bread straight from the oven.

Something was wrong. She quickly got to her feet and backed away. She could feel an urge. An urge to kill. An urge to kill Patrick.

She turned and began to run before she did anything she'd regret.

Trees, branches, nothing but a blur. This wasn't even her top speed, nowhere near.

She came to a stop. She wasn't out of breath. In fact, she wasn't breathing in the first place.

She placed one hand on the closest tree for a few seconds. The feeling of the bark, its texture, it seemed to keep her tethered to reality.

The taste of blood filled her mouth all of a sudden, and she quickly threw up a few mouthfuls of blood onto the grass below.

The smell of blood hit her nose instantly. Her sense of smell was much better than before.

She turned away from the blood stain. She heard a slight movement in the trees above, and the beating of a heart.

It wasn't a human heart; it was much smaller. She sped up into the branches and grabbed the squirrel.

The small creature squirmed and wriggled in an attempt to escape her grip. After a few seconds, it resorted to biting at her hand.

She felt the pain as the squirrel's teeth sunk into her skin, but it didn't bother her.

"Pain means a lot less when you die." She muttered as she increased her grip on it.

She watched as the squirrel slowly suffocated as its lungs collapsed from the pressure. Once it finally stopped moving, she brought it up to her mouth.

Two fangs grew out of her normal set of teeth and sunk into the squirrel's body.

***

The feeling of an undead feeding off a living body is one that cannot be described with words from any kind of language. However, someone very close to me once tried to describe it as best as she could.

It's sort of like the warm feeling you get when you eat your favourite food, mixed with intense pleasure and satisfaction that cannot be beaten by any other experience. If you are human, then you will also experience horror and disgust at the same time as these other feelings, and some may even go as far as fear for both themselves and of the living beings around them.

I was also told that although it gets better over time, it doesn't get that much better. The first time is the worse, but not by much, and the added memory as you continue to do this to survive drills a hole right through whatever morals and respect for life you once had.

As human beings we handle this burden rather poorly, it is very possible that this will break you, which will tend to happen more for those who value life a lot more, or have a fear or reaction to the sight, smell or texture of blood.

This can sometimes lead to suicide, and in fact many end up crossing that line no matter which way they take it. If you find some way of avoiding this fate, you will instead learn to disregard life. The lives of your friends, family, loved ones, all become worthless to you as your mind adapts to be able to take lives without a care in the world.

The moral of this small section is that there is a price for a second chance, and you won't know the full extent until you pay it yourself, but take it from me, from what I have seen, it really isn't worth it.

***

The dried-up corpse of the squirrel dropped to the forest floor.

Amy's bloodied hands reached for her mouth, where her fingers began to feel her own teeth. No fangs, but they had definitely been there before.

She looked down at her blood covered hands. She could feel it dripping down the side of her mouth as well, slowly reaching the tip of her chin as it began to drip off her face.

The taste was intoxicating. She spent a few minutes simply getting over the pleasure of it. The rush that instantly became addictive. She needed more.

Just as Amy managed to climb down from the tree, she got a sharp pain in her stomach. She quickly threw up what she assumed was her last normal meal all over the trunk.

She made sure all of it was out before she wiped her mouth with her bloody hands.

"Not great." She muttered to herself as she realised how messy she was.

The blood had already dried, but she cleaned the vomit off with a few leaves before she began to walk in a completely random direction.

She was deep in the forest now, with no idea which direction home was, although at the moment she was quite thankful of that.

She had a hunger to deal with, one that she wouldn't satisfy with just squirrels.

***

From a small, shady cave, Amy watched the last of the sunlight slowly vanish behind the horizon. Somehow once the last of the light vanished from sight, she seemed to be able to see better than she had during the day.

She was hungry. Starving. She needed something big to eat. She closed her eyes and focused on the surrounding sounds.

Heartbeats of all kinds. Many different rhythms, some big, most small. Her ears seemed to lock onto a pack of heartbeats. They'd kept themselves low and quiet up until now, but now they were keeping just out of her sight.

"Mother taught me about you lot." She muttered with a smile, "You've already figured out how good my hearing is haven't you?" She chuckled. With a bit of focus, her eyes began to spot the odd wild cat creatures that had craftily surrounded her, "You were waiting until I went to sleep."

She was answered with a chorus of growls. They knew they'd been spotted now, but there was enough of them around to take on a whole group of humans.

The first wave charged forwards towards her at lightning speed. Yet before they even left the treeline, they all collapsed to the floor dead.

The remaining beasts stared at Amy, who was standing at the mouth of her small cave with a pile of still beating hearts in her arms. She took one and bit into it. The others could do nothing but watch as she slowly sucked the blood out of each heart.

There wasn't enough to feed her. Both the beasts and Amy knew that. She was doing it for show, to teach these creatures that they weren't the top predator out here anymore.

CHAPTER 27; THE WILDERNESS

A now freshly clean Amy walked out of the now red river. She watched the washed off blood travel downstream and eventually disappear around a meander as she grabbed her clothes from the nearby bush that she'd hidden them in.

Before putting them on she carefully moved into a patch of sunlight. Her skin quickly turned red, so she jumped back into the shade. The sunlight seemed to set her skin ablaze every time she entered it now. It hurt, but for a short bit of time it was a neat trick to get dry quickly.

She watched her skin quickly heal as she began to get dressed. It had taken quite some time to find a river deep enough to wash in while having a shaded patch for her to keep to, but it was nice to not have the constant stench of dried blood around her.

Within a blur she was at the mouth of a cave a kilometre away. Deep in the heart of Death Valley, it wasn't a particularly big cave, but the best she could find for now.

Despite being rather cramped for even a single person, it had its perks. She looked down at the two cat-like creatures in front of her. They had their snouts to the ground with a freshly killed deer.

Amy gave them a nod, picked up the dead animal with a single hand and walked past them into the cave. The moment she passed them; they both ran as fast as possible away from the cave.

Amy carefully put down the deer inside the cave. She really didn't want to get blood all over herself just after cleaning herself. It had taken forever to get the blood out of her clothes, some dried stains still remained.

It hadn't exactly been her idea to receive such offers from the previous rulers of this valley, but after seeing what she was capable of doing they seemed very eager to buy her kindness.

It wasn't a bad deal. Free food to not kill the lot of them. Now she was wondering how to drink the blood without causing a huge mess.

Her fangs were sharp and precise, but not much could be said for the rest of her teeth. She had a bad habit of trying to bite with full force, but before she'd been ravenously hungry.

With a quick and precise bite to the beasts neck she found it rather easy to drink the blood without any spillage. It took a lot longer for her to completely drain the body, but that made sense considering she was only making two small holes to drink from instead of ripping half the neck off.

She found herself preferring this method even more now that she could take her time to slowly enjoy every single drop.

By the time she was done the sun was beginning to set. She didn't have too much of a problem moving about in the thick forest during the day, but she was pretty much trapped in it until night fell.

She waited a little longer so that the sun dipped below the horizon before she left. The deer had been a nice meal, but she was already craving the next.

She'd spent an entire week living off what the creatures had brought her, but now she was itching to stretch her own legs. She hadn't even come close to seeing how fast she could move, nor come across anything she couldn't lift with ease.

She pointed herself towards the sea. If she ended up going too far, she didn't risk slamming into a mountain or something. She made sure she stuck close to the winding river so that she avoided any risk of hitting trees.

Once again, she became a blur as she sped off at full speed. She suddenly came to a stop, however. The ground was no longer at her feet, but a long way beneath her. As she began to fall, she looked behind her. A cliff edge. She'd run off a cliff.

She landed rather heavily on the open plains. She certainly felt the pain that time, but after a few minutes her legs seemed to recover from it rather well.

***

As Patrick continued his journey, the love heart arrow suddenly completely changed direction. Tom had mentioned something being able to move at a great speed. It seemed to either be Amy herself, or something that had her.

He quickly changed direction as he headed towards the direction of the plains.

***

Most of the creatures nearby had scarpered. Spooked by her sudden landing. One however instead seemed to get closer.

Amy could hear its heartbeat, its footsteps, but for some reason she couldn't see it.

Whatever it was, it suddenly pounced at great speed towards her. She quickly sped to the side a short distance. Grass and dirt were thrown into the air from where she had previously stood.

"So you can sense me." A voice chuckled. The heartbeat had moved too fast for her to realise it was now behind her.

She turned around, but there was nothing. The heartbeat was still very much there though.

Slowly, a creature began to appear as if from thin air. A pitch-black dragon with a huge, teeth filled grin, which was less than an arm's length from her.

"My mother taught me all about the dragons of this world. She never mentioned a black one."

"You speak of the humans, who know almost nothing about anything." The dragon chuckled, "And you seem surprised to find a gap in their knowledge."

"What are you? No dragon I've heard of could match my speed."

"Perhaps the better question is, what are you?" The dragon responded, "The look of a human, but the smell of a predator almost as strong as I."

"I'm still trying to figure that out myself."

"I'm rather curious to see what your capable of." The dragon spoke as it seemed to vanish into thin air. He also seemed to be slowly backing away from her, "You might even prove yourself worthy of surviving my presence."

Amy quickly sped off to the side once more. This time the heartbeat hadn't even alerted her to the attack, her reaction seemed to be purely instinct. Once more the attack landed where she'd been less than a second ago.

A creature who can hide from sight even on the open plains. A creature that can attack at speeds too fast for her to detect. Was it in her capabilities to defend herself from such a beast? She didn't want to find out.

She sped off in a completely random direction, only to hit an invisible wall, "You can't run from me, little girl." The dragon's voice chuckled.

It hadn't been a wall she'd run into; it was the dragon.

Her new speed and strength were seemingly easy for this dragon to counter, but she wasn't limited to her newest bag of tricks. As she stumbled backwards, she managed to roughly draw a triangle in the dirt with one of her heels before she regained her balance and sped off in the opposite direction of the dragon.

She watched the barrier shatter and dirt around it fly into the air as if something big had just fallen over. Unfortunately, she hadn't been paying attention to the direction she was headed in. She turned her head just in time to see the cliff face in front of her.

After trying her best to slow down, Amy managed to only make a small human shaped hole in the cliff edge. She quickly composed herself as her wounds from the sharp rocky edge began to heal. Whatever time she'd bought herself with that barrier she'd wasted. She'd also managed to corner herself.

The dragon was visible now that it was covered in a layer of dirt, but that didn't stop it charging towards her at full speed.

Before Amy could even react, the dragon seemed to violently change course. As the side of the dragon revealed itself, a single cat like creature had gone claws first at its side. She watched as its sharp claws pierced the dragon's thick skin and drew blood.

The dragon rolled to get the creature off it, but the creature had known better and withdrew from its attack before it was even in danger.

She watched the creature run over to her. It presented the object which had been sitting in its mouth. A bow. Her bow, to be precise.

Amy could smell Charlie's blood all over it. The wood and rope had both been drenched red, presumably by laying in a puddle of blood. She found it rather worrying that she knew the blood was Charlie's.

She cautiously took the bow from the creature. The moment she did, it turned and began to growl at the recovering dragon.

The dragon got back to its feet and slowly began to walk towards them, "How very annoying." It boomed, "I'm aware you think you stand a chance little beast, since your kind specialise in killing dragons, but I don't see your pack, nor am I your typical dragon."

"Can you get me something sharp?" Amy asked the creature as she gave her bow a test pull. With no response, the creature charged forwards towards the dragon.

Amy could do nothing but watch as the dragon seemed to release an attack from its mouth. The creature quickly changed its pace, hopping side to side with each stride. The attack missed but threw up a cloud of dirt between Amy and the other two.

There was a growl as the dirt settled. The creature had bitten the dragon's front paw. The dragon lifted its paw up and shook it violently. The creature was flung back towards Amy. It rolled as it landed, but quickly got back on its feet beside her.

Amy suddenly found a dragon claw in her hand. Forced into her grip by the creatures bloodied mouth. It had bitten a claw off the dragon.

Initially she'd wanted to be able to build an arrow. The task would have been difficult, and she would have had to have done it fast while the creature distracted the dragon, but this was much better. She slung her bow over her torso and held the freshly bitten off claw like a small sword.

She watched the dragon's eyes widen as he noticed the sword stance she'd taken.

"Red hair, sword and monstrous strength." The dragon listed, "I did not realise I was facing the fabled Catahyme Clawson." It added as it bowed its head.

"Clawson? You know one of my family?" Amy asked him.

"I see, not Catahyme herself but a close relative. The red hair alone should have told me you were at least a Clawson." The dragon sighed, "This is what I get for being curious. Messing with a key player of the continuum."

"Afraid you aren't making much sense to me. I recognise the name Clawson but not the first. I'm also sure that none of my family have ever come across a dragon like you." The dragon simply chuckled at this statement as it shook the dirt off its skin and began to vanish into thin air.

"No. Not for a while anyway." It added before completely disappearing.

It's heartbeat quickly vanished. Had it found a way to completely hide from her? A few minutes passed with the two of them on edge. The creature beside her then began to relax, realising that the dragon had fled.

The plains seemed to return to normal. The frightened animals slowly returned with time but kept their distance from the two of them.

The creature began to rub its side against Amy's leg, and began to purr.

"Don't you have a pack to be with?" She asked the creature with curiosity as to why it was here of all places. They were far from the valley of death. On top of that, it had found her bow for her.

The creature nudged its head against the tip of her bow and made a sniffing sound. It had tracked her scent down from the bow. Impressive considering that it had been drenched in another human's blood.

She then noticed three scars on one of its back legs. Claw marks. Made by its kind. Cuts made to cut tendons. It had been left for dead by whatever pack it had been part of. Clearly it had no intention of re-joining them.

Up until now no human or dragon had really managed to get a very good look at one of these creatures. They were almost always hidden or moving at great speed, normally with sharp teeth and claws pointed right at you. Not exactly an ideal time to take a good look at what the creature's appearance actually was other than how many teeth and claws it had.

Built like a cheetah. The cat like creature had eyes that shone with intellect. Biologically designed to be a solo hunter, but with the brains to be able to work together instead of fighting its own kind. A creature to be rivalled by no other, although it didn't seem as scary now that it was curling around her legs and continuing to purr.

Its sleek grey fur was smooth to the touch, but she could feel the almost armour like skin underneath anytime it put just a bit too much weight into its rub, "I guess since you helped me out back there, I can let you tag along."

The creature seemed satisfied with this answer. It stopped begging and simply lay on the grass by her feet. It certainly behaved like a cat. Something told her it wouldn't have the loyalty of a dog, but it seemed to like her enough to keep her alive.

It began to lick at the blood on its two front paws. The blue dragon blood was neatly cleaned up. It then began to tidy the blood around its mouth as well, "So what do I call you then?" She asked it. The creature seemed to look up at her rather blankly.

Clearly the idea of a name was more of a human or dragon thing. The fact that it seemed to understand what she was saying was rather impressive. It's ears quickly pricked up as an animal wondered just a little bit too close to them. It seemed to track it with its eyes even through the long grass until the animal had realised its mistake and fled to the safety of the other side of the plains.

She had to call it something, but she had the feeling it wouldn't appreciate the tamed pet names that she'd brought to mind from her experience in the other universe. One word sprung to mind. She'd heard it before, from the other Tom's mouth. He never did explain what it meant to her, but she liked the way it sounded.

The creature continued to methodically groom itself. "How about Jubatus?" The creature's ears pricked up as it looked up at her. "Juba?", It quickly gave its own snout a lick before standing up.

She wasn't exactly hearing any complaints from the name. To be honest it probably didn't care what it was being called as long as it was something nice, "How fast can you run?" She asked it.

***

Patrick barely came to a stop before almost running off the cliff edge himself. He'd been paying too much attention to the orange glowing arrow and not where he was going. The only thing that had tipped him off was that the arrow began to sharply point downwards.

The moon was nothing but a small white sliver in the sky, offering little light. However, whatever moonlight there was gently bounced off the calm surface of the sea beyond the plains beneath him.

Between him and the sea, two silhouettes stood out from the tall grass. One with trailing hair and what appeared to be a bow on her back. The other a cat of some kind, keeping pace beside her.

At first, he thought the creature was chasing her, but after a few seconds, even from this distance it became obvious the creature was with the figure. Cathie wouldn't be so reckless as to let a creature like that near her. It had to be Amy. He watched as the arrow slowly moved to continue pointing to the figure.

"That confirms it." He sighed as he examined the cliff in front of him. Even if he found a way to quickly get down unharmed, they were the other side of the plains from him. They were also heading to the shore, where the cliffs sloped down and eventually met the ground of the plains, shortly before vanishing under the waves.

She wasn't moving at the insane speed she had been before, but she was certainly moving faster than Patrick could run. He had to quickly think of something before he lost her. He quickly got out a book with a flame on the cover and began to flick through the pages.

***

Just as Amy and Juba made it to the shoreline, the sky lit up with a blinding light.

The two of them turned to see a huge ball of flames shoot into the sky from the top of the cliffs on the other side of the plains. A fire dragon? They would have been able to see that. In which case that meant only one thing.

"Patrick." She muttered. At first with relieve, but then with horror. Images of him covered in blood began to fill her mind. It took her a good few seconds to get her mind in a fit state to think again, during which she hadn't noticed Juba begin to growl and hiss at the path ahead of them.

Just as she regained her senses and decided to run as far as she could from this place, an earth dragon emerged from the ground in front of the two of them, "Shit." She cursed as a rock narrowly missed her. She'd managed to dodge the surprise attack, but the dragon remained in her way.

She felt the ground rumble as four more earth dragons appeared beside the first. More and more then began to appear behind them.

"How nice of our food to invite us." One of them chuckled as they eyed what remained of the flames above. The sky eventually darkened once more as the flames died out. Flames so bright that even an earth dragon could notice it.

Killing multiple small animals was one thing for Amy to do. Killing a whole pack of earth dragons was a challenge in of itself. Their armour was going to be tough to get through, plus she wasn't even sure how much of a beating she could take. One hit might be all it would take to kill her.

She reached for her bow, but quickly remembered she had no arrows. Instead, she took out the dragon claw that had been tucked into her trousers and held it like a sword once more. It was shorter than any sword she'd used, but then again, she was used to using her mother's large and heavy swords. Being small and not made of metal made it really light. Speed was clearly going to be the key to this fight.

With a blur she found herself deep in the ranks of the dragon pack. She'd sliced at the first six or so dragons in her path, but she heard none of them fall.

She quickly sped out of danger and back towards the plains. Her sharp eyes focused on where she'd attacked the dragons. There were certainly a few scratch marks on their armour, but she hadn't broken through.

She watched as a dragon on the right side of the pack quickly fell to its feet. Juba pounced from the dead dragons back and began to use the confused dragons as steppingstones. She watched the creature bounce from dragon to dragon, causing confusion and breaking their focus from Amy.

Unfortunately, it didn't distract the ones still underground. Teeth surrounded Amy from below. She sped out just before the powerful jaws snapped shut, but she'd moved right into the path of another open mouth. They'd predicted her movements.

Amy was sharply pushed just out of biting reach of the second mouth and harshly landed back within the long grass of the plains. Juba stood above her. Out of breath, he began to quickly scout their immediate surroundings with its eyes, ears and snout.

Amy wasn't partially happy how she'd found out Juba was a he, but given he'd just saved her life once again she wasn't about to complain at the beast.

Juba quickly moved off her and took a defensive stance between her and the shoreline. Her view was blocked by the tall grass from down on the floor, so Amy quickly tried to get to her feet. Before she did however, Juba's ears twitched. He quickly turned around and pounced onto her. She was once again thrown to the floor.

There was a loud whoosh. Shortly after, the tops of the tall grass began to flutter to the floor. There was a huge thud right above the two of them as a bare human foot appeared in Amy's vision. The growl of an earth dragon right above her shook her to her core, but the human foot stood strong.

There was only one human capable of holding an entire earth dragon back on their own.

More dragons attacked from all sides. Amy could do nothing but listen as sword cut through armour and flesh above her. She was sheltered from most of the blue blood by Juba, who had continued to keep Amy pinned to the ground as low as possible.

She noticed that Juba's eyes were shut, and the creature was shaking with fear. The slaughter above them eventually came to a stop. A few dragons limped away as fast as they could, but only a few.

"Care to explain what this thing is doing?" Cathie's voice hissed as Juba was lifted off Amy and held at arm's length away from them both.

"Protecting me." Amy answered as she quickly got onto her feet. She grabbed the arm Cathie was using to hold him, "Let him go."

Cathie's eyes thoroughly examined the beast. She quickly noticed the scars on the back of its leg. She then began to pay close attention to its front paws.

There it was. Another scar. Small but circular, dead in the middle of one of its front paws.

"You." She scorned at the beast. Juba hissed back. He seemed to remember her as well.

She threw Juba onto the floor and redrew her blue blood covered heavy sword. Amy quickly blocked her mothers' advances on the beast.

"Don't." She protested.

"I tracked every single one down, except you." Cathie continued to address the creature, completely ignoring Amy.

"He was abandoned by his pack. They cut his back legs and left him for dead."

"Yes, they did." Cathie finally acknowledged her, "For failing to kill me." She added, "I found every one of the creatures with the arrow wound Tom inflicted on them and killed them myself, all except one that I never found."

"He's saved my life." Amy revealed, "More than once."

"Bullshit."

"It's true." Patrick's voice confirmed. He walked over to join them as he continued to brush his clothes free of small bits of rock. He'd come from the direction of the cliff that he'd been on before, "Watched the beast save her life with my own eyes during my climb."

Cathie hesitated as she gave his words some thought. She then lowered her blade.

"You've earnt your freedom, this time, beast." She hissed as it. Juba didn't waste a second. He made for the shoreline at full speed. He then vanished into the nearby treeline to the side.

Amy attempted to speed off in the same direction, but she came to a violent stop before she'd even started. Cathie had grabbed her arm. As fast and strong as Amy was now, she still couldn't make her mother even budge, "Where are you going?" She asked her. From the tone alone Amy could tell she was pissed off, but her fierce eyes certainly helped to confirm the fact.

"I can't be around other humans." She calmly answered as she relaxed the arm Cathie had grabbed.

"Any particular reason you wish to give?" Cathie asked her. Most of the anger had now drained away. She was still trying to hold the pissed off mother act, but deep down she could sense the concern.

Amy could feel her fangs begin to grow the more she looked at the two of them. She sheepishly turned to look away.

"I didn't come back the same. I don't want anyone to get hurt." She muttered. Until now she'd managed to block it out, but the beating sound of two human hearts was becoming overwhelming very quickly. Her nose was also ringing with a smell she could only describe as delicious. Despite turning away from them, her fangs came fully out.

"Hurt us?" Patrick asked her, but his words vanished against the smell and sound of their blood pumping around their bodies. It took everything she had not to try and take a bite, but then it suddenly wasn't enough.

Amy quickly turned around and pounced at Patrick with her sharp fangs nicely aimed at one side of his neck.

What was she doing? She felt as though she wasn't in control anymore.

Just before her fangs reached Patrick's skin, an arm came between Amy's mouth and Patrick's neck. Despite her hunger, she'd been smart enough to go for Patrick instead of her mother, but it was still an uncontrollable impulse. Her fangs wouldn't be a match for Cathie's seemingly impenetrable skin.

She just about managed to close her mouth to protect her fangs from the impact of her mouth against Cathie's arm. Cathie quickly used the position she was in, to lever Amy away from Patrick.

The two of them took a step back in surprise from her. Amy quickly snapped out of it and covered her mouth. She felt the fangs retract, but not fully. She turned to flee with tears flicking off her face as she did so, but once again she was brought to a stop before she could even move.

This time the arm hadn't grabbed hers but had wrapped around her waist. A second arm landed on her shoulder and span her back around to face her mother. As her fangs grew once more, Cathie quickly tightened her hug on Amy, forcing her mouth against her chest.

"That's some bite you have there." Cathie sighed as she felt Amy's fangs slowly retract. They knew there was no hope of food now. She could both feel and here Amy sobbing against her chest. Amy of all people knew how powerful Cathie was, so she wouldn't have intentionally tried to kill Patrick in front of her, not normally anyway. The tears added to Cathie's first suspicions. Her words now made sense, and her attempt to run away from them.

"I'm sorry." She cried into Cathie's chest. Cathie kept one arm firmly around her to keep her pressed up against her but used the other to stroke her head.

"It's alright. You won't hurt anyone while I'm around."

"Fangs and superspeed." Patrick sighed, "Not exactly the typical side effects of magic."

"How about we save the theorising to when we get home."

CHAPTER 28; ADJUSTMENTS

Tom continued to closely examine the two large fangs in Amy's mouth. Cathie had both hands firmly on Amy's shoulders from behind just in case. She was sat on Cathie's bed, with Tom on his knees to get a good look at the top of her mouth.

"Those things are sharp, even for teeth." He muttered as he backed off, letting Amy close her mouth.

"What's the verdict then?" Patrick asked from behind Tom.

"Ability to heal, impressive speed and strength, not to mention those heightened senses. One would see it as an improvement if not for the oddly specific appetite and skin condition." He answered as he stood up.

"Anything you can do to stop me constantly wanting to eat the lot of you?" Amy asked him. Tom considered this for a few seconds before an idea clicked into his head. He walked out of Cathie's room and into his own, then back again holding a vial of red liquid.

"I know this isn't the real stuff, but it seems to have a lot in common with human blood."

"That the stuff you use to cut the black material?" Patrick asked him.

"Yeah, have a taste." He answered as he handed the vial to Amy. She slowly took a sip of the liquid.

"Disgusting." She coughed as she struggled to swallow it, "But bearable." She added. She quickly downed the rest of it. The bitter taste scrunched her face up as she swallowed.

"Not much I can do about the senses though. I'm afraid that's something you'll have to learn to control on your own." Tom added.

"Which means it's probably safer for me to stick around until you do." Cathie suggested. Tom nodded at this.

"Best we can do."

"What about the whole sunlight thing?" Patrick asked them. Tom shrugged.

"No clue. Thick clothing perhaps? Make sure none of her skin gets exposed to the sunlight."

"I'd prefer to just simply go out at night instead of the day. My senses seem to work a lot better in the dark." Amy revealed.

"I still can't believe magic managed to achieve all of this." Tom muttered.

"Death is a tricky subject when it comes to magic. Until now no one has dared to mess with it and succeed, those that were foolish enough didn't ever survive the process." Patrick explained.

"Which begs the question of how you pulled it off in the first place." Tom responded as he turned to face Patrick. Clearly, he was waiting for an answer. Patrick sighed and took in a deep breath.

"Since I was a kid, I had the unique ability to strengthen my own magic by turning it orange. A dangerous power that pretty much nearly killed me whenever I used it, but with it, I was able to achieve the impossible, even for other magicians."

"Do go on."

"I could turn a simple liquid to solid spell into a spell that made roughly ten times the solid than any other mage could achieve. Ten times the mass of the liquid I started with."

"Do you have any idea how many laws of the universe that breaks?" Tom asked him, "I'll give you a clue, all of them."

"Just telling you the facts. This power is how those arrows of yours tore through the earth dragon that attacked us. In Amy's case, I took the life circle of a tree, amplified it with my power and used it to restart her own life circle."

"Eventually creating more life than there was to begin with, just like the liquid to solid reaction, right?" Tom asked him. Patrick nodded.

"That doesn't explain these changes." Amy pointed out. Tom shook his head.

"Oh, but it does." He sighed, "Creating more mass than he started with was bad enough but doing the same with life itself must have seriously messed with the rules of the universe. Such a thing shouldn't be possible for either science or magic."

"Not even the other universe had the power to bring anything back from the dead." Cathie added.

"Which means we're dealing with something other than magic, other than science." Tom concluded.

"There is more." Patrick announced, "Something seems rather impressed with my power. Some guy called Will."

"Another human?" Tom asked him. Patrick shook his head.

"I know this will sound crazy, but I felt more like I was being spoken to by a god."

There was silence in the room for a few seconds.

"The word Neutral wasn't ever brought up was it?" Tom asked him. Patrick shook his head.

"No, he was something different, and whatever power I have seems to come from him."

"Some good news at least." Tom sighed, "Because if one of us turns out to be the reincarnation of this Neutral god figure, we're all as good as dead."

"I guess it should go without saying that the dragons probably shouldn't be made aware of this power." Cathie added.

"Speaking of the dragons. That's our next major issue." Tom was reminded.

***

Amy was now alone in Charlie's room. Although it was now her room. Empty of everything except a few spare clothes just a little bit too big for her and a few weapons against the walls.

She watched as Patrick slowly opened the door, walked in, then carefully shut the door behind him, clearly making sure the other two didn't notice him enter.

"You shouldn't be here without Cathie."

"I'm sure I can raise a barrier in time if needed." He responded as he walked further into the room, "Just wanted to talk to you more about what happened."

"Dad told me you went to a lot of effort to find me. Sorry I made it so hard."

"None of that matters. I'm talking about what happened just before you ran."

"Yeah. That." She sighed as Patrick sat beside her.

"I know I didn't exactly give you a choice about the whole thing. It's fine if you want to blame everything that you're going through on me."

"Why did you risk everything to bring me back?" Amy asked him. She seemed to reach into her pocket and take out an old, folded sheet of paper.

"Because Cathie would have killed me for sure." Patrick answered. Amy gave a small chuckle at this, but quickly turned to face him.

"The real reason." She pushed. Despite the danger she posed right now, Patrick could do nothing but take in her beauty. He's spent the little time they'd spent together trying his best to avoid her noticing the looks he'd been giving her. So much so that he hadn't even had the chance to fully embrace her finer details.

Her red hair, although the exact same shade as her mothers, was a different shade to her eyes. Her eyes were still red, but much lighter, closer to pink if anything. Her hair was also neater than Cathie's. It had been brushed many times during its life, unlike Cathie's more chaotic locks.

"I…" His throat choked up. He hadn't felt this feeling for a long time. Since he'd first met Cathie in fact, but even then, not with this intensity.

Amy slowly unfolded the paper in her hands and showed it to Patrick. It was a sketch of a face. Detailed and very well drawn, it had clearly taken a lot of time and effort to draw. Love hearts of different shapes and sizes surrounded the face, but Patrick didn't recognise the man.

"The original plan was for me to stay in the other world. A world I'd grown up in and was used to. Yet I decided to come to this one instead with full knowledge of what was here."

"I'm guessing Cathie told you many stories about this world."

"Too many to count. Within a lot of these stories, was this guy."

"Someone from Cathie's past?" Amy gave another small laugh.

"You have to remember I'd only heard of this guy from stories told by mouth. I honestly had no clue what he looked like, but I drew him anyway."

"With love hearts?"

"A man who gave everything up in order to keep my mother safe. A man whose magical knowledge I'd barely scratched the surface of. A man who happened to be the last single guy in this world that wouldn't try to kill me."

"This is starting to sound all rather familiar."

"This is a drawing of you Patrick." She revealed, "At least, what I thought you'd look like before we met."

"So those love hearts…" Amy slowly started to blush.

"A girl doesn't just decide to spend the rest of her life in a world with one unspoken for man just for the hell of it." She muttered. Slowly, she folded the paper up and put it back in her pocket, "I know we've pretty much only just met, but I've been surrounded by stories of you my whole life."

"Not really sure what to say about that." Amy gave a smile.

"Nothing, for now. If for any reason, right now it's far too dangerous for me to be close to anyone. But if I can manage to control these urges to kill, I was hoping to hear your thoughts on the matter then."

***

Frost carefully landed on top of a high and sharp mountain peak covered in snow. The next mountain across however despite being of similar height was completely void of snow.

Flame was perched atop it. Eyes trained on him. She turned her attention to lower down on the hill he himself was perched on. A cave. She opened her wings, then swooped down into it, disappearing into the hillside.

Frost hesitated but decided to follow with caution. The entrance to the cave itself was rather small, but it quickly expanded out into a large cavern. The light of Flame's fiery skin did little to the surrounding darkness.

"A message with no content other than an invitation. Rather unusual for someone like you, Flame." Frost spoke as he came to a stop a comfortable distance away from her. No fire dragon would be able to hide in such a place without him spotting it. If this was a trap, it was either a very bad one, or a very good one.

"The invitation was not from me." Flame revealed as she turned to face the overwhelming darkness that was the rest of the cavern. Frost himself began to peer into the shadows. He watched as two eyes opened themselves.

Two eyes in the pitch-black darkness were unnerving enough, but it was the fact that each eye was roughly the size of Frost himself that really unsettled him.

"Frost. Welcome." A voice calmly but firmly spoke. The voice itself sounded godlike in nature, but that was to be expected if this was who Frost suspected it was.

"I was not aware the divine had returned." Frost responded as he bowed his head towards the set of eyes. A bright, golden skin began to reveal itself attached to the eyes. Before long, the two leaders were looking at a bright, golden dragon figure standing before them, dwarfing them in size and stature alike.

"It has come to my attention that my last orders have not been carried out to completion." The divine spoke, "To which both of you are partially responsible."

"Apologies to your greatness, but I have my reasons." Frost apologised.

"I am aware. Flame has informed me of the apparent absence of the Neutral's presence despite my concerns."

"You have my word that if I even suspected the Neutral had reincarnated in one of the remaining humans, I would have killed every last one of them myself." Frost added.

"Of course. I did not call you here to question your loyalty Frost. Flame has also informed me that of all the dragon's, you have the closest relationship with these remaining humans."

"The truth as far as I am aware."

"The time the Neutral can survive without a body will soon be at its end. If it still lives, it will have to act soon." The divine revealed.

"How much time does it have?" Flame asked.

"A few hours."

"None of the current humans show signs of pregnancy. Not in that time frame at least."

"The human does not have to be born as the Neutral. It can become one with its power even in adulthood should it be required." The divine explained, "I have already had the opportunity to check the four humans for the power of the Neutral thanks to Flame. However, between then and now the Neutral may have made its move."

"Perhaps a second test? After the time the Neutral would have been forced to act?" Flame suggested.

"Indeed. I require you to bring the humans to the round table. Should they all pass, I shall allow this complex web of politics you seem so eager to place the humans at the centre of Frost."

"And if they fail?" Frost asked.

"Then I expect you to keep to your previous words. I have other more pressing matters to attend to instead of chasing ghosts, you have a week to bring them before me. Be gone, you have your tasks." He announced as his golden figure began to vanish until it was just his eyes, which then slowly closed. Soon there was nothing but the darkness.

Frost was the first to head for the exit of the cave, followed by Flame, at a safe distance away from him. Frost came to a stop right at the mouth of the cave as the sun began to slowly rise. Flame kept a safe distance away for a few seconds, before quickly walking over and standing beside him.

Steam began to slowly come off Frost's body as Flame's heat began to lower further than normally possible for a fire dragon.

"You wish to talk?" She asked, "You'd better be quick."

"Hiding the divine amongst your own." Frost simply spoke.

"You know fully well I wouldn't have, if I'd been given the choice."

"I've always known of your hatred to the legends of old."

"It is not the legends I detest."

"More of who the legends are about, right?" Frost asked with a small chuckle. He made sure his words wouldn't be heard outside their conversation, considering where they were.

"He nearly drove our race into the ground because of this silly fear of a ghost that probably never truly existed." She sighed in a hushed tone.

"Say's the one who seems most insistent about the Neutral not being amongst the humans."

"An act I must maintain. For he was always close by, within my own kind as you stated earlier."

"So you are also not pleased of his return?"

"The sooner he abandons this world, the better. However, I suspect the entire story of the Neutral was really a ploy to wipe out humanity."

"Propaganda? From a god?" Frost asked her.

"Something tells me the humans will fail this test. A rather conveniently diplomatic way of convincing us all that although we were not wrong to begin talking with the humans, we were not right either."

"I do agree the convenient timing does seem odd. Do you have a plan then?"

"Still working on it, I suggest you come up with one yourself just in case."

"Who would have thought the two of us would have to outwit our own god?" Frost quietly chuckled, "Reminds me of an earlier time."

"A time long since passed, as well you know Frost. A time when we both dreamed a dream that can never be." Flame sighed as she gestured to his own melting body and her own shivering one.

"How cruel fate can be." He sighed, "It's been too long since we last spoke like this."

"I'm afraid we're out of time for a catch-up chat." Flame muttered as she opened her wings.

"Another time then, but sooner rather than later." He suggested as he too opened his wings. Flame gave a small nod before taking to the sky.

Flame kept herself in a straight path towards home, but she carefully looked back to spot Frost flying in the opposite direction to her. North instead of south. She turned her head back to the way she was heading. She took a few seconds dive as she used the end of one wing to wipe a warm, fiery tear from her eye before she levelled out. After a shake of her head, her flames intensified in order to stop her body from shivering.

Being close to Frost had taken a toll on her, but not just a physical one.

She distracted herself by thinking about the future. The fateful day to come where she'd have to challenge her own god. Deep down she knew that not even the might of every dragon within this world would be enough to stand against their own god, even if they would have wanted to. Right now, it seemed to be the day humanity would be snuffed out forever. A fate she had little confidence of changing.

Tom flashed into her head. A man she'd persecuted time and again for being the very thing the divine seemed to fear. This Neutral may never have truly existed, but that man seemed the closest thing to it.

She quickly changed her direction, towards the rising sun. No time to gather guards for an escort, she'd have to make the trip alone. If only she'd had the idea before she'd separated from Frost, but it was too late to catch up to him now.

Just as the sun made it over the treeline of what was left of the forest outside the cave, Flame gracefully landed in front of Patrick, who'd just returned from morning patrol.

"I must speak with you all." She quickly huffed as she folded her wings up. Patrick quickly raced into the cave, but shortly returned, followed by Tom, Cathie and Amy.

"What is it?" Tom asked her, noticing that she'd both come alone and in a hurry. Flame opened her mouth to speak, but she was distracted by the purple colour that had suddenly appeared underneath them all.

The ground beneath their very feet no longer supported them. Down they fell into the waiting purple swirls of the portal underneath.

CHAPTER 29; EDWARD

Thomas carefully watched a screen in front of him. At first, it was blank, but soon it filled with thousands of numbers and calculations.

"Fuck." He cursed as he turned away and opened the door to the small, dark room he was in, "The bastard pulled it off."

***

The five of them were thrown onto a hard, smooth floor unlike any other they'd come across. As they all got to their feet, someone standing above them all slowly clapped at them. Bright lights were shone in their direction from multiple angles.

"Did you have to bring the lizard as well?" The clapping figure asked as he turned to someone behind the lights.

"Sorry sir, portal radius was bigger than calculations predicted."

"No matter." The figure sighed, "Weapons live!" He seemed to order. The sound of a charging gun echoed through whatever large room they were in. Red lasers were pointed at the lot of them, most trained on Flame.

"What is this?" She asked as she struggled to see past the lights.

"You probably have no idea what is currently being pointed at you all right now, so I'll explain. A military issued laser riffle. Capable of punching a nice, crispy hole through even the toughest of dragon armour." The figure explained as he took a few steps back and spread his arms out to gesture to the many red lights.

Now that the man had taken a few steps back, they could all get a look at him. Hair as black as the night, eyes as sharp as a fox and as grey as the clouds on a rainy day. Wearing a white, long coat with many pockets and black trousers that contrasted the bright lights either side of him.

"Any particular reason you decided to capture us?" Tom asked the man. The man gave a small chuckle.

"You really do look alike, you and your counterpart." He continued to chuckle, "The shivers down my spine when I stare at that face, although the yellow eyes are different. Don't quite give the same effect."

"Who the hell are you?" Patrick asked him. Tom noted that both Cathie and Amy had moved very close to one another and were being rather quiet about the whole thing. Cathie's mouth opened with a quiver of fear.

"That's Edward." She spoke. Eyes trained on the man like a deer watches a tiger for signs of an attack.

"The fabled Thomas Thomson of Universe One." Edward chucked as he seemed to pat himself on the back, "And I thought you'd be as challenging to beat as my last opponent."

"What have you done with Thomas?" Amy asked him.

"A container dropped to the bottom of the sea was all it took in the end." He answered with another, now sick and sinister chuckle, "I'm sure right as we speak, he's breathing his last breath."

"Bastard." Cathie cursed. None of the lasers were pointed her way, but she knew the moment she even flinched, Edward would order one of the others to be shot down instead. Edward seemed to smile from her remark instead of take offence to it.

"Now then, hopefully for the very last time. Hand the child over." He demanded as his face turned serious, "For every ten seconds you don't, I'll shoot one of them at random." He added.

Amy slowly let go of her mother and walked over to him. A second figure grabbed her and quickly restrained her with some kind of metal contraption that seemed very much overkill for restraining a little girl, "Of course I'm all too aware that your family has a habit of breaking the unbreakable, so this time I'm not taking any chances."

"You'll pay for this." Cathie spat at him.

"Now for the next problem." Edward sighed as he looked at the four of them, "How I'd very much like to kill you all right now, but one of you happens to be unkillable, and I'd prefer to keep my bargaining chips."

"So you'll take us prisoner instead then." Tom responded. Edward smiled at this.

"Oh but you'd like that. Experience has taught me that Thomas Thomson isn't someone you can keep prisoner for long." Tom seemed impressed with his response.

"Can't kill us, can't take us prisoner. What now then?" Tom asked him.

"Now you return to a place I can reach you, but you can't reach her." He answered as he pulled out a small laser rifle and pointed it directly at Tom, "Clawson first, followed by the lizard." Tom squinted in annoyance. This guy was good. He'd spent seventeen years dealing with Cathie and who knows how long dealing with his apparent twin in this world. What he hadn't dealt with however, was someone named Patrick.

"Barrier, now!" Tom seemed to order as he reached into his bag and pulled out his bow. Red hot shots fired at the speed of light towards them. They smashed through the magical barrier but stopped once they hit a transparent orange one just behind it.

Cathie was already vaulting over the top of it, sword already drawn with burning red eyes solely fixed on Edward. Shots smacked right into her, but she charged on anyway. Despite the clear pain they were causing her, and the fact that her skin slowly but surely began to show signs of charring where multiple shots had hit, she ploughed forwards until her sword was in reach of him.

As she made her swing, an armour seemed to construct itself around him. Cathie's blade smacked right into the familiar sight of black material.

More streamlined than Tom's version, it also seemed to cover his entire body, with no vulnerable points to exploit. Even Edward's face had been covered, but Cathie knew all too well that he could still see.

"Jealous?" Patrick asked Tom as he wiped the blood from his nose.

"Flame, aim for the lights." Tom ordered. Flame rather quickly decided she was better off listening to them than trying to ask what the hell was going on.

Bursts of fire methodically took out each light source, which then revealed the humans behind. A large cloud of flames quickly began to engulf them and block all visible exits to the room.

The flames died down to reveal that it was now just them and Edward left in the room.

A brown sword seemed to remove itself from the back of Edward's armour and find itself in his hand as Cathie regained her footing. The moment she noticed the sword, her eyes widened as it started to swipe towards her.

She didn't attempt to block it, because she knew she couldn't. Instead, she moved back, but it wasn't quite enough. The others watched as the tip of this odd sword sliced a shallow cut across Cathie's lower torso. Blood appeared and began to slowly drip out as she winced.

A sword that could cut the indestructible. A hole in Patrick's barrier opened up in front of Tom as he aimed his bow. Patrick noticed the arrow heads had been stained in blood that also dripped down Tom's bow strings from his hand as he carefully aimed.

Ten arrows were released, but none of them hit. The arrows instead struck a crystal-like structure that had quickly formed just in front of Edward.

"Smarter than you look Thomson, but you're badly outmatched." Edward chuckled as the structure seemed to repair itself, pushing the arrows out and to the floor.

"A barrier?" Patrick asked.

"If you ever wanted proof that science and magic were one and the same." Tom muttered as for once he was completely stumped. The barrier slowly vanished before them.

Cathie quickly came in for another attack, this time with her own blood covering her blade, but she too struck a barrier that formed to protect Edward from her strike. Cathie's sword seemed to remain jammed into the crumbling structure that seemed rather different to Patrick's smooth and glass like barriers.

Edward tried to stab her with his sword, but Cathie grabbed his arm with her free one. Instead, Edward smacked her right in the stomach with a punch.

She lost her grip on her sword and was flung back against Patrick's barrier, leaving a trail of blood that splattered onto the floor.

Edward examined his gauntlet which had been slightly dissolved by her blood, but it seemed to remain reasonably intact. That confirmed it. He was wearing an armour made from the black material.

Charlie's sword fell to the floor as the barrier close to Edward vanished. Tom watched the shards of the barrier fall to the floor beside the blade and watched as they remained despite the shield vanishing.

"Matter to energy formation." He muttered to himself. He eyed Edward's armour with questioning but methodical eyes. It had to be. Patrick's barriers were simply a magical force that couldn't last very long without fuel from a shape, but he was seeing Edward do no such thing, yet the broken shards seemed to remain even without anything fuelling them, as if they'd been permanently brought into this world.

If that was the case, then surely Edward was capable of keeping that barrier up indefinably, so why didn't he? He pictured the shield as it appeared to block Tom's shots. It seemed to focus on the point he was aiming but didn't entirely surround Edward himself. Then he lowered it before raising it somewhere else near his body to stop Cathie's attack.

That was it. The limit. He was forming matter from something, most likely energy. He didn't understand the technology behind it, but he understood the science. He was turning the energy to matter, then back again. That meant he had a limited amount at his disposal, with perhaps some form of restoring the energy used up over time for the repair they'd witnessed.

If that was the case, then there was a limit. Enough damage over a short period of time, and they might get lucky. Spread the damage out to spread out his resources, it was worth a shot.

"What now?" Patrick asked him. Tom gave a small but confident smile. They could win.

"Cathie, think you can harass him up close?" He asked her as she slowly got to her feet. She wiped some blood that had come from her mouth as her eyes quickly locked back onto Edward.

"Yeah." She answered as she began to run forwards again, this time with just her fists, covered in her own blood. Patrick watched as Tom cut his hand once more with an arrowhead and dipped another ten in it.

"You too Patrick. As many shots as you can manage. Mix and match, so he doesn't know which ones to block and which ones to take." Patrick nodded as he took out a dagger and sliced his own hand open. The blood dripped out into a liquid ball that floated in front of him. His barrier fully dropped as he lit a fire ball in his other hand.

"Thomson." Flame spoke as she peered behind them. Tom looked behind to see the portal they had come from had now closed, "We don't have a way out."

"We'll worry about that once we deal with this guy."

Cathie went in for punch after punch. Each time her fist smacked into a shield, but that just seemed to piss her off even more. Her punches got faster, stronger. Tom watched the shield as she did so. Despite her speed, only one shield was active at a time. It was quick to activate and deactivate, but only one at a time.

As Patrick began to unleash shots of fire and blood, the shield still seemed capable of handling the number of attacks.

"It reclaims the energy and then redistributes." Tom realised, "But that leaves it one weakness." He added as he carefully aimed his shot.

Two arrows shot off towards Edward's leg, timed perfectly between Cathie's punches so that she was just out of the way. However, those two arrows weren't the only ones in flight.

Two more were aimed at his other leg, while another two were aimed at his chest. The final two were aimed at his head.

A shield appeared in front of Edward's head, stopping the two arrows, but the rest of them struck their target. Edward began to chuckle as Cathie pulled away from him. He hadn't had a chance to swing that sword at her, but she knew not to push her luck.

"It seems I was right to be cautious of you, despite your lack of technology." He continued to chuckle as the shield in front of his face deactivated, dropping the two bloodied arrows to the ground.

One by one, he easily removed the remaining arrows from his armour. They hadn't gone through. They'd barely made a dent despite the blood, "Close. If that had been a gun instead of that primitive bow, you might have gotten through, but I'm afraid your way out of your depth here."

His sword seemed to pack itself away, back into the rear of his armour. Instead, he took out the weapon from before. A small laser gun and aimed it at Tom. The shot smacked into an orange barrier as Cathie came in for another swing, but Edward hit her with his own.

This one was aimed right at her ribs. She smacked right into one of the side walls, covering the floor in front of her with blood as her head remained still and looking down. She was out cold this time.

The other three could do nothing but watch as Edward walked over to the orange barrier between the two of them. He placed his armour covered hand against the barrier. As he applied pressure, it began to crack.

The barrier began to seal itself up as Patrick put more into it, but Edward effortlessly increased the pressure on it, "A magician, a dragon, an immortal girl and an excellent mind. All nothing against this world's greatest achievements." He spoke as the barrier shattered.

Patrick fell to his knees, his lower face now covered in blood, "The very finest of your world beaten so easily. Perhaps now you realise just how much you didn't stand a chance." He sighed as he kicked Patrick to the ground. He then aimed the laser rifle at Tom once more.

A deafening sound rang thought the entire room. Tom could do nothing but watch as a slug smashed straight through the crystal shield that had formed to stop it. It then broke apart, splashing a surprising amount of what appeared to be human blood right onto the side of Edward's head.

Edward's left eye suddenly became visible, and it revealed his shock matched Tom's own. A second shot almost immediately after the first struck the side of his body. Once again smashing through the shield. Once again blood was splashed all over the now vulnerable armour. The shots had brought Edward off balance, the weapon was now no longer pointed directly at Tom.

Tom used this opportunity to land a punch squarely in Edward's face before he had the chance to react. Before Edward even hit the floor however, he vanished into a portal that quickly closed behind him.

Tom quickly looked over to where the shots had come from. On the other side of the room, holding a rather large rifle, an exact copy of him stood, panting and huffing.

"Welcome to Universe Two."

CHAPTER 30; THOMAS THOMSON

Tom's copy quickly dropped the rifle and ran over to Cathie, who was still out cold against one of the walls. He sat her upright and took a quick look at her wounds. Tom did the same for Patrick, although Patrick seemed to be more or less ok, just some rest was required.

"And now there are two of you?" Flame asked. She'd not understood anything that had occurred since she'd first come through the portal, but things were now starting to get confusingly bizarre.

"Oh shit." Tom's copy exclaimed as he seemed to only just notice Flame, "No joke about the dragons I see." Tom walked over to his copy and curiously eyed him up.

"I take it you're this Thomas Thomson I've heard so much about." Tom asked him.

"First things first, I'm Thomas, your Tom alright? Saves a lot of confusion later down the road." Tom nodded at this, "Secondly, damn I knew she said we looked alike, but we really look alike." He added as he seemed to eye Tom with the same curiosity.

"He managed to take Amy. Don't suppose you know where he'd take her?" Tom asked him. Thomas nodded.

"His main lab most likely. Had a special place all nice and set out for her for years now."

"Where is it?"

"Later. Right now, you guys aren't exactly in a shape to pick a fight. Not to mention the state of the AG-Project." He sighed.

"I've heard that name before."

"It's the organisation I work for. Not important but right now we can't count on their help either. This is all we got." The two of them looked around the slightly charred and blood covered room.

"That weapon of yours, more than one use?" Tom asked him. Thomas smiled.

"Like I'd be some hack that made a single use weapon. The ammo is a pain in the ass to make but I've still got a few rounds spare."

"These weapons…" Flame seemed to mutter as she paid close attention to the charred laser rifles littered around the room, "They remind me of your father's weapon of choice." She revealed.

Her previous words flooded Tom's mind. A stick that shot red death towards its victim at unimaginable speed, capable of bringing down a dragon in one shot from range.

"More questions to answer later." Tom sighed.

"Does the dragon know how much trouble we're in?" Thomas asked Tom. Tom shook his head.

"Perhaps the quick explanation then." He sighed.

"Once we have these two somewhere safe." Tom suggested.

"Not going to be easy, especially with a dragon that size."

"How bad are we talking?" Tom asked him.

"We're pretty near the edge of the city but hiding something that size through the back alleys is going to be impossible."

"A what now?" Tom asked him.

"Right, forgot you don't have cities in your world." Thomas sighed, "Alright we'll have to run for it. You fast?" He seemed to ask the dragon.

"I can be." Flame answered.

"I'm going to have to ask you to not kill anything or anyone while we do this. Last thing I need is more innocent blood on my hands." Thomas sighed, "You're about to run through a crowded street."

"Crowded with what?" Flame asked him.

"Humans."

***

The walls of the building were tougher than anything Flame had come across before. It took a good few minutes for her to melt her way through and into the outside world.

The sunlight of another world shone brightly in the sky. The air was rough and polluted. It had a horrible taste to it that was indescribable.

In front of them, a straight pathway perfectly flat. Either side of the pathway, concrete towers that seemed impossibly high. The glass windows shimmered in the sunlight as the noise finally hit them.

Horns, walkway lights beeping, engine noises and the constant low mutter of a crowd of people walking along the flat pathways, either side of metal boxes that seemed to move unaided.

There were more humans in Tom's view right now than he'd ever seen in his entire life. Humans calmly walking, talking, going about what appeared to be everyday business.

"A forest of concrete. At least that's how she first described them." Thomas chuckled as he shuffled his grip of Patrick over his shoulder. Tom himself was holding a still wounded Cathie in his own arms.

The view was a wonder to look at. That was until someone noticed the rather large and flaming dragon which had just melted its way through half a building.

Screams filled the air as the once calm and peaceful crowd began to panic. The crowd dispersed as far from the lot of them as humanly possible, which Tom noticed was slower than he'd expected them to move, "Make a dash for the end of the street. Edge of the city isn't too far."

The two of them started off at full sprint. Yet despite Cathie being heavier than Patrick, Tom seemed to easily out pace his counterpart. Flame kept behind them, doing her best to watch her footing as the surrounding humans panicked in all kinds of chaotic and rather idiotic fashion. She found some almost run into her, which she didn't expect, while others tripped and fell over themselves and one another to try and get away.

What was this world? She understood the desire to run at the sight of a dragon, but it was as if these people had never run from anything in their lives until now.

Sirens began to sound from far off, but their source, metal boxes with flashing lights of blue and red, quickly came into sight. Humans dressed in blue got out of the boxes and stared in amazement at Flame's presence.

"Trouble?" Tom asked.

"Damn, faster than I expected. Keep running!" Thomas ordered. Flame picked up her pace as she watched even these blue humans back away from her in shock and awe.

As they reached the end of the street, Tom found a view he was somewhat more familiar with. Fields of grass that spanned as far as the eye could see. He'd never seen so much flat ground before, but at least this was something more comprehensible than what lay behind him.

The metal boxes with flashing lights and sirens began to follow the three of them but seemed to keep their distance more than chase them down.

One of the officers in the car behind Flame reached for the radio.

"This is four seven three currently in pursuit of... well... a giant... flaming lizard." He spoke into it. He gave his partner, who was driving a rather confused and baffled look, which she returned.

"Copy four seven three. Could you repeat the description of the pursuit target? Sounded rather crazy our end." A voice spoke from the radio.

"I say again, a giant flaming lizard."

"A... giant... flaming lizard?"

"Correct. Please... advise?" There was a pause for a few seconds.

"Roger four seven three... keep... keep it as far away from populated areas as possible. Maintain safe distance and visual contact if possible until further advisement... should we figure out how to procced."

"Station please be advised that the flaming lizard now appears to be picking up the two unknown males running ahead of it and is currently showing signs of taking flight."

"Umm... right... any idea where it's heading?" The voice over the radio asked.

"Seems to be trying to get away from the city for now." The officer reported.

"Fall back then four seven three. We'll try to get more specialised units to track and peruse it."

"Roger that. Be advised the target is now airborne and heading… south by south west."

***

The calm ocean quietly lapped at the sides of the large aircraft carrier that calmly continued a current course as far from land as possible. On the main deck, no aircraft were sat. Instead, however, Flame did her best to keep herself steady despite the unfamiliar method of transportation. The deck also had the words AG-Project in large, bold letters.

Tom and Thomas carried Cathie and Patrick below deck, where Thomas showed his counterpart a room with two rather comfortable looking beds. Just as Tom finished lowering Cathie onto one, a red head caught his eye peaking in from the door.

"Damn. When you said he looked like you, I didn't think to this extent." The red-headed girl exclaimed as she got a good look at Tom. To Tom's surprise, he was staring at another version of Cathie.

"Thought I told you not to poke around until I explained things." Thomas sighed as he walked over to her.

"Guess I'm not the only one with an equivalent other." Tom worked out as he looked back at his Cathie.

"Holy shit. That's me!"

"Come on, things are confusing enough as they are." Thomas sighed as he took her arm and more or less began dragging her away from the room.

"Oh, come on. It's not every day you get to see yourself from another universe." She protested as she was dragged out of Tom's view.

"If you really want to poke your nose around, I'm sure the dragon currently on the deck will be wonderous enough on its own."

"A dragon? Here?" Tom heard the sounds of light footsteps running away from the room, "No way." Her voice echoed from around a corner now.

Thomas returned to the room.

"Sorry about that. Wanted to avoid too many shocks all at once."

"I'll be alright. Are you two… well…"

"Together?" Thomas asked as he rubbed the back of his head, "It's complicated." He answered with some hesitation, "Since these two are out, now might be a good time for a little chat."

"My thoughts exactly." Tom sighed as both of them left the room.

***

The two of them sat down on opposite sides of a small, metal table. On chairs made from what appeared to be metal poles and a smoother, flexible but durable material Tom hadn't come across before.

The room they were in was lit by a single light bulb that hung above the table and slowly rocked with the ship.

"How about the most awkward question first?" Tom began, "Is Amy mine or yours?" Thomas chucked at this.

"I knew it was coming, but I didn't expect it right off the bat." He sighed, "She's yours. Probably won't understand much of this, but despite our looks there are a few genetic differences between what we would both define as human. Amy is one hundred percent a human from Universe One by all genetic accounts."

"Good to know."

"How are you and Cathie doing by the way? I take it her seventeen-year holiday was a rather big shock."

"Still working things out. It's complicated, you could say."

"Fair enough."

"This world, do your best to explain it to me."

"The short version, or the extremely long version?" Thomas asked him.

"Whatever I need to know."

"World is ruled by humans. Most of which live in various cities dotted about the globe. Science is a keystone of our culture, and we take it very seriously. Many technological advancements have been made faster than ever originally thought possible. Given we're currently in the twenty-first century compared to the relatively short history of your world, I can imagine even our most trivial scientific breakthroughs would be incomprehensible to you."

"At this point I've more or less leaned to accept certain things as fact than try and work it out as I normally would."

"Perhaps the best approach for now, but since we're planning to go toe to toe against Edward, you'll want to know what you're up against."

"That armour of his…"

"Thick plated armour made from a material I'm told you're familiar with. Only weakness is human blood which seems to dissolve it rather nicely given enough of it."

"Something I considered unbeatable when I designed a crude version for Cathie."

"Yes, she told me about that. Rather impressive work considering your limitations."

"Now isn't the time for complements."

"I'm sure you are more than aware by now that this isn't all the armour is capable of. Installed within is an energy source linked to a shield generating device. The energy source is very versatile and can handle any additional energy absorbed by the armour. The sensors on that thing can react to a speeding bullet as well."

"I figured something like that. Energy to mass conversion, right? Instead of the energy becoming more mass for the armour he uses it to protect himself with a barrier."

"Oh, you're aware of such a possibility?" Tom reached into his bag and pulled out an air crystal.

"This is a dragon crystal taken from an air dragon. Energy goes in, pressurised air comes out." He explained as he squeezed the crystal. For once, nothing happened, "That's odd."

"You'd need more energy than a squeeze of a hand to make any considerable amount of mass. Chemical energy wouldn't be enough either."

"But that's how dragons do it. They fuel the thing with chemical energy from their body."

"Wouldn't be anywhere near enough. Not unless those dragons are lugging a massive nuclear reactor with them." Thomas answered as he shook his head, "The energy to mass conversion can be described with the equation E equals M C squared. Where E is the energy, M is the mass and C is the speed of light, and that's assuming perfect conversion, which is never the case."

"I think you'll find it's E equals M times a constant dependent on the material the energy is transferring from or to, and everything I've come across matches the pattern perfectly." Tom responded as he folded his arms, "For instance that black material seems to have a value close to one."

"Interesting. Based off readings?"

"My mother was the best at what she did. I doubt her numbers were wrong. As for the black material I'm simply guessing, but it can't be more than a factor of ten conversion."

"Perhaps a difference between your universe and this one."

"If the conversion is so one-sided in this world, then how come Edward can do it?"

"The only way anyone can do it in this world. A lot of energy."

"Hence why he can only produce one shield at a time." Tom realised.

"Exactly. However, every time we face him, he always has a new bag of tricks to play with. That sword for example."

"I've never seen another human mess Cathie up so badly, even when she wasn't invincible."

"Honestly I don't want you to know too much about the material it's made of, because once I tell you how even you might be able to manage it."

"Sounds like a challenge." Tom chuckled to himself, but Thomas rather forcefully slammed his hands on the table.

"Look, you probably don't know about this given that you've barely scratched the surface of what science can achieve, but science is a double-edged sword." He mumbled through gritted teeth, "That material has already brought enough trouble to this world as it is, I won't let it destroy another one."

"Fine, but I still need to be aware of its capabilities." Tom huffed. He didn't like being kept in the dark, but he knew himself well enough that he wasn't going to get an answer.

"It's stronger than anything we've ever encountered. Even that black material."

"It can cut through that?" Tom asked him. Thomas nodded.

"To add to it, it doesn't share the black materials' weakness of human blood."

"How do we beat it then?" Tom asked him. Thomas sighed.

"We don't. It's a rare material that's difficult to mass produce ethically. Unlike us, Edward has a lot of red tape to get around to achieve things."

"Not familiar with the expression, but I think I get the message. He can't make an armour out of it."

"For now, yes. The sword is the only evidence of the material we've come across but be aware of it just in case he's made something else small but crucial from it."

"I'll keep it in mind."

"Our last problem is his newly acquired portal technology."

"Something I've at least had some time to look at myself. Albeit I didn't get very far."

"Good to hear. I can't even imagine what portals would mean for your world. Their bad enough in this one."

"Says the inventor of it."

"What makes you think I invented it?" Thomas asked him.

"Jordan let slip the name of his creator. Thomas Thomson."

"Jordan?" Thomas asked him.

"An A.I. inside the portal device that made its way to our universe. Cathie mentioned that Edward got his hands on him."

"Oh, that. It claimed that I created it?" Thomas asked. He seemed rather confused by this fact.

"Thomas Thomson. List of achievements include discovery of the Flipside, discovery of portal technology and discovery of alternate universes." Tom listed. Thomas seemed surprised by this.

"You know about the Flipside?"

"So, you are the guy." Tom sighed, "That was Jordan's description of his creator."

"Those are a list of my achievements. Yet I don't have a clue how it works."

"Haven't suffered a head injury recently have you?"

"I have had trouble in the past with memory, but that's all been sorted out."

"How certain are you that you remember everything?"

"Very certain." Thomas answered.

"The more I learn, the more questions I find myself asking."

"Better get used to that I'm afraid." Thomas sighed, "Anyway, since he's got this new tech, he can escape any situation with a click of his finger, not to mention travel to your world."

"Him being in our world is a scary thought." Tom sighed.

"One we both dread. You fear what will become of your world once he arrives, I fear what he'd return with."

"As much black material as he can bring with him." Tom realised.

"Which is why I'm going to ask for your help." Tom took a few seconds to make sure that his counterpart was being serious.

"You want a bunch of cave dwellers to help you take on someone who quite frankly seems to possess the powers of a god compared to us."

"Yes." He responded rather seriously, "In this world Edward is almost untouchable. The only time he'll be vulnerable is when he's in yours. Limited resources and no help from others."

"But our world doesn't stand a chance against his power, as you saw."

"A fact that needs to be changed. Quickly. I can cut him off from this end, stop him from getting back up and more resources, but if his armour is still functional then that won't matter."

"Nothing you can do to help us beat him?"

"What do you think I'm currently doing?" Thomas asked him, "I've given you as much knowledge as I dare. Think it's enough to beat him?"

"Depends how much time we'll have to prepare."

"The portals he creates seems to follow laminar time flow. Unlike the one I created for Cathie, which fixes itself to the point in time I managed to accidentally magnetise both of our universes."

"But as you stated before, your world is a lot older than mine. That means we've been brought forwards in time as well as across universe."

"I've no idea how that all works, but I have a feeling it has something to do with my mistake. Our two universes seem irreversibly linked between this point and whatever point you're currently at in your world."

"Something to figure out once I crack portal technology myself then."

"Don't you dare."

"Let me guess, another technology too powerful to be created in the first place?"

"Dead on the mark. Like I stated before, this world has an abundance of technology already, to the point that dangerous discoveries that should have never been discovered are beginning to be made."

"Is that your role in this world? Is that the role of this AG-Project?" He asked, as he looked around the room.

"AG stands for anti-god." Thomas revealed. Tom smiled at this.

"Come up with that yourself?"

"No. But a fitting name."

"Sounds to me like you're fighting against the tide. Not something I myself would advise."

"You got a better solution?"

"You fear technology not yet ready for the world around it. I embrace the knowledge granted to me despite the lack of it within my surrounding world."

"I'm not going to dictate how to proceed in your own universe, all I ask is that you take my warnings to heart." Thomas sighed.

"Fine. Consider them noted."

"Now then. On to the current issue. We need to get you, your family and Patrick back to your world in one piece."

"So, we need to get both Amy and portal technology from Edward." Tom concluded.

"Correct. We're heading to his main lab as we speak, but it's going to take us a while to reach it. He's already there though, most likely."

"So, he'll be ready for us."

"Place is a bunker. Luckily for us though I have access to an old device of mine, plus Edward isn't aware I've regained my memories, so he won't expect me to use it."

"Will it help us get inside?"

"Yes, but that's all it will be able to do. It's something I've used against him before, so he'll easily counter it once he realises what's going on."

"I assume the same can be said for my earlier tactic."

"He might not be able to improve the weakness of his technology, but he'll certainly expect you to try and exploit it in a similar fashion."

"Meaning I'll have to find another way of beating the guy."

"Leave Edward to me. My rifle poses the most threat, so he'll focus on me. I should be able to buy you enough time to grab Amy and get back to your world."

"Alright." Tom sighed, "One more thing." He reached back into his bag and began pulling out a series of books of different shapes and sizes.

"Quite the collection you have there."

"My mother's notes. Scientific masterpieces to which I have barely scratched the surface. Sound familiar?"

"You suspect your mother came from this world?"

"I cannot overlook the fact that my own father was seen wielding the weapons of this world. As we make our way towards Edward's lab, I want you to read these books and tell me how advanced these notes truly are compared to this world."

CHAPTER 31; GODLIKE POWER

Flame continued to cough as her flames seemed to become less and less intense by the second. After a while they seemed to stabilise, but they wouldn't last.

"It seems we were right about this universe." Tom sighed as a large wave crashed into the side of the deck. Water spayed just shy of Flame, who had taken shelter near the main structure of the aircraft carrier, as close to the door inside as possible. Thomas nodded in agreement.

"The crystal fuelling your flames won't work here. I'm afraid you're on a timer dragon." He added.

"I feel hungry, yet nothing I eat helps." Flame coughed as she struggled to keep her balance as another wave hit the other side of the craft. The open water wasn't as calm as before.

"Because you can't turn the energy from your food into fire." Tom explained, "Nor will you be able to until we return home."

"By the looks of things, your own heat reserves should keep you going for a while, but you'll only get worse with time."

"How long do I have to last?" She asked them. Thomas turned to look towards the horizon, covered in dark clouds that lay right in their path.

"Another day by boat." He answered her.

"She won't last that long." Tom sighed.

"Then I suggest we change things up. The other two are more or less recovered, so it's not like we need the ship anymore, just a way of getting there fast."

"What do you suggest?" Tom asked him.

"Normally a plane. Unfortunately, we don't have any on hand, but we have the next best thing."

"Which is?"

"You're worlds equivalent." Thomas responded as he turned back to Flame, "You any good in a storm?" Flame looked over to the dark clouds that occasionally lit up with lightning.

"I take it that is a natural lightning storm?" Flame asked them.

"What other kind would there be?" Thomas asked her.

"The unnatural kind. A harsh environment but one I have dealt with before under far more dangerous circumstances." Flame sighed.

"Such as?" Tom asked her.

"Well I very much doubt that there will be a lightning dragon in the centre of this one."

"Better pack my bag then." Tom muttered.

"One last thing, Thomson." Flame added, "Should I lose the chance to tell you later, I have something you need to hear."

"That wouldn't be the thing you wanted to say before we were pulled into this world?"

"It is."

"I'm all ears."

***

The flight had been rough. A lightning storm was no joke when you were in one with almost no protection but Flame clearly hadn't lied about her past experiences and managed to fly through it with a surprising amount of ease.

They now stood upon a white shoreline cliff with grass covering the top. Off in the distance, a small building sat in the middle of nowhere. Fields as far as the eye could see.

"Security isn't very high here; he doesn't know I found this place. Even so, the walls are thick enough to shrug a nuclear blast off, as far as you guys are concerned, pretty indestructible." Thomas revealed as Patrick finished climbing off Flame. She began to shiver in the light draft from the coast. The storm was coming their way.

"So, he won't be expecting an attack." Cathie muttered as she checked her sword blade for dents. The blade had dulled in places, but it wasn't too bad. Charlie had certainly made it well.

"At first, but make no mistake, he'll respond to us faster than you expect."

"Not if we expect him to instantly respond." Tom responded as he checked the strap on his bag. It had made it through the storm unharmed. Thomas smiled at his remark.

"Like I said before, we'll need to distract Edward long enough for us to rescue Amy and find his unstable portal device."

"The unstable one? Surely we want the stable one instead?" Tom asked him. Thomas shook his head.

"Only stable one Edward has is embedded into his armour. But since he has access to it, he won't really be guarding the unstable one very well."

"How are we going to get back using the unstable ones then? Pretty sure you said unstable means we die if we go through." Patrick asked him. Thomas took out what appeared to be a small ring of black material and handed it to Tom.

"Edward doesn't know this, but for his original portal design I swapped this out for one cut just lightly wrong." He revealed. Tom nodded with approval.

"So the shape does matter." He chuckled as he pocketed the ring, "Good to know."

"I'm sure I don't have to tell you to not leave the device here once you correct it."

"You're going to let us take it with us?" Tom asked him. Thomas sighed.

"As much as it pains me, I'd rather have you have it than Edward. I trust you'll heed my earlier warnings and do the sensible thing."

"Edward already has access to it though." Tom reminded him.

"Something I plan on changing while you're rescuing Amy. Enough shots from my rifle and I can completely destroy his armour, the portal device with it. If I succeed here, I won't need your help later on."

"You're going to need help if you're going to get a clean shot." Cathie pointed out, "I'd like to help you with the distraction."

"Your priority is Amy."

"Which means I can buy her double the time to escape should you fail." She added. Thomas realised he wasn't going to convince her otherwise.

"What about miss campfire over here?" Patrick asked.

"Right now she needs to conserve as much heat as possible. Fighting in the state you're in is far too risky." Tom explained, "We'll have to make a quick stop with the portal device to pick you up before calibrating it to home."

"Which reminds me." Thomas added as he delved into his lab coat pockets. He brought out a small high-tech looking object and also handed it to Tom, "I was scanning when Edward pulled you through. Plug than in and it should produce the same readings I measured, should get you back where you started, plus or minus a few hours perhaps."

"So how are we getting in this place then?" Tom asked as he pocketed the object.

"The device I stored inside your bag." Thomas revealed. Tom first took out the large rifle, which he handed to him, but then also brought out a second device.

A metal glove by the looks of it at first, but the many wires and peculiar design around the palm of the hand seemed to suggest it did something other than look fashionable.

"This thing?"

"Don't worry too much about it. Very much out of your league." Thomas answered as he put the glove on. He also slung the rifle over his shoulder, with the strap attached around him.

***

The rest of them watched in complete amazement as the red light coming from the glove seemed to make a large chunk of the exterior wall in front of them vanish. Tom began to open his mouth as the glove powered down, but he was quickly interrupted by Thomas.

"Forget it." He answered before Tom had even begun, "This is but the surface of this things potential. I wouldn't trust this to you no matter what the stakes."

"You make it sound like it can destroy anything." Tom seemed to probe.

"It can, given enough time. But even that is only one aspect of things' function. Now on to other matters." He answered as he desperately changed the subject. He brought out a phone like device and looked down at the screen.

Once more Tom very nearly began a series of questions, but his own mind stopped him. The time for questions was over, "Amy is somewhere that way, but her life signs are weak. I'm also reading another weak life sign near her, so be cautious."

"What about Edward?" Cathie asked him.

"This direction." He answered as he pointed elsewhere, "He seems to be alone for now."

"Wouldn't have really made a difference." She sighed as she walked through the fresh hole and into a corridor. Thomas followed her as the two walked off in roughly the direction Thomas had pointed to.

"Let's go." Patrick added as he patted Tom on the shoulder. The two of them entered the hole and began to make their way in the rough direction Thomas had also pointed to.

***

Thomas put away the phone like device as the two of them came up to a double door at the end of the corridor.

"Just through there." He revealed as he took out his rifle. He made sure the sleeve of his lab coat hid most of the glove before he took aim at the door from a distance.

Cathie took out her sword and approached the door slowly. Just before she was about to push it open, Thomas noticed something off.

Too late, Cathie had already pushed it open. They watched the pin leave the grenade as she did so. Her eyes widened as her instincts told her to run. She turned and did so, but the blast was quick.

As the smoke cleared, Edward walked through the now hole in the wall instead of the doors with his armour donned.

He came across the sight of Cathie's back, riddled with the shards of brown material he'd used as frag in the bomb. She was still standing, but not for long.

She fell to her knees, then face first onto the floor. However, Edward didn't have much time to celebrate. As she fell, Thomas' barrel came into view. Charred floor either side of him, but he himself had been protected my Cathie's body.

A slug fired at full speed. It hit a shield, but it smashed right through it. Instead, it deflected off the blade of Edward's brown sword. Blood splattered onto the corridor floor right at his feet.

"Nice shot." He chuckled as he checked the blade edge of his sword. No damage, as always. He pulled his attention back to Thomas as he took out a laser gun and aimed it at him, but Tom had already closed in on him.

He'd adapted to the rifle shots, so now for something old and unexpected. Thomas' glove grabbed a hold of Edward's blade and surrounded the entire thing with a red light. Edward's eyes widened as his blade at first shattered, but then completely disappeared within the red light.

He quickly threw an elbow towards Thomas, but he'd already had the sense to back off all the way back to Cathie. He revealed the glove under his lab coat sleeve and seemed to look at a small display on the forearm.

"As I thought, Karathus." He scoffed as he turned his attention back to Edward, "How many people did you have to kill to make that blade?"

"Three." Edward answered with a chuckle, "I see old habits die hard. Thought you vowed never to use that thing again."

"For you Edward, I'll make an exception."

"A risky game you're playing here Tom, should that thing fall into my hands we'll have a repeat of last time. A time I assume that you now remember considering you have that working again."

"Better to risk one world's fate instead of two. Then again, math was never your strength, was it?"

"Insulting me already." He spoke as he shook his head, "Talking as if you've already won." Thomas seemed to spin a part of his rifle by only a few degrees as he began to aim it once more.

This time instead of firing a single slug, the gun let loose with smaller projectiles. Each one seemed to get stuck in the new shield in front of them, but their tips had made it through. The tips opened and before Edward knew it, multiple small streams of blood were being squirted at his chest.

The shield disabled and the bullets dropped to the floor. It wasn't enough to completely break through the armour, but it certainly weakened it.

Another boom confirmed that another large slug was on its way. Edward did his best to move to the side, but it caught his left arm dead on. He watched as his elbow and upper left arm became exposed.

"Overconfidence is your real weakness Edward. Apparently, you seem incapable of overcoming such a thing."

***

Tom and Patrick arrived at an almost completely empty room. In the middle however stood two large glass chambers filled with both liquid, and bodies.

As the two of them ran over to them, they were rather puzzled to find that both bodies were in fact exactly the same, and both were Amy.

"What the hell are we looking at?" Patrick asked as Tom began to examine the small amount of machinery that both bodies were hooked up to. The glass chambers each had a label. One said 'Original' the other read 'Clone'.

"This thing seems to extract samples from specimens placed in the original labelled chamber. Most likely our Amy. Sample goes through a lot of shit I can't even begin to work out, but it all ends in the second chamber."

"Is it possible they made a second Amy from part of her?" He asked. Right now, what was in front of him didn't seem at all possible.

"Can't tell. Try and see if either of them are conscious while I figure out if it's safe to open these things up." Tom suggested as he began to dig through a few loose wires.

Patrick began by tapping on the glass for the one labelled as a clone. If they had created a second Amy, was it alive? To his surprise, her eyes shot open. She seemed to instantly panic at the sight of the many wires coming out of her, and the fact that she was submerged in some form of liquid.

"That's not possible." Patrick muttered as Tom resurfaced from checking out the machinery.

"Seems safe enough. Let's get them out." It didn't take much force to smash through the glass. Tom caught the original as she was washed out of her glass prison by the liquid while Patrick caught her copy.

Both were rather confused, shaken and unclothed. Tom quickly brought out a fur blanket from his bag and wrapped both of them in it, "Only have the one I'm afraid, so you'll have to share for now." He added as the two of them suddenly noticed one another.

"Wait, that's me." Both of them spoke as they got a good look at one another. The cold from the large empty room began to make both of them shiver. They were both soaking wet still.

"We'll figure everything out once we're safe." Tom sighed as he pointed to the one who'd come out of the original chamber, "You're O." He spoke, he turned to the other one, "You're C. Remember that, both of you."

They both gave a rather confused but compliant nod as they tightened the single blanket around the two of them.

"Now to get out of here." Patrick reminded Tom. Tom nodded.

"I saw another room that seemed important earlier. Might be the portal device."

***

A wave of energy made its way throughout the building. Thomas watched as his rifle lost power and deactivated. Now it was nothing more than scrap metal.

"I'm more than aware that you two are a distraction. That EMP should take out the unstable portal device as well as your weapon. Only thing that will work now is my armour." He explained. Thomas dropped the rifle and pointed the glove towards Edward.

"That's not exactly true. This thing doesn't rely on electric charge for energy storage. As well, you know."

"Honestly forgot about that, but I see you're correct." He responded as he caught the display on the forearm was still on, "No matter."

"Pun intended that time?" Thomas asked him.

"Guess I'll just have to fight you like old times." He chuckled as he began to walk towards Thomas. Thomas in turn began to walk towards him until they were both in arm's reach.

Edward threw the first punch with his right fist. Green light shot from the glove and within it, a concrete block quickly formed. The block absorbed the blow as Thomas side stepped and aimed the glove at Edward's exposed elbow. More green light as this time a pole of metal shot from the glove.

Edward managed to move his arm, but the pole managed a small injury as he failed to completely avoid the attack. Edward threw a second punch with his left, now too close to Thomas for anything to form. The pole fell to the floor as Thomas ducked and grabbed a hold of Edward's left leg.

Red light surrounded the leg as the armour began to thin. The red light seemed to focus more on cutting pieces off instead of total destruction, since that would be faster at creating vulnerabilities. The leg armour shattered into large chunks of black material that joined the metal pole on the floor.

A kick from the right flung Thomas against the wall of the corridor. He'd just about created a thin layer of impact resistant material, but despite this he spat out the blood in his mouth as he struggled to his feet. Edward's armour was of course power assisted. Which meant a single direct punch or kick could go through tank armour, let alone a normal human body.

The impact resistant layer vanished in a cloud of red light, along with the pole and chunks of concrete. The red light seemed to return to the glove.

"I'll admit you still pack as much of a punch as last time." Thomas winced as he managed to finally get himself upright.

"The power to create and destroy. For a man so hell bent on stopping man from becoming a god, you alone are responsible for the invention of a device that grants the user that very same godlike power."

"I'm fully aware of the irony, trust me."

"And yet I still manage to land a hit." Edward chuckled, "It seems that both of us have become gods amongst man."

"There's that overconfidence again." Thomas sighed as he wiped some blood from his lips, "You're a fool if you think you're a god. Last I checked you needed this thing to achieve that dream of immortality you seemed so desperate to make a reality."

"A dream I have found other methods of achieving." Edward revealed as he closed the distance between the two of them once more.

Edward's eyes moved left, to where he was expecting Thomas to attack given the broken armour, but instead he found himself staring at nothing but the empty corridor.

"Not if I finish this now." He heard a ring through his right ear as the glove landed on his back. Edward raised a shield, but it merely surrounded Thomas' arm as the red light surrounded the thick back of the armour. The rear of the armour was not very thick armour, however. Not only were there storage components, but most of the systems onboard were stored in the back. These systems were what Thomas had been after all along.

Edward felt his armour slug as the power assistance failed. He was now supporting the whole weight on his own. The shield around Thomas' arm also failed as the power source crumbled. Edward turned and smacked Thomas' hand out of the way, but the damage had been done.

Movement was hard now. No shields either. Not to mention the on heads display. He was now blind as well as slow. He took off the helmet to see that Thomas was holding a perfectly cut ring of the black material in his glove. The ring from his on-board portal device.

As the red light began to surround it, Edward shot forwards and managed to grab it right out of the glove, but his hand now felt the wrath of the glove. The armour around his left fist shattered. The armour of the left forearm fell off with it as he managed to pull his hand back just in time to avoid damage to his flesh.

Thomas made a grab for the ring, but Edward threw an unexpected right hook into his stomach. Thomas keeled over as Edward tried his best to get away, retreating into the room he'd originally come from.

"Activate backup!" Thomas heard Edward shout as he disappeared from view. The sound of armour coming off began to worry him greatly. Backup… he had another armour!

He got to his feet, ignoring the pain. Now wasn't the time for hesitation. He ran through into the room just in time to see Edward's face disappear inside of his second suit of armour.

"Bastard!"

"Always helps to have a spare. Afraid this one doesn't have a portal device on-board, but easily fixed since I still have the ring." He explained as he took a fist fighting stance. Thomas made a desperate sprint around the side of him to get to his back. He needed to get to that storage device no matter what.

Edward however saw this coming. Before Thomas got too close, he shot him in the chest with a laser gun. Thomas fell to his knees clutching his wound. Green light surrounded it and the bleeding quickly stopped, but it wasn't a good fix.

"Fuck." He cursed as the pain of both the wound and the rough patch job hit him like a brick wall.

"A handy device to be sure, but I know for a fact you didn't calibrate it well enough to be used for medical treatment." Edward chuckled as he aimed the gun at

Thomas' head. He hadn't really had time to aim with the last shot, but this one would kill him for sure.

A noise came from down the corridor, but he disregarded it as some leftover rubble from their earlier brawl. He went to pull the trigger, but then suddenly remembered what else was in that corridor.

He quickly spun around and raised a shield as a bare fist smacked into it at full force. The fist shattered the shield and with ever so slightly less force, smashed into his chest.

A pain shot through him as his eyes finally looked at the face that until now had been distorted by the shield.

The blood on her face made it hard to tell where the blood stopped, and her hair began. Eyes of pure fire stared back at him. They were no longer just red anymore; they were glowing a bright but sinister red that screamed hatred right into the depths of his mind. Despite being drenched in her own blood, her hair seemed to give off a similar energy as it waved slightly unnaturally in the still air of the room.

His eyes followed her arm right up to his chest. In her attacking hand, she had a tight grasp of a shard of Karathus, so tight her hands were covered in large, deep cuts. The shard had punctured his armour. He watched his own blood begin to make a bigger hole as his armour slowly sizzled and dissolved.

Jets fired from a concealed compartment on his back. The two of them slowly lifted into the air as Cathie kept her firm grip on the shard. She plunged it deeper into his body, her fingers now flush with his bare skin.

As he looked back at her, he noticed that her eyes and hair had calmed down and returned to normal. He felt her arm now tremble with weakness.

"For my daughter." She spat as she felt her own grip fail. She fell to the floor.

"You Cathie Clawson, are one scary person." Edward winced as he did his best to keep the shard in his wound. He shot through the roof of the room and out into the world beyond.

"Damn it." Thomas frustratingly exclaimed as he struggled to his feet, "I didn't get the portal technology from him."

"A problem for later." Cathie winced as she herself struggled to stay on her feet. The shards hadn't caused too much damage to her back, but that last move had taken almost everything out of her, "Hopefully the others found Amy."

"You'd be right about that." Tom spoke as he walked into the room, first taking in the destruction of the doors, then realising how wounded the two of them were, "You two good?"

"We'll last." Thomas muttered as the two of them did their best to hold one another up, "You get the portal device?"

"Fully operational." Tom revealed as he waved about the small gun like device. Patrick walked into the room, closely followed by two Amy's and Flame, "Already made the detour."

"How? Edward set off an EMP, it should have fried it."

"You mean that energy wave thing?" Tom asked, "Yeah, didn't work at all, not even the unstable portals generated, until I switched the rings."

"Ah, the stored-up energy in the ring I gave you, but it should be empty if memory serves. What the hell charged it?"

"If it wasn't the device, best guess is that wave thing itself. Anyway, we need to be getting home, Flame doesn't have long."

CHAPTER 32; FATE

Tom stared at the open portal in front of him as Cathie walked through it. The others had already made their way through, leaving just him and Thomas.

"You sure you're alright?" Tom asked as he tried to get a good look at Thomas' wound. He simply waved him away.

"I'm good. My Cathie's still on her way remember? She'll make sure I'm still alive." He spoke as a light rain began to dribble through the hole in the roof.

Tom then turned his attention to the portal device in his hands. He took the high-tech looking object out of it and crushed it in his hands.

"If all goes to plan, this will be the last time we meet." He added as he let the pieces fall to the floor.

"If all goes to plan." Thomas smirked between winces, "Take good care of those girls Tom. They fought battles like this every day just to return to you."

"I'll certainly keep that in mind." Tom replied with a smile as he walked towards the portal.

As he stepped through, lightning struck the portal dead on. The portal closed instantly, leaving just a charred floor.

***

Tom walked out of the portal, but not where he was expecting to end up. He stood in a room that was massively out of proportion to him. He seemed like an ant compared with the glass see-though table he was standing on. The view underneath made Tom want to throw up with the sheer height.

Stood around this table, were three gigantic figures. One red, one blue and one green.

"At last, a chance to finally speak with the fabled Thomas Thomson." The red one boomed as they all seemed rather pleased to see him.

"I'm afraid there is a chance you've got the wrong guy." Tom responded, worried that they might not even hear him from where he was standing.

"We are certain you are the one. Thomas Thomson, son of Kara and Maximus, although you knew him as Jack Thomson, correct?" The blue one asked.

"That is I." Tom answered.

"We've had our eye on you for many days now. Even sent an old friend to bring you to us." The green one spoke as Charlie seemed to form into existence beside him.

Almost instantly, he drew a sword and charged at Tom, but seemed to freeze before he could attack.

"You are no longer necessary." The red one spoke as he waved his giant hand. Tom could to nothing but watch as Charlie dissolved into nothing.

"Who are you three? Why did you send Charlie to kill me?" Tom began to ask.

"We have a limited presence in the material realm. Your death, we could intercept and bring you here, as we did with your friend. However, thanks to some crafty planning, we have brought you here by other means." The blue one spoke.

"As for who we are." The green one began, "I am Creation. The blue one is Essence and the red one is Destruction." He listed, "The three of us are known as the higher powers."

"So, I take it I'm addressing some form of gods?" He asked the three of them.

"To you, yes." Essence answered.

"Gods of humanity." Destruction quickly added, "Gods that require your assistance."

"I'm not sure if you've noticed, but I've kind of got my hands full at the moment." Tom sighed as he folded his arms.

"Oh, I'm more than aware." Another voice spoke. Tom turned to face the figure behind him. Black hair, crafty, almost evil smile across his face. Edward. Dressed in fur skin clothes, but definitely Edward.

"Do not be alarmed Thomas Thomson." Creation announced before Tom had a chance to react. Edward walked over to him and seemed to admiringly look him up and down, "For he is not the Edward you have been facing."

"No, but my world's equivalent, right?" He asked Edward. Edward seemed to smile at this.

"Fast, isn't he?" He began to chuckle as he finished inspecting him and held out a hand. Tom hesitantly shook it, "They brought me here too, just like you."

"Why?" Tom asked them.

"Two souls fated to oppose one another. A fate that transcends worlds as you have discovered. A fate we wish to exploit in order to restore humanity."

"If you are the gods you claim to be, surely you can just make more humans with a clap of your hands." Tom pointed out.

"They can." Edward responded, "But these three are rather useless at looking after things. Current human population is all their doing." He added.

"Harsh, but perhaps somewhat deserving." Essence sighed, "We lack the understand and craftiness required to keep humanity ticking. However, we have noticed that when under pressure and danger, humanity thrives like nothing else."

"Unless the danger is too much too fast." Tom added, "Then you just end up wiping us out."

"See now why they need us?" Edward pointed out.

"We will remake humanity. After which it will be your job to create these scenarios to further push them at every step."

"What about this fate thing you mentioned. If we're both working on this, surely fighting one another is counterproductive?" Tom asked.

"No, fighting one another is the whole point." Edward revealed, "I get to play the bad guy, you get to play the good guy. Either you defeat me and progress humanity, or I win, and humanity gets wiped out."

"Risking everything on the hope that I'll win every time?" Tom asked him. Edward gave a small smile.

"I'm certainly not going to hold back just because humanity will die as a consequence. Personally, I don't like the idea of helping them, but I do enjoy a challenge." He explained.

"Regrettably, as I stated before, I've got my hands full with matters of more concern to me." Tom spoke as he turned to face the three higher powers.

"The world is not ready for humanities return, but after this threat from another world is dealt with, then we shall end the age of dragons and begin the age of humanity." Destruction revealed.

"Defeat the other world, defeat the divine, save your world." Essence added.

"About the divine. Since your gods and all, wouldn't mind some advice on how to take him down."

"Most gods have strength beyond your ability to comprehend, yet most gods fuel this power by way of worship."

"I don't see many humans worshiping you."

"Our power comes from…" Destruction paused for a second, "Other means."

"A god without worship will possess no power other than any physical form they take up."

"Certainly, a massive help." Tom sighed with relief. He'd thus far struggled to work out exactly how to go toe to toe with such a being, but now his next move seemed clear.

"Of course. The four of us need you to succeed." Edward added as he gave Tom a pat on the back slightly harder than Tom was ok with, "Try not to disappoint me."

***

Tom emerged from the portal. Cathie, Patrick, Amy, Flame and Amy were waiting for him.

"You certainly took your time." Patrick muttered, "Thomas had a lot of goodbyes to say?"

"More or less." Tom answered as he looked down at the portal device in his hand.

Tomorrow they were going to take on a god, but he couldn't get the image of Thomas' rather pissed off face from his mind.

He dropped the device, then put his foot through it. He bent down, took out the ring of black material and threw it into the forest beyond.

"You sure about that?" Flame asked him.

"Never learnt how it worked, never will. Nothing wrong with our deal is there?" Tom asked her. She thought about this for a few seconds.

"No." She simply responded.

"We leave something like that anywhere and something or someone in this world will take up the role that Edward seems to play in the other. Something we shouldn't risk."

"Right." Patrick agreed, "One nutcase is enough for me." They all nodded in agreement as they began to walk.

"Figured out where we are?" Tom asked them. Cathie nodded.

"Not too far from the cave. But perhaps you should look up."

Tom looked up at the sky in between the thick leaves above them. The moon hung over them.

"The night before we were pulled into the other world." He realised, "That gives us enough time."

"Enough time for what?" Patrick asked him. Tom turned to Flame.

"Your god gets his power from worship. Every dragon that looks up to him makes him stronger." He explained to her.

"You know this because?" Tom smiled at this.

"Please, who do you take me for?" Flame nodded at this.

"I take it you wish for me to reduce his followers."

"The more you do, the less trouble we'll have."

"If this works Thomas Thomson, you might end up being the first god slayer amongst us."

"You've witnessed the other world with your own eyes. You've seen the things us humans face. What is another god?"

***

Cathie stared at the two Amy's in front of her as they finished getting themselves properly clothed from some fresh wolf skin.

"I don't remember giving birth to twins." She muttered as Tom joined her after filling his bag with salted meat, "And I'm sure I'd remember. I was very much awake and screaming at the time."

"Not entirely sure what Edward did, but he seemed to make another living and breathing Amy." He answered her.

"So now we have two bloodthirsty, adorable children."

"Don't look at me. I didn't have any a few days ago." He shrugged.

"Well, we're going to have to do something about their names. Twins with the same names are just asking for trouble." Tom nodded at this.

"Sooner the better." He muttered as he walked over to the two of them, "Alright, which one is C and O?"

"I'm O." One of them answered.

"C." The other answered.

"C means copy. O is the original." He revealed to them.

"So, I'm a copy of her?"

"Afraid so. Also means we can't just call you Amy either. Far too confusing."

"So, what name should I have?" She asked, "I really like Amy."

"Amelia?" Cathie suggested as she joined them, "Long version of the name."

"No better than Tom and Thomas." Tom sighed, "But probably good enough."

***

After watching themselves fall through a portal just outside their cave from the treeline, they made their way back into the cave. The night outside had been rough, but nothing compared to what they'd all just been through.

Cathie was quick to gently tug at Tom's arm in the direction of his room. Noticing her serious face, he quickly led her there.

Once the door was shut, Cathie turned to face him.

"My wound… I… ummm…"

"Lied about it healing?" He asked. He didn't seem surprised by this.

"A bit worse… I… I keep reopening it… on purpose…" Tom gave a slow nod of understanding.

"Right. Didn't even occur to me that this is the first time you've been cut in seventeen years." He sighed as he quickly reached into his bag and grabbed a few bandages.

"I wanted to tell you sooner but…"

"Wanted to enjoy it while it lasted right?" He filled in as she lifted her top up halfway. He started to bandage it up.

"Sorry."

"It's alright. Should have spotted it myself." As he finished tying the bandage their eyes met.

Thomas' last words quickly popped back into his head. Seventeen years of fighting that monster just to get back to him. Of course, she would. She'd have fought for much longer if she'd had to.

He realised he truly was staring at the same obsessed, broken girl he'd for some reason fallen in love with.

"Are you alright?" She asked as she lowered her top. They'd been looking at one another for longer than a minute now.

"Yeah." Tom muttered before kissing her. Her face blushed the same bright red it always did.

"Since you have to keep an eye on me until this heals anyway, mind making the whole thing easier for me?" She asked with a smile as their arms wrapped around one another.

"Depends on what I have to do." She quickly gave him a peck on the lips.

"I'm sure you can do something to keep my mind off it." She whispered.

***

Meanwhile, Patrick was left in the main room with both Amy and Amelia.

"You two alright?" He asked them both as they both sat down at the table.

"Kind of still taking the whole thing in still." Amelia responded as Patrick stood at the head of the table. The two of them had sat either side. Every now and again he'd catch one of them checking that the other was in fact still real.

"So, you both remember everything from before this happened, or is your memory clear Amelia?" Patrick asked her.

"I remember everything up until we lost consciousness after we were taken away from you guys." Amelia answered.

"Same here." Amy added, "Guess we really are exactly the same."

"I don't know about that." Amelia muttered as she eyed Patrick up, "See I remember having a massive crush on you, but now I don't really see why." Amy's face turned bright red.

"Do you have to be so blunt?" She asked her.

"You're saying your feelings are different?" Patrick asked.

"Well since I've apparently only just begun feeling, yeah. Can't explain why but half the stuff I used to like I can't see myself liking anymore." Amelia explained.

"I guess that makes things a little less complicated between the three of us." Amy muttered, face still bright red. Amelia stood up and quickly walked into Cathie's room. She returned with a small one-handed sword.

"Hope you guys don't mind, but I really need to figure out who I am. Right now, all I see myself as, is a copy of an original. I don't want to live like that."

"You sure you want to be out there alone?" Patrick asked her. Amelia nodded as she headed towards the front door.

"Got a memories worth of knowledge to help me out there." She added just before leaving.

***

The sun was now up in the sky and as bright as ever. Amelia quickly sped from the front door of the cave to the nearby treeline. Her skin turned red, but quickly healed once she was in the shade. She tucked the one-handed sword down the back of her top, with the hilt hanging off the rather hastily fashioned fur collar. The point poked out of the bottom of her top, with the cold blade itself against her bare skin.

She quickly sped off into a completely random part of the woods, but on purposely far from the cave. She needed to make sure she was outside her sister's earshot completely. She finally came to a stop and slowly backed into a tree.

She began to tear up as her blade protected back slid down the bark of the tree until she was sitting with her legs tucked right up to her chest. She quickly let loose the wall of tears she'd just about managed to keep at bay throughout that talk.

She reached into her pocket but found it empty. That's right, her sister was the one who had what she was looking for. She took a good few minutes to get a loud, wet and messy cry out while she could.

After a few minutes she managed to calm herself. Slowly, she began to wipe the tears from her face. Her cheeks were still puffed up and her eyes were bloodshot from it all, but with only a few snivels she was back on her feet.

She picked a random direction and started to walk. Thoughts of Patrick filled her head, but she quickly blocked them. If one of them was going to be happy then this was something she just had to do. She had to get those thoughts to stop no matter what.

This was going to be harder than she'd first thought.

CHAPTER 33; THE DIVINE

To say that none of the four of them were frightened to enter the large ice dragon doors to the building within the swamps that housed the round table would be a complete lie.

A god, seeming hellbent on destroying humanity would soon stand before them. One who has had their claws in too many pies for each of their liking.

For some reason, this very god wanted both the Thomson's and Clawson's dead above all others. The dragon's natural fear of magic probably meant that Patrick wouldn't be in any nicer position than Tom and Cathie right now and Amy… well. A Clawson and a Thomson. She was perhaps the most at risk from this all.

Behind them, Frost slowly shepherded them in as four ice dragons, Shard among them, opened the doors ahead. Cathie had Charlie's sword on her back, but with arms ready to pull it out in less than a second if need be. Patrick's satchel was filled to the brim with both books and ingredients of all varieties. Amy herself had a bow over her shoulder, but also a light one-handed sword strapped to a belt just in case.

Tom simply had his bag over his shoulder. No weapons on display for now, but the bag alone was perhaps the most dangerous thing the four of them were carrying.

The four of them all swallowed rather nervously as the doors slammed shut behind them. No turning back now.

They made their way into the large room with the round table at the centre. To their surprise, this time a metal staircase the perfect size for them led from directly in front of them onto the top of the table. Taking the hint, the four of them walked up and onto the table once more.

It was only now that they were able to get a view of the whole room themselves. Unexpectedly, almost every single seat was filled.

Flint and Flame were here, as well as the water, lava, earth and air dragon leaders. Only two slabs were currently empty. The mysterious slab of metal that quietly hummed, and the grand slab that was within the middle of the table.

Flame's message had reached Frost. They assumed she'd managed the same for the rest of the alliance, but the air and earth dragons would be a problem. Everyone in the room could feel the tension in the air barely holding either side at bay from an all-out fight right here and now.

A sparkle appeared above the centre slab. Small at first but it seemed to disperse golden glitter that quickly grew into golden bubbles, before beginning to form a shape as a collective.

The shape sharpened, until there before them stood a golden dragon that towered over the rest more so than the dragons themselves towered over the humans.

This dragon's mere presence seemed to cut right through any tension within the room. All rose to their feet and bowed their heads with respect. The guards behind each leader made certain their snouts were against the floor of the room like their life depended on it.

"It has been a long time since you've all been in my presence." The divine spoke in a voice that could only be described as godlike. If the four humans hadn't been nervous before, they certainly were now, "It has come to my attention that my last orders before leaving this world have not been carried out to completion. The four who stand before me are proof of this fact. Explain!"

"We have been carrying out your orders for many years now your greatness." The earth dragon leader began, "More so than any other dragon type. Yet these four have proven a challenge for us to find and kill."

The divine seemed to nod at this, then turned to Frost.

"The ice dragons have also followed this path for many years, oh great one." Frost began, "However I decided to instead use these humans to heal the divide left after your absence. I saw it wiser to avoid our own self-destruction than complete the task given to us many years previously." He explained.

"All present fall on one of these two sides, correct?" The divine asked as he looked around the room. Everyone nodded. He seemed to take in each of their responses carefully to make sure no one was overlooked.

"Perhaps the honour of slaying the last of the humans should fall to you yourself, great divine." The leader of the air dragons proposed.

"We shall see." The divine responded as he turned and looked down towards the four humans beneath him. Before their very eyes, the golden dragon shrank in size as he took a step onto the table. His shape seemed to swirl and stir as he shrunk, until he stood as a golden suited human. A gold tie and cuff links constructed themselves at the click of his finger as he now stood before the four of them.

"I have many questions." Tom spoke as the divine's attention turned to him. He seemed to note the lack of weapons on his person.

"Thomas Thomson. The man this world seems to revolve around." The divine chuckled as he took a good look at him, "Ask away."

"Why order humanities destruction?" He asked. The divine gave a rather understanding and expected look.

"I am what is referred to as a celestial. A being of power no one in this room could comprehend. I rather enjoy this thing you refer to as life, even play god for a species or two. The dragons being one of these. However another celestial entered this world I'd built a home for my worshipers for."

"The Neutral." Tom interrupted. The divine smiled.

"A name that has been thrown at you many times I am sure."

"I've heard this and that. Not all the pieces fit together just yet though." He responded.

"The Neutral and I had a… disagreement. Difference of opinion at first, but he soon took it much further than that. Meanwhile in this rather beautiful world, a new creature was being born and beginning to slowly spread throughout the known world. Human beings. Not very strong, but especially crafty. I myself wished to take your race under my nurturing wing like the dragon race, but alas, it was not to be."

"What happened?"

"Battles between celestials are messy things. Given there are only three of us, until this point it had never happened. Instead of fighting the Neutral directly and risking those in my care, I trapped the Neutral in a human body. I gave him the option to act as your god as I did for so many others instead of continuing the conflict."

"But he didn't take that well, did he?" Tom asked him, "He used our kind to try and fight you despite his entrapment." He guessed.

"Yes, he did. It was then I realised that there was no longer a way of reasoning with the Neutral. The two of us fought it out, but with the whole human race behind him, I was forced to get my own precious children involved as well."

"The beginning of dragons against humans."

"Once the Neutral was defeated, I realised I'd merely destroyed his human body, not the celestial inside. Thanks to my earlier efforts though, he still needed a human body to survive and interact with anything. I could not risk more bloodshed on those under my care, so I ordered the genocide of the human race."

"Because you feared one of us would carry this Neutral within us. What about the Thomson's and the Clawson's?" Tom asked him. The divine seemed rather uneasy at this request.

"The Thomson's were not of this world. Humans from another world, one with more knowledge and science than any could achieve here. A threat should they ever have allied with a reincarnation of the Neutral." He answered.

"And the Clawson's?" Cathie reminded him. He turned to look at her and noticed her fiery red hair and eyes.

"Angel Clawson and her fierce husband Fire, god of the fire dragons, actively opposed me. They posed a very dangerous threat to my children, so I eliminated them." He explained, "Catahyme, a name of death and loss. Such a fierce warrior despite you're minimal training. I'm sure you could all imagine how much of a threat you yourself would have posed to dragon kind had you properly learnt the skills of your mother."

"But since she didn't, there shouldn't be a need to kill her." Tom argued. The divine seemed hesitant at this.

"Your family blood is a risk I would have snuffed out long ago had I been aware you had survived. However, without the Neutral you pose little threat to me. Her fate shall, like the rest of you, depend on whether one of you is currently holding the Neutral inside you." He answered, "Speaking of which."

"So, if none of us hold this Neutral, you'll let us live?" Tom asked him.

"How ever much I would love to eliminate every threat to my children and reunite them myself, I do not have the time for such things anymore. There are more important matters to consider than the fate of this world. If the Neutral is dead, then none present threaten to hinder me." The divine answered as he raised a hand and pointed it towards Amy, "Human dragon hybrid with a few abnormalities unique to your kind. Nothing too special about you." His hand turned to point towards Patrick.

As it did so, Patrick seemed to uncontrollably glow orange, "The presence of Will?" The divine chuckled, "Now that's an old face, but not one I have a quarrel with. Consider yourself blessed, Patrick of the clan of magic."

His hand then turned to Cathie. As it did so, Cathie held Tom's hand and held it tightly beside her.

***

Tom suddenly found himself inside a white, blank room that seemed to continue onwards to infinity in all directions. A shapeless figure appeared before him. It seemed to take on the form of a human, but with so little detail it was all he could take from the shape. Tom then realised the feeling of Cathie's hand hadn't disappeared.

He turned to his side and there she was. Standing beside him, looking at the figure before them as well. More figures stood behind Cathie, but Tom didn't recognise them at all. He turned his attention back to the one that seemed to want their attention.

The figure seemed to form a mouth and fingers.

"Shhhhhhh." It hushed as it placed one finger over its mouth. The two of them suddenly felt a wave of power move through the room. It hit them, the figures behind Cathie, but it seemed to gently pass through the figure in front of them. It slowly vanished.

"Was that...?" Cathie began but trailed off.

"Hopefully not." Tom answered as he turned to face her. His attention was drawn back to the other figures behind her, "Who are they?"

The other figures all turned to face him, seemingly surprised that he was here. One was a large tank of a man; one was a thin but tall girl whose hair seemed to blow in the non-existent wind. The third seemed to be a very hazy version of Cathie, with red floating hair and eyes of pure fire.

"Some of us are spells fused to Cathie when she fell through the portal." The tall but thin woman spoke, "Big guy here is why she's immortal. But miss crazy was here from birth."

"As was he, I take it." Cathie added as she pointed to Tom's side. Tom turned completely around to spot the figure which until now had been standing behind him. He looked like him in every single way apart from the purple hair and eyes.

"Analysis has determined that this is a physical manifestation of our combined minds." He spoke rather coldly, "I represent the ability to break the minds limits. Clearly the third one behind Cathie represents her ability to break her bodies limits." It hypothesized.

"I don't sound like that, do I?" Tom asked Cathie.

"Sometimes." She answered. There was a sudden white flash.

***

They were back. The divine's hand lowered, but he didn't seem concerned.

"None of you are harbouring the Neutral. It appears I no longer have to fear its return." He sighed. The sudden tension that had been unnoticed reached an all-time high, but then quickly lowered with his words, "So you were ready to attack should I have revealed otherwise." He chuckled as he turned to face Frost, and then Flame. Both were standing combat ready.

All eyes on the room fell on the two of them.

"If it came to it." Tom spoke, "We certainly weren't just going to let you kill us." He revealed.

"Turning my own children against me." The divine sighed as Flame and Frost slowly backed down, "Let me guess, those want to be gods known as the higher powers told you that my power relies on worshipers, right?" He asked Tom. Tom slowly nodded.

"Friends of yours?" The divine laughed at this.

"As much as you are a friend to an ant under your foot. Rather ironic that you of all people chose to side with them, considering what they did to your family."

"My family was killed by a pack of three earth dragons." Tom reminded him. He simply smiled.

"Many beings of power much greater than you'll ever understand can take many forms Thomas Thomson. Funny though, if memory serves correctly, your mother trapped them inside a very secure box. Wonder how they got out." He asked with a huge grin on his face.

Tom's mind instantly flashed back to the cube he'd broken on the huge chunk of black material. His eyes widened, "But anyway, I care not of this betrayal now. Since the Neutral is no longer a concern I am done with this world."

"Thought you said you liked playing god to your people." Tom pointed out.

"I do, but I have a greater goal I must achieve. One that requires many sacrifices from me. I've got rather a long way to go still. I see no reason for these human's death. Juggle them around your pointless politics if you so wish. I shall not be returning, nor do I care for what this world becomes."

The golden suited man seemed to collapse in on himself until he was a cloud of golden glitter that slowly faded into nothing. The room was left silent.

"Our... our god has abandoned us." The earth dragon leader spoke. There were a few seconds of complete silence as everyone in the room began to process such a statement.

"Then was he ever really your god?" Tom asked the room. All were shocked that he'd spoken up, "Way I see it, beings of which we do not understand have been playing us all for puppets. The Neutral, the Divine. How much blood has been spilt because of those two words?"

The room began to murmur.

"Too much." Frost boomed. Slowly but surely, the entire room began to agree with him.

"So what now?" Flame asked. Tom straightened himself out and prepared to speak.

"Right now, this world of ours is in danger. Humans from another world, humans who wish to do us all harm, are on their way here." He announced. Uproar and panic spread through the room, but the respective leaders remained calm and steady.

"How many?" Frost asked them.

"It is not the number we should fear." Flame responded, "But their might. I myself have seen them wield powers that make Thomson achievements look tacky and pathetic." She revealed.

"How do we stand a chance against such a thing?" The air dragon leader asked.

"We will win." Tom answered, "We will win because as dragons you've been killing humans for years. Yes, these are more dangerous than normal, but this time you've got four crafty and more importantly, loyal humans to help even the odds."

The room slowly began to regain order at his words.

"You speak as if you already have a plan, Thomas Thomson." Flame seemed to probe. Tom smiled at this.

"The four of us walked into this room prepared to fight a god. You really think a couple of humans are even on the same level?" He asked them.

"If we do this, we'll need to do it together." Frost added. After some hesitation, all of the leaders finally nodded to this.

"Then it is settled. One full alliance between us all. One last fight against those who dare to enter our world from outside it." Flame rallied. Cheers from all around the room followed her words, "One last spilling of blood between our races and humanity."

CHAPTER 34; NOSTALGIA

A whole month passed. The calm autumn skies turned to harsh winter. The four humans spent this time living a rather normal everyday life. Cathie would hunt while Tom continued his work on this or that contraption. He'd ramped up his work now that it was very much going to be needed for the coming battle, which could happen at any moment.

Patrick continued to teach Amy magic. The two of them also ventured out to a lot of the different dragon leaders to report on progress and get updates of the situation. With everyone busy preparing for the fight of their lives, co-ordination between them all was key.

Thanks to the cold Cathie was forced to move her usual hunting areas with the change of behaviour from her prey. The creatures of this world had switched from gathering food and building fat to hibernating and avoiding the cold snow.

On a search for a cave perfect for a bear or two to hibernate in, she came across a rather large hole in the ground. She looked down to find a tunnel that levelled out and continued underground. An earth dragon tunnel. What was it doing this far north?

She'd heard nothing about the earth dragons doing anything way up here, now deep in ice dragon territory. Something was fishy about this. A quick look at the edges of the tunnel told her that it had been dug some time ago, but fresh tracks less than a few hours old littered the area.

With only her sword and a rather empty sack, she wasn't really equipped for the situation, but that didn't exactly stop her. The earth dragons used vibrations in the ground to see in the darkness that Cathie quickly found herself in as she continued forwards into the tunnel. She walked slowly, carefully placing each of her bare feet as she did so. She wasn't as good as an earth dragon, but then again, when trying to detect something as large as a dragon down here, she didn't have to be.

For now she left Charlie's sword in its sheath on her back. Didn't want to give the wrong impression considering they were supposed to all be working together now.

After half an hour of straight walking and cluelessly navigating the many forks and crossroads she'd come across, she eventually reached a tunnel she recognised. A tunnel where the sides were lined with glowing rocks. She followed her memory for a few more long minutes before coming up on the tunnel they'd used to escape with Flint, up to the cave at the top of the cliff.

That settled it. She was currently under the valley of Certain Death. Why had an earth dragon tunnel led here? It certainly hadn't been a stone dragon given how much the tunnel avoided outcrops of dense stone for the most part, but now she was in tunnels surrounded by the stone that earth dragons couldn't dig through.

She climbed her way up until she was standing at the top of an all too familiar cliff.

***

(Years earlier)

Cathie was on her own. She had got trapped by a pack of wild animals in the forest; nine wild cat like creatures surrounded her, except on one side where there was a tall cliff, too high to climb. Her spear; broken, from all that she had killed before. The previous fight with the other hundred or so cat like creatures had taken its toll on her.

She was out of breath. She felt a pain on her knee. She looked down. Her knee was badly bitten. She watched the blood oose out of it as if it were a waterfall. She'd seen blood before but not so much of her own. She nearly passed out just at the sight of it. She looked up at the creatures, they were all about to lunge.

She was going to die.

The whoosh sound as ten arrows struck, she would never forget such a sound. She was sure that one of them had even passed right by her left ear. Nine hit the creatures in the legs pinning them to the ground, and the tenth was attached to a rope which led from the tree it had struck, towards the top of the cliff. The arrow had a bit of paper on it reading 'Climb up' In rushed handwriting.

She looked at the creatures; they were breaking free of the arrows, slowly. She grabbed hold of the rope and swung her leg over it, which released a burst of pain. She ignored it and began to climb up the rope.

She remembered climbing up the rope and almost reaching the end but not much else.

When Cathie woke up, she was no longer on the rope but was at the top of the cliff, there were the remains of a campfire and the arrow with the rope.

She was being watched.

Cathie looked around. She tried to stand up, but her leg was hurting too much, she slowly crawled to the entrance of a small cave she was in front of. She used the walls of the cave to help stand up.

"I'm unarmed!" She announced, limping out of the cave. The sound of footsteps behind her caused her to turn around. She watched as a shape appeared out of the cave.

There he was, with his special bow. Looking at her with questioning eyes, as if he'd never seen another human before. A look that she returned. Right there, right then, it was love at first sight for her.

***

She folded her arms as the wind picked up and brought her back into the present. Then her ears twitched as something caught her attention from behind.

She quickly turned and drew her sword to find one of the cat-like creatures standing in the entrance of the cave behind her.

She prepared for an attack, but the beast seemed to just stand there and look at her. Her eyes were drawn to the small circular scar on one of its front paws.

"Oh, it's you." She sighed as she lowered her sword. The moment she did so, Jubatus walked over to her side and sat down. The mountain had changed shape slightly since she was last here, but that was probably due to the stone dragons. Other than that, same old cave, same old cliff.

As she turned to face the rather spectacular view of the valley however, she noticed that something had changed.

Other than the obvious layer of snow over everything, a hole in the treeline not too far from where they were. The ground in this new clearing also seemed to be raised, as if someone had piled a huge amount of dirt on top of something. She then remembered the earth dragon tunnels she'd just made her way though.

Jubatus got to his feet, gently licked Cathie's hand, then began to walk off in a particular direction. After a few paces he turned, as if waiting for her to follow, "You know what that is?" She asked him. Of course, he didn't answer, he just turned and continued his previous path.

Cathie took another second to take the view in before following him down the mountain.

The pathway down the mountain and into the dangerous chaos that was the valley bellow was a single straight pathway calved by long extinct animals migrating up the hill for safety during the night. Sheltered by the mountains either side, it was perhaps one of the best obstacles to have between the valley and the cave back when Tom and she had lived up there.

Easy to defend, plus the constantly dwindling amount of greenery as you made your way further and further up deterred anything from venturing this far up. That and the fact it was the only way up apart from the shear climb up the cliff face. A safe haven amongst the dangerous chaos of this place.

***

(A few less years earlier)

A fifteen-year-old Patrick slowly made his way up that very same pathway. Tired and lost, he seemed to be heading to higher ground for scouting rather than safety. Nothing was chasing him, but that just added to the other two's suspicions.

A spear landed at his feet. Unsurprisingly Patrick came to a stop and jumped back slightly in surprise. His rather high-quality silk and cloth robes of orange and blue flailed rather un-majestically for someone dressed so well.

Cathie stood a few metres off, further up the path. She at first seemed to eye his clothes with curiosity until he managed to regain his composure, where she quickly switched back into alert and dangerous.

"Leave." She demanded. Patrick very quickly put his hands up in the air as she took out another spear from the many tied to her back.

"I mean no harm. Just wanted to see where the rest of my clan is." He nervously explained.

"You mean the people dressed like you but in many different colours, right?" She asked him. A sense of hope filled Patrick's face.

"Have you seen them?"

"Watched the massacre, yeah." She answered. Every bit of hope on Patrick's face quickly drained away. His entire figure slouched out of his rather straight standing appearance, "But that's what you get for wandering into this place."

"I take it there were no survivors then?" He asked her. Cathie simply shook her head, "Then I'm on my own."

"On your way." She demanded. A small and quick wiggle of the spear in her hand quickly reminded Patrick of the position he was in.

"Could I not pass simply to try and plan a safe passage from this place?" He asked her. Cathie sighed and lowered her spear.

"There is no safe passage out of this place." She answered as she slid the spear back into the small bunch tied to her back, "Leave."

"Perhaps someone like you, who seems rather at home here could at least help me leave this place?" He asked of her.

"No." She simply stated as she turned her back on him and began to walk back up the path. Patrick's eyes narrowed. If she wouldn't help, then she was just in his way at this point.

A ball of fire shot towards Cathie at full speed. Cathie heard the flames approach and quickly turned around. With a quick but accurate slap, the fireball hit the loose rock in front of her bare feet.

This caught him rather off guard. She'd used her quick movements to push it off course with air. A smart move from someone who seemed more bully like than educated. Then he noticed the arrow.

The arrow that had sunk itself into the very same hand he'd used to cast the spell. Precisely aimed to make sure whatever he just did couldn't happen a second time. He had the feeling that even moving his other hand would bring a similar fate to it.

Small loose rocks tumbled down the hillside as Tom slid down and aimed his bow at Patrick's side. It hadn't been a smart move to reveal himself, but as Patrick stared into this man's eyes, he had the feeling that he wasn't the kind of person who would make such a mistake.

"That's quite the trick you have there." He spoke as he eyed Patrick's hand, still pointed towards Cathie. Cathie had backed off somewhat. She hadn't drawn another weapon, but she seemed ready for anything else thrown her way. Patrick also noted that she'd rather tactfully placed her feet ready to switch to a sprint at a second's notice. Attacking the archer would mean she'd charge head on, attacking her would provoke the archer.

These two seemed to work rather well together.

"Interested in my magic, are you?" Patrick asked as he slowly lowered his injured hand. He removed the arrow from it and held it close to his body to stop the bleeding as best as he could.

"A man who can produce fire from thin air certainly piques my interest." Tom responded.

"What should we do with him?" Cathie asked him. Tom seemed to consider this for a few seconds.

"You see, Cathie and I aren't really keen on other humans." Tom sighed, "But someone with your skills is not only something I'd like to research but could prove very handy."

"So you're willing to take me in?" Patrick asked the two of them. Tom lowered his bow.

"Provided you pull your weight. Better than letting that talent die out there."

***

The start of the forest. This marked the point where the real danger of the valley started. Cathie drew her sword as Jubatus seemed to walk on lighter heels, ears twitching at every slight noise for miles around them, or more importantly, the lack of noise.

After a pause, he continued forwards into the snow-covered forest ahead. The snow hadn't really stuck to the rock of the mountains here, but now that they were low down and slightly sheltered by the sun by the bare tree branches above, the ground was covered in the stuff.

The odd track here or there, but that wasn't going to tell Cathie much. She watched as Jubatus expertly spread out his paws with each step and seemed to analyse the snow ahead. He was walking over its surface leaving almost no paw print at all. In a few minutes it would be impossible to tell that he had been here.

Cathie on the other hand couldn't manage such a thing. Her bare feet sank into the almost knee-high snow with every step. The lack of colour and the more sunlight than at any other time during the year made it rather easy to spot anything within the forest beyond, but the snow also made it painfully easy for something to track Cathie at a distance unseen, ready to strike the moment she was vulnerable.

Climbing a tree and moving through the branches wasn't really an option either. Each branch had its own small layer of snow on the top. Any expert hunter would be able to track her just as easily up there too.

Yet despite all of this, no attack seemed to come. After a while even Jubatus began to seem less and less concerned about surrounding danger as they got closer and closer to their destination.

A cave, of course. Nothing in this world ever felt safe exposed on the surface, most likely due to what lurked in the sky above.

The entrance was half blocked up with snow, but there was enough of a gap for the two of them to get through and down a packed ramp of snow. Cathie's feet finally met stone. Still cold, but a blessing compared to the snow outside.

She quickly drew her sword as other catlike creatures slowly showed themselves from inside the cave, however Jubatus growled at her. She stopped, then slowly put her sword away as the catlike creatures produced a chorus of low growls towards her.

Many were covered in scars, some of which Cathie remembered inflicting herself. A quick hiss from Juba however and they parted, leaving a clear path deeper into the cave.

The fact that they weren't attacking her was something she really wasn't used to. All of her instincts told her to either run or fight with every small move any of them made. Slowly, she followed Jubatus through the crowd of them.

Some gave vicious growls that clearly had a lot of hurt feelings and history behind them. She had lived in this valley for many years, some of these beasts she'd bested, others may have lost friends or family to her as well.

Eyes watched her from all angles. Most trained on her hands, some trained on the sword on her back. It seemed to only get worse as they came into a large cavern filled with more of them. Jubatus quickly showed her down a passageway and into another cavern of a similar size, however this one was almost empty.

At the centre, a fur dressed Amelia sat on a bed of fur. Disturbingly, the fur she was dressed in and sitting on was that of the very same catlike creatures that seemed to be guarding her.

Others had followed her and Juba into the large room but kept their intrusion strictly at the entrance. Cathie stopped and took the whole place in for a few seconds as Juba made his way over to Amelia.

He curled up beside her, resting his head on her warm lap after giving her shoulder a nuzzle. He began to give a low but satisfying purr as Amelia began to stroke his back.

"I see you've got yourself a nice place." Cathie broke the silence as she looked from the pile of fresh meat on one side to the assortment of clothes made out of the same fur she was wearing on the other.

"Are you all missing me already?" Amelia chuckled, "Didn't expect to see a human so soon."

"Honestly didn't expect to find you here either. That thing picked me up while I was checking out an earth dragon mound."

"Ah yes, that thing." She sighed, "Normally not a challenge for these guys, but apparently whenever they get near the thing rocks begin falling from the sky."

"Earth dragons in the air?" Cathie asked her. Amelia shook her head.

"No. These creatures don't have complex enough language to describe it perfectly, but the words purple, and circle seem consistent with all I have sent."

"A portal device?"

"My best guess. Mind coming with me to check it out?" Cathie took a few seconds to consider this as she looked at the creatures behind her.

Narrow eyes and scowls were thrown her way from the crowd. Clearly the pack had some hurt feelings they wanted to address with their leader.

One of the creatures snared and growled at her as it made its way to the front of the pack. As it did this, Juba calmly lifted his head off Amelia's lap. Knowing full well what was about to happen.

With a blur, the one who'd snared at her turned from a beast to a horrific work of art. Its bones held up the strung-up intestines and other components of the meat sculpture like a frame. Its limbs had been rearranged and shoved through other parts of the body.

The rest of them backed away from the sculpture as blood finally hit the floor underneath it. Amelia was sat back where she'd been before, only now both of her hands were covered in fresh blood. She presented one to Juba, who began to cleanly lick the blood off it one finger at a time, while she did the same with her other hand.

CHAPTER 35; BURIED SECRETS

The two of them now stood at the base of the mound of dirt. The constantly rumbling ground confirmed that earth dragons were in fact present.

The rumbling got louder and louder. Something was coming their way. Amelia pulled her sword from her clothing as Cathie pulled hers from her sheath.

Dirt flew everywhere as something emerged from the mound. The two of them raised, but then quickly lowered their swords. Flint stood before them.

"The hell are you doing here?" Cathie asked her.

"I could ask the same of you two." She replied.

"Investigating portals that drop rocks from the sky." Cathie answered her. Flint seemed to nod at this.

"I see." She sighed. She gestured that the two of them follow before turning and walking back down the freshly dug tunnel.

The two of them put their swords away, then followed Flint into the mound.

As they made their way through more winding tunnels, they passed both stone and earth dragons mixed in with one another. They continued onwards until they reached a tunnel that hit a dead end. The tunnel was clearly blocked off by the uniform sheet of metal ahead of them.

Rather surprisingly, beside the metal stood Frost.

"The humans?" Frost asked as he noticed them approach.

"They saw how we defended this place from the beasts of this valley." Flint explained. Frost gave an understanding nod.

"So I assume you'll both be looking for an explanation."

"The way it seems to me Frost, is that you've been hiding a portal device from us." Cathie accused as she folded her arms.

"The air dragons had two devices to begin with. The earth dragons captured the one in the ice cave while you stole the one on the mountain." Frost began, "We learned of this once the earth dragons finally allied with us. However, we soon discovered this place."

"What's behind the metal?" Amelia asked him.

"A place I feared you humans would get access to if you knew about the portal device. We cannot get inside without the portals, and honestly I'm still not certain I should permit you access to this place." Frost answered.

"We should show them." Flint argued, "It's risky, but they have more of a chance of understanding what is inside than I do."

***

Flint, Amelia, Frost and Cathie all walked out of a portal, inside a fully metal room dimly lit by small glowing rocks that had been placed on the floor like someone leaving a trail of breadcrumbs.

The first thing to hit them was the smell. Decaying bodies. A smell Cathie was well acquainted with. The smell was strong but grew weaker with every breath of air that came through the portal behind them.

Drag marks on the floor and the lack of the decaying bodies in question suggested that the dragons had already removed the corpses.

The room itself was massive. Even the two dragons had no issues at all moving about and actually seemed quite small in comparison.

On the walls, words had been etched into the solid metal. Human words. Human drawings had also been calved here and there to add to the story that the words seemed to tell.

"What is this place?" Cathie asked. Frost and Flint walked over to one particular wall.

"It is this part that is the reason we did not want you to freely enter this place." Frost explained as he looked at the wall. Amelia picked up one of the glowing rocks in her hand and pointed it, so it illuminated the dark wall.

Neutral.

The first word the two of them noticed. Etched in letters the size of a person. Five lines seemed to run from this word and down to eye level, where they ended with five different words.

Mind. Body. Spirit. Skill. Unity.

Cathie walked over to these five words, which each had a picture representing what the words meant. She found herself oddly drawn to the second word. Body.

Her hand seemed to move on its own. She placed it where the word was etched. A red glow suddenly surrounded her. The word itself also seemed to glow bright red. The line all the way up to the word Neutral began to light up with the same red glow as well.

"It is as I thought." Frost sighed, "Five humans would be able to activate the ancient magic of this place."

"Mind…Tom." Amelia realised as she thought out loud.

"Spirit is Patrick. Skill is Charlie." Cathie added.

"But Charlie's dead." Amelia pointed out.

"You are very skilled with a bow are you not?" Frost reminded Amelia.

"She is, but not as good as Charlie was with his sword. He really was the embodiment of skill, like I am the embodiment of strength." Cathie explained.

"Then who is unity?" Flint asked them. Cathie seemed to shrug at this as she pulled her hand off. She stopped glowing, and so did the rest of the wall.

"No idea. None of us are really any good at bringing others together. That's more of your thing, right Frost?" She pointed out.

"I see, so even with everyone you have now, you don't possess the pieces to unlock this." Frost sighed, "Then perhaps our caution was for nothing."

"Five aspects of humanity. Ever since the start we've been missing one." Cathie muttered.

"Do you think that suggests another human is out there still?" Amelia asked her. Cathie shook her head.

"Someone who is apparently the embodiment of unity, wouldn't last this long on their own in this world." She answered.

"We found many human remains in here. We cleared the bones out and buried them as you humans do, but one of them had their hand on the unity calving." Frost revealed, "Couldn't tell how they died, but clearly they shut themselves out from the rest of the world."

Cathie began to look around the rest of the walls. She came across a door, although it had been welded shut. She took a few quick glances at the many words and pictures on the walls. There were many words she didn't recognise, but then again, she'd never been the best at reading.

"I bet Tom would love to read all of this. Probably a lot of history we don't know about. History told from a human perspective instead of a dragon one."

"Perhaps that is the next step. Of course, I'll also allow him access to the portal device."

***

Tom and Patrick both emerged from a portal in front of Frost, Flint, Amy, Amelia and Cathie. Both were holding newly bound books and pencils, with many notes written down. The two of them seemed to compare notes with one another for a few minutes before facing the others.

"Alright, pretty sure we have an idea of it all." Tom revealed. The others stood, waiting to hear their findings.

"It seems humans first built this place way back when the Neutral was a thing." Patrick began.

"I thought we decided the Neutral was nothing but a myth." Amy seemed to point out.

"Unfortunately, this proves otherwise." Tom revealed as he continued to look down at his notes, "You were right to fear giving us access Frost. If we possessed all the pieces required, I believe this is the place the Neutral was to be reincarnated."

"But we never did get all the pieces together." Cathie added. Tom nodded at this.

"Let's try to keep it all in chronological order." Patrick suggested.

"This place was built as a temple, a safe haven during the war between the Neutral and the Divine." Tom revealed, "When the Neutral fell, most of what was left of humanity retreated here."

"There wasn't enough room or resources to keep them all here though, so some were forced out into the world above to live in caves, hiding from dragons." Patrick continued.

"Over time the humans here began to run out of resources. Desperate, they turned to their dead god. That is when the calving of the five pieces seemed to appear to them."

"Appear?" Frost asked. Tom nodded at this.

"Even human hands aren't skilled enough to calve in the quality of that calving in particular. Plus the stories all seem to detail the calving drawing itself." He explained, "Clearly the Neutral wasn't quite as dead as first believed."

"Many theorised that the Neutral could be brought back if all five pieces could be brought to the calving."

"Stories say that their leader was able to light up the unity symbol. However, no matter how strong anyone else was, how smart they were, how skilled or faithful, no one could light up any of the other four."

"Meanwhile, other stories of those who dared to venture outside seem to suggest that the valley above went under a drastic change shortly after the Neutral was first killed. Creatures that could outwit their prey and hunt in large numbers seemed to surround them to the point that they were forced to seal themselves underground."

"Trapped inside, knowing that the four missing pieces were in the outside world somewhere, two were sent to find them all and return, instead of the large parties they'd tried to send previously, who never made it out of the valley." Tom continued.

"Lucky enough their names were documented." Patrick added as he looked down at his notes, "And luckily enough Charlie once told me about his past many years ago."

"What does this have to do with Charlie?" Cathie asked him.

"Those two were his parents." Tom answered.

"Don't know why they never told stories to Charlie about this place." Patrick muttered.

"Honestly, they'd probably lost hope. They'd been lucky enough to escape the fate of those trapped here and didn't have any plans on returning."

"Even with the rest of them relying on them?" Amy asked.

"Harsh, but honestly a decision I would have made myself under similar circumstances. It makes sense to preserve oneself when the group is clearly doomed." Tom answered.

"But that is where the stories end. Starvation is the most likely cause of death." Patrick concluded.

"But not the complete end of this story, because around the time those inside perished, the four pieces were slowly meeting one another." Tom pointed out, "These people were on their last legs around the time Cathie and I ran into each other in this very valley. A few years later you came across us, and a year or so after that we found Charlie."

"It seems fate messed up by a few years." Frost sighed, "So does this mean the Neutral really is dead now?"

"From everything the Divine said, the Neutral seems to be able to survive a limited time without a human body. This place seemed to be how it would re-enter one, but clearly this never happened. The Divine also stated that the Neutral's time was up, it would be dead by now if it hadn't been able to get back into human form." Tom explained, "So yes, it's dead."

"Rather silly for it to have such high requirements to re-incarnate." Flint pointed out.

"Some earlier stories suggest that the Neutral was responsible for creating humanity in the first place. Most seem like religious storytelling, but if the Neutral was the god of humanity, then we represent parts of itself perhaps." Patrick suggested, "Parts needed to repair or restore it."

"But as a god it made one mistake." Tom sighed, "It was arrogant enough to ask for the best of the best of each aspect and nothing less. Even in such a desperate time."

"Are you saying that after all this, arrogance is what killed the one thing our god feared?" Frost chuckled.

"We've only ever actually met one god, but stories of almost every god seem to show how arrogant the gods of this world truly are." Patrick answered, "Isn't too much of a stretch to perhaps suggest it's their shared weakness."

Tom remained quiet as he thought to himself for a few minutes. The other's voices blended into the background as he did so. His thoughts were on the higher powers.

Clearly gods in their own right. They did seem slightly arrogant, but the fact that they'd asked him for help seemed to suggest otherwise. Somehow, he had the feeling that simple fact made them all the more dangerous. The Divine's words also replayed in his head.

They'd been responsible for his parent's death. Parents that possessed a map identical to Cathie's parents, one allowing them to meet at the very valley they were under. Was that what had gone wrong?

That and the Divine's orders for Cathie's parents may have inadvertently been the final nails in the coffin that was the Neutral. Yet his mind reminded him about the figure that had appeared to both himself and Cathie when the Divine was searching them.

Had that in fact been the Neutral? If so, how? How had it survived? How didn't the Divine sense it?

It couldn't be within him, because Cathie saw the same thing. That room hadn't been a representation of just his mind but Cathie's as well- Hold on!

Something clicked in Tom's head. Was it possible? Perhaps. While he'd been thinking about all of it, in the back of his head he seemed to have asked himself one big question.

If I were a god in the Neutral's position, how would I have survived while making the Divine think I didn't?

Tom indeed had an answer, and it seemed to match the current facts just a little bit too closely for his liking.

Step One, set up requirements for the resurrection. Ones that made sense and seemed possible, but ultimately fate wouldn't be kind enough for everything to perfectly align.

Step Two, secretly come back. Skip the ritual, skip the false requirements. Come back somewhere hidden and out of sight. Come back in a vessel that stopped you from being detected.

Come back in a form the Divine wouldn't recognise. Hide your power as something else, something the Divine wouldn't expect. Blend it in with an existing power.

Within the infinitely large blank room that represented Tom's mind, Tom turned to the purple haired, purple eyed version of himself.

"You are the power of the mind. Something taught to me by my mother from a young age, correct?" He asked him. His purple counterpart tilted its head rather suddenly. He seemed puzzled as to why he was being asked this.

"Correct." He answered plainly.

"An ability that allowed me to think like no other, but one that until recently was nothing more than that."

"Correct."

"So why the sudden change? Why could I suddenly push my mind not just beyond its own limits, but dangerously far above them?" He asked. His purple other seemed to consider this for a few seconds.

"Unknown." He finally answered. Tom slowly nodded at this.

"I don't recall Cathie's ability to push the limits of her body ever being able to go far enough to take on a stone dragon barehanded either. It seems both of us have gone through a change."

"What are you suggesting?"

"I'm not sure about Charlie, but Patrick doesn't seem to have had any change to his own power. As he told us, he's been that powerful with magic since he was a child."

"Are you suggesting that something happened to you and Cathie to increase how far you could go above your respective limits?"

Tom began to look around the blank room.

"I know you're here!" He shouted, "Show yourself!"

***

Tom seemed to be forced back into the real world. His sudden departure caught him rather off guard, but luckily the others were paying no attention to him. They were still all theorising about what they'd found in the temple of the Neutral, except Cathie, who had started to hold his hand.

"All the pieces fitting together yet?" She asked as she turned to face him. She'd done so in a hushed voice so that the others didn't hear her. She didn't know everything, but she knew enough that with time she'd eventually figure enough out to cause both of them quite the bit of danger if she let slip about it around a dragon.

Tom slowly nodded.

"Not here." He quietly told her. Her eyes turned in the direction of Frost and Flint. She clearly understood who's ears Tom wanted to avoid. He wanted to be wrong, so very wrong. Would such a being be smart enough to pull something like this off?

The Neutral had suffered defeat, would that have been enough to shatter the arrogance of a god enough for them to resort to such a desperate tactic? He honestly didn't have the answer, but too many things were falling almost perfectly into the place of the plan he had concocted.

Not everything had been explained by his theory, however. If his mind did in fact contain the Neutral, how had it completely hidden itself from the Divine? On top of that, Cathie's mind was somehow linked in with this as well… no… it wasn't making complete sense.

Perhaps he was jumping to conclusions. Patrick had mentioned the presence of a god talking to him at some point as well, something clearly not linked to the Neutral. Even Charlie rambled about voices in his head, who clearly ended up being the higher powers using him like a puppet.

Too many gods, too many answers that all seemed likely. If the Neutral possessed the intellect to deceive the Divine so easily, then it wouldn't have lost in the first place.

***

A very young Tom looked very curiously at the black, box shaped bag with the word Kara painted on the side.

"Mommy?" Tom asked as he looked around to speak to a woman that towered over him.

"Yes honey?" She replied as she bent down to his eye level. Her brown long hair oddly contrasted with her purple eyes.

"How does this small bag fit all of your things inside?" He asked her. She gave a small smile.

"That's a rather hard question to answer." She replied. Tom began to pout.

His mother gave a sigh and stood up. She walked over to the bag and picked it up, "The question you should be asking is why it's almost completely weightless despite having many things in it." She added.

She knelt down and handed the bag to Tom. His small hands barely wrapped around the strap, and yet he lifted it as if it were a feather.

His mother looked around and found a small rock. She picked it up and dropped it in the bag while Tom was still holding it up.

The bag didn't seem to gain any weight whatsoever.

"Is it magic? Like those people you told me about?" Tom asked her.

"I'm afraid I'm no magician." She answered. Tom put the bag down and peered into the zipped opening on the top. The stone was nowhere in sight.

He put his hand in to feel around, but found that his hand found nothing to touch, not even the side or bottom of the bag.

"It's bigger on the inside?" Tom asked her.

"Sort of... I guess that's the simple version." Tom reached further into the bag, leaning over it precariously His mother's hands gently lifted him from under his shoulders, "Careful, the last thing you want is to fall in."

"What happens if I do?" Tom asked as she gently put him back down.

"You'll get lost in all my stuff, and I'll have to come in and look for you."

"Don't you think pocket universes are a little bit advanced for the kid?" A man asked from behind Tom. Both Tom and his mother looked up to face him.

Of course, Tom was still only a child. The two words that perfectly described the inside of the bag simply washed right over his head.

"Back already?" His mother asked as she stood up.

The man gestured his head to speak with her on the other side of the door behind him.

Once both of them had left the room, Tom quietly walked over to the door, and opened it a tiny bit.

"They're closing in again." The man muttered. His mother gave a sigh and almost instinctively looked towards the door. Tom made sure she didn't notice that it was slightly open, "I know, don't worry. It means moving again but I spotted them early."

"We can't keep doing this. They're going to find out I have a child eventually."

"It's the only option we have at the moment. Normally I'd confront them, but it's not worth risking Tom." The man gave his mother a hug, and a peck on the cheek.

***

Tom looked down at the black box shaped bag.

They had clearly been protecting him from something, and the only thing he remembered attacking them were Earth dragons.

Now he knew that the higher powers were in fact the ones they were hiding him from. From what had been said, Tom realised that they'd been after his mother.

The Divine also mentioned that she'd trapped them in the very prison that he'd earlier smashed.

He cursed his own ignorance. Yet they were asking for his help. They hadn't tried to kill him or take him prisoner. They knew his last name, so they were very much aware of who he was.

He desperately wanted to ask them many questions, but he had the feeling that they wouldn't like him doing so. They were planning to use him for something, under the guise of keeping the human race going. The feeling that told him the moment they figured out he suspected as such, they'd end him just like his family, was incredibly strong.

He lay awake in his bed beside a fast-asleep Cathie. His head filled to the brim with these thoughts.

CHAPTER 36; ARRIVAL

As the winter sun hung low in the sky despite it being midday, the wind gently picked up on the plains for a few minutes. The long grass danced to the breeze and the chorus of rustling leaves from far off trees.

The wind slowly died down. Everything slowly calmed and came to a stop. That was until, a loud tearing noise echoed throughout.

A large purple portal ripped itself open. The size of a house at least. Small metal spiders emerged and seemed to sweep the area as the grazing animals fled from the unnatural event. The spiders eventually seemed satisfied and returned through the portal.

Shortly afterwards, men and women wearing camouflaged gear began to march through. Each one carrying a laser weapon of some form.

Entire squads spread out and began to sweep their surroundings. Eventually, a large vehicle on tracks emerged from the portal as well. The tank slowly came to a stop a few metres ahead of the portal. Edward popped his head out of the top.

He took a good look around before completely climbing out of it. He took a large breath of fresh air into his lungs as he seemed to marvel at everything around him. He began to laugh.

"Another world." He continued to laugh as he spun around to take the whole world in, "Ours for the taking."

***

Amelia watched from the table in the main room as Amy and Patrick quietly entered Patrick's room. The two of them had gotten even closer than when she'd left.

Despite everything she'd done, every time she saw the two of them together, she felt like she was being stabbed in the chest with a sharp rock. Not a fine blade, a sharp but jagged rock that left a messy wound instead of a clean cut.

Juba caught her attention by licking the back of her hand, before returning his head to her lap. She wasn't entirely sure if he'd done it to comfort her or simply because he wanted more petting. She hoped for the first, but knew it was far more likely to be the second.

She both watched and listened as he fell asleep on her lap as she gently stroked the back of his head. When she looked back up, Cathie was standing in the room, staring at Juba.

"Please tell me you didn't bring them all." She sighed as she sat down at the table with a wooden slab with some cooked meat on it.

"Just him." Amelia answered as she watched her mother dig into her food. Originally Tom had been the only one of the group to ever use cutlery, since he'd grown up with it. Yet seventeen years of practice had in fact worn off on Cathie, meaning she no longer ate with her bare hands.

Granted, she wasn't used to wooden cutlery, but it wasn't that much of a change, "They have a word for you, you know."

"Oh? Just for me?" She smiled before finishing her meal.

"More of a specific noise really, but they all know it."

"Glad to see my efforts are at least recognised."

"I miss anything important while I was away?"

"Oh, you know, confronted the god of dragons. Started preparing to fight the humans from another universe. Nothing too much." She listed with a smile, "How about you?"

"Mainly been trying to find myself."

"How did that go?"

"I'm certainly closer to the answer." Her eyes shifted to Patrick's door. Her heightened hearing managed to pick up Amy giggling despite trying her best efforts to not hear anything in that direction, "Not quite there yet though." She mumbled.

***

Cathie made sure to close the door to Tom's room behind her before walking further into the room. Tom took notice of this as he looked up from a book he was reading while rocking on his chair, which was facing the door so that his desk would catch his chair should he fall backwards by mistake. Something he'd learnt to do the hard way.

"Are you ok?" He asked her as he noticed her becoming rather uncomfortable, which wasn't normally the case while the two of them were alone together.

"We need to talk. About a matter I've been worrying about quite a bit since Amy and I escaped the other world."

"Must be something serious if it's worrying you." He muttered as he stood up and put his book down. He walked over to her and put his arms around her waist.

"It's about you and Amy, Amelia too."

"You worried about the fight ahead?"

"I am, but I'm also thinking about after that as well." She went quiet for a few seconds, "You see, I don't age anymore. For seventeen years I've stayed exactly the same. I was wondering how we'd end up after all of this is over."

"I see. You're worried we'll both leave you behind while you remain alone in this world." Tom sighed as he tightened his hug around her. He felt her arms hug him just as tightly.

"I don't want to be alone in this world. Trapped here by my own stupid body that won't let me leave."

"Well from what I can tell, Amy doesn't seem to age either." Tom revealed. He felt her relax slightly at his words, "Turns out whatever she is, doesn't age. I've seen no evidence of it in her tests. Provided she continues to drink blood and avoids burning in sunlight, she'll be right beside you. I assume the same for Amelia given their twins."

"That doesn't fix everything though. I don't want to lose any of you." Tom slowly nodded at this.

The concept of his own mortality wasn't something Tom pondered about often. He knew one day his life would end, and he was ok with that. Up until recently life wasn't much to him anyway.

That had changed, however. He had Cathie, Amy and Amelia. People who depended on him a lot more than anyone else ever would.

"I've got a possible solution." He finally muttered, "But it will probably cost us."

"I'd honestly pay anything."

"I'll keep pursuing it then. I'll let you know when I've figured out all the details, alright?" He pulled his head back to look into her eyes. She nodded before wiping a tear from her eye. She seemed to get a hold of herself before giving him another hug.

The higher powers needed him. That much was clear. Under the guise of fighting Edward throughout human history, which meant they'd need to keep them both alive for a rather long time.

Trouble was, given that they most likely have ulterior motives, the chance of them allowing his family to be by his side was low.

The cost of his lifespan being lengthened would be that he wouldn't be able to be with her. Cathie was strong, the strongest person he'd ever met, but that price would hit her right in her main weakness.

Her love for him was borderline obsessive, which was for the moment rather flattering for him, but she'd already moved heaven and earth just to come back to him once. Something told him she might not be able to handle it again.

***

Amelia had spent most of the night outside the cave. The fresh air helped, and it meant she wasn't anywhere near her sister and Patrick. After filling the caves supply of meat and berries to keep herself occupied, she sat on the rock outside the front door as she watched sunlight begin to peak above the horizon that was now clearly visible due to the half-destroyed forest in front of the cave.

As the sun just began to catch the top of the hill that the cave was dug into, the front door of the cave opened. She turned to see Patrick, who seemed to be looking for her.

"There you are." He spoke as he noticed her. He walked over and sat beside her on the stone, "Haven't really had the chance to talk since you left."

"Been trying my best to distance myself from Amy. She's normally right beside you these days." Amelia muttered in response. She turned back to looking at the sunrise, which brought Patrick's attention to it.

"I… umm… made this a while back." He continued as he reached into his satchel and brought out a necklace made from what looked like a dragon tooth and some string.

Her first reaction was to get all flustered, but before she gave anything away, she quickly forced a confused face instead.

"Patrick, I told you I-"

"It's not what you think." Patrick interrupted, "I attached a spell to it." He revealed.

"What kind of spell?" She asked him. He gestured to her to take it. With some hesitation, she did. Slowly she put it around her neck.

"More impressive if I show you." He answered as he held out a hand for her to take. She slowly took it, all the while trying her best to control herself.

He began to lead her up the hill. She followed until he stepped into the sunlight. She stopped just before it, then backed away as it continued to move down the hill.

Patrick walked back down and took her hand once more. This time, though, he simply lifted it slowly into the sunlight above her. She watched as she prepared for the pain, but none came.

She looked at her hand in surprise as she felt the warm and soothing sunlight upon her hand. Not quite as warm as she remembered, but it was a winter sun, and it had been quite some time since she last felt it.

Before she knew it, the sun had moved past, engulfing the whole of her body in sunlight. When she finally broke free from her amazement, she turned to Patrick. She at first went for a kiss, but once more quickly stopped herself and went for a hug instead, "Made one for Amy a while back, made a second one with it just in case you came back."

"You didn't think I'd come back?" She asked him as she slowly let go of him. Anymore and she wouldn't have been able to stop herself.

"Were you?" He asked her in response. She fell quiet as her gaze slowly fell to her feet.

"It had crossed my mind."

"Ever since we came back to this world you've always been off around Amy and me. I get it, it's weird. But I don't want that to scare you off."

"You're talking as if I'm planning on leaving again."

"Are you?" She fell silence once more, "I can't make you stay, but I know for a fact that your parents worry for you every day you aren't around."

"They aren't my parents." She mumbled as she turned away from him and folded her arms, "They're her parents." Patrick gently took her hand.

"They certainly think of you as a daughter." He muttered as he squeezed her hand. He let go of it and began to walk back down the hill, "Just like she sees you as a sister." He added before he reached flat ground. He disappeared into the front door of the cave.

She brought the hand he'd taken up to her face and gave it a quick sniff. His scent was driving her crazy. She finally dropped the act and began to blush as she admired the necklace around her neck.

After a few seconds she let it go as she realised what she was doing. She slowly walked down the hill and onto the flat ground that was now bathed in sunlight just like the rest of the world.

She found the largest rock that wasn't directly against the walls of the cave and kicked it hard. She felt the bones in her foot snap and crunch as she chipped a large chunk of rock off.

After everything she'd put herself through, she still couldn't let go. Her foot throbbed with pain as it slowly began to put itself back together. She waited until it had finished before she put any weight on it and once it was done, she managed to walk without any issues.

"That's quite the temper." A voice spoke behind her. She turned to see Breath. Of course, only an air dragon would be capable of sneaking up on her, even so she'd done it very well, or perhaps she didn't notice due to her mind being elsewhere.

"What do you want?" She quietly snapped at her.

"Our scouts have found a portal. A big one. The humans from the other world surround it on the plains." She revealed.

"I'm sure if you shout loud enough one of them will come out to hear your news." She sighed shortly before speeding off into what remained of the forest beyond.

***

Amelia stood against a tree that very nearly hung over the edge of the cliff that overlooked the plains. She watched people in the process of setting up a small mobile trailer that seemed to act as the main base for them. They just about finished locking its wheels to stop it from rolling off somewhere unexpectedly. Around that were many tents and tarpaulins held up by thin metal poles. Some covered equipment that she recognised from the other world. Some housed soldiers. Off towards the sea, on the other side of the large portal that stood beside the trailer was what appeared to be an armoured tank that was slowly exploring around the coast.

They seemed to be looking for a way to get it though one of the surrounding forests to take it around the surrounding cliff faces. Honestly, they'd picked a rather bad spot for it, which suggested that they probably didn't have much control on where the portal ended up.

The forests either side were very thick. Even with the manpower they had it would take them forever to cut a path through it big enough for that thing. A fact they were just about to learn themselves.

She was rather glad that the huge thing was more or less stuck to the coast and the plains.

She also watched a couple of soldiers working on what appeared to be a large flat track that led from the portal and towards the sea. They seemed very keen on keeping it flat, to the point that they'd built it up on sturdy stilts when the ground lowered as they approached the coast.

She'd seen boats before, but surely it would make sense to have a ramp down to the sea. This seemed to continue straight for quite some distance.

Amelia looked down at her new necklace once more, then up at the midday sun. She'd been watching them for some time now, but there was still no sign of him.

That was until she caught the sight of something shiny coming from a window on the side of the trailer. She focused on it to find herself looking down a pair of binoculars pointed right at her. She watched the figure lower the binoculars, to reveal Edward's face covered in a large grin.

Edward turned away from the window to find the door to the trailer off its hinges, and Amelia standing in front of him.

"Came alone, did you?" He asked her as soldiers rushed to the door with their weapons raised at her.

"I wanted to ask you a few questions." She responded. Edward waved at the soldiers, who then stood down. They however remained nearby with their weapons still armed and loaded.

"Questioning things? Your own existence perhaps? I take it I'm talking to the clone, not the original then."

"I get why you made me. You wanted an Amy you could hold onto and experiment with, but why did I get her memories and feelings as well? Why give me those?"

"The cloning technology I used was recently stolen from Thomas Thomson. I wasn't aware you'd be a perfect copy, mind and all." Edward chuckled as he seemed to admire her, "Got to say, not bad for my first try. Most other first attempts end in horrific mistakes that have to be put out of their misery shortly after being born."

Amelia tried her best not to throw up at those words as rather horrific images of herself appeared in her head.

"I have all of Amy's memories. All those times you hunted Amy and her mother. They always assumed you were after all this knowledge and research just to get rich, but I don't buy it."

"I see you don't share everything with your sister then. I certainly didn't expect you to come to that conclusion based solely on what you have from Amy."

"Answer the question." She demanded.

"Why are you so interested in my motives?" Edward responded, "Got some reason to consider helping me?" Amelia fell silent at this for a few seconds.

"I mean… if my… original had some tragic accident that allowed me to take her place. I wouldn't exactly complain." Edward smiled at this before walking over to her.

He passed her and grabbed a cup containing some form of hot beverage. He took a sip and placed the mug down.

"See, if I was a master manipulator, I'd take you up on your offer, but regrettably I'm not. I'm a determined genius with a goal far beyond petty squabbling."

"I'll take that as a no then." She sighed as she turned to leave.

"You wished to know my motives, right?" She stopped just before leaving through the doorway and turned to look at him, "The reason I try to get my hands on every single piece of technology I can, collect powerful materials and push the boundaries of my very own universe, is very simple."

"As I said before, it can't be to sell it all. I also don't see you conquering worlds either."

"I may conquer a few. Including this one. The reason is though, is because I aspire to be something more than I already am. I wish to be immortal, all powerful."

"You wish to be a god?" Amelia almost laughed out loud at his explanation.

"I do." He answered, "Because you see it's all almost in my grasp. Thomas Thomson just barely stopped me from achieving immortality a number of times, but I can recreate my machine to do so. It's currently under construction, and the best thing is the current Thomas Thomson has no idea I can even do it. The black material of this world will provide me with new technologies that no other has access to. These portals will allow me access to universes beyond any of our understanding. Do you not already see how close I am to achieving my goals?"

"You're not immortal yet. I'm sure someone will make sure it stays that way. Besides, from what I hear being a god isn't all that great."

"Many have tried, but as all good people do, I learn from my mistakes. Unlike the gods of any world I started from the bottom and built my way up to their level."

"Speaking as if you've already won."

"Look around you my dear. I already have. Tom and your mother will do their best to try and stop me, but I have an army, my armour and more of everything you see here waiting just the other side of that portal. While they have a few flying lizards." Amelia smiled at his statement.

"You certainly have the arrogance of a god. Perhaps you are closer than anyone else to your goal."

"I'm flattered to hear you say so, but I'm afraid I've been burnt once by a double agent in the past. Learn from my mistakes remember? Whether you like it or not, your side has been chosen."

"No one chooses anything for me." Edward burst out in laughter at this.

"Reached the difficult, rebellious teen phase, have you?" He squeezed in between bursts of laughter, "And I always took Amy as a mother's girl."

"I'm not Amy." Edward calmed his laughter but still kept his smile as wide as ever.

"My dear, Amy defines everything about you. Most of your experiences, thoughts and memories are Amy. You honestly sound like a dog trying to run from the owner it is leashed to. No matter how hard you pull you'll either not move or take the owner along with you." He explained as he walked past her and out of the doorway to the trailer.

"If I can't free myself of her, then I guess I'll just have to do the next best thing." She sighed as Edward came to a stop a few metres away from the trailer. She stepped out onto the dirt.

The two of them were surrounded by an arc of soldiers who slowly raised their weapons at her as Edward raised his hand.

"Let me guess, kill the one responsible, right?" He chuckled as armour began to construct itself around him.

***

After shoving one last thing into his bag, Tom slung it around his shoulder and turned to the front door of the cave. He walked through it to find Cathie, Amy and Patrick waiting for him.

"Where is Amelia?" He asked them.

"Breath said she sped off somewhere after I said some things she needed to hear." Patrick sighed, "My fault, shouldn't have been so direct."

"She's still trying to distance herself from me?" Amy asked him. Patrick nodded in response.

"As much as I'd love to go and find her, we don't have time. If we give Edward enough time to prepare, he'll be unbeatable." Cathie reminded them.

"She also said she'd mentioned the plains before she took off. If she wants to help us, then she'll be there eventually." Patrick added.

"Guess we'll just have to hope she comes to her senses then." Tom sighed, "Are we ready?" The three of them nodded, "Let's get a move on then."

Tom pulled out a portal device from his bag.

Despite listening to his counterpart's advice, another device had somehow found its way into this world anyway. Clearly this universe decided its fate separately from the other. His counterpart's ideals and motives wouldn't be effective here. Still... fate was kind this time that the device had ended up in his hands... despite Thomas being wrong, perhaps it wasn't as simple as being wrong or right about such things.

Tom had spent most of his life not believing in something as fickle as fate, but the universe seemed to be throwing him bones left right and centre to prove him otherwise.

He was never religious either, yet they'd all met a god in person. The world was more complex than he could ever dream, and he'd barely scratched the surface.

Whatever fate had in store for them now, for the first time in his life, he prayed that it would be good.

CHAPTER 37; GRAVESTONES

Slightly earlier….

Cathie poked her head into Tom's room. He was sat on his chair at his desk, working on what appeared to be some rather complex mathematics.

"That was Breath. It's time, they're here." She spoke before disappearing into the rest of the cave. Tom slowly got out of his chair as he nodded.

Time was up. Hopefully it would be enough. He grabbed his bag and began packing things. He started with his bow, then a few other creations he'd made over the past month. Not all of them were going to be useful, but he wanted to be prepared for every situation.

Tom's door opened once more, but this time it wasn't Cathie. It wasn't Amy or Patrick either, or Amelia. It also wasn't his door, or at least not his current one.

The one who had opened his door, was his mother.

"Honey listen to me, we are going on a trip, somewhere safe." His mother spoke, looking him right in his yellow eyes to the point that she could see the purple of hers reflected off them.

"But Mom why is it not safe here?" A childish Tom's voice spoke. Tom's mum smiled.

"Come on." She gestured for him to follow, clearly hesitant to answer. Tom's mum picked up a bag and stood next to a taller man, with a laser rifle, his father.

"How's that talking potion coming along?" He asked her.

"Not good, I can't figure out the last ingredient, but I think I could once we are safe."

"They'll keep following us."

"We keep to the pattern, that way we will be safe." Kara suggested, "No time to pack the doors this time, we'll make new ones." She added as she headed towards the front door of the cave they were in. Tom who was holding her hand followed with his father behind.

***

He was in a cave, making a bow out of a stick he had found. A bow like no other worthy enough for his father to wield.

The cave was empty, except Tom. His parents were out getting food; it was hard living by yourself, but the three of them seemed to manage. A boom came from outside the cave as his mother rushed in, covered with dirt.

"Small quake sweetheart, we need to move." She told him, trying to smile.

"Mom, I am not stupid. It's a dragon." Tom responded as he walked over to her and hugged her legs.

"Alright, let's get you somewhere safe." She muttered, she took his hand and took him deeper into the cave,

"Daddy's going to deal with it." She added. They entered the room Tom used to sleep in, "Now you know the drill."

"Yes, don't come out of this room until you or dad come and get me." Tom said as if those words had been drilled into his head.

"Good boy, mummy's going to be back ok?"

"Ok." Tom answered as he sat on his bed. His mum closed the door behind her and left Tom in his room. The sound of a dragon screeching reassured Tom that his dad had won the fight. Tom's mum came back into the room.

"Ok honey, time to pack."

Every time they kill a dragon they had to move, otherwise the other dragons would find the dead body and them.

Tom grabbed his mother's bag and quickly began packing everything he could. He walked out of the room with all his things, his mother was unscrewing the doors to the cave, folding them up and packing them, better to take the doors with you than make new ones. He walked to the front door to where his father was.

"Ok son, is your mother behind you?"

"She is doing the doors."

"Done the doors." She said appearing behind Tom, "All ready?"

"Ready." Tom said with a small, childish smile.

They walked for about a kilometre or so before they heard a deafening screech coming from behind them.

"They found the body." Kara announced. They broke into a sprint. Running as fast as they could away from the body, but it was not fast enough. Tom had the bow he had made for his dad in his bag, although he had only had time to make three arrows and half of the strings, but if used correctly it could be fired.

"Get down!" Tom's dad yelled. They all ducked as a huge bolder flew above them. Another bolder few over them and another. No earth dragon could fire that fast, there had to be at least three, possibly more. Tom and his parents took cover in a ditch.

A bolder landed between Tom and his parents. Dirt nearly completely buried him from the impact, but his panicked motions quickly managed to break him free from the fine soil.

"Tom? Honey?" He heard his mother shout.

"I'm ok mom!" He shouted back. He saw the dragons for the first time. They didn't notice him, but they were standing in front of where his parents were on the other side of the bolder.

Tom closed his eyes and curled up as dragon screeches and loud electrical charges ramped up and discharged.

The loud weapon fire suddenly stopped, however. Tom opened his eyes to a flash of purple that outshone the sun. More dragon screeches, but now large thumps began to sound, as if blows were being exchanged on a scale that shook the planet to its core.

However, soon these came to a stop as well. Tom's eyes quickly flashed purple for just a second. His yellow eyes searched in panic for his bag. He found its strap stuck under some dirt beside him, too deep for him to dig out in time. Yet something had been flung out of the bag in the confusion. His bow, and the three arrows tied to it so that he wouldn't lose them were right at his side.

With only some slight hesitation from his dirt covered little hands, he grabbed the bow and loaded the first arrow.

He came out of the ditch to find himself right in the view of the three earth dragons. They'd backed off a bit, and two of them had some rather bad wounds, but no fatal ones.

Tom aimed his bow at the closest one and almost immediately realised the dragon's thick armour. It began to charge towards him at full speed.

His eyes flashed purple for a split second as they were drawn to the dragon's eye sockets. Instead of following his instinct to run, he adjusted his aim and let the arrow fly.

The arrow struck its target dead on. The dragon collapsed, its body sliding towards him from its momentum. That had been the first time he'd ever fired a bow. He moved to the side to avoid being hit by the body as it slowly came to a stop.

As he did so, he noticed the second dragon already at full speed and far too close for him to have a chance of aiming. Tom instead used his small size to duck under the dragon and load his second arrow as he did so. He managed to roll onto his knees as he aimed his bow at the third dragon.

Second shot, second hit. The third dragon came crashing down just like the first.

The sound of metal being torn apart caught his attention. He turned to see the second dragon, who had just ripped through a metal dome that had been over both his mother and his father as his mother seemed to be bandaging a wound on his father's chest.

There was another purple flash, just as bright as the first, followed by more screaming from his mother. When the purple light died down, the dragon quickly turned to face Tom.

Tom quickly loaded his third arrow as it began to charge towards him, blood covering its teeth. One final shot, one final hit.

Three for three, but even that hadn't been enough.

Nothing made a little boy run faster than the thought that his mother and father were hurt, or worse. He'd thrown all caution to the wind, so he nearly tripped twice before making it to the ditch.

The first thing he saw was the blood. That enough was a sight he very much wasn't ready for. Then there was his father's body. It was clear even to a five-year-old that he was dead. He lay in a puddle of his own blood beside the broken remains of his weapon.

Sharing his pool, was his mother, who was coughing up her own blood. He quickly came to her side, knees fully into the thick red puddle. Despite her injuries she began to smile the moment he came into her view.

"How's dad looking?" She asked him in between coughs. She was doing rather well considering a lot of her insides were no longer where they were supposed to be.

Tom tried to speak, but his voice simply didn't know what to say. She seemed to get the idea from his expression, "Listen, inside my bag is a potion. I need you to finish it. There is also a map."

"Mum I-" Tom's voice finally managed to get out.

"I know. Promise me." She seemed to beg. Tom slowly nodded, "Good boy. The bag should have everything… everything you need." She winced from the pain. Her eyes were slowly starting to close.

Her breathing stopped.

Tom was there for hours crying over their bodies. He piled some dirt on top of them and made a marker with a few sticks. He calved some writing into a stone and placed it in between the two graves, it read;

Here lies Kara and Jack Thomson

It started to rain as he walked away from the bodies of his parents. He carried his bag, now full of his stuff.

His tears slowly stopped as his eyes turned from sorrow to narrow determination over the course of a few minutes. If he was to make it to the next day, he couldn't afford such things distracting him anymore.

His slow walk switched to a faster pace. Despite his focus he could feel his pain even in the background. His best efforts to drown it out never fully succeeding. That was a problem. Something he'd have to fix.

***

Tom slowly came to his senses as he continued to pack his bag. He'd only ever had to make two graves in his life so far. Hopefully over the next few days he wouldn't have to make anymore.

He found himself over a puddle of his own tears next to his bag. He wiped his face and turned his mind to happier thoughts.

His hand searched his desk for one final thing to pack from his room. A sheet of paper. He gently unfolded it to see the drawing. A drawing of Cathie.

Other than the grey pencil lines, the only other colour he had used was red for her hair and her eyes, yet that was all the colour needed to capture her.

***

He was on a mountain. He was fifteen years old now, he had been living by himself, eating off the berry's which grew there and the birds that flew over, the dragons never seemed to come up his mountain, probably had no reason to.

He heard a girl, she was not screaming, she was fighting. He watched her from the top of a cliff. She was a good fighter, but she was also human. The last humans, the only humans he'd ever seen had been his parents, so he decided to simply watch her. Would she suffer the same inevitable fate? Most likely. A shame, but nothing of concern to him.

She was suddenly surrounded by a group of nine cats like creatures, he looked at her closely. She was badly bitten on the leg. She was going to die.

In the middle of nowhere, only this time no one would be there to carve the gravestone. He could save her. To make up for his failure, he could save her.

Tom couldn't help it, sure he could watch her die, but she was certainly determined to keep on living. He saw nothing of himself in her, she was preparing to take her foes on despite the clear odds against her. She had to be everything he wasn't, a purple glow briefly replaced his yellow eyes.

He grabbed his bow, tied a rope and a note to one arrow and fired. Nine arrows struck the creatures and the tenth struck a tree next to her, the arrow with the note and the rope.

She read the note and then started to climb. She made it halfway before she passed out, but Tom pulled her up. She had a tight grip on the rope, but he got her hand off eventually. He patched up the wound on her leg and then stepped back to look at her.

He felt something. He did not know what, he'd turned his emotions off years ago, but this girl made the memories return, only… different. Tom placed her slightly down the mountain away from his cave and hid in a smaller cave, with his bow. He left the remains of a campfire and the arrow with the bit of rope next to her.

When she woke up, she looked around, at first scared, but then she saw the arrow and the campfire. She tried standing up with little success, so she crawled over to the wall of the cave and used that to aid her. After standing up she looked back at where she had been.

"I'm unarmed!" She shouted. She could tell Tom was there, so there was no point in hiding. He walked out of the cave into her view. Something in her face changed, as soon as she saw him, it was probably shock, but Tom didn't really think about it. He raised his bow at her.

"Why are you on your own?" He asked as he pulled back the strings.

"I could ask you the same question." She responded as she eyed the tip of the arrows, "Let's just say I don't get on very well with others." Tom lowered the bow.

"Well looks like we have something in common." He slung his bow over his shoulder, "What's your name?"

"Cathie, yours?"

"Tom."

"Ok, so what now?"

"I don't know. You're in no shape to travel, so I guess you will have to stay here for a few days." He felt a connection with this girl somehow; she seemed to trigger some emotion that Tom had long forgotten about.

"Ok, so you live on your own?" She asked him as she got a good look at him.

"Most people would think I am crazy." Tom revealed. The concern on her face shot out like a fireball, "But I am not, just clever."

"How's my leg doing?"

"It's ok, it should heal in a week or so, it didn't get infected, so you should be fine."

***

Tom made his way from his room to the main area of the cave where he grabbed a quiver full of many different looking arrows and shoved it into his bag as well.

He then walked over to the front door of the cave and made his way outside.

"Where is Amelia?"

CHAPTER 38; LOYALTY AND DEVOTION

Shots flashed her way so fast that she didn't have time to dodge them. Yet none of them seemed to hit her. The soldiers stopped firing after noticing that their weapons seemed to have no effect whatsoever.

"How interesting." Edward spoke from inside his armour, "The light seems to be changing to a very specific wavelength the moment it gets anywhere near you. Not just the laser fire either, the sunlight as well." He explained, "How on earth are you achieving that?"

Amelia looked down at the necklace Patrick had given to her. That must be how it worked. It turned the sunlight down to something that didn't burn her. It seemed to do the same for their weapon blasts as well.

"Lucky me." She muttered as she cracked her knuckles. The soldiers all took a few steps back, but Edward instead took a step forward.

Amelia charged at full speed towards him while throwing a punch. She felt each individual bone shatter in her hand after making contact. Blood spilled out of it and on to the armour, which seemed to catch Edward by surprise.

She continued her path forwards, pushing Edward aside before coming to a stop behind him. She carefully watched her own hand rebuild itself as Edward turned around to face her.

"I've seen evidence of your speed, but that…" He spoke as he too seemed fixed on her repairing hand, "That's something new."

Her hand quickly snapped back into its proper shape and the wounds sealed shut. She hadn't managed to dissolve all the way through the chest plate, but she'd certainly made a dent in it. He hadn't even raised a shield, because he hadn't expected her to break her own hands to cause damage.

Her next punch was blocked by a shield. And the next, and the next. The shield wasn't hard enough for her to break her hands on, but it stopped all of her attacks despite her strength.

She quickly switched things up by at first going for a leg sweep, which was blocked by a shield, but using her speed to throw a punch almost instantly after the shield formed. Another smack to the chest, another broken hand.

This time however Edward had punched her right in the gut at the same time. She went flying back between two tents and slid across the exposed dirt for a few seconds before coming to a stop.

The grazes were painful but healed rather quickly as she got back up to her feet. Her vison began to waver for just a little bit.

Using blood from her own body to break through the armour was a good surprise tactic but given that it wasn't exactly her blood coursing through her veins, it didn't have as much of an effect as she'd hoped.

She was lucky that she'd managed to down a meal of Tom's bootleg blood, but now it was getting to the point that she'd have to feed again, and animal blood wouldn't have any effect against Edward's armour.

Amelia looked down at the brown liquid that was now covering both of her hands. A mixture of the dissolved black material and blood. It stung her cuts; she could feel the liquid replacing the blood around her skin.

A memory from Amy suddenly showed itself to her. The colour of this liquid was exactly the same as the colour of Edward's sword. A sword capable of cutting even Cathie. Was this how Edward had made it?

She heard his power assisted armour walking towards her. She had to act quickly. She had to think quickly. Liquid to solid. You'd cool it right? Like water to ice, but Edward's sword was solid at room temperature while this was liquid.

Her hands stung once more. She paid closer attention to what was going on under her skin. The liquid seemed to be soaking itself in even more blood. It seemed to harden the more blood it drained from her.

She took out a knife from her pocket and slit her own wrist as deeply as she could without chopping her whole hand off. She held the wound open, preventing it from healing as she poured the gushing blood down her wrist and onto her hand. She waited for a sizable puddle to form itself in the palm of her own hand, then let go of the wound and soaked her other hand in it.

She felt the liquid harden over her knuckles as she did her best to shape it before it became completely solid. Eventually, it wouldn't budge anymore.

It was a rough job. Not every knuckle was covered, and bits of the material were still painfully sticking into her hand, but it would have to do for now.

A punch was thrown her way, but she used her own speed to punch the incoming fist. The whole of Edward's armour on his arm shattered from the impact. Yet once more Edward had punched her with his other hand.

This time she went flying up into the air with blood trailing behind her. She blacked out for a second until the ground beneath her started getting closer again.

She landed at the base of the cliff face. She did her best to get back up again, but it was no good this time. Her chest seemed to be full of constant pain. The cuts on her arms and legs from the impact weren't healing anymore. She'd run out of blood. She'd run out of food.

There was nothing now. Her strength, her speed, all without the fuel they drew their power from. Her wrist hadn't properly healed either. That had probably been where she'd lost most of it.

She felt the hunger kick in, but it was already too late, her body didn't have anything left in it to get the food it so badly needed right now.

Something was approaching her, but she could barely keep her own eyes open, let alone try and work out what she already suspected it being. Edward had come to finish her off.

As her eyes slowly closed, a set of teeth appeared in her view. She felt a mouth grab and tug at her at first. When that didn't seem to move her, she felt herself being rolled over onto her front.

A head managed to wedge its way under her and once it stood up, she seemed to be over some animal's back. There was only one creature in this world that ever would come to her rescue, but before anything else, she completely lost consciousness.

Juba looked on at the soldiers quickly making their way over to him. With her on his back his movement would be limited. He didn't know much about human bodies but from the state of her alone he could tell she didn't have long left.

The soldiers closest to him raised their weapons. Weapons he'd never seen before, but he was smart enough to realise that they were dangerous. He shot off as fast as he dared without dropping her. He wasn't exactly high off the ground, so he had to take extra care not to bash her head into anything or let her legs drag enough to slow him down.

Red flashes surrounded him as bits of dirt set alight where they hit. That confirmed his suspicions. Weapons of fire, weapons of death. They seemed to be able to attack at range as well. A bow with arrows of fiery death that seemed to travel faster than his own eyes could see.

He quickly looped into the camp. Using tents and other items to dodge and weave as if they were trees in a forest. More of them seemed to be around the camp, but right now he needed the cover.

He shot past the portal. A purple swirly thing that instincts told him not to go near. There were less armed humans behind it. Most were busy trying to for some reason flatten the ground into a straight line. He'd never understood humans' fascinations with straight lines.

Swords, bows. All straight. That was normally the first clue that something had been made by a human. The unarmed humans seemed to flee from him as the armed humans gave chase from behind.

Pain shot through one of his back legs. It had just scratched him, but it stung like hell. It didn't matter though; her life was on the line still. He simply pushed through the searing pain and in fact picked up speed.

A large metal box with what appeared to be a large metal pole for a face came to a stop in front of him. He quickly changed direction to head towards the nearest forest now that he was close enough to the coast to go around the cliffs. The top of the metal box turned so that the metal pole began to point his way.

Death! His own instincts shouted at him. He quickly pounced to the side, nearly throwing her off, but he managed to balance her just at the last second.

A huge explosion went off where he'd just been. It had only just missed him. The shear sound of it shook him to his core. He'd never heard a noise so loud before in his life.

Whatever that thing was, it was big and slow compared to him. He made a quick dash for the trees. As he turned, he felt a small pain in his chest, but once more ignored it. He flew past the tree line almost at his full pace now.

He could hear the metal box moving, as well as steps from the armed humans chasing him, but they were in his world now. Now they played by his rules. Unable to simply jump, he instead found a fallen over tree thick enough to be raised up from the snow that he now sank in with every step. He carefully hopped onto it and onto a low, thick branch. He'd have to be extra careful with her still balanced on his back, but up here, even without the leaves, he could disappear into the branches.

***

Amelia slowly awoke to the taste of meat in her mouth. She couldn't quite tell what it was, but it was fresh and dripping with blood.

Her teeth quickly sank into it. She felt every one of her wounds slowly begin to heal instead of her hunger being satisfied. As she finished, she began to pay attention to the small and quiet sound in the background.

She slowly sat up to find herself surrounded by deep snow. She was sitting on a patch of ground that had been quickly cleared of most of it, but a white layer still remained.

Upon the white layer were many stains of blood. Some were hers that had just spilled while her body slowly repaired, some were of her food which seemed to have been dragged towards her, but the rest followed the path the food had been dragged from for a bit.

The drag marks ended with what appeared to be half a dear carcase, while the other trail of blood ended with Jubatus, who after noticing that she was awake, slowly limped his way over to her.

His most obvious wound was the laser shot he'd taken to the back leg, which was the cause of his limp. It had barely grazed him but had still taken a sizable chunk of flesh. That wasn't the source of the bleeding however, in fact that wound had been burnt shut.

The cause of the bleeding only became clear as he curled up to the side of her. Shards of metal had gone into his chest and his side. She found similar shards just falling from her back as she realised his wounds.

They were deep, and they'd been bleeding for some time. He'd been running with them as well, which only made them worse.

She tried her best to get a better look, but she wasn't the best at dealing with injuries. The metal showed signs of being warped by heat and kinetic force, an explosion. In places it had fused to his thick skin, while in others his movements had sliced the wounds open more. She wasn't even sure if she could remove them or not.

As she reached for them, he slowly got up and began to curl up on her lap instead. His whole weight was a bit more than she was used to, but he seemed to spread it out over her legs as he curled up, keeping his wounds curled away from her.

Jubatus was many things, but a fool wasn't one of them. He knew a fatal wound when he saw one. He began to shiver as the wind slowly picked up, blowing loose snow into their faces.

Amelia gave him a large hug that shielded most of him from the cold breeze.

"Thank you." She whispered with tears building in her eyes. He brought his head up and gave her face a small lick, before resting it in her lap once more.

He closed his eyes and fell asleep. A few minutes later she could do nothing but hold him tight as his breathing slowly stopped, and his heartbeat slowly faded with it.

***

The door to the cave was blown off Its hinges as Amelia furiously sped through it. All the fires were out, not a sound either. As she'd thought, they'd left to deal with Edward, but it wasn't them she was looking for. She sped into Tom's room, destroying his door in a similar fashion.

Tom normally had many a contraption lying about in his room, but no longer. Her eyes finally settled on what she was looking for. A small rack of wooden bottles with caps that were kept hidden under the desk. She grabbed some rope and speedily began to tie each one to her waist.

She was beyond enraged, but she also still had her wits about her. She'd gotten her ass handed to her last time, and it had cost Jubatus his life. She wouldn't make the same mistake twice, nor would she let the bastard get away with it either.

When she'd finished, she sped back out of the cave and off into the wilderness. She had hunting to do.

CHAPTER 39; GRAVITY

Tom continued to look through a crudely made telescope, using precisely shaped ice instead of glass for the lenses. His sights were set on Edward's military camp below. His eyes spotted the trailer and the portal, and the tank too. He also spotted the large number of soldiers and the construction work going on between the portal and the sea.

Tom lowered the telescope and shortened it until it could fit back into this bag. Now he instead looked down with his own eyes, although it was hard to see that much detail from such a height.

His feet sat just a little bit too close to the edge of the icy floor beneath him than he'd have liked, but he needed to get a first-hand look at what they were going to have to deal with.

He took a few steps back and took in the rest of the mouth of the ice cave, as well as the clear skies beyond. The air was thin and cold, but enough for him to manage for short periods of time. He turned and walked deeper into the cave.

After this battle, the age of dragons would end. Those words rang through Tom's head as he came to a stop by a putty lined door.

The temptation to warn Frost and the others was consuming his every thought. No not yet. If they knew now, they wouldn't be focused on the fight right now.

Perhaps once all of this was over, he could convince them to shelter in universe two for a bit. They couldn't last forever there but they could survive.

He shook his own head. He was doing the very thing the dragons would, had he said anything. Right now, he needed to be focused on the here and now. He opened the door that was lined with putty. Once closed, he got himself a good breath of more concentrated air.

"How's it looking?" Frost asked him as he noticed he'd entered the room. Tom gave a large grin.

"They're about to get quite the shock." He chuckled.

***

The ice cave that hung in the air was rather different to the original ice cave which the air dragons had originally used. Like the original, this one was mainly made of ice, however near the centre of the long structure, the material switched to calved rock, then metal plates which glowed hot in rather specific dragon shaped places. In the middle of the metal plate was a large hole that lead into the bottom of the cave.

Meanwhile, the back of the cave and the underneath were both littered with large fans with metal blades that seemed to spin on their own. Holes where air dragons blew into pipes also littered the base, although not quite as many as the original had.

The cave also boasted two large wings also made out of thick, study ice, with air crystals linked to wires on the bottom for even more lift. At the top, a metal rudder. There were also two other small cave mouths at the top, with dragons waiting patiently to be given the order to fly.

A fortress of the sky. One that planned to use one of the universes most basic forces as a weapon.

Gravity.

Lava slowly began to pour out of one side of the hole at the bottom. A slow dribble at first but it soon picked up to the point that it was now raining lava over the camp below. Rocks that had been set ablaze then began to be thrown out of the same hole.

It took a while for both to actually reach the camp due to the height they were at, but once they did... it was utter chaos.

***

Edward could do nothing but watch as flaming boulders smashed into the ground as if someone had summoned a meteor shower upon them. This itself brought utter panic as tents set ablaze and flaming body parts and charred chunks of dirt were thrown into the air with every impact.

He quickly looked up to just about see the small speck that was the floating cave above them. Just in time to see the lava begin to shower down on them in massive blobs of hot red jelly.

The smaller blobs cooled into rock before they hit the ground, which didn't exactly make things better, but the larger blobs splashed onto the camp with a fiery consuming vengeance. Everything underneath instantly melted or vaporised depending on what it was. Half melted men fully ablaze ran past desperately searching for a nearby stream, but it was already too late for them.

"Well played Thomson." He spoke through gritted teeth as his repaired armour constructed around him, "Is the runway ready?"

"We only got it half done sir." A voice reported over an internal radio in his armour.

"Alright switch to plan B. I want those jets airborne now." He ordered. He watched as the portal flickered.

Luckily, he'd planned ahead. It was rather ambitious to build a runway before they would be attacked, but luckily by moving the portal entrance back at their world, they didn't need to have a runway this side.

Unfortunately, it meant repositioning the portal once more for any further reinforcements other than aircraft, but right now any more soldiers would just die to the falling rocks and lava.

***

Tom watched though his telescope as an oddly shaped metal box exited the portal at a high speed. He struggled to follow it as it lifted off into the sky and began to climb in height.

His eyes widened.

"That's new." He muttered as he watched the aircraft begin to circle around towards them. He watched closely as the craft quickly broke through the sound barrier, something Tom had never even seen before.

He then watched as more began to one by one shoot out from the portal, "Well shit."

He ran from the mouth of the cave and through the airtight doors as the cave shook from a few impacts. The loud roar of the aircraft passing by alerted everyone in the room he'd just run into.

Frost, Wave and Breath all turned to face him from the map they were all looking at on the large table in front of them all.

"The hell was that?" Frost asked.

"They have flying machines. Fast ones. Probably have weapons of some kind as well." He explained.

"And here we thought we'd have the advantage." Wave sighed, "What do we do?"

"We lose this thing now and the battles over." Tom answered, "I'd mobilise the air dragons. These machines seem impossibly fast in a straight line but seem to need a wide turning angle. Chances are dragons are more agile."

"Anything else that could help?" She asked him. He seemed to think about this.

"Flying machines by principle rely on differences in air pressure for lift. That's how this thing flies. I'm sure it's using its wings and its speed to keep itself in the air.

Disrupt either, you might be able to get them to drop out of the sky." He theorised, "But that's just a guess."

"I'll do my best to explain it to the others then." She added before slithering out of the room via a second exit. Frost and Breath remained rather concerned, however.

"We might have suspected they had some form of flying machine, but not one this advanced." Frost sighed.

"I'm sure the cloud cover could also prove useful." Tom suggested as he turned to Breath. Breath nodded, then quickly left the room.

"I don't like surprises Tom."

"Now, now Frost. There were bound to be a few as far as Edward is concerned. Thankfully we have the resources to combat this threat." Tom responded as the cave shook once more.

"For now." He muttered, "For now." He repeated in a quieter tone filled with hope that his own instincts were wrong.

***

From small holes in the top of the cave, water began to sprinkle to the point that it spread out either side of the cave. The whole thing was suddenly covered in beautiful rainbows, but not for long. As the water fell below the cave and towards the now constant stream of lava pouring out of it, it began to evaporate. Yet the moment the hot steam began to rise it was quickly cooled once more by the high altitude.

After a minute or so, the whole cave was completely surrounded by an artificial cloud.

Air dragons began to shoot in and out of the cloud at great speeds, constantly moving and constantly changing position. As a jet came in for an attack run, a few shot out from different points of the cloud and blasted it with high pressured air from multiple random directions.

The jet quickly span out of control as it continued to shoot across the sky. It missed the cave and eventually splashed into the sea far off in the distance.

***

Tom quickly ran back to the mouth of the cave only to find his view now blocked by cloud, which began to seep into the cave all the way to the airtight door.

He began to make his way back, until a purple light began to shine through the now cloud engulfed room. He watched as the purple swirling light vanished after briefly illuminating an armoured figure.

"Shit." Tom cursed to himself as he reached into his bag and pulled out his bow and his quiver. He quickly slung the quiver over his shoulder, took an arrow and aimed in the general direction Edward had first appeared.

There was silence for a few seconds. A jet shot past, followed by red flashes from outside the mouth of the cave.

"Impressive work." Edward's voice echoed throughout the large space, "Guess you've had quite the time to prepare for me since our last encounter."

"Still hiding behind that armour of yours?" Tom asked into the white mist as he slowly began to change his position the moment he spoke. He did so with the lightest of footsteps to not give himself away. He could feel the bulky armour shake the floor ever so slightly with every step. He wasn't very close, but he was getting closer.

"As you hide behind everyone else." He responded. He'd definitely gotten closer. Close enough for him to locate despite the echo. He aimed his bow and fired.

He heard the tip of the arrow smash and the blood contained within splatter. He then heard the armour begin to slowly sizzle as he quickly changed position as light footed as before.

"The cowards roll has its perks."

"You really have upped your arsenal. Glass in such primitive times. Not very good quality of course, but still." Now that Tom had moved, he was too far for him to locate once more. He loaded another arrow and aimed blindly into the white fog.

He decided to move a little more.

"Just a bit of heat and sand. Afraid I don't have the craftmanship of my mother to please your high standards, but the arrow heads do what they are designed for."

"Tell me Tom, what drives you?" Edward asked him seemingly out of the blue, "You see, your counterpart I understand, he fears that myself and others will achieve my goals."

"Which are?" Tom asked before quickly changing positions once more. From the pattern of his footsteps he seemed to be just as aimlessly moving about, hoping that Tom would somehow slip up and reveal his position, but Tom was keeping one step ahead of him for now.

"Why, to become a god of course." He revealed. Tom slowly chuckled at this, "You think my goal laughable?" He asked.

"No. In fact to this world you might as well be a god." Tom responded, "But oddly enough your goal is somewhat linked to my own."

"Oh, and what is yours then?"

"You see, I'm rather sick of the gods of this world. Most have tried to kill me and my friends at one point or another."

"So what, you want to give them all a slap on the wrist?" Edward chuckled. He'd gotten closer again. Tom quickly moved to avoid the two of them meeting.

"Most would think your goal arrogant and unreachable, but I can't exactly talk given that mine is even more so."

"Oh? You've certainly got my attention."

"You see Edward, I aspire to become someone capable of killing the gods of this world."

Suddenly, a step in the right direction put Tom right behind him. He released four of the ten loaded arrows right into his back. Each one only had a small bit of blood inside, but this wasn't his bootleg blood. It was pure, authentic human blood.

The four arrows seemed to be just enough to dissolve a small hole in his back before he turned to face Tom, but Tom had already backed away into the cloud.

After a few more seconds, Edward was alerted to the sound of more arrows flying through the air. He quickly moved, but then realised that not only were they regular arrows, but that they'd been shot blindly into the cloud.

A volley of ten arrows quickly struck him seconds afterwards as if from nowhere. He'd fashioned arrows that made a loud noise in the air on purpose to get him to move just so that he could locate him.

This time however the arrows had all hit a shield.

"Impressive work. Nearly caught me off guard. My targeting system isn't fairing very well in this mist, but the moment it worked out your firing position it could block your next shots I'm afraid." He explained as the glass tipped arrows fell to the floor and shattered, leaving a small puddle of blood.

Edward listened closely to the sound of buckles being tightened from the same position Tom had fired from just now.

"Guess I'll have to improvise then." His voice spoke from the same location. A single arrow shot towards him. Once more the arrow was blocked by a shield, but this time the arrow exploded violently on impact. Edward was thrown backwards. He expected to land on his back, but instead he found himself continuing to fall through cloud, until he came out of the bottom of it.

Out of the cloud shot Tom, with wings attached to his back, "See you on the ground." He chuckled as he shot past him and dived down towards the chaos below. He continued to watch as the lava stopped flowing, and the fiery rocks also seemed to stop as well.

Clearly Tom wanted to fight him where the air wasn't so thin. His army had been more or less destroyed, but some remnants remained.

"I might need some reinforces."

"Sorry sir, we're a bit busy at our end. We can only spare the odd man or two." A voice spoke over the radio. Edward sighed.

"Let me guess, Thomas Thomson."

"Afraid so sir. We could probably bring through the last resort."

"Bring it through, but don't make it obvious. Once I'm done with the annoyance over here, I'll return to crush him once more."

CHAPTER 40; TO BEAT A GOD

Most of the lava had now cooled to rock. Tom slowly walked between the now towering solid structures that still radiated quite a large amount of heat despite their now solid state.

His eyes caught a figure move across a gap between two lava casts. He quickly raised his bow towards the gap, but slowly lowered it as his mind replayed what he saw. A woman with brown hair and purple eyes. He was seeing things again.

A noise from behind caught him off-guard, and he quickly spun around to aim his bow at Patrick.

"Little jumpy there. You alright?" He asked him as Tom slowly relaxed. Tom hesitated for a second before deciding whether or not to reveal that couldn't trust his own eyes right now.

"No, starting to see shit again." He sighed. They couldn't afford a fuck up this time, and his hallucinations would only make things worse unchecked. Patrick nodded at this, he seemed to appreciate the honesty.

"Save your arrows for the endgame then." He suggested, "Cathie and Amy are getting ready to strike. Probably best if you're with someone else right now."

"And you?"

"I'll wear him down with my magic. He isn't going to run if we hold back, so we need to time this perfectly." Tom nodded at his suggestion as a purple light caught both of their eyes just a few lava casts away from them.

"He's here."

"Go, I'll handle him for now."

Tom unloaded his bow and began to run in and out of the lava casts until he vanished into what remained of the battlefield. Patrick turned all of his attention towards the purple light, which quickly died out.

"You wanted me down here Tom, so, where are you?" Edward shouted as he walked through the lava casts. He eventually came across Patrick.

"Afraid I'm the one you're dealing with for now." Patrick responded as he began to draw triangles in the scorching rock ground with his foot. As well as Patrick's satchel, he also had quite a few wooden bottles tied to his belt with the lids on.

"Ah, the magician. Tell me, you didn't happen to bring all of your books with you, did you?" Edward asked him.

"Like I'd tell you."

"No matter. Ideally I'd like to take you alive but finding the books won't be that much of a task should I end up killing you."

"Good luck with that. Not even Tom could figure my magic out." Edward chuckled at this.

"I don't think you understand who you're dealing with, magician. I myself already have quite the history of outsmarting the Tom of my world, and he's whole millennia ahead of your worlds equivalent. I'm fully aware that right now he's busy setting up whatever plan he has made, but I guarantee it won't even hold a light to what I've gotten myself out of."

"We'll see." Patrick darted forwards as he undid a bottle lid. Liquid quickly shot out of it and towards a lava cast.

Edward quickly raised a shield, but the liquid missed it and instead bounced off the lava cast. The water was suddenly around Edward's arm.

Patrick quickly took out a small dagger as the water turned to a block of ice. Edward seemed unphased by the move and in fact rather confused as to what he was trying to do. Before he knew it, Patrick had calved a triangle in the ice, with his arm in the centre.

"What?" He asked as Patrick closed his eyes while backing away.

"Shatter." Patrick muttered as the triangle glowed red. The armour around Edward's arm shattered to pieces, much to his surprise. Patrick himself seemed rather stunned that it had actually worked, given he hadn't tested the spell on something thought to be unbreakable, "I guess it isn't resistant to magic."

"Apparently not." Edward cursed through gritted teeth. That had been a good trick, but one he wouldn't get away with using again. He went to take a step forwards to try and land a blow, but then remembered the triangles on the floor between the two of them.

He looked down at what was probably the equivalent of a magical minefield. One step in one of the many triangles that littered the floor would cost him leg armour, not to mention what would happen should he put his bare leg in one.

He couldn't get close enough for a strike now, but that was alright. He'd held back a few secret weapons just for a scenario like this.

Edward aimed his other arm at Patrick as a small gun popped out of the forearm. A black beam shot out of it but stopped right in front of Patrick's raised barrier. At the end of the beam, a small mass started to build up. It continued to grow as light began to warp around it.

Patrick's barrier began to flex as loose rock began to get sucked up into this mass, further adding to its size. Patrick rightly listened to his instincts and ran as fast as he could while putting as many lava casts between him and this mass.

The beam died down as the light bending object shot off into the distance, calving a circular hole though everything that it passed through.

"It seems I'm not the only magician here." Patrick muttered as he caught his breath. Whatever the hell that was, it was beyond dangerous.

"I was saving it to surprise Tom. Not sure if he's aware of the existence of black holes or not, but he certainly would have appreciated the knowledge." Edward sighed as he moved from lava cast to lava cast searching for him, with the weapon on his arm raised and armed.

"What possible science could bring about a weapon of death like that?" Patrick asked as Edward began to draw closer to him. Edward aimed his weapon at where the question had come from and fired. He watched the black hole rip through multiple lava casts without finding a victim before vanishing into the distance.

"Science that to you might as well be the power of a god." Edward chuckled in response, "Which is why I'm going to win."

An arrow shot high into the air. Normally at such a height, most on the ground wouldn't notice it, but it not only left a bright red trail behind it but shone bright red at the tip as well. Patrick smiled as he noticed this, "A signal?"

Patrick closed his eyes. The entire battlefield began to glow the same red as Patrick's earlier spell.

Edward's eyes widened as he realised what was happening. The others had surrounded the area in one very large triangle after seeing that Patrick's spell did in fact work against his armour.

It was too late. The whole of his armour shattered as the red light died down. He quickly looked down at his arm that hadn't been protected by the armour. It was still there and completely fine.

He also noticed that his clothing underneath hadn't been affected either. His white lab coat and black trousers and shirt. However, the stone lava casts around them had shattered, revealing the boiling hot liquid within, which then quickly cooled into more, smaller lava casts.

He smiled and nodded as he finally came to his conclusion, "I see, the triangle represents strength, structure. That nasty trick of yours can only break materials which are designed to be as such."

"That's quite the observation, but in the end, it doesn't matter, does it?" Patrick asked as he came out from behind a lava cast to appear behind Edward. A fireball lit in his hand which he aimed towards Edward's now unprotected body, "No protection, no hidden tricks left." Edward smiled at this last remark, which quickly put Patrick on guard.

"Do you really think that armour was my only weapon against you all?" He asked as what seemed to be a black cloud began to surround him. Patrick took a few steps back, not really sure what was happening.

"What magic are you conjuring now?" He asked as he quickly brought out some small wooden triangles from his satchel.

"I'll forgive you for not knowing about nanotechnology, let alone nano construction and deconstruction, given that even in my world its rather new and unheard of." Some of the cloud seemed to cover a bag on his back, while the rest swirled around him like a swarm of insects looking for their next prey, "A good attempt to bring me down, but I can adapt to your little spell by simply not forming anything ridged."

Out of curiosity, Patrick threw the fireball in his hand towards Edward. The black cloud seemed to consume it before impact.

"Well then… time for something different." He muttered to himself. He turned around and ran as fast as he could, tossing a handful of the small wooden triangles behind him as he did so. The black cloud shot towards him but smacked into the many shields now between the two of them.

Just as Patrick vanished from sight, an arrow shot towards Edward at an impressive speed. More of the black cloud seemed to seep out of hidden containers under his lab coat and caught the arrow just before the arrowhead reached his head. He turned to face it, then the direction it had come from.

Amy stood a little way off loading another arrow into her bow. She seemed to smile as she noticed her arrow had been caught. The arrow suddenly lit up with a flash that blinded Edward for a few seconds.

During his confusion, another arrow shot towards him, but the black cloud managed to catch that one as well. This time it quickly threw the arrow as far away as possible in a random direction as Edward regained his senses.

By now, the first black cloud had returned to him and combined with the second, making an even bigger cloud that now circled Edward protectively.

Part of it shot towards Amy and struck her, only for the image of her to shatter like a mirror. Another arrow shot towards him just in time for the black cloud to once more protect him. She'd tried to get him during his attack so that he wouldn't be as protected.

He looked towards where the other arrow had been shot from, but she was no longer there. He recalled Amelia's speed and strength. He had to be careful with this one.

His eyes found her once more, only this time she was slowly walking towards him, rather pissed off. Edward noted the belt of wooden bottles she hadn't been wearing before, and the hand covered by bits of a brown solid he knew all too well. This one wasn't Amy; her clone had returned to face him once more.

"And here I thought you and that pet of yours ran off to lick your wounds." Edward chuckled as she drew closer, but his words simply seemed to piss her off even more. Her own fiery red hair and eyes suddenly began to remind him of Cathie, which triggered a sense of terror few could instil.

Suddenly something fast grabbed her and pulled her out of Edward's sight.

"So you decided to show after all." Amy huffed as she made sure they'd taken cover behind a lava cast far enough away to get away with talking.

"Don't interrupt me. I've got a score to settle with him." Amelia seemed to hiss. Amy took a good look at her and noticed that her clothes were drenched in a lot of blood. From the smell alone Amy could tell that not all of it was hers either.

Amelia began to walk past her, but Amy put her hand out to stop her.

"Is he alright?" She simply asked. Amelia closed her eyes and took in a calming breath.

"No." She simply answered. She couldn't hide it any longer. She could do nothing but watch as Amy saw her pain in her own eyes. She very quickly put two and two together. She then watched Amy's eyes fill with a similar pain, but it quickly vanished the moment she remembered where they were.

"Patrick took out his armour, but now he seems even stronger than before." She explained to her.

"Considering he beat my ass in his armour, that isn't a good sign." Amelia sighed. She oddly found some comfort in Amy's words. Not the words themselves, but what Amy meant by them.

"That cloud of his seems to evenly spread-out attack and defence, unlike his armour which was mainly defensive. But we land a single hit and the bastard falls."

"I assume the others are up to something?" Amelia asked her. Amy quickly nodded, "Tom's got his eye on the whole thing. We simply need to keep attacking until he finds a weakness for this thing, then he'll either send Patrick or mum in to take over with the new information."

"So, we have to do all the hard work then." Amelia sighed.

"For now. Once we get him to turn tail, Tom will play his part." She revealed. Amelia slowly nodded at this. She took out her sword and handed it to Amy.

"You aren't going to land a shot on him with your bow." She explained.

"What about you?" Amy asked her as she slowly took it after slinging her bow over her shoulder. Amelia looked down at her fist covered in bits of the mysterious brown material.

"I'd rather kill him with my own bare hands given the opportunity."

***

Edward continued to walk between the many lava casts of varying sizes. Most still gave off heat that made it unbearable to stand close to them, which he now felt a lot now that he was out of his armour. The twins had run off somewhere, which wasn't making too much sense.

Tom knew that he probably had a spare set of armour somewhere, so letting up on the attacks just gave him the opportunity to find it amongst the chaos that was the battlefield. Eventually, he came up on what was left of the trailer that had been their headquarters.

Most of it was under a lava cast, but luckily the door wasn't. He slowly opened it, burning his hand as he did so. The whole structure was burning hot. The inside was a sauna. He hesitated to step inside for a few seconds. If he wasn't careful then he might fry himself trying to get to his spare armour.

Yet before he could decide whether to enter or not, he was alerted to the sound of incredibly fast movements coming his way.

The black cloud moved and blocked a sword that had tried to strike him from behind at quite an impressive speed. As he turned to face Amy, Amelia came in from the side. Part of the black cloud separated to block Amelia's punch while the first half pushed Amy backwards and away from him. Yet Amelia's punch wasn't stopped by the cloud. Edward just about managed to dodge her fist, noticing the shards of brown material on her fist once more.

Right, that was going to be a problem. Instead, the black cloud grabbed her arm and quickly seemed to eat through it. Amelia sped backwards with now only half of her arm. Blood began to drip from her wound until she quickly gulped down one of the many bottles of liquid strapped to her. Bottles filled with freshly collected blood.

Evidence of her arm starting to grow back quickly began to show itself to her relief before she sped away, out of sight. Edward turned to Amy, but she too had vanished.

He looked down at Amelia's severed arm, which seemed to quickly turn to dust.

"What are you two?" He asked himself as he bent down and examined the dust. Ash.

Regeneration, speed and strength. Plus, a necklace designed to protect them from light. Dots began to connect. He couldn't exactly be sure, but then again this was another world after all. Anything could be possible here, "Vampires?" He seemed to ask himself. He found it rather unfortunate that he hadn't exactly brought garlic and a stake with him, but nevertheless he seemed to be able to damage them quite easily considering.

Another attack, from behind once again. Edward turned to face Amy as her sword was blocked by the black cloud once more. This time however flames began to burn either side of the red-hot sword. She'd heated the blades using one of the lava casts.

Edward's black cloud began to burn slightly as tiny parts of it fell to the ground. The black cloud quickly pushed her blade away before dispersing to put out the flames. It then quickly reformed once it had cooled itself in the air.

It all made sense now. He kicked himself for not working it out sooner. Tom was taking this time to learn every one of his tricks, to analyse all of his weaknesses. Right now he was inside a huge experiment to see what it would take to beat him.

Something in the air caught his attention. Something that shimmered. A sword, heading right for him. Cathie's sword to be exact.

Just as he moved his cloud to block, Amy sped out of hiding with her bow drawn, and Amelia did the same with her sword. They'd changed things up once again.

Edward quickly split up his cloud to try and block all three attacks before realising they were all diversions. He split the cloud protecting his backpack to counter the other unseen attacks.

Amy's arrows were caught, Amelia's sword was stopped. Patrick's rather sneaky fireball was consumed, and Tom's volley of arrows were slapped out of the air. Cathie's sword was also caught behind him now as he faced the four of them, but then realised that Cathie herself was missing.

A foot landed on either side of the hilt to Cathie's sword with considerable force. So much so that the blade was pushed through the cloud and into the bag on Edward's back. The blade seemed to break something important inside.

All of his cloud instantly fell out of the sky and to his feet, "Well shit." He cursed as he quickly reached into his lab coat and brought out a portal device. Surrounded on all sides, he quickly fired it at his feet, but Tom was already right beside him.

CHAPTER 41; BETWEEN WORLDS

As Tom grabbed Edward, both of them fell though the freshly formed portal beneath them. As they came out the other side still falling, Edward noticed the portal device already in Tom's hand.

A second one? Had he made it himself? Impossible!

Tom pointed it down and fired, so that they fell straight through the portal he'd formed. They came out the other side, but only to fall back into Edward's original portal.

Edward quickly began to fiddle with the controls to his portal device, but Tom quickly knocked it out of his hands before shoving his own portal device into his bag.

Edward made a desperate grab for the bag, but the moment he put his hand in he seemed to only be able to grab at an endless void.

"What the-"

"Never come across a pocket dimension hidden in a bag?" Tom laughed as the two of them continued to endlessly fall, "And here I thought you knew everything."

"A pocket dimension? How the hell did you manage that?" Edward asked, now completely confused.

"My mothers work. You're lucky she died many years ago, because unlike me, she would have schooled your ass a hundred times over by now."

"That kind of technology isn't possible in your world."

"Then it stands to reason that my mother wasn't of my world. Afraid you aren't the first person to cross the line we are constantly crossing now." The two of them looked around at their situation.

They were both falling so fast now that everything in either world was a complete blur. It was hard to tell what universe they were in, or whether they were somewhere in between.

"So, what now?" Edward asked him.

"Now we settle things the good old-fashioned way." Tom answered as he threw a punch at Edward's stomach. It hit, causing Edward to fly back into the seemingly continuous edge of the portals they were falling though. He harshly bounced off it and steadied himself in the fall.

The impact had slowed his fall, but he quickly dived so that he caught Tom up again. Edward threw a similar punch towards Tom, but Tom had been ready for it.

Despite Tom's weak figure he seemed surprisingly strong. Strong enough to grab Edward's arm to stop his punch and twist it until it burned, "See in my world I'm considered weak. Not really the fighting type. I'm sure the same could be said for you as well, but unfortunately for you our worlds differ in what we consider weak."

He began to lecture as Edward slowly broke free of his grip just in time to receive a smack to the face.

"Clearly your world demands far more from the human body than mine, but that fact isn't going to win you this fight." Edward spat as he wiped some blood from his lower lip. Tom went in for another punch, but Edward managed to block and counterattack.

Once more however Tom seemed to expect this and simply moved himself out of the way by gripping Edward and tugging himself to the side.

By doing this, the two were pulled closer to one another, but Edward felt the pain of something stabbing into his lower torso.

"As I said, I'm not a fighter. I'm a coward." He muttered as he shoved the dagger as far in as he could. Edward tensed and grunted in pain.

"Unfortunately for you." He managed to get out between groans and winces of pain, "Playing dirty is my specialty."

He spread his body out as wide as he could, causing Tom to quickly pull away from him. The dagger remained in Edward as he grabbed his portal device, which had been falling with them.

He hesitated as he tried to work out the timings and the coordinates required, but that hesitation cost him. A black material tipped arrow shot into his portal device from below and struck the carefully calved ring within, chipping it.

The device was now useless.

Edward's portals collapsed. Edward slammed rather violently into the ground of Universe One's charred, lava cast filled battleground.

Tom on the other hand gently came to a stop while continuing to squeeze an air crystal in his hand. He hastily landed without a scratch on him.

Edward on the other hand felt a few of his ribs break from the impact. One of his legs also hurt like hell and was probably broken.

The knife that had been stuck in him had been pushed all the way through. The handle end now flushes with his skin. He yelled out as the pain from that eventually hit him.

There was a sudden blast. Both of them flew off to the side. They both rolled along the charred floor before eventually coming to a stop. The ringing in both of their ears continued as they both got to their feet, rather disorientated.

When their hearing finally returned, the sound of mechanical tracks echoed throughout the battlefield. The lava cast beside them had been blown to smithereens, spraying fresh lava around before it quickly cooled in the air. A few other lava casts had been blown up as well.

"Shit." Tom cursed as he recovered his bow and quickly got some distance from Edward, "The bloody armoured box." He muttered as he watched the large tank aim its turret towards him. He quickly took cover behind some undamaged lava casts but knew it wouldn't offer much protection.

As he heard it open fire, he quickly dived to another nearby lava cast. The explosion just about threw him off his feet as his ears began to ring once more.

Tom quickly got back up, swung around the lava cast while the machine was reloading and let loose a volley of black material tipped arrows. He watched as they began to glow orange as they passed through the air.

Nine massive holes all the way through the tank appeared shortly after as Tom took cover once more. He waited for the next attack, but one didn't come. He looked out from cover to see the now completely wrecked machine.

"Nice shot." Patrick muttered from beside him. He'd been so focused on the metal box that he hadn't even noticed him.

"Thanks for the assist." Tom responded as he noticed Patrick's nose start to bleed.

"We've got bigger problems."

"I'll admit, you almost had me." Edward chuckled as he emerged from the trailer. A new suit of armour constructed around him, "But luck just happened to be on my side today." He added as he charged towards Tom.

"Going to risk the only working portal gun, are you?" Tom asked him as he came into punching range. Edward came to a stop, then remembered that now the only working portal device was in Tom's bag. A bag he couldn't seem to take anything out of no matter how hard he tried.

"Fuck." He cursed as he aborted the attack. He couldn't just kill Tom right now. He was the last man standing on this side, and he didn't possess nearly enough manpower to produce a new portal device. His only way back now was that one.

Wait. The loop they'd just been in. He looked back to find Tom's portal had closed.

"No way back, and any minute now the other me will have taken over everything you have back in your world."

"This was all his idea, wasn't it? He asked you for help."

"You knew from the beginning that you'd be fighting both of us. But if you're under the impression that was the last trick up my sleeve, your very much mistaken."

"Did you manage to deliver the package?" Edward seemed to ask a non-existent person.

"Yes sir. The portal closed shortly afterwards, should we be concerned?"

"Begin working on opening a portal here from your end. I might be here a while. What's the situation with Thomson?"

"Communicating to home base?" Tom asked him.

"Dire sir. They've gained access to most of the complex."

"Just keep them out of the portal departments at all cost. Last thing I need is two Thomson's." Edward sighed. He then began to pay attention to the Tom in front of him, who'd reloaded with the glass tipped arrows filled with blood.

"How about dealing with the issue at hand?" Tom asked him.

"I'm afraid this is game over for you Tom. If you want your friends and family to survive that is." Edward threatened.

There was a large thump as a fire dragon landed behind Patrick.

"Thomson. The humans managed to get something through the large portal before it disappeared." Flame revealed. Tom looked at Flame, then narrowed his eyes as he looked back at Edward.

"What have you done?" Tom asked him.

"I assume that you're familiar with the concept of a bomb, right?" Edward asked with a small chuckle, "Now imagine one that could wipe out all life in this world with a single explosion."

"You can't be serious."

"Better hurry. Won't be long until it goes off. Think you can work out how to disable it?" Edward asked him with a loud chuckle, "Of course, I could tell you how, for a very reasonable price."

"The portal device." Tom sighed. He didn't know whether or not to believe him. If he was serious, then he couldn't afford not to believe him – and with everything else he'd seen from the other world such a bomb suddenly seemed possible. He turned back to Flame, "Finish off the flying machines, I'll deal with this."

He lowered his bow and ran off to where the portal had been, with Patrick in tow.

Amy, Cathie and Amelia were all standing around a large cylinder that seemed to be designed sort of like a giant metal arrow, although Tom highly doubted the metal tip was the dangerous part of this thing.

On the side he noticed a symbol. A yellow dot surrounded by a circle broken up into sixths, with three of the sixths being yellow, and the other three black.

Naturally Tom had no idea what this symbol meant, but he had a rather nasty feeling that it wasn't good. He found a panel that he could see large screws for, "Going to need to see inside." He said as he turned to Cathie.

She grabbed the panel and tore it off as quickly as she could. Inside was a mixture of wires and mechanisms that all seemed simple enough, but in the grand scheme of things made no sense as to what it was trying to do.

Tom quickly reached into his bag and pulled out a specific book titled 'Scientific symbols'. He quickly flicked through the pages until he found what he was looking for. He held the open page next to the yellow symbol. A perfect match to the one on the page.

He began to read, but quickly slammed the book shut without warning, "Fuck." He cursed. Now he'd wished he didn't know what the symbol meant. He shook his head as he backed away from it.

"Tom?" Patrick asked. Tom turned to look at them all, worry painted across his face.

"I can't disarm this." He revealed to them all.

"Let's see." Edward chuckled as he joined the rest of them, "One minute, forty-eight seconds." He read from a small hologram display on his wrist.

CHAPTER 42; 00:01:47

Edward quickly found Cathie right in front of him going for a punch. Amy's bow released an arrow that quickly glowed bright orange as Amelia came in from the side with her sword covered in blood.

A shield blocked Amelia's sword. Amy's shot struck Edward's chest, but the orange glow seemed to simply dissipate into the armour before vanishing. The arrow barely made a scratch. Edward also smacked Cathie in the gut as she landed a blow herself, but it achieved nothing, while she was flung backwards a few paces.

"This isn't the strategy of someone who wants to become a god." Tom spoke through gritted teeth as Patrick and his family backed away from their failed attacks, "You have an exit strategy."

"My exit strategy is your portal device Tom. You made sure of that yourself." Edward responded.

00:01:32

"So, you'd be willing to die along with the rest of this world?"

"This armour can easily withstand a nuclear warhead. Tried and tested. Sure, I might be the only thing alive here, and I might not have a way home, but I'm sure I can make a new home here. A world all to myself doesn't sound so bad now, does it? A world where I alone resound as a god."

"You're insane."

"But we both know it won't come to that, will it?" Edward asked him, "Not even you are determined enough to win to sacrifice both yourself and your friends."

Tom looked at them all, then looked up at the sky, the floating cave, and the many dragons that swarmed around it. He then looked back at Edward. No time to save the dragons. Barely enough to save his family.

Damn him. An impossible decision with no way out without heavy losses.

00:01:28

"Better one world burns than both." He simply spoke. His determined eyes stared deep into the armour covering Edward's face. Edward narrowed his own eyes at the image of Tom's face in front of him inside the armour.

There were a few seconds of tense silence.

"Now that sounds more like the coward you really are." Edward sighed as he realised that Tom wouldn't in fact yield, "What was it you told me, you wished to be a man capable of killing gods? I don't see that dream being fulfilled here, do you?"

There was more silence for a few more seconds.

"I won't stop you from disarming this bomb Edward."

"And the begging starts." Edward laughed.

00:01:04

"Never asked you to, just saying I won't stop you."

"I'll see this through to the end Tom, no bluffs on my side. Either way I get what I want, but you only win if you give me the portal device."

"I give you the device, and you leave this thing here. Unless you disarm that thing, this world is going to burn no matter what I do." Tom explained.

"Perhaps. Perhaps I might consider being merciful."

"We both know that won't happen."

"I guess you're right, no point hiding it then." Damn him. He was seriously going to make him burn a whole world just to win.

After a few more seconds of silence, Tom slowly reached into his bag. He removed the portal device from it. He had no way of generating a portal big enough for the bomb, this device was already low on power, perhaps enough for three, maybe four-person sized portals before it was dead.

00:00:55

"Of course, there is one other person capable of disarming this thing." He added as he began to set co-ordinates into it. One small idea, one last desperate shot. If this didn't work...

Edward charged forwards towards the device. He hit a magical barrier, but he simply smashed his way through it. He then hit a second barrier, this time an orange coloured one.

Tom opened a portal to the side of him, "Keep him busy."

***

Thomas stood in what was left of a room inside of what was left of a building. The roof and the above floors had all collapsed, revealing the night sky. His lab coat was riddled with burn marks, blood and dirt. His face and hands seemed to match this same pattern.

He watched as Tom stepped through a portal in front of him with urgency in his stride.

"Need your help."

"What now?" Thomas huffed. The fight this side had been a long one, and a bloody one.

"Does the term nuclear warhead mean anything to you?" Tom asked him.

"Fuck, he didn't, did he?"

"I need your help disarming it. I don't even know where to begin."

"Tom… I hate to break this to you, but I would have as much of a clue as you." Thomas revealed, "I know nothing about them."

"It's either that or I somehow trick Edward into disarming it."

"Edward wouldn't know how to either. Their archaic weapons in this world. Banned and discarded before most of us were even born." Thomas revealed.

"Are you saying there is no way to save my world?" Thomas shook his head.

"Save as many as you can, quickly!" Tom quickly turned and ran back through the portal.

***

He came out to find the others locked in a fierce battle against Edward.

"Everyone through. NOW!" Tom ordered. His eyes looked back up to the hovering ice cave. Damn it. There was no saving them now.

00:00:39

Amy quickly grabbed Amelia, stopping her from charging headfirst towards Edward and more or less threw her towards the direction of Tom.

Cathie did her best to follow, but Edward himself was hot on her tail. Just before he managed to grab her, an orange barrier blocked him.

00:00:20

As Cathie ran past Tom and through the portal behind him, Tom's concern switched to the last remaining member of the group. Patrick.

00:00:16

The orange glow around his entire body seemed to flicker as he struggled to hold the barrier between the portal and Edward. Stuck on the other side of it with

Edward as he continued to punch at the sheet of pure will power blocking his path.

Cracks formed where Edward's fists landed, but quickly sealed themselves up, although every time they did, Patrick seemed to get weaker and weaker.

00:00:10

Tom and Patrick's eyes met. Patrick's now pure orange eyes burning brighter than ever.

"You better protect her." He quietly muttered, yet Tom could hear him despite Edward's fit of rage as he continued to constantly hammer at the barrier.

00:00:05

Tom's eyes began to turn from yellow to purple. Lines began to paint themselves across his vision. Numbers began to calculate, but his attention was quickly brought to Patrick's shaking head, "Go."

00:00:02

The purple colour drained from his eyes, now being overtaken by the original yellow colour. He turned, and quickly ran through the portal with genuine tears building up.

Edward turned towards Patrick, who passed out the moment he saw the portal close behind Tom. His body slowly began to dissolve into an orange powder that seemed to dissipate into the air above.

Will stood above him. Invisible to Edward, he simply slowly shook his head.

"Pushing your limit with anything else, you might have gotten away with, but your human body just cannot take my power any more than you have already been doing so." He sighed as he looked over towards the bomb.

He then looked over to Edward, and then looked up at the ice cave above, "Choosing to sacrifice a whole world to save another. Of all of the continuums, of all of the many versions of Universe One, this one seems particularly interesting."

An orange portal appeared above him, then quickly came down over him, causing him to vanish.

00:00:00

***

"Any chance anyone survived?" Cathie asked Thomas. They were both siting in a room along with Tom. The three of them had remained rather silence until now.

"The initial explosion would have taken out everyone near the battlefield. If that didn't kill them, the radiation will. Anyone unlucky enough to survive that then has to go through a nuclear winter thanks to all the dust thrown into the air."

"In other words... no." Tom muttered from the corner of the room. He was still staring off into space, while the other two were sat either side of a table.

"So, what now?" Cathie asked them both.

"The AG-Project should be able to look after you all. Afraid we can't let you roam freely, every single one of your bodies is a walking miracle in this world." Thomas suggested.

"As if something like your organisation could keep us safe." Tom muttered, "Could barely keep portal technology from a madman."

"Now isn't the time to be throwing blame around." Thomas sighed. Tom got to his feet rather quickly.

"All of this happened because you couldn't outsmart a man off his head. Instead you had to rely on humans from another, less developed world. I fail to see exactly how this isn't your fault." He calmly but fiercely pointed out.

"Fine. I failed, I'm sorry. Happy?" Thomas snapped at him.

"Not until you say that to the girl crying in the other room." Tom calmly snapped back at him. Those words seemed to really hit Thomas deep.

"This isn't going to get us anywhere." Cathie sighed as she reminded the two of them that she was in fact present.

Tom turned away and headed for the door to the room.

"No shit." He muttered as he slammed the door shut behind him. Thomas continued to be rather uncomfortable in his chair as Cathie turned to look at him.

"I get it, he just lost a world. A home. You all did."

"Tom was given a choice. A big one. End the battle against Edward there and then, or let him return here, making him nothing but your problem once again."

"So, he chose to end the fight, despite it costing your world?"

"He chose to end the fight so that you wouldn't have to continue it." Cathie answered, "He did you one hell of a favour, one he paid the price for."

"Guess I owe him, big time." Thomas sighed.

"You owe a little more than that Thomas." Cathie muttered as she stood up. She too began to head for the door. As she opened it, she turned to look at him again, "You owe him a world." She slowly began to close the door, but stopped as it was about halfway shut, "And just as importantly, a friend."

***

Rather tactfully, Cathie had left Tom for a few hours now. She'd spent the time instead trying to unravel the mess that was Amy right now, to little success. For once Amelia seemed rather close to her sister. If it was an act for Amy's sake, it was a good one, but either way, she was making a lot more progress with her than Cathie was.

She slowly opened the door to the room that she knew Tom had been sitting in alone with his thoughts.

He was sitting on the opposite side of the room, on the floor, with his back against the wall. As he noticed her, he gave a weak smile.

She walked over and sat down beside him. As she did so he put his arm around her and let her lean her head on his shoulder.

"How's she doing?" He asked.

"She's certainly inherited our ability to cope with things."

"That bad?"

"Close to it, yeah. Tried my best to help but… well."

"We're not exactly the right people to be giving her advice right now, are we?" Tom took a few seconds of silent thought, "Ironically Patrick would have been the perfect man for her right now."

"Fate certainly likes to play with us."

Fate. A word that reminded Tom of what was to come.

"You remember our chat about the future, right?" He asked her. She brought her head off his shoulder and faced him.

"Am I finally going to hear this plan of yours?" She asked him.

"You are… but you're also going to hear what I think the price for it will be."

***

Amelia gently shut the door to the room behind her. She closed her eyes and leaned back against it. Two whole hours and she'd just about stopped her from bursting into tears every few seconds, but right now she couldn't spend another second inside that room.

She sped down the corridors at full speed until she came to a door that led outside. She needed fresh air, and a lot of it.

She opened the door to see the sun high in the sky above the open sea. The deck of the aircraft carrier lay empty before her.

She took in the salty sea air as she walked out fully into the sunlight. She stopped and basked in its warmth for a few seconds, before tears of her own began to flood down her face. She did her best to hold them back like she'd been doing for so long now, but it was no use now.

She fell to her knees. She went to throw her fist as hard as she could at the deck beneath her, but after almost doing so, decided that would probably end up causing more issues than it was worth.

She wanted to hit something, anything, but the empty deck that slowly rocked with the gentle waves offered her nothing.

CHAPTER 43; STRINGS

Edward's eyes slowly opened to the screen in front of him. He was looking up at a fiery red sky. He slowly began to move his arms and legs to make sure he was still all in one piece. He seemed fine.

On his screen, a bright red radiation symbol was flashing, but that was to be expected. He should be fine as long as his armour wasn't compromised. He sat up and checked himself. No holes.

He was sat in an Edward shaped hole in a thick layer of snow some way off from what remained of the mushroom cloud in the distance. The trees that had been in this area had been blown down and torn from their roots by the blast. He slowly got to his feet as he began to notice a fizzing sound. A pain shot through his lower torso.

He put his hand against where the pain was. The dagger wound. The blood was slowly going to make a hole in his armour, and there wasn't much he could do about it.

Taking the armour off this close would be certain death by radiation poisoning, which was not a nice death at all. Edward slowly smiled and slowly began to chuckle to himself.

"Bastard." He cursed at Tom, "You got me in the end."

"I take it your referring to the wound that's slowly eating through the armour, right?" A voice asked from the side of him.

Edward turned to look at the figure that until now he hadn't noticed standing right beside him. He looked down at the snow. No evidence of any footprints. He seemed to calmly stand on top of the snow as if he weighed nothing at all, but that wasn't the strangest thing about this figure.

As Edward looked at the figures face, he realised that he was looking at another version of himself.

Dressed in black leather from head to toe. He stood in complete contrast to the white snowy background that glowed slightly red due to the current state of the sky.

"You're this worlds equivalent of me, aren't you?" Edward asked him. His counterpart slowly nodded.

"As much as it pains me to admit it, yes."

"You're not keen on the idea of more than one of yourself?"

"I actually find it more amusing than anything else." He revealed. He slowly turned to look towards him, "But I am rather disappointed with your performance."

"Disappointed? I drove your Tom out of this world, I killed everything that was once here. How are you not impressed?" Edward asked his mysterious counterpart.

"You achieved nothing." He sighed. He truly did seem disappointed in him, "And after all the effort I put into you."

"How so?"

"You burnt a world that was already set to be burnt one way or another. You simply saved the gods of this world a few seconds of effort. You drove Tom away, yes, but he'll be back in no time at all to fulfil his role in the world to follow this one. As I said, you have achieved nothing. The end result of your life's work has amounted to nothing more than saving the odd second of a few gods time that in the end serves no purpose at all other than granting me some trivial amusement."

"I fail to see any of your accomplishments." The Edward dressed in all leather slowly smiled at this as he looked back towards the mushroom cloud.

"You see, I wanted to test Tom. See what he was made of, see if another version of me was capable of beating him before I even gave it a shot myself."

"Why would you do something like that?"

"Because I've faced others like him before and been greatly disappointed. I like a challenge, no, I live for the chance to face someone willing to challenge me at every turn. I simply wanted to see if Thomas Thomson was up to my expectations."

"And you used me to do it? That isn't possible."

"Oh it was quite possible. I knew of your existence from the moment you opened your very own unstable portal to this world by accident. Thanks to another random portal opening to your world I even got my hands on two portal devices, which I decided to let out into this world simply to see what would happen."

"That explains where he got those two." Edward finally understood.

"All it took was for me to simply guide your portals to this world again and again. Tom himself acted as the perfect bait for you to come here and face him."

"While you sat back and watched. Tell me, how are you capable of all of this in this world?" Edward asked him.

"Because as a mere child I achieved the very same dream you have failed to reach your whole life." He turned to face Edward once more, "I am a god in this world."

"How did you achieve such a thing in a world as primitive as this?"

"Technology is not the only pathway to becoming a god. Although it is the easiest." He spoke as he turned and began to walk away from him. Edward looked back down at his slowly dissolving armour.

"I doubt it so, but you wouldn't happen to be more merciful than myself?" He asked his other.

"No." He spoke as he seemed to fade from existence as he continued to walk away.

"Fair enough."

Edward simply sat and watched the fiery red sky. He'd lived a long life filled with many conflicts and challenges. He'd fought against the living legend of his universe, Thomas Thomson, and more or less come out victorious. He'd nearly completed his life's goal as well.

It stung his pride that he was to die to the actions of a more primitive version of Thomson, but at the very least he found comfort that his death was at least at the hands of a version of him. There was honestly no one else in either universe he would have let deliver the final blow.

He thought his own universe had been messed up and heading for disaster in the hands of Thomson, but the complexities of his world clearly were nothing compared to whatever this world was headed for.

Universe One. Originally, he'd designated his own universe this, but after beginning to map out the surrounding universes, one thing became very clear about this particular one.

The original universe. The one all others branch out from in every conceivable direction, and every inconceivable one as well. A universe that seemed to be special in every single way. A universe like no other.

A Universe already more fucked up than his own, and it had only just gotten started. A universe deserving of its name far more than his own universe deserved the name Universe Two.

Edward slowly smiled as the armour covering his head deconstructed. The blood had broken through, there was no point protecting himself now, "A shame." He muttered to himself, "I'd have liked to see the fate of this world."

***

Tom continued to carry his bag though a long, straight corridor towards a set of double doors. He noticed the sound of footsteps trailing behind him.

"A word?" Thomas spoke from behind him. Tom stopped and turned to face him.

"This better be good." He sighed.

"What I told you before we set off to save Amy, about those books of yours."

"My mother's books, yeah I remember. You said that they contained knowledge even this world hasn't stumbled upon yet."

"You never figured out anything more about that, did you?"

"Why do you want to know?"

"I'm not a fool Tom. Your mother clearly came from a place even more technologically advanced than this universe. Surely it's no surprise that I'd be interested in such a place."

"What, so you can find it and restrict it with your technophobic principles you're so very proud of?"

"To learn how they advanced so quickly without destroying themselves. To learn the secret of not constantly being one step away from disaster."

"No, I didn't learn anything. But hopefully I will in the many years to come."

"I'm not even going to pretend that I understood half of what you talked about in front of the others, but they seemed to understand enough for now. It seems you still have much to do. Problems only someone from your universe can solve by the sounds of it."

"As do you. I catch another one of you lot in my universe again I'll personally come back here and gut you myself."

"Understood. Are you sure going back is the right choice? A life for you all here is still possible."

"It would be, but we all have our roles to play back in our world." Thomas nodded at this. The two of them then began to walk towards the doors together.

Cathie, Amy and Amelia were waiting on the other side of the doors. The three of them stood in front of an already open portal.

"You sure you three are ok with this?" Tom asked the three of them. Cathie walked over to him and have him a large hug.

"Someone needs to make us a new home." She answered as she brought her nose right up to his, "Besides, I'd rather live in the hope of seeing you again than watch you age and die without me." She added shortly before kissing him.

When the two of them eventually stopped, Tom handed her his bag.

"You'll need this more than I will."

"You sure?" She asked him.

"Just take good care of it. I'll be wanting it back. Make sure it doesn't fall into the wrong hands either."

"Promise. Just make sure you come back for it."

CHAPTER 44; THE END OF THE BEGINNING

Edward stood and watched as Tom walked out of a portal and onto the massive table that the higher powers all sat at. He then watched the portal close behind him.

"You got what you wanted, right?" He asked them. The three of them nodded.

"Granted we didn't expect you to destroy the current world. That was supposed to be our job, but I suppose the result is more important than the method." Destruction answered.

"You're first task shall be assisting us on creating a new world for humanity." Creation added.

"May I suggest we take inspiration from the other universe?" Edward contributed, "Planets and stars of all shapes and sizes. A lot to play with, and plenty of growing room."

"Sounds promising. I assume you two will have no issues designing such a system?" Essence asked them. Tom and Edward looked at one another.

"I'm sure between the two of us we can figure it out." Tom answered.

"Good. Once this task is complete, we shall recreate humanity. That is when the rivalry between the two of you shall begin." Destruction explained.

"May I ask a favour?" Tom asked them. The three of them were rather surprised by this, but Edward simply smiled, seeing what was coming next.

"Speak." Essence ordered.

"My family is currently without a home. They won't exactly pose any form of threat to this new humanity. I ask that they are allowed to find a home in this new world. It would certainly put my mind at rest to know they are safe."

"I don't see why not." Creation responded, "Do what you must, but you are forbidden any form of interaction or communication. We want your mind solely on the tasks at hand." Tom nodded at this.

As expected, they'd played right into his hands. So, they did share the theoretical weakness of gods after all. Granted not to the same extent, he had to be cautious with his every word.

"Of course. Thank you."

Tom and Edward both watched as the three beings before them vanished. After a few seconds of silence, Edward turned to address Tom.

"Tell me... that goal you have which you told to my counterpart, is it true?" He asked with his eyes quickly sharpening, showing the tactful mind hiding behind them.

"You heard that, did you? So, what if it is?"

"If so, you're either a fool, or you have a plan of some kind."

"Perhaps not a full plan, but I guess I have plenty of time to change that." Edward gave a small smirk at this.

"So, you are planning for the long haul?"

"Don't tell me I have to worry about you tattling on me now, do I?"

"On the contrary, I'm rather intrigued as to how your plan eventually unfolds. Provided you don't interfere with my own goals, you'll have nothing to fear from me."

"Well, you're already a god, or close to it. What does one desire after that?"

"God is a very relative term Thomson. To the average humans, we shall become gods, to the higher powers, nothing more than pets. I'm certain the ladder of power continues much higher up than them. The Divine for instance…"

"So, you've been watching me for some time then."

"Yes, they decided I should pick the best candidate to face me, I chose you. I'll keep your secret provided you play along with these games between us. Once I beat you, wipe out humanity for good, I'll have gained enough power to truly call myself a god."

"Sounds like a plan then. I get my revenge; you get your power. Not so stoked about destroying humanity, but I guess the only way to stop that is for me to win." Edward laughed at his statement, but it wasn't an insulting or mocking laughter, it was a laughter of understanding and respect.

"May the best man win."

***

A god's weakness is first and foremost their arrogance. Any who claimed the title of god had clearly never met anything or anyone able to best them.

The idea that anything or anyone could pose a threat to a god would clearly never even cross a god's mind. The higher powers were very different in this regard. They had seen power greater than their own, but more importantly, they had noticed when such power had itself fallen low enough for them to reach.

For now, their arrogance was quiet and hidden in the backgrounds of their minds. They were not gods. They were not the all-powerful beings they had once believed themselves to be, but it wouldn't be long until they were.

***

Deep in the heart of a void so vast it was impossible to imagine even a sizable fraction of it all at once, lay a small spiral galaxy, freshly born from the power of the gods themselves.

Fitted rather comfortable between two arms of this spiral galaxy sat a lonely star, far off from most others of its kind. Around this star, many rocks of all shapes and sizes orbited at varying speeds and distances.

One rock in particular seemed far more special than the rest. A small, blue and green rock that had its own pet moon slowly circling it. Upon this rock, a purple portal appeared. Cathie, Amy and Amelia quickly emerged from it, ready to explore the new world in front of them.

This new world was much larger than the last. No black mountains, no black cliffs. Sea's that spanned much further than the eye could possibly see. Land enough to house humans in the billions at least.

Varying from desert to tundra, and everything in between. Upon this spectacular little rock, the first of the new human race slowly began to appear.

***

A brown haired, purple eyed woman continued to pace within the endless grey void that surrounded her.

She came to a stop all of a sudden, for seemingly no reason.

"An alert." She muttered to herself. She began staring off into the distance, seemingly rummaging through her memories for something, until she found what she was after.

She quickly looked up as dread filled her face, "Tom… Oh, no… They found you…"

Her hair quickly flared as purple as her eyes. A huge power surged through her and lashed out violently against the invisible confines of her prison.

Before any damage could be done however, her powers quickly flickered, before dissipating. Her hair returned to its brown state, and she fell to her knees with tears in her eyes.

Those tears however quickly vanished. A face of fear and despair quickly turned to determination and thought.

Trapped in a prison she'd constructed herself. Designed to trap the most ambitious and patient beings in the universe. One built to last indefinitely without ever yielding. She was good at outsmarting others, but this time she had to outsmart herself.

She had to escape that which she herself deemed unescapable. A thought that she hadn't even entertained until now, for one very good reason. She had no drive to leave until now.

Her son was in trouble. Far more trouble than he could possibly hope to imagine.

***

This maybe the end of this book but this shattered story has only just left contact with the hammer, there is still more shards to be revealed. Some maybe big, others are so small you would almost miss them. However, the whole shall not be revealed until the pieces are picked up and fitted back together.

FIN

TABLE OF CONTENTS

CHAPTER 1; INTRODUCTIONS 13

CHAPTER 2; THE START 41

CHAPTER 3; OUT OF THE FRYING PAN AND INTO THE FIRE 55

CHAPTER 4; PAINFUL PASTS 93

CHAPTER 5; WATER AND FIRE 105

CHAPTER 6; THE CLIFF EDGE AWAITS 127

CHAPTER 7; NOT SO EXTINCT 135

CHAPTER 8; LIMITS 155

CHAPTER 9; BODY 169

CHAPTER 10; MADNESS 185

CHAPTER 11; THE ENEMY ABOVE 199

CHAPTER 12; SOMETHING NEW 215

CHAPTER 13; MURPHEY'S LAW 229

CHAPTER 14; THE COWARD 241

CHAPTER 15; THE VENGEFUL 247

CHAPTER 16; VENUS FLY 257

CHAPTER 17; MAGIC 267

CHAPTER 18; REALITY CHECK 281

CHAPTER 19; POLITICS 299

- CHAPTER 20; CONSEQUENCES OF PREVIOUS ACTIONS 321
- CHAPTER 21; NEWTON'S THIRD LAW 335
- CHAPTER 22; EXPANDING HORIZONS 353
- CHAPTER 23; GONE 369
- CHAPTER 24; AMY 377
- CHAPTER 25; SOMEONE'S GOING TO DIE 397
- CHAPTER 26; COST 411
- CHAPTER 27; THE WILDERNESS 427
- CHAPTER 28; ADJUSTMENTS 447
- CHAPTER 29; EDWARD 461
- CHAPTER 30; THOMAS THOMSON 473
- CHAPTER 31; GODLIKE POWER 493
- CHAPTER 32; FATE 513
- CHAPTER 33; THE DIVINE 527
- CHAPTER 34; NOSTALGIA 539
- CHAPTER 35; BURIED SECRETS 553
- CHAPTER 36; ARRIVAL 571
- CHAPTER 37; GRAVESTONES 589
- CHAPTER 38; LOYALTY AND DEVOTION 601
- CHAPTER 39; GRAVITY 611

CHAPTER 40; TO BEAT A GOD *623*

CHAPTER 41; BETWEEN WORLDS................... *637*

CHAPTER 42; 00:01:47... *647*

CHAPTER 43; STRINGS.. *659*

CHAPTER 44; THE END OF THE BEGINNING 667

europe books